HEAVEN
SENT

HEAVEN SENT

A novel by

DYNAH ZALE

www.urbanbooks.net

Urban Books, LLC
78 East Industry Court
Deer Park, NY 11729

ISBN-13: 978-1-60162-217-4
ISBN-10: 1-60162-217-1

First Trade Paperback Printing August 2007
First Mass Paperback Printing June 2010
Printed in the United States of America

10   9   8   7   6   5   4   3   2   1

Distributed by Kensington Publishing Corp.
Submit Wholesale Orders to:
Kensington Publishing Corp.
C/O Penguin Group (USA) Inc.
Attention: Order Processing
405 Murray Hill Parkway
East Rutherford, NJ 07073-2316
Phone: 1-800-526-0275
Fax: 1-800-227-9604

Dedication

In Loving Memory of
Alberta M. Evans
&
Lillian L. Evans

Acknowledgments

My Lord, I thank you for the burdens I bear—because they only make me stronger. Because of your strength the heavy load I carry may weigh me down, but it never takes me out. There is nothing you can't do. The difficulties in my life that hold me hostage are only temporary. I've seen the consequences of being addicted to alcohol, shopping, drugs, cigarettes, gambling, food, financial debt, sex, and work and nothing can compare to you. These things can only continue as long as we hold on to them and never let them go. That's why I'm blessed to know you and have you as my father. Love, Dynah

Lorraine Evans, mom, thanks for doing whatever I needed whenever I asked. I thank my aunties for their support: Aunt Babes, Aunt Jessie, Aunt Stump, Aunt Effie and Aunt Skins and the friends who have lobbied for my books to do well. Dana "Munchie" Williams and Tyrone Hargrove. Tyrone,

I can count on one hand the number of men I would label "A Good Man." Your name happens to fall on that list. Please don't allow anyone to change who you are.

I appreciate the different authors who gave me advice and were so kind to me when I was out traveling the roads for different book signings and events. Allison Hobbs, Monica Frazier Anderson, Lizette Carter I hope to see you again soon.

Mrs. Bebe Moore Campbell, you will never be forgotten because I will always admire and look up to your work. Thank you for sharing your talent and allowing your readers to see the world through your eyes.

The WOMAN IN ME 2002 BOOKCLUB, thank you for being the first book club to send me an invitation to have lunch with you. Everyone was so kind and Naloe Ervin, thank you for making me feel special.

AS THE PAGE TURNS BOOK CLUB in Philadelphia, we discussed so much church drama when I met with you girls I still laugh out loud to myself. I enjoyed my time with you and thank you, Nakea, for inviting me.

The JUST US BOOKCLUB in Atlanta, I thoroughly enjoyed the time I spent with you. As I listened to each of you speak about DITC I felt like you really could relate with the point I was trying to make. I can't wait to see you all again.

I received hoards of emails regarding DITC but one reader who wrote to me made me realize that my writing was not in vain. Mrs. Delores Collins from Michigan; just when I was beginning to doubt myself you sent me enough encouragement to finish this book. Thank you Mrs. Collins, I appreciate every word you dropped.

A heartfelt thanks goes out to all the different African American bookstores that welcomed me to promote my books in their stores Karibu, Urban Knowledge, Horizon, and Ligorious.

Special shout outs to the entire staff at Q-boro Books that assisted me in this project. Without you none of this would have been possible.

To Gwendolyn Marcus, I appreciate you sharing your life with me. You are one of the strongest women I know. With everything you've been through you have managed to overcome it all and become someone I admire. May God Bless You!

Lastly, to the Heaven in my life who endured so much heartache and pain when the only thing she was looking for was acceptance and love, may you rcst in pcacc.

Love,

Dynah

Dynah.Zale@comcast.net

Prologue

The early morning light rained through Courtney's window. Rays of sunlight surrounded his six-year-old face and gently roused him for the start of a new day. Courtney opened his eyes and a cold chill caressed his bare arms. Lying next to him in bed was his three-year-old sister, Odyssey. She peacefully slept with the covers pulled tight around her neck.

Courtney's stomach growled loudly. He was hungry and he knew when Odyssey woke up she would be hungry too. Their mother made them go to bed hungry the night before. She promised them a big breakfast this morning. Courtney got up out of bed expecting to see his mom in the kitchen cooking, but she was nowhere around. He searched the living room and her bedroom, but there was no sign of her.

"Courtney, where's Mommy?" Odyssey's question startled him. He didn't know she had gotten up out of bed. Odyssey stood in their bedroom doorway hanging onto the yellow security blanket she carried around with her everywhere she went.

"I don't know," Courtney replied. "But let's sit in the kitchen until she comes back." He led her to the kitchen table and pulled out a chair for her to sit in. While waiting on his mother to return, he remembered his mother's instructions.

"Courtney, if you ever get up and I'm not here I want you to sit in the kitchen and wait for me to get back."

"Courtney, I'm hungry. When is Mommy coming home?" Odyssey whined.

Courtney shrugged his shoulders in response and Odyssey sneezed twice, inciting a stream of mucus to flow from her nose. Courtney ran into the bathroom and grabbed some toilet tissue from the roll. He held it up to her nose and told her to blow. Her puffy red eyes and constant sneezing throughout the night was evidence that Odyssey's allergies were bothering her again. When his mom had money, she usually got some medicine to make Odyssey feel better. "Courtney, I'm hungry." Odyssey breathed through her mouth because her nose was stuffed up.

Courtney wished there was something he could do to make his sister feel better. "Mommy told me to sit here until she gets home."

An hour passed before Heaven stormed into the house, ignoring her children. Not noticing her children sitting at the kitchen table, she went straight to her bedroom and locked the door behind her. Behind closed doors Heaven ran to her dresser drawer and pulled out her kit. A lighter, hose, needle, and rusty spoon were the instruments she needed. She pulled an enormous bag of dope from her front pocket and examined it closely. She lightly plucked the bag with her finger and calculated how many hits she could get off the dope in her mind. She cooked the drugs and prepared to get high when she heard Courtney banging on her bedroom door.

"Mommy, we're hungry," he cried. "Can you fix us something to eat?"

"In a minute," she yelled back through the door. Heaven needed to get in one hit to make her feel better. The sensation from that initial hit would help her make it through the next few hours. She tied the hose around her arm and searched for a vein that had not collapsed yet.

"Mommy." Courtney wouldn't leave her alone until she unlatched the door and came out.

She stomped her foot on the ground upset that Courtney wouldn't leave her alone. She jumped up from the side of her bed and swung her bedroom door wide open.

"Courtney, what do you want?" Heaven yelled at the boy.

"Mommy, we're hungry." His small eyes pleaded with her to feed him.

She remembered her children hadn't eaten since the day before. The layers of aggravation she felt a moment ago faded away and unveiled a compassionate caring mother.

"I'm sorry, Courtney. I know you guys are hungry." She quickly grabbed her kit and walked back into the kitchen with Courtney following close behind her. She placed her things down on the kitchen table and pulled her last two stale fortune cookies down from off the top of the refrigerator.

Heaven knelt down in front of her son, "I'm sorry for yelling at you. Remember when Mommy told you sometimes she gets really sick and that makes her be a mean mommy?"

Courtney nodded his head.

"Well, now is one of those times. Mommy really has to take some of her medicine before she gets any sicker. Take these." She handed him the two fortune cookies. "You eat one and give one to your sister and go into the living room with your sister. Watch TV until I call you. Okay?"

He carried the fortune cookies in one hand and his sister's hand in the other. They sat down on the living room floor in front of the couch and watched cartoons. Courtney and Odyssey broke open their cookies and pulled their fortunes out. Then they ate the hard outer shell; a temporary cure to their hunger.

Odyssey laughed at the cartoons on television screen while Courtney's attention was directed toward his mother. He watched as she took the rubber hose and tied it tight around her arm. Plenty of times he watched his mother poke herself with that needle to make her feel better. He had memorized her routine. She would push the lever on the needle only halfway down, lay her head back, and allow the medicine to take effect. The medicine she used always seemed to have a magical affect on her. Before she took the medicine she was mean and selfish, but afterward, she was pleasant and more fun to be around.

Heaven placed the needle down on the table and lit a cigarette. Suddenly a loud banging sound at their front door scared her. His mother looked at them and smiled. Courtney was frightened. It sounded like someone was trying to tear into their home.

"Heaven, come out here. I know you're in there."

Heaven lifted herself from the raggedy, but comfortable chair she was sitting in and dragged herself to answer the front door. When she opened the front door, her next door neighbor, Art, verbally attacked her.

"Heaven, where's my stuff?" he yelled at her.

"Art, I don't know what you're talking about." she replied with a straight face.

"Don't play games with me, Heaven. You came to my house late last night talking about you missed me and had been waiting for me. I took you to bed and when I woke up this morning, you're gone and so is my last bag of dope. If you stand there and lie in my face about taking my stuff, then you leave me no choice but to beat the truth out of you," Art threatened.

"I didn't take your stuff. I just borrowed it."

"Borrowed it!" he yelled. "You can't borrow dope. What, you think you can give it back to me when you're done?"

"I was going to replace it."

"That's bull. Heaven, if you don't return my stuff right now." Art tried to open the screen door, but Heaven had it locked. "Where is it?"

"Gone."

"Gone. What do you mean by gone? You couldn't have used all that dope that quickly."

"Art, it wasn't that much in the bag to begin with. But if you want proof I'll show you the empty bag." She opened the door and invited him in.

They stepped inside and when they reached the living room, Heaven watched in horror as her son took the needle and injected the remaining amount of dope into his sister's arm.

"No!" Heaven screamed. She dashed to her daughter and the moment she wrapped her fingers around her daughter's arms as the girl's body fell cold. She screamed Odyssey's name, trying to wake her up.

"Mommy, I was just trying to give her some of your medicine so she would stop sneezing," Courtney explained.

The child was pronounced dead on arrival and Heaven was charged with endangering the welfare of her children.

Chapter 1

Six Years Later

Freedom never looked so good. After six long years, Heaven was finally leaving Jefferson State Reformatory for Women. A smile that stretched from here to Texas spread across her face. Today she said a final good-bye to the barbwire fences and prison bars that had kept her in bondage for so long.

With Heaven's hands securely fastened behind her back, the prison guard pushed her tall, slender frame through the gate and over the border into deliverance. Stepping over that threshold meant more to Heaven than simply leaving prison; it meant she was being given a second chance. The slate was being wiped clean for her and she had made a promise to herself that she would leave all remnants of her former life in the past and only look toward the future.

Jefferson State was the first women's prison in

the country built on the shores of the Atlantic Ocean. It had been standing since the early nineteen twenties. At night, Heaven could see the bright lights advertising each Casino along the Atlantic City Boardwalk from her prison cell. The smell of salt water that lingered in the air around the prison would forever be a reminder of her time there.

Only two prisoners were being transported from the prison to a halfway house that morning. One was Heaven and the other female inmate stood in line a few feet behind her, waiting her turn to board the van. A male prison guard stepped off the van and carefully read her name from the clipboard. "Heaven Stansfield."

She stepped forward and he gestured for her to board the van first. Once she was seated he handcuffed her hands and legs to the seat in front of her and did the same to the other prisoner.

The two guards who would be accompanying them on their journey this morning reminded Heaven of Michael Jackson and Paul McCartney. The black guard's hair was dripping with activator trying to keep the moisture in his jheri curl and was very thin. The white guard was just as thin with olive skin and hair that reached no longer then the top of his neck. The black guard volunteered to drive, leaving the other guard the task of riding in the back with the prisoners.

For twenty minutes, Heaven watched the dimwit guards argue over the best route to get to the halfway house. The mere sight of them spitting words and saliva at one another made her stomach upset.

She laid her head against the passenger side window and tried to get some sleep.

Once the guards had come to an agreement, the driver announced they were ready to go. Behind the wheel, he buckled his seat belt and the other guard got up to slam the passenger sliding door shut. The veins in his arm bulged out, showing the strength he had to use to seal the door.

The driver started the engine and just before the door was closed they heard a voice in the distance shout, "Wait." The voice sounded familiar to Heaven, but she didn't want to believe it was him. Officer Jennings ran toward them waving his hands to stop the van before it pulled off. Sweat poured off his face, wet hair swung in his eyes, and wet spots formed under his armpits.

"The warden wants to see you before you leave," Jennings said to the driver. Upset by the summons, the guard sucked his teeth and complained that the delay would throw them off schedule, but he knew he couldn't leave without first reporting to his boss. Jumping out the van, he told his companion he would be right back.

"Good luck, Heaven," Jennings hollered out, still panting and out of breath. "It's going to be hard to replace you. No one can clean that floor like you did," he snickered.

Jennings was the main reason Heaven was fleeing to a halfway house. He had made her time there a living hell by feeding her heroin habit. The drugs he supplied kept her under the influence most of the time. When she came to prison she was a twenty-two-year-old addict who would do anything for a hit and six years later nothing had changed but her age.

Behind bars each inmate had a job and Heaven's job was to mop the cafeteria floor every afternoon after lunch. Scrubbing eight hundred feet of cold, hard floor every day was backbreaking work and laboring in the hot August weather was even worse. During the summer months the temperature in the cafeteria stayed ten degrees hotter than outside, but the guards were kind by letting her use the water fountain that sat right outside the cafeteria doors whenever she needed a break from the heat.

The afternoon Heaven and Jennings met, she had just come back from getting a drink from the fountain when she found him waiting for her. He stood with his back and left foot placed flat against the wall. A wooden toothpick hung out his mouth and he perspired profusely. She tried to ignore his presence and continued with her chores.

"Little lady, you can stop anytime you want," he said out loud.

She stuck the head of her mop back into the sudsy bucket and used her hands to wring it dry. Heaven had made up her mind she was going to do her time without getting into any trouble and Jennings looked like a rebel looking to cause a disturbance to her peaceful alliance. "I'm not going to say a word if you decide to take a break. I know this job can be tiring; especially for a beautiful woman like yourself."

"I've already taken a break." She moved the bucket a few feet away from him, but he followed,

"You sure you don't want to take a break? I have

something I'm sure you'll like." He dangled a small bag filled with a white powdery substance in front of her face.

Her eyes grew to the size of ping-pong balls and she fell into a trance. That familiar desire she had when all she cared about was drugs took over her body. Her focus was no longer on cleaning the cafeteria floor, but on finding out what was in that bag. Jennings pulled her behind some crates stored in the kitchen storage room and gently placed the clear plastic baggie in her hand.

Like a woman starving for food, she dumped the contents in a hurry on the back of her hand and snorted it up her nose. The sensation that ran through her welcomed the heroin back into her body like it was a long lost friend. Since heroin was her drug of choice on the streets she immediately recognized its presence. That first sniff hit her so hard she held her hand out against the crates to maintain her balance.

"Don't use too much of that stuff too fast," Jennings warned her. "I don't want you to overdose on me."

That is how their relationship began. He would faithfully supply her with a dime bag of dope and never ask for anything in return. One day, paranoia took over and she got suspicious about why Jennings was putting himself at risk by sneaking drugs into the prison for her.

"Why are you doing this?" she screamed in his face. "You're up to something. Are you trying to set me up?"

"You dumb broad," he shouted back. "You black people always think somebody is out to get you.

Don't think you're special because I bring you drugs. I supply plenty of women in here with this stuff and they not only pay me but they always leave me with a little for myself. That's how I can get you all this dope for free." He pushed her up against the wall and breathed into her face. "But since you think I want something in return why don't we start settling your tab right now?"

Swinging his hand back, he punched her in the face and she fell back onto the storage crates. Then he jumped on top of her. He forced his hand underneath her skirt and tore her panties away. While holding her down with one arm, he unbuckled his pants and dropped them to the floor. He laughed as he forced himself on her with a satisfied look on his face. She knew that this was what he wanted from the beginning. He was just waiting for the right time.

Jennings was surprised Heaven didn't put up much of a fight. He did what he wanted to do and she allowed it. *What is the point of putting up a fight?* she thought. No one was around to save her. She had been raped plenty of times over drugs when she was on the streets. Coming to jail and finding herself in the same predicament wasn't surprising; just annoying. It seemed no matter how many problems drugs seemed to bring her way, she couldn't seem to leave them alone.

A couple minutes later, Jennings pulled out of her. Still high and in a daze, she watched him put his clothes back on. Her torn panties lay on the floor next to her foot. When she bent down to pick them up, Jennings dug his dirty nails into her arm and pulled her close to him. "If you ever tell anyone about this, I'll kill you," he threatened.

She was scared, but not because of his threat. What frightened her was the emptiness she saw when she looked in his eyes. Her nana always told her that if a person looked hard enough then they would be able to see the soul of everyone they met through their eyes. Staring into Jennings's empty eyes was like looking into outer space. The depth of his eyes was never ending. It felt like she was looking into the eyes of someone evil.

Officer Jennings continued to supply her with drugs and he was compensated with sex.

On the one year anniversary of her incarceration, Heaven made plans to do something special for herself. She had developed a routine of going to the library in the mornings before going to work, but today she felt like being lazy and had decided to sleep in until noon.

Half asleep in her cell, she was awakened by her cellmate coughing up mucus and spitting in the toilet. The loud thumping sound splashing against the toilet water made Heaven nauseous. The urge to throw up overwhelmed her and she started to gag on her own vomit. Heaven jumped out of bed and pushed her cellmate out of the way just as she started throwing up everything she had eaten the night before. She clutched her belly to stop the raging war inside of her and cradled the commode in her arms until the CO's rushed her to the infirmary.

The doctor performed several tests to determine the cause of Heaven's illness. Hours later, she had diagnosed the problem. "Heaven, you're pregnant."

The doctor's news caught Heaven by surprise. She sat with her mouth hanging wide open for ten minutes before she could say anything. "Doc, there has got to be a mistake." Heaven was scared the doctor would tell the prison warden.

"It's no mistake. I had them run the test a few times. They all came back with the same result."

Heaven knew the doctor was curious as to how she had managed to get pregnant in a woman's prison, but she wasn't ready to answer that question yet. "Doc, I'm tired. Can I get some rest?"

"Sure, I'll come back and check on you later."

The moment she left, Heaven turned her back away from everyone and closed her eyes. All she could think about was the baby she carried belonged to Jennings. He was untrustworthy and she was sure once he heard about her pregnancy, he would deny everything in order to save his own behind.

"Heaven!" Before she turned over she had already recognized the signature hillbilly call that could only come from "her baby daddy." She turned around just in time to see him fill her presence with his arrogance. He grabbed a nearby chair, straddled it between his legs, and winked his crooked eye at her. "Listen, I'm going to take care of everything."

How did he find out about the baby so quickly? She hadn't planned on sharing her secret with him, but now that he knew, she wondered what he was going to do about it.

"How are you going to do that?" Panic filled her

voice. "I'm pregnant and the doctor knows. It won't be long before the warden finds out, too."

"Listen, no one is ever going to say anything." He stuck his plump fingers into his front pocket, pulled out a small white pill, and placed it in her hand.

She examined it closely. "What is it?" she asked.

"Take it!" he screamed, causing her to jump and nearly drop it on the floor. She popped the pill in her mouth, using her own spit to wash it down.

"I'll be around to check on you tomorrow." He got up to leave. "Make sure you get some rest."

The doctor released her from the infirmary and she returned to her cell. That night she lay in her bunk hoping the pill Jennings had given her would take her to another place. She was looking forward to escaping her problems even if it would be only in her mind.

Hours passed and she didn't feel any euphoric feelings. No matter how hard she closed her eyes, she didn't feel any different. Around midnight she concluded that somebody had probably sold Jennings some aspirin telling him it was drugs. She couldn't wait to tell him he had been played.

Before leaving the infirmary, the doctor suggested she take a week off from work. Being confined to her cell meant she had no way of getting in touch with Jennings unless he came to her and he did—two nights later.

"That pill you gave me did nothing for me. I thought it was going to make me high. I felt nothing."

With a devilish grin on his face he replied. "Don't worry, you will." He then handed her another pill but this one was peach. She took the pill and went to bed thinking Jennings was a fool.

Around midnight, Heaven was jolted out of her sleep with severe abdominal cramps. The sensation she felt was worse than labor. A sharp pain stabbed her in her side repeatedly. It was paralyzing. She feared the pain would grow worse if she moved so she laid completely still. Unable to endure the suffering any longer, she decided to get up and yell to a guard for help. When she pushed the blankets off her she looked down between her legs and her pants were covered with blood. She was hemorrhaging.

Again she was rushed to the infirmary on a stretcher. When they wheeled her in this time, her doctor was waiting for her at the entrance. The doctor told her not to worry then she told the nurses Heaven had a rare stomach virus and to hook her up to an IV. But Heaven was in so much pain she couldn't bear for anyone to touch her. She squeezed the doctor's hand, begging her to stop the pain.

For a split second, Heaven thought about the baby and wondered if she was having a miscarriage. The pain in her abdomen had spread to her back and she heard a nurse say she was bleeding so heavily she needed a heavy-duty pad to control the flow of blood. Suddenly, her dinner splattered out her mouth and all over the doctor, guards, and herself. Pain gripped her stomach again and she doubled over. She had the urge to use the bathroom and she tried to tell the doctor she needed to go, but the pain prevented her from speaking.

Suddenly, her bowels let loose and she went right to the bathroom right on the bed sheets.

The doctor instructed the nurses to help her into the bathroom. Heaven sat on the commode and she could feel several blood clots pass through her. The more blood clots she felt the less pain she felt. By morning her rare stomach virus had passed and a nurse came in to help clean her up. They put her in a clean bed and she slept for the rest of the morning.

A few hours later, Jennings woke her up. "How do you feel?" He chewed on a piece of gum.

"Horrible." She could barely open her eyes.

"Listen, I took care of your problem. The pregnancy was terminated." Her eyes shot wide open in disbelief. "Those pills I gave you make a woman's body dispose of a baby without the mother having to get an abortion." Heaven tried to sit up. Her abdomen was still sore so she remained lying on her side, but she could see her doctor standing at the foot of the bed.

"Heaven, what Officer Jennings is trying to say is the medication he gave you caused you to have a chemical abortion. It feels like a miscarriage, but there is no surgical procedure needed. It's perfectly safe and the body disposes of the baby on its own. That is why you bled so much. In a few days, I will do a follow-up exam on you to make sure the baby has completely expelled itself from inside your womb."

"What if there are parts still hanging around in there?" she asked.

The doctor and Jennings looked at one another.

Both seemed unsure how to answer her question. "That doesn't happen too often, but if that is the case, we'll have to consider taking you to an abortion clinic."

"But won't the warden get suspicious?"

"Don't worry about that," Jennings barked at her. "Let's just hope those pills did the trick."

A week later she was released from the infirmary with a clean bill of health. Following another week of rest, she was allowed to go back to work.

That wasn't the last time she was rushed to the infirmary for a so-called stomach virus. She was rushed there at least three more times over the next five years.

Chapter 2

Heaven's release from prison to a halfway house in Camden started out as a joyous event. The simple one-hour drive from Atlantic City to Camden seemed a lot longer than it was because the other female prisoner who was traveling with her was a talker. The minute the van merged onto the Atlantic City Expressway she started talking non-stop. Heaven's head ached and her ears hurt from listening to the girl soar from one topic to another. The guards even gave her dirty looks that said she was gnawing at their last nerves.

"Am I talking too much? My momma often told me that I was a talker. I've been like this since I was a little girl. She believes I'm bi-polar. One minute I'm up and the next minute I'm down." Gently bobbing to a tune in her head, she quieted down. It was so quiet in the van that Heaven laid her head back on the seat and closed her eyes to get some sleep. "I'm sorry, I didn't introduce myself.

My name is Ebony. How long were you locked up for?"

"Six years."

"Wow that's weird!" Ebony exclaimed. "You've been there for six years and I was there for two years and we've never run into one another.

Heaven had never met Ebony before that morning, but she was somebody she would never forget. "A lot of people are surprised when I say my name is Ebony. It's not too often they meet a white girl with the name Ebony." Using her hands to express herself, she pointed her finger in the air. "When I was born, my momma thought my father was a black man. His parents weren't too thrilled to hear he was having a baby with a white woman so to make sure they accepted me, my momma named me Ebony. By my first birthday, my bright red hair and Howdy Doody freckles made my father and his momma question whether I was really his child. A blood test later confirmed what my momma had probably known all along. He wasn't my father. To this day my momma swears that I'm half black, but she refuses to tell me who my daddy is." Ebony looked down at her pale arms. "Do I look half black to you?"

Heaven glanced at Ebony's milky white skin compared to her copper complexion. She had to admit, Ebony didn't look like she had any black in her. Heaven would have told her that if she hadn't started talking again.

"I can tell just by looking at you that you're mixed; your beautiful, curly, honey blonde hair practically reaches down to your behind and emerald green eyes. Is your momma white and daddy black? Or is it reversed?" Ebony fiddled her fingers around one another.

Heaven didn't like talking about her parents. In fact, she didn't like talking about herself at all. The less other people knew about her the better. "My mom is black," she answered, hoping that bit of information would satisfy her curiosity.

Distracted by Ebony's question, Heaven hadn't noticed the prison van had come to a stop. The prison guard unlocked and slid the van doors wide open.

The guard helped them off and unlocked the handcuffs from around their wrists. Heaven stood with the bright morning sun beating down on her back and inhaled the familiar smells and sounds of the city she was born in. At last she was home. It seemed so unreal. Seeing all the familiar sights stirred her soul and took her breath away. She took a deep breath to hold back the tears in her eyes.

The aroma of fried chicken from the corner res-taurant drifted past her nose. Young mothers talk-ing on cell phones and pushing baby strollers passed her by, the sounds of ambulance sirens blared in the distance. These things she used to take for granted now welcomed her back home.

"Aren't you excited?" Ebony softly patted her hands together. "So many times I thought about never coming back here, still I can't stay away. It's in my blood. I was born here and I'll probably die here." Her smile glowed with joy. Heaven thought Ebony was just happy to be out of prison, but she later learned she was full of cheer every day, always keeping a smile on her face. She was kind to everyone she met and her unselfishness caused her to always put the needs of other's before hers— she was an all around generous person.

The guard ordered them to stand still while he checked off a few items on his clipboard. Checking his watch, he wrote down the time.

They stood in front of a small red brick building with a white door. Above the door hung a tattered wooden sign that read G.I.S.A. Ebony, Heaven, and the guard turned their attention to the sound of the doorknob being jingled. They watched the knob twist from left to right and then they heard someone struggling on the other side to pull it open. One firm attempt to pull the door open and it finally gave way.

The blinding sun hindered them from clearly seeing who stood in the doorway. The three of them stared at the six-foot outline that weighed well over three hundred pounds. The figure quickly descended the five steps that led to the sidewalk and her face was revealed to them. Her large facial features stood out—plump nose, wide eyes, and big teeth. Even the wig she wore was huge. "Welcome, ladies." She greeted them then turned her attention to the prison guard. "Hey, Barney. How you today?"

"I can't complain, Ms. Campbell." He handed her the clipboard and the pen. "Two more for you." Ms. Campbell signed for them like they were property; then handed the clipboard back to Barney. "Good luck, ladies." He waved farewell, climbed in the passenger side, and the van sped off.

"I'm Ms. Campbell, the director at G.I.S.A." She

addressed the women like they were soldiers in the army. "Follow me," she ordered.

Ebony gestured for Heaven to follow first because she didn't want to be the one standing next to the drill sergeant. Heaven wasn't scared so she followed the walking titanic inside the halfway house. Despite her huge frame, Ms. Campbell was a fast walker. Heaven had to practically run to keep up with her. Halfway up the second flight of stairs, Heaven had to stop a moment to catch her breath. Ms. Campbell turned and looked back when she heard Heaven's heavy breathing.

"Come on, Stansfield. A skinny girl like yourself can take a few flights of steps."

Heaven looked perplexed at her assumption. She may have been skinny, but she was also out of shape.

Their journey came to a stop on the third floor in front of room 305. Ms. Campbell opened the door. They stepped inside and looked around the neatly decorated bedroom. The first things they saw were two twin beds separated by a nightstand and an antique lamp. The room had tattered linen drapes hanging from the windows and multi-colored throw rugs on the floor. Ms. Campbell showed them the interior as if they were tenants renting a room. Behind one door there was a private bathroom and there was also a small closet they had to share.

"Ladies, this will be your room for the duration of your stay. Last week, two residents were sent back to the prison. It's not often we have two openings in the same room, but the two women who were here before you broke the house rules. They snuck out in the middle of the night and visited a bar. I still don't know how they climbed up and down that tree in stilettos." She pointed to a huge oak tree that sat outside the window. "But when they climbed back in that window at four o'clock in the morning, I had prison guards waiting for them. You should have seen the look on their faces," she laughed to herself.

"Don't allow my story to scare you. If you want to stay in this program until you are officially released, all you have to do is follow a simple set of rules." Ms. Campbell pointed toward one of the twin beds and asked them to sit. She then handed each of them a thirty-page manual that detailed every rule, regulation, and procedure set by the halfway house.

"The reason you are here is because you messed up somewhere along the way. Every resident who comes through here was incarcerated for a non-violent drug-related crime. G.I.S.A is here to help you regain control over your life. All our principles focus on Christ and we teach you how to turn your life over to him. I've been where you girls are today. I was addicted to crack for over twelve years. For years, I stood on the corner of Kaighn and Mount Ephraim Avenue so high I couldn't even tell you what year it was. I lived my life with my head in the clouds for over a decade and I still can't remember all the things I did, but I can tell you the day it all stopped. It was a Sunday morning when the image of a man stood before me, calling out my name. He was dressed in all white and with open arms told me he loved me."

"Was it Jesus?" Ebony asked with the innocence of a child.

"I believe it was, because he is the only one who could have saved me from that potent drug I was addicted to. After I heard his voice I got up and walked out the crack house, but in my heart I wasn't ready to give up the drugs. Not yet, because if I was, I would have left that crack pipe behind. Instead, I carried it with me for three blocks until I came to a church.

"From outside I could hear the church choir singing praises to God. I stumbled up the church steps one at a time and pushed open the heavy wooden doors. My legs carried me down the center aisle and my vision was blurred from getting high all night. No one tried to stop me or block my way to the altar. The choir never stopped singing and through their bold and loud voices I felt the presence of the Lord. When I reached the altar I heard him whisper in my ear, 'Let go.' I dropped to my knees; laid that crack pipe on the altar and never picked it up again. I haven't touched any drugs since. At that moment, I realized I couldn't kick this habit alone. I needed a friend and his name was Jesus."

Heaven glanced at Ebony from the corner of her eye. The gullible look on Ebony's face said she believed every word from Ms. Campbell's mouth. But Heaven wasn't buying it. She knew who Jesus was and she believed in him, but she had enough sense to know that Jesus was not going to show up in Camden, New Jersey; especially not in a crack house.

"The staff at G.I.S.A are here to help you on

your journey to recovery in any way we can." She opened the booklet to the first page and provided them with a brief overview of what was inside. "I'm not going to discuss this entire booklet with you. I will leave that to your assessment counselor, who you will meet with later on, but I do want to point out one important rule." She turned a few pages over and pointed to a line in the book. "At no time are drugs allowed in this building. I don't care if it's aspirin, cough syrup, or any over-the-counter drugs. If you have a headache we have a nurse on duty who can provide you with medication. I will not tolerate marijuana, coke, crack, aspirin, prescription drugs, or any kind of drug paraphernalia. That means no blunts in your possession." Ms. Campbell was very serious. "If you break any of these rules your things will be immediately packed and you will be sent back to the prison. We have had many people successfully released and plenty of people who were sent back to the prison. Ladies, I hope both of you will return back to the community as productive members of society. Any questions?"

They shook their heads and Ms. Campbell stood up to leave, but before she did, Heaven had to ask her one last question. "What does G.I.S.A stand for?"

She smiled to herself. "A lot of people ask me that. I like for residents to figure out the meaning for themselves. Some figure it out—some never do. Many haven't figured it out until they were released from the program. I pray the both of you will one day experience its true meaning."

Chapter 3

Before Ms. Campbell left, she suggested that the two women sit in on a group meeting that was currently underway in the annex adjacent to the halfway house. "That would be a good place to start your recovery," she said.

While still in prison, Heaven made a promise to herself that once she was released, she would do whatever she had to do to get her life in order and stay clean. She knew by attending this meeting, she was taking the first step necessary to accomplish those goals.

When they arrived at the meeting, everyone's head was bowed in prayer. Ebony and Heaven slipped into a couple of seats in the back without being noticed. Heaven was surprised to see the number of people in attendance. The room was sparsely full. She expected there to be standing room only. Thousands of junkies lived in Camden. It's a shame when only one or two people have the desire to seek help to get clean, especially when meetings, like this one, were open to the public for free.

Once the prayer was over another woman introduced herself to the crowd. Her name was Fatima and she had a story to tell. "The best thing that could have ever happened to me was being sent away to prison. Before that day, everything was a blur. Except for the day I sacrificed my kid for a few vials of crack.

"It had been a rough day for me. I was worn out from chasing dope all day. Being an addict is a full-time job." Several women in the room nodded their heads in agreement.

"Tossing and turning from one side of the bed to the other; slow moving pictures of my lips wrapped around a crack pipe flashed through my mind. My body shook involuntarily. I felt like I was being weighed down by a ton of bricks. I was so tired. I couldn't even lift my head. This wasn't the first time I had felt this way. If more than two hours passed without me inhaling on a pipe or shooting dope into my arm, my body reacted this way.

"It was October twenty-ninth; my baby's twelfth birthday. I spent my last ten dollars on a dime bag of dope and I didn't even have enough money to buy a birthday card. Barricading myself away in my bedroom, I hid from the embarrassment and shame drugs had over me. I pulled the covers up over my head and tried to escape the voices in my head, but it was pointless. Something kept telling me if I didn't get a hit soon I was going to die," Fatima stretched her finger to the sky. "Crack was my god. I worshipped it and I couldn't live without it." Then she massaged her temples. "Earlier that day I had gone to see if I could get a hook up from one of the young boys who hustled drugs around the corner from my house."

"I've been there, girl! Lord knows I've been there," a woman the color of coffee screamed out as she raised her arm and pumped her fist in the air, as if she was at a rap concert.

"I didn't have any money, but you know how it is when you're an addict. You don't need money if you know how to hustle and I could hustle lunch money from every fifth grader in the neighborhood if I had to. I figured it would be no problem talking the dope man into giving me something for free.

"I made that hike around the corner with the hood of my sweatshirt pulled up over my head; hoping to conceal my identity. As I got closer to the block, I looked around for the boy they called Upshaw. At first, I didn't notice him staring at me from the stoop where he usually sold drugs. The black on black clothes he wore made him blend in with the darkness of the corner.

"When I finally spotted him I headed in his direction. It must have been obvious by the look on my face that I didn't have a dime to my name because as soon as I got close to him he said, 'Sorry. No money. No credit. No dope.'

"In a split second, he took away any hope I had of getting high that night. I had heard those same words before, but the rejection always hurt like it was the first time. Probably because I would trick myself into thinking each time would be different. This would be the day one of those dope dealers would have sympathy for an addict," she laughed to herself. "I don't know what I was thinking. Those dealers care about nobody but themselves.

"While standing on that corner my need to get high grew. My flesh burned like it was a gas fire that couldn't be put out. My heart hammered against my chest. I thought I was going to have a heart attack right there on the corner, but I didn't care. I wasn't leaving. My number one priority was to get high.

"I strutted up to Upshaw and offered him a sexual excursion in exchange for some drugs." Fatima giggled to herself. "That must have been funny to him because he laughed in my face. He said whatever I was giving away I could keep, but if I really wanted some free dope there was one thing I could do for him. I thought to myself, whatever he wanted I would get."

Fatima's words labored with pain. "He told me he would give me two free bags if I brought my kid down to see him. At first I was confused. I didn't understand what my child had to do with me getting some drugs, but when the corners of his mouth turned up into one of Satan's smiles, I fully understood what he meant. He wanted to steal my baby's innocence. This low-down, dirty drug dealer wanted to soil the only good and pure thing the Lord had ever blessed me with. Thoughts of my twelve-year-old performing the same sexual acts on him I had done in the past made me sick."

Her shame-filled eyes looked down at the floor. "I got down on my knees like a dog and begged him. I promised him I would get him whatever he wanted; but not my baby.

"He didn't care. Lifting his foot, he kicked me in my face. I fell over onto the ground and he stood towering over me like a king. He ordered me to go and not come back unless I had my son with me. I cried all the way home.

"When I walked in the front door I was greeted with the usual 'Hey Mommy,' from my son. I didn't even bother to say happy birthday. I walked straight back to my bedroom and stayed there until I heard him go to bed.

Several people including Ebony were crying tears over Fatima's ordeal.

"I finally drifted off to sleep around midnight, and I wish I hadn't because my mind was invaded with nightmares of smoking crack. I dreamt I was running through Centerville Projects and every-one I passed would call out my name. I'd stop and they would hold out a pipe full of crack; offering me a hit. Thankful that someone was willing to share their high with me, I'd run over and reach out for their pipe but every time I did the pipe would disappear. My dream played over again four or five times before I finally woke up.

"Tangled inside my bed sheets, I threw the cov-ers off me and jumped out of bed. Running into my son's room, I ordered him to get up and get dressed. I can still see the confused look on his face when I told him that we were going out. 'Where are we going, Mommy? Where are we going?' He kept asking me. The sound of his voice made me angry. I guess my conscience was over-loaded with guilt because I yelled at him and told him to shut his mouth and not ask me any more questions.

"Less then fifteen minutes later, we stood in front of Upshaw. 'Here he is,' I said. Upshaw immediately grabbed hold of my boy's wrist and pulled him from my side. Unaware of what was going on, my son struggled to break free from his strong grasp. Through my son's screams I unconvincingly tried to reassure him that everything was going to be all right.

"Upshaw threw the two bags he promised me to the ground. When I stooped down to pick them up I noticed two young fellows come over to help hold down my son's arms. 'Hold up!' I yelled. "Wait a minute!" The four of them stopped and looked at me. I saw my son's tear-stained face and it broke my heart, but the call of the drugs was stronger. I went up to them and spoke to the two faces that were unfamiliar to me. "If you two want a piece of my son you're going to have to give me some more bags. This arrangement ain't free." They thought for a minute before nodding their heads in agreement and each boy threw me two bags.

"I trailed the boys, along with my son, to the nearest crack house. When we reached the front door, Upshaw kicked it in like he was the police. Inside, dozens of addicts ran for cover. Upshaw ordered the boys to take my son upstairs to one of the abandoned bedrooms and I found a dark, discreet corner to get high and hide from my guilt over what I had done. Placing my back against the wall, I slid down to the floor. Pulling out my lighter, I ignited the flame. I was drawn to the light but I just couldn't live in the light. Instead, I choose to live in total darkness with the only light I saw burning from a crack pipe.

"Upshaw came and knelt down beside me. He tried being friendly by flashing his pearly white teeth, but I still didn't trust him. I feared he was going to try and renege on our agreement so I turned toward the wall and hovered over my drugs. I was caught off guard when he thanked me for coming through with my son. He then reached into his pocket and in the palm of his hand he held a small pink vile full of crack.

"It's for you," he told me and I quickly snatched it up before he could change his mind. I heard him give a cocky chuckle as he walked away.

"My son's piercing cries and screams for help from anyone who would come to his rescue didn't bother my high. From that day forward, I entered a world I couldn't escape from."

Someone offered Fatima a tissue to wipe away the tears from her face. "For the next nine months, I set my child up to be raped over and over again by Upshaw and his friends. Those rapes resulted in major damage to my son's . . ." Fatima searched for the proper word to use. ". . . rectum. He began having problems controlling his bowels. He would have bowel movements any where, at any time. The kids teased him so badly at school he stopped going."

"One day I came home from working the corners all day searching for my next high, and all my son's things were gone. No note. No phone call. Nothing. I haven't heard from him since. Drugs can and will destroy your life. I thank the Lord for helping me stop because I couldn't do it on my own. God is so amazing!" she wailed. "God is so amazing."

A pointy elbow jabbed Heaven in the ribs. "Heaven, you believe that?" Ebony whispered in her ear. "She must feel horrible." Ebony rose from her seat and joined in on the group hug.

Chapter 4

Ten minutes passed before a loud buzzer sounded throughout the room. Ms. Griffin, the group facilitator, spoke loudly above the noise in the room, "Ladies, this afternoon we have another speaker. A highly respected man in our community is here to share his story with you." Ms. Griffin led a futile attempt at applause and stepped away from the podium before taking a seat in the audience.

The speaker stepped up, straightened his tie, and grabbed the microphone. "Ladies." His strong baritone voice contradicted his short five-foot-four stature. "I'm Reverend Stansfield and I feel honored to have been asked to come speak with you today. The reason I feel so honored is because at one time in my life I was facing the same issues a lot of you are today."

Reverend Stansfield paced back and forth in front of his audience and Heaven turned her attention toward him. "I spent thirty years in Rahway

State Prison for murder. I was married to a beautiful woman who carried the burden of my drug addiction for over fifteen years before she put me and my things out on the curb. She shut the door on me and our life together.

"The day my life changed forever began with me waking up to the smell of urine and funk in the air. That scent was a reminder that I had again spent the night in a crack house." Reverend Stansfield rubbed his hand over his face.

"I remember my stomach growling loudly from lack of food. I had no choice but to get up and find myself something to eat. I didn't have any money, so I had to do what I had done in the past, go rummaging through the dumpster that sat behind the McDonald's until I found enough food to fill my belly. Lifting myself up from the floor, I walked toward the exit."

Reverend Stansfield held up one finger. "On my way to the door, I passed by a man lying in the corner. Now, it wasn't unusual to find a dead body lying around in a crack house. On any given day, somebody may lay down to rest their eyes and never open them again.

"I had a habit of checking on people to make sure they were all right. So I went over and lightly shook him. When he didn't move, I knelt down to turn him over and when I did, I was surprised to see it was my next-door neighbor, Shane. Pressing my fingers against his neck, I prayed he still had a pulse. Suddenly, Shane's eyes opened in a panic. The look in his eyes made me think I was looking straight into the eyes of death. His hair was full of lint balls, teeth were yellow, clothes soiled, and he smelled like he hadn't bathed in weeks. Black circles surrounded his eyes. Shane grabbed my shirt and begged me to share my dope with him. He even offered me sex for just a small hit.

"I couldn't believe how low my neighbor would go just for some drugs. Isn't that just like an addict? I could criticize somebody else for their faults, but I couldn't see my own." He laughed at himself.

"I ran out the door leaving Shane to fend for himself. On my way to McDonald's, I managed to beg a few city workers for spare change. By noon, I had collected enough money to buy a coffee so I went to Dunkin Donuts. As I was sitting on a bench in a nearby park enjoying my coffee, a former co-worker happened to pass me by. He stopped and preached to me about how drugs were bad. All the things he said I had heard before, but one thing he said stuck in my mind. 'Drugs had brought me down.' After he walked away, I laughed at everything he said. I was aware there were some things I could improve about myself, but I wasn't as bad as Shane and in my eyes that made me okay. But the truth was, I was worse than Shane because I couldn't admit I had a problem. I sat on that bench all day thinking about what that man had said to me. Ultimately, I knew he was right. I was just as messed up as Shane. At one time, we both had families, houses, and cars but by that time, we were homeless, sleeping in crack houses, and addicted to drugs.

"I couldn't live like that any longer. I needed my wife and family back and it had to start that day. I went home to talk things over with my wife, but instead of a blessed reunion I witnessed the greatest betrayal.

"When I reached the house I was surprised to find the door open and screen door unlocked. I knew my wife must have been home and once I heard her laughter in the air I knew I was right. I decided to enter without knocking; knowing I had to take the only chance I would have to get back into my house. Her voice lured me to our bedroom. I approached the doorway, unprepared for what my eyes would see; my wife in the arms of another man. I can't even describe the anger that stirred like a storm inside of me. I roared like a lion and pounced on the man who lay in my bed."

Reverend Stansfield grabbed his head to illustrate his state of mind. "I could hear my wife's screams telling me to stop. Her soft punches landed on my back. With little effort I threw her off me and slammed her lover into the dresser. He came toward me and I hit him with all my might. I hit him so hard he stumbled backward tripped over my wife's high heel shoe and hit his head on the corner of a wooden chest that sat in the room. Her lover lay on the floor, lifeless. She ran to his naked body, cradling his head while screaming obscenities at me. He was dead."

The reverend leaned against the podium. "I pleaded self-defense. It wasn't until the trial and my wife was on the stand testifying that I remembered. She told the jury how we were no longer married and had been divorced for over three years. The man I murdered was her new husband. They had just gotten married two weeks prior."

He sighed heavily. "My mind was so fried from doing drugs I had forgotten three entire years out of my life. I felt so guilty and ashamed I wished I had been the one to die that night. I went through hell before Jesus saved me, and if he can save me, I know he can save you. But you have to be willing to make Christ the center of your life."

Heaven was moved by the reverend's words. She sat for a moment and reflected on what he'd said. She wanted to do the right thing, but she was unsure whether she could do it. Her past was full of so much failure. When she looked at Fatima and Reverend Stansfield, they appeared strong and confident. That wasn't her. She felt best about herself when she was getting high or was around people who got high. None of the women in the room looked the way she felt. She still had doubts about whether she could successfully complete the program, but she was willing to give it a try.

"The deacons from my church have bought each of you a Bible," Reverend Stansfield announced. "They will pass one out to each of you." Then Reverend Stansfield mingled with the women in the meeting. Ebony had never returned to her seat, leaving Heaven with no one to talk with.

Heaven was picking at her nails to pass the time when she saw a man approaching in her peripheral vision. When she looked up, the face that looked back at her was identical to her grandfather, "Uncle Avery," she said.

"Hey, baby girl." They hugged. "When Ms. Campbell asked me if I was related to a woman named Heaven Stansfield who would be staying at the halfway house, I couldn't believe my niece was finally coming home." Heaven blushed. "Why didn't you write? You know Mom thinks about you every day."

"That's why I didn't get in touch with anybody. She needs to stop worrying about me," Heaven said.

"As long as she has breath inside of her she will worry about you." He snatched up her hand and told her to sit. "You know you're not the only one in this family who has had a drug problem. Just like I told those ladies, you can beat your addiction. Stop relying on yourself. Lean on me. Lean on Nana. Lean on God." They hugged again.

Then one of the deacons walked up to them and handed Heaven a Bible. "Deacon Washington, this is my niece, Heaven."

She looked up at a fine man who stood at least six-foot-two with an athletic slender build. He had the kind of look that would make any women look twice. His dark smooth skin glistened under the lights and a strong jaw line was the foundation for voluptuous lips.

"Hello, Heaven. That's a beautiful name." He reached out to shake her hand and flashed a brilliant smile. Her eyes followed him as he continued giving out Bibles.

"I have to finish up, but we'll talk later." Avery went back to the podium then asked everyone to turn to I Corinthians 10:12-13. Heaven hadn't read a Bible in years. She heard people around her flipping pages, trying to find the scripture. Everyone around her had successfully found the verse, except for her. She felt stupid. While those around her read the scripture together out loud, she was still trying to find I Corinthians.

Flipping one page at a time, she became frustrated and set the Bible down on the chair next to her. She was slouched down in her chair when Deacon Washington came to her rescue. He opened her Bible to the verse with ease and pointed it out to her. They read along with the group and as he held the Bible open, she noticed a wedding ring on his finger. Her heart shattered from disappointment. She had hoped he was single.

After scripture was over Mr. Good Looking remained seated next to her until the meeting concluded. "Thanks, I really appreciate you saving me," she said to him. "I'm really embarrassed by my lack of knowledge about the Bible."

"Don't be, green eyes. Everyone has a little trouble once in a while. Sometimes I even forget where a few of the books are located." He smiled. "So, what's it like being the reverend's niece?"

"It's not that bad."

"I also knew your grandfather before he passed. He was a good man."

Heaven remembered the day the warden called her into his office to tell her that her grandfather had died. It was hard to believe he was gone. "Yes, he was," she replied.

As they talked, a woman from the group approached them and reached out to hug the deacon. Her flirting was obvious. After they finished hugging, she reached out to give Heaven a hug. But Heaven instinctively threw up her hands to ward her off. "Oh no, I'm sorry!" She shielded herself from the embrace. "I don't hug people I don't know. I have a phobia about hugging strangers. You understand, don't you?"

Not offended by her words, the woman simply smiled and moved on to the next person.

"So I guess that means I can't get a hug from you?" the deacon asked.

"No. You can have a hug." she had quickly rescinded her words. "I just don't like to hug strangers; especially addicts." As soon as the words left her mouth she regretted it. "I'm sorry I didn't mean that the way it sounded it's just that . . ."

"You don't have to explain." He nonchalantly changed the subject. "So I guess I'll be seeing you in church on Sunday?"

"Church?" Heaven questioned.

"Of course she'll be in church." Avery walked up behind them. "Listen, Mom is gonna be gone all summer. She went down south to stay with Aunt Matilda. I'm not going to tell her you're home. I'll leave you that honor. So that gives you all summer to prepare and get yourself together. Is that fair?"

"That's fair."

Light chimes rang out and pulled Deacon Washington away from them and to his cell phone. "Excuse me a moment." Turning his back to them, he answered his phone. "All right, honey. I'll meet you there." She overheard him tell the caller as he ended the call. "I'm sorry, I have to go. My wife just went into labor. My sister is rushing her to the hospital. I have to meet them there."

"That's great news. Congratulations," Avery shouted. "Let me walk you to the car."

Heaven forced a smile on her face as she watched Avery and Deacon Washington hurry off. Ebony leaned over her shoulder and whispered in her ear. "I heard what he just said. It's too bad the good ones are always taken."

"Yeah," she solemnly replied. "I guess some things aren't meant to be."

Chapter 5

Heaven's first day at the halfway house had been a long one and it wasn't over yet. After dinner she was scheduled to have her first one on one meeting with Ms. Griffin, her assessment counselor. Her journey through a maze of halls ended at the last office at the end of a desolate hall. Ms. Griffin's door was already slightly ajar and Heaven could see her typing away on her computer.

She noticed Heaven standing in the hall and waved her in. She told her to close the door behind her and have a seat. Ms. Griffin's office was neatly decorated. Every pen, paper, and file on her desk was arranged in an order that was specific to her needs.

Sorority paraphernalia decorated three of the four walls and against the fourth wall hung a portrait of praying hands with the Lord's Prayer inscribed beside it. Heaven's grandmother had the same exact picture hanging on her living room wall.

Taking a seat in one of the empty chairs in front of Ms. Griffin's desk, Heaven watched her pull out a file and quickly look it over. "Did you go out for dinner?"

"I went out, but I didn't have much money to buy anything to eat. Two dollars and eighty seven cents isn't enough to even buy a Happy Meal."

Ms. Griffin laughed. "How does it feel to be back home?" Folding her hands in her lap she focused her attention on Heaven.

"It's strange to come back after all these years and see the old buildings I grew up with replaced with newer ones."

"I agree. I grew up in the Parkside section of the city and I can see the city is trying to make a change for the good." The two chatted a bit about the neighborhood and the improvements the city was trying to make through the urban revitalization project before Ms. Griffin asked about her. "Heaven, what made you sign up to come to the halfway house, besides the obvious reason of leaving the prison early?"

"My prison assessment counselor and I had been talking about it for a while. She wouldn't let me forget that once I was within nine months of being released on parole I was eligible to come to the halfway house. She gave me some pamphlets about this place and once I read you were a Christian halfway house that helped women with substance abuse problems coming out of prison, I felt like this program was made specifically for me."

"A lot of women feel the same way. That is why a lot of the women who leave here never return to prison. They see and hear that everyone here is in the same fight." Ms. Griffin's office phone rang loudly, disrupting their talk. Instead of answering it, she pushed a button that sent the caller straight to voice mail. "What did you think of the group session today?" she asked.

"It was sad."

"Yes, the stories shared with us today were sad, but that's why it was so important they shared their story with the group. Fatima has had all that sorrow and regret bottled up inside of her for years, and today was the first day she was able to release it. With all that pain inside of her, there was never enough room for her to begin healing. I like to encourage the ladies to give their burdens to the Lord because it will make life so much more fulfilling. A lot of the women say once they tell their story it's like being baptized because they are letting go and letting God."

The joy Ms. Griffin spoke about was evident on her face. She really believed Jesus was the key to sober living.

"Heaven, it's obvious by the expression on your face you don't agree with me."

"It's not that I don't believe what you said, but if Jesus really is the key to cleaning up, then that meeting would have been full of addicts who want to get close to Christ."

"You are absolutely right." Heaven was shocked Ms. Griffin agreed with her. "Addiction is not a good thing and people turn to drugs for different reasons. For some, life becomes too much of a burden. Others have endured a personal tragedy they are trying to forget. Whatever the reason, these people are making the wrong choices. They are disillusioned into thinking drugs will make them feel better when the only thing that can permanently cure them of this disease is submitting to God."

"So we're wrong?" she asked.

"No. I would never judge or blame anyone because of their choice to abuse drugs. Perhaps at the time they didn't know God existed, but G.I.S.A is here to show you that have another option. Instead of being enslaved to something that will bring you down every time, I want to introduce everyone to someone who will lift them up and take them places they never thought were possible. I want everyone to see how amazing God can be."

Hearing her speak made Heaven feel good. Ms. Griffin was inspiring and encouraged Heaven to believe in herself. That was something she hadn't done in a long time.

When Heaven returned to her room, Ebony was already sound asleep in her bed. It had been a long day for both of them and Heaven couldn't wait to hit the sheets. After taking a shower, she slipped on her pajamas and got into bed. The first thing she noticed about her bed was that it was so much softer than her bunk at the prison. She could no longer feel the bed springs in her back. The bed was so comfortable she was sure she would have no problem falling fast asleep.

An hour later, she lay in her bed still unable to get any rest. She kicked the covers off and sat up. It felt like somebody had turned on the heat, although the heat wasn't on and the window was open. She placed the back of her hand against her forehead. A dry mouth forced her to get a cup of water from the bathroom. Heaven was jealous that Ebony slept soundly while she suffered restlessly from the heat.

Heaven walked over and stuck her head out the window trying to catch a breeze. The weather outside was not offering any relief from the heat so she had no choice but to strip down to her bra and panties.

Ebony finally stirred from her sleep. Rubbing the sleep from out of her eyes, she turned on the lamp. "Are you all right?" she asked. When she glanced at Heaven, she stared in awe and then sprung out of bed and to Heaven's side. "Heaven, are you feeling all right? You're drenched with sweat."

Heaven looked down at herself. Suddenly she felt weak and a bit groggy. Her body swayed and she held out her hand to steady herself against the wall. Ebony panicked and raced out their room yelling for help.

There was nothing anyone could do to help Heaven. Going through withdrawal was hard and the only way she knew how to free her body from its dependency was to do it cold turkey. She had expected to experience the usual symptoms but she had never become light-headed before. By the time she had made it back to bed, Ebony had returned with Ms. Campbell.

Ms. Campbell was the last person she wanted to see. Heaven was scared that if Ms. Campbell knew she was going through withdrawal, she was going to send her back to the prison.

"What's wrong with you, Stansfield?" Ms. Campbell asked with her stern voice.

"Nothing; it's just the twenty-four-hour flu."

Ms. Campbell walked up to her and pulled Heaven's face up toward hers. "Look at those dilated pupils." Ms. Campbell left the room and within fifteen minutes, the paramedics were at Heaven's side taking her vitals. They told Ms. Campbell they needed to take Heaven to the emergency room.

They kept her at the hospital overnight and gave her methadone to help alleviate the uncomfortable feeling from withdrawal. When Heaven returned to the halfway house, she was surprised when Ms. Campbell said she wasn't going to send her back to the prison. Instead, she told Heaven she was not the first resident in the house she had seen detox from drugs they had gotten inside the prison. Ms. Campbell told her she was being given a second chance and how important it was to stay clean. Heaven was thankful and promised not to let her down.

Chapter 6

One week had passed and Ebony started her job as a cashier at a nearby supermarket. Heaven was also hired as a cashier but she wasn't scheduled to begin until the next day. They hadn't even been looking for jobs, but when Ms. Griffin came to them and said she could help them get jobs, they jumped at the chance.

Seven days of rooming with Ebony had been exhausting. Heaven thought Ebony displayed signs of Attention Deficit Disorder. The girl wouldn't leave her alone. She had not had one day alone since they arrived.

Residents in the halfway house were required to attend group meetings at least three times a week, one-on-one meetings twice a week, and keep up with daily chores. Heaven felt like she had left the prison to come to work camp, and to make matters worse, Ebony followed her everywhere she went.

Ebony's hyperactive behavior was irritating. The

girl not only talked non-stop, she couldn't sit still. She was the first one up in the morning and usually the last to lay her head down. Ebony completed her chores every morning, did laundry for the entire floor, and helped cook breakfast, lunch, and dinner for every resident in the house. Her energy was mentally draining on those who watched her, but with Ebony being at work for eight whole hours, Heaven had time for herself.

So far, she had slept till noon, took a long hot bath, and now she was about to take her third nap of the day. When Heaven laid her head down, she thought she was dreaming when she heard Ebony's voice drift in from the hallway. *She couldn't be back already.* It was too soon. Time sure did fly when she wasn't around.

"Heaven!" She stumbled into their room carrying an arm full of clothes. "Remember Deacon Washington? The man you were talking to last week."

"How could I forget?" Heaven wished Ebony would be a little quieter. She covered her head with a blanket.

"His wife died," she blurted out while looking through the pile of clothes.

Pushing the blanket to the side Heaven sat straight up in bed. The smile on her face resembled the joker. Ebony had her back turned to Heaven so she couldn't see her reaction. "What happened?" Heaven asked, disguising the joy she felt.

Ebony shook her head in disbelief. "She died during childbirth. Her funeral is today. Ms. Campbell said it would be nice if the house showed its support for the deacon in his time of need since he's always been around to support everyone here."

What a coincidence, Heaven thought. *His wife dying the same day we meet. Maybe some things were meant to be after all.* "What time does it start?" she asked.

"Two o'clock," Ebony replied, while digging through her top dresser drawer for underwear.

A quick glance at the digital clock that sat on their nightstand told Heaven she had less than three hours to get ready. "Where did you get those clothes from?" Heaven asked. Ebony had several pairs of pants, shirts, skirts, and dresses out on her bed.

"The Salvation Army truck is downstairs. Ms. Campbell said if we needed some clothes we could have anything off it we wanted." She held up a dark brown, flowery, sheer blouse against her chest and posed in the mirror. "Do you like this?"

"It's okay, but you're going to need something on underneath that." Ebony tossed the top back into her pile of clothes and dug for something else.

The secondhand clothes Ebony was given may have been good enough for her, but not Heaven. "I'll be right back," Heaven hollered out as she left the room. "I'm going to see if Fatima has anything I can borrow."

Fatima was the only other size six in the house. Plus, she worked part-time as a sales clerk at one of the department stores at the mall and always had the best clothes in the house.

Fatima wasn't planning on attending the funeral and that was good because a few hours later,

Heaven stood at Celeste Washington's burial feeling like a perfect ten. Convincing Fatima to allow her to borrow her black, wrap around dress was not easy. Initially, she had told her no. Fatima complained about how she wasn't going to allow anyone to wear something of hers that still had the tags on it, but Heaven was desperate to get her hands on that dress. She had to promise to do her household chores for two months in exchange for the dress. She knew it would look great on her. She just hoped that the good Deacon was worth all the trouble.

Ms. Griffin had warned Heaven that since her body was still cleansing itself from the drugs she used while behind bars, she may begin to look worse before she looked any healthier. She saw what Ms. Griffin was referring to when she saw how Fatima's dress hung off her like a hanger. Her rapid weight loss left her with no booty and flat breasts. Her caramel complexion had turned pale so she had to use plenty of foundation and blush to get her face to look natural again.

During the funeral she learned Deacon Washington and his wife had three children together, including the newborn. The two had been members of Mount Olive Baptist Church for over seven years and were very active in the community. It was quite clear by the number of speakers and the long line of people waiting to pay their last respects, his wife was admired by many.

From a distance, Heaven watched Deacon Washington mourn the loss of his wife. He leaned over and laid a single red rose down on her casket and mouthed the words, "I will always love you."

Tears fell down his cheeks from beneath his dark sunglasses. His pain was understandable to everyone in attendance and the sorrow he tried to bury deep inside escaped his soul. He collapsed to the ground and wept beside his wife's casket. His display of devotion set off outward cries of grief from everyone in attendance.

Heaven had the urge to rush to his side and soothe his broken heart. The longer he cried the more his pain weighed heavily on her heart. She couldn't bear to see this handsome man endure any more heartache. Stepping forward, she pushed people out of the way as she tried to get to him, but before she could, a couple of deacons grabbed him and helped him back to the limo.

Grieving church folk each placed roses down on Celeste's casket and left the cemetery. Heaven stared at her casket wondering what kind of woman Celeste was. She had heard all the nice things people said about her at the funeral but she wondered if she was really a good wife. Was she spontaneous and fun? Did she take care of her husband behind closed doors?

"Heaven, are you coming?" Ebony nudged her lightly.

"In a minute. I want to pay my last respects."

"We'll wait for you back at the van," she said.

Heaven looked around to see who was left. There weren't many people around as she stepped up to Celeste's casket and lightly brushed her hand along side the beautifully polished wooden box. "Celeste, you don't have to worry. I'll see to it that your husband is taken care of. You don't have to worry about a thing." The van horn blew twice and Heaven looked up just in time to see Ebony waving her hand telling her to come on. Heaven attempted to drop the rose on top of Celeste's casket, but she missed and it fell to the ground. She quietly left Celeste to her final resting place.

Chapter 7

After they left the cemetery, a few of the girls insisted they stop by the deacon's house to grab a bite to eat. Ebony objected to the idea. She thought it was tacky for them to take advantage of the Washington family's hospitality just to fill their empty stomachs, but a simple vote among the girls outnumbered her five to one.

Back at the deacon's house, they stood in a long line that extended out the front door and down the walkway. At the front of the line two women greeted guests and accepted sympathy cards. Heaven overheard someone from behind her say the women were the deacon's mother and sister, Emalee.

She stretched her neck to get a good look at them, but was only able to clearly see the sister. After studying her appearance, Heaven came to the conclusion she was a common looking girl. The woman was of average height with a run of the mill hairdo and ordinary looking prescription glasses. There was nothing extraordinary about her. She was the sort of woman who could easily blend into any crowd.

"I'm so sorry for your loss." Ebony gave Ms. Washington and her daughter a comforting smile when they finally reached the front of the line.

"Thank you," Ms. Washington replied. "It's been hard on my son and his children. Hasani is so used to being the strong one. He has always been known for putting other people's needs before his. It's good to know he has so many people who care. It's hard for him to allow others to help. Celeste was his only love."

"Is he around?" Heaven spoke up from behind Ebony. "My name is Heaven." She reached out to shake her hand. "I'm Reverend Stansfield's niece and I would love to give your son my condolences in person."

His mother smiled back at her and gripped her hand lovingly. "No, dear. He went up to his room to lie down. Today has been rough for him. I'm counting on God to pull him through this. He needs some time alone. God is so amazing and only he can mend a broken heart."

The genuine warmth that rose from Ms. Washington's voice made Heaven feel at ease. Love showered her words when she spoke about her son and the love of God was reflected in her gentle touch and soft eyes. Her spirit was something one Heaven not only admired, but she coveted for herself.

"Reverend Stansfield's niece? I've never heard him mention a niece before." Emalee shot daggers of bitterness in Heaven's direction. After Emalee looked Heaven over from head to toe, she sucked her teeth and rolled her eyes, exhibiting extreme hostility toward her.

"I've been away for a while and I'm just getting reacquainted with my family," Heaven replied to Ms. Washington.

"Ms. Washington, if you need any help with anything, please let me know. I don't mind helping out," Ebony offered.

"Thank you, dear."

"I'm also available to help," Heaven added. "I'll help with whatever you need." Heaven threw a callous look Emalee's way.

Emalee wasted no time moving them along so she could greet the guests standing behind them. When the ladies stepped into the deacon's home, Heaven immediately fell in love with the impressive décor. The entire house had a homey, rustic feel to it; from the living room walls made of brick face and stucco, to the kitchen painted in different shades of yellow and orange.

Ebony and Heaven grabbed a couple of empty seats at the dining room table. It wasn't surprising when Ebony struck up a conversation with the other women at the table while Heaven sat watching guests enter the house one at a time.

Without any warning, a woman wearing a chic, simple black dress offset by gold-plated accessories entered the house. Her short hairstyle was regal and made her look like a queen. She could have been a spokes model for confidence, beauty, and modesty.

Several guests on their way out the door stopped and greeted her with warm hugs and kisses.

"Hello, Sister Washington." The woman screamed straight into Ms. Washington's ear.

"Hello, Sister Stewart, and how are Grand-momma's babies doing?" Standing next to Sister Stewart were two small children; six-year-old Samuel and three-year-old Imani. Ms. Washington looked Sister Stewart in the eye. "Thanks for keeping an eye on them."

"No problem, but I think somebody's hungry." Sister Stewart pointed to the infant cradled in her arms.

"Hey, little Wesley, are you hungry?" Emalee lifted the baby from Sister Stewart's arms. "I guess all the children are hungry."

"I'm sorry I can't stay any longer, but I have to get back home," Sister Stewart apologized. "You know my son is still battling that illness and he isn't doing too well today."

"I will continue to pray for you." The two women shared a warm hug before the Sister rushed out the door.

"Mom, why don't we feed the children first and then I'll fix a plate for Hasani?" Emalee suggested.

"Why don't I just run upstairs and get Celeste? She'll help us out with the children," her mother replied loud enough for just about everyone in the house to hear.

Ms. Washington's remark stood out like a sore thumb, making her the center of attention. Emalee prayed her mother would go through the day without having an episode, but it just wasn't meant to be. Dementia was deteriorating her mother's mind and memory. She walked over and took her mother's hand in hers. "Mom, don't you remember? Celeste is gone," Emalee reminded her.

Always ready to lend a helping hand, Ebony went to Emalee and again offered her help, "If it's all right with you, I would love to help you with the children."

Emalee agreed. "Thank you, girl! I could really use an extra pairs of hands today." Emalee walked toward the kitchen with the baby in her arms with her mother following not too far behind.

Ebony lowered herself eye level with the children. "How you guys holding up today?" she asked.

The children looked so sad. The usual sparkle you expect to see in a child's eyes was gone and in its place was a lot of unhappiness. Imani attempted to give Ebony a smile, but Samuel didn't even try to put up any effort.

"Today is not a good day is it?" Ebony asked.

"My mommy is dead," Samuel mumbled.

Ebony took Samuel's hand in hers, "Sweetie, your mommy is an angel now. God took her from you so she could be with Him."

A single tear fell from Samuel's eye and landed on the collar of his white button-up shirt. That one tear released a stream of tears and he threw his arms around Ebony's neck to hide his face from the guests in the room.

Imani patted her brother on the back. "Sam, don't cry. Mommy's not here to wipe them away."

Ebony pulled Samuel back so he could see her face. "Do you want to see if we can find something good to eat in the kitchen? Earlier, I saw someone carrying a chocolate cake. Would you like that?"

Wiping the tears away with the back of his hand and using his dress pants to dry his hand off he nodded.

"I don't like chocolate cake," Imani screamed, letting the entire room know her preference.

"I'm sure there are different kinds of cake in the kitchen. We'll just have to look until we find something you like." Ebony held out her hand and the three slowly shuffled toward the kitchen.

While Ebony assisted in the kitchen, Heaven took the liberty of checking out Deacon Washington's home. Scattered on walls and table tops were dozens of pictures of him and Celeste together. Pictures of the children hung against another wall and separated from all family photos was a picture of Deacon Washington shaking hands with the former President Bill Clinton.

Every painting, picture, and art sculpture seemed to sit perfectly in its own place. Heaven wondered if Celeste decorated herself or hired someone. Either way, the woman definitely had a sense of style.

A lifelike portrait of Celeste sat above the fireplace. The painter had used such detail that it captured the realness of her piercing black eyes, her flawless mocha brown skin, and thick black hair that fell in layers around her face.

Other guest standing around commented on how elegant and at peace Celeste looked in the picture. For Heaven, the picture was mesmerizing. She couldn't tear her eyes away from it. She forced herself to look elsewhere, but her curiosity about this woman drew her back.

Heaven looked into Celeste's eyes trying to learn more about who the woman really was. At the funeral, everyone who spoke had something nice to say about her, but Heaven thought there had to be someone in the church who held a grudge against Celeste because of something she did or said.

"Celeste was an angel." Avery seemed to appear out of thin air and startled Heaven. "She was everything to this church. Kind. Considerate. Thoughtful. No one ever had an unkind word to say against her. She will surely be missed." Then he walked away.

Heaven watched him disappear in the crowd. "That was bizarre." It felt like her uncle had come by just to answer the questions Heaven had been thinking to herself.

A loud crashing sound came from the kitchen and Heaven could hear Ebony say, "I'm sorry, Ms. Washington." Ebony's attempt at being helpful wasn't going as well as planned.

Heaven had to use the ladies' room. So, using the same directions Emalee had given some guests earlier, she climbed the stairs to the second floor, turned left, and entered the first door on the right.

She pulled a comb and tube of lipstick from her purse and set them down on the counter. Before she freshened up her lipstick, she noticed several bottles and jars sitting on the counter. Heaven browsed through a collection of women's perfumes until she found one she was not familiar with. She sprayed a dab on her wrists and took a whiff. "Phew, this stuff stinks." She quickly put the cap back on it and tried to place everything back in its place before walking out.

Instead of heading back downstairs, Heaven focused her attention on four closed doors. She knew one of them had to be the Deacon's bedroom. She knocked at a couple of doors before she succeeded in finding him.

Deacon Washington was laid out on his king size bed, still dressed in black slacks and a button-down shirt. He was balled up in a fetal position, facing the window and staring into the sky. He did a quick change of position and turned over in her direction, stretching out his long legs. His eyes fixed on her, but he didn't look startled or surprised by her presence. The way he stared at Heaven made her stomach nervous.

"I'm sorry. I was looking for the bathroom." His eyes gazed straight through her, making her feel guilty for lying. "Are you all right?" She walked farther into his bedroom. "Everyone's worried about you and you didn't look too good at the cemetery."

He was looking in her direction, but she didn't think he knew she was there. She watched his eyes and he didn't blink once while she was talking to him. Heaven began to rethink the decision she made to go searching for him, but before she could leave, he stopped her.

"That perfume you're wearing. It's my wife's favorite."

"I'm sorry. I didn't mean to . . ."

"No. It's okay." He beckoned for her to come closer, and then he remembered her. "Heaven?" She sat on the edge of his bed and she nodded her head. "I remembered you by those green eyes. I appreciate you attending my wife's funeral. I know you didn't know her, but it was thoughtful of you to come."

"It was a beautiful service."

"Yes it was. My wife would have loved it. The church was full of purple and white lilies; her favorite flower." He appeared to go back over the day's events in his mind.

"Would you like something to eat?" Heaven tried to change the subject. She didn't want to talk about his wife. "I can run downstairs and fix you a plate," she offered.

"No, thank you. I'm not hungry. Can we just talk?" he asked.

She shifted her body uncomfortably and prayed he didn't want to talk about Celeste.

"You're scared I'm going to talk about my wife." He chuckled out loud. "I can read body language pretty well."

She laughed along with him and was ashamed she was so transparent. She laid her hand on top of his and squeezed it lightly. "If you want to talk about your wife, I'm fine with it. I feel honored you feel comfortable enough to discuss her with me."

"You are probably the only person I have mentioned Celeste to. Up until now, I haven't really been in the mood for a lot of company. Celeste's death happened so suddenly. It was a surprise to all of us." He closed his eyes. "After she delivered the baby, the doctors took him to check his vitals. The nurse handed him back to me and I held him up so Celeste could get a look at him. She smiled and reached out her hand, and then her hand went limp in mid-air. Monitors started beeping, one nurse snatched Wesley from me and another escorted me out the room. I tried to ask them what was going on, but no one would answer my questions. Then the doctor came out to tell me she had passed on."

He sat quiet for a moment, leaving Heaven at a loss for words. How was she supposed to comfort him over the loss of his wife when all she could think about was how inviting his lips were?

A light tapping on his bedroom door interrupted them and when he yelled out for the guest to come in, Emalee entered with a tray full of food for her brother. She was smiling until she saw Heaven and then that nasty smirk reappeared on her face. "I'm sorry. I don't mean to interrupt," she said, although Heaven didn't believe a word out her mouth.

"No, that's okay. Heaven, I would like for you to meet my sister."

Emalee plastered a phony smile on her face for the sake of her brother. "It is nice meeting you." She turned back to her brother. "Hasani, I thought you might be hungry. I brought you up something to eat." She placed the tray down on the bed and pulled up a chair that sat in the corner of the bedroom.

"I have to go." Heaven wasn't allowing Emalee to run her off, but it was getting late. Ebony was probably looking for her so they could go. "It was really nice talking with you, Deacon Washington; I hope to see you in church soon."

"Likewise," he replied.

Chapter 8

When Heaven told Ebony she was going to church on Sunday, she wasn't surprised when she asked to tag along. Ebony had made it known she was willing to try anything that would help her get her life together.

It had been a long time since Heaven had been on the inside of her grandfather's church. The closer they got to the building with a white wooden cross perched on the top the more Heaven was reminded of how Nana would sit in the front pew every Sunday morning and listen to her grandfather preach the Gospel.

Mount Olive looked rather busy this Sunday morning. Men in fancy double breasted suits escorted women in big, elaborate, feathery hats. Dozens of people stood around, chatting and greeting one another.

When they reached the top of the stairs leading into the church, they were stopped by a young man who looked no older than twenty years old.

"Ladies, welcome to Mount Olive Baptist Church."
He handed them each a program. "Let me guess.
Is this your first time here?" Ebony nodded her
head. "I knew that. I've been a member of this
church since I was a little boy. I know just about
everyone who comes through these doors and
your faces were not familiar to me."

"I'm Ebony and this is Heaven." They shook
hands. "Heaven is not really a stranger to this
church. She used to come here when she was a little girl. She's the pastor's niece."

"Welcome back!" He hugged both girls, then
Levi Wright introduced himself. The first thing
Heaven noticed was that he was just as friendly as
Ebony; maybe even friendlier. The two of them hit
it off right away and talked as if they were old
friends.

In order for Heaven to tolerate being friends
with Ebony, she quickly learned it would be wise to
mentally tune her out when she started talking too
much. This was one of those times.

While Heaven waited on Ebony, she saw a man
pull into the church parking lot driving one the
most expensive Lexuses on the market. The white
Lexus with gold trim and rims that sparkled in the
sunlight slowly crept through the lot.

The driver lightly blew the horn to get the attention of another man who happened to be walking. They spoke for a brief second before the
Lexus sped into the first available parking space.

From where Heaven was standing, she couldn't
get a good look at the driver, but that didn't matter. She could see herself dating a good, *rich*,
church-going man. If someone had told her she

could find an eligible bachelor at church, she would have been there a whole lot sooner.

Minutes passed and he still hadn't gotten out of his car. She wondered what could be taking him so long. If he took too much longer, she wouldn't be able to introduce herself until after church.

"Heaven, come on." Ebony held the door open for her to follow. She wasn't ready to go in yet, but feared she would get left behind. She extended her neck one last time to see if the driver had exited the car. He was still sitting. So she would have to wait to meet him.

Levi escorted them down the aisle to their seats. "If you need anything, just raise your hand and I'll be here." He quickly walked away to usher other guests.

"He's a nice young man," Ebony commented. "I wish more kids were like him."

From the back of the church the alto, soprano, tenor, and bass choir members warmed up their voices in harmony. Standing in the front of the church, the choir director motioned for the choir to march toward him. Men and woman dressed in white robes with burgundy trim hummed a soft melody as they marched. Sister Stewart stood at the front of the line, lending her loud voice as a guide for everyone to follow.

Once the singers were seated in the choir box, service began. Right before the offering was collected, Reverend Stansfield reminded members of the congregation not to call Deacon Washington regarding any church matters. He was taking a three-month leave of absence and would return at the end of summer.

Then Reverend Stansfield asked Heaven to stand. "This is my niece," he announced. "And sitting next to her is her friend, Ebony. I want everyone to make sure they welcome her back to the house of the Lord. I've got a feeling we'll be seeing a lot of them around here," he teased.

After the offering, Reverend Stansfield stood before the congregation to deliver his sermon. "Mount Olive, I know you've been reading the paper and I know you've seen the news." The congregation declared amen. "You may think you know what's going on in the streets of Camden, but let me tell you what's really going on. If you look outside these doors you will see people are sleepwalking; addicted to drugs. Our brothers and sisters are screaming out for help. Friends and family are dying in the streets, unaware that taking that one hit could be their last.

"A deadly concoction of heroin laced with Fentanyl has hit our streets and it's laying out bodies so fast, the hospital is running out of room in the morgue. People are dying within minutes of one another.

"It's being promoted by the dope dealers as stuff that can give any user the ultimate high. Fentanyl is a drug that is eighty times more powerful than morphine. Imagine combining that with heroin!"

Reverend Stansfield stormed down from the pulpit and into the aisles. "This new kind of drug is making people go crazy. Addicts are lining up around the corner. Can you imagine waiting for your turn to die? Our future is fading right before our eyes," he screamed. "Doesn't that make you mad? Don't you want to do something?"

One of the six deacons who sat in the front pew handed the pastor a handkerchief to wipe the sweat from his forehead. Reverend Stansfield then dropped to one knee and bowed his head. "Church, heroin isn't the only thing killing our community."

"Amen," several people yelled out.

"There is a serial killer terrorizing the streets of Camden. The Grim Reaper, that's what the papers are calling him. They have identified this man as a follower of the Christian faith. Clues left at the scene of each murder have led investigators to believe after he has killed his victims, he reads a Bible passage over them for repentance. This monster is claiming the lives of the elderly."

"Preach!" The congregation was in an uproar. All the commotion made Heaven sit up and pay attention.

"These are old people who can't defend themselves. This man is a coward." Reverend Stansfield told everyone to turn to the book of Obadiah.

While everyone flipped through the pages searching for scripture, Heaven's mind stayed on the Grim Reaper. She was concerned for Nana's safety. Her grandmother fit the profile for becoming one of the serial killer's victims. She was glad nothing had happened to Nana while she was in jail.

While in prison, Heaven withdrew from her grandmother and everyone else she had ever loved. That was a painful time in her life. She had not been allowed to mourn the loss of her daughter because of her arrest. She missed the funeral and then had to live with the guilt of it all. That's probably why it was so easy for her to take drugs from Jennings.

Nana tried reaching out to her several times, but Heaven rejected her each time. Every letter from Nana was sent back unopened. Every visit she made Heaven refused. She loved her grandmother, but she was scared to face her after all the wrong she had done. Heaven couldn't bear to see that look of pity in Nana's eyes. That would be the same look Heaven had seen in Nana's eyes every time she looked at Heaven's mother. That's why she hid from her for the past six years.

Reverend Stansfield asked the congregation to read the scripture together. To avoid the hassle of looking for the book of Obadiah, Heaven huddled close to Ebony and read from her Bible. From across the aisle, Heaven caught the eye of a guy who reminded her of Boris Kodjoe. A flirtatious smile and sexy wink from her had him salivating like a hungry dog. She slowly inched her skirt up her thigh and stopped right before crossing over that line of risqué. He turned red in the face and bashfully looked away. After her performance, she was sure he would approach her after church.

After an hour of watching just about every member in the church catch the Holy Spirit, Reverend Stansfield dismissed church.

Ebony slipped her purse strap over her shoulder and picked up her Bible. "Heaven, I'll be right back. I need to go speak with Reverend Stansfield." Before Heaven had a chance to say anything, Ebony bolted away.

Crowds of people came and hugged Heaven and welcomed her back to church. With so many people crowded around her, they had blocked her suitor's view of her. Once the crowd started to thin out, Heaven heard a man's voice invade her ears.

"Excuse me."

She turned around and her eyes unexpectedly landed on metal crutches that were holding up the same guy she had been smiling at all morning. He tightly gripped the crutch with one arm and balanced himself to shake her hand. "My name is Davis. I hope you didn't mind me staring at you today. I couldn't help but admire your beauty." His compliment made her blush, but the interest she had in him disintegrated. "Welcome to our church."

"Thank you." She played with the clasp on her purse to avoid staring at his crutches. If she had known the guy was handicapped she would have never flirted with him. "Are you a member here?" she asked.

"I became a member a few years ago. I love it here."

The hands on the wall clock moved just as slowly as Ebony. Without trying to be rude, Heaven tried to run out on Davis. "It was really nice talking with you, but I need to go find my friend. We have to get going." She picked up her Bible and stepped away.

Davis grabbed her blouse before she could flee the scene. "If you need a ride home, I can take you," he offered.

"I really don't want to inconvenience you."

"It would be my pleasure." Before she could object, he used his crutches to help turn himself around and hobbled out the doors.

Ebony snuck up behind her and whispered in her ear. "I should have known the rich guy would be attracted to you."

"Rich?"

"That was Davis Davies you were talking to wasn't it?" she asked.

"You know him?"

"I met him at the outreach service that night the church came to the halfway house to worship with us. You may not remember him because you were talking with Deacon Washington, but he was there. He's a really nice guy and he loves the church. Reverend Stansfield speaks highly of him. He said Davis is a faithful member of his flock." Ebony then whispered in her ear. "Plus, I heard he's generous. He gives thousands of dollars to the Lord."

"Thousands of dollars?"

"Yeah, Davis received a huge financial settlement when he turned eighteen. Remember years ago when a bunch of kids were contaminated by hazardous waste that was being illegally dumped in Camden by a company in Freehold?"

"I remember. That happened when I was a kid."

"Well, Davis was one of the kids who got infected. Those chemicals did something to his legs and he had to have them amputated. His parents sued the company and he was awarded millions of dollars."

This new information changed how she looked at Davis. She rushed Ebony out the church and she scanned the block for Davis. Disabled or not, she needed to see what Davis could do for her.

The Lexus slowly paraded through the parking

lot until it came to a complete stop in front of her. She had no idea he was the one driving the Lexus. She felt like she had just hit the jackpot. Like a gentlemen, Davis got out as fast as he could and opened the passenger side doors for Ebony and her.

"Buckle up, ladies," Davis instructed before he pulled off into a steady stream of traffic. Davis's Lexus was an example of world class luxury at its finest. A voice-operated navigational system, DVD entertainment system, massage equipped rear seats, and individual climate control were just a few of its first class amenities.

"This car is really nice," Ebony complimented.

"Thanks! I got it a few months ago." Davis drove through the streets of Camden with no difficulties from his handicap. When he offered to give them a ride, Heaven was leery of his driving skills, but he proved her wrong. He was a good driver who obeyed all traffic laws. As he was driving, he turned a few knobs and pushed a few gadgets. Heaven couldn't help but stare at all the different instruments he used to drive.

"It's all right. You can ask me about these buttons." he said to Heaven. "I'm not ashamed of my handicap. Everything was placed in here as a safety precaution so I wouldn't lose control of the car. My prosthetic legs are the reason I have the crutches. Modern technology has made it so I can do a lot of the things that normal people do. I can drive a car, ride a bike, or run a marathon, if I wanted. I can't do everything you do, but I can still do a lot for myself."

"I admire you," Ebony said.

"And I admire you ladies." The women gave him a bewildered look. "I like the way you two are changing your life. Jesus is in the business of changing lives and I can tell the Lord is going to bless both of you," he pointed his finger at Heaven. "You just watch and see. God is so amazing."

"I believe you're right, Davis," Ebony agreed and the two of them chatted for the remainder of the ride.

By the time Davis stopped in front of the half-way house, he looked worn out from Ebony's conversation. He probably didn't expect her to talk so much in such a short amount of time. Ebony thanked Davis for the ride and went into the house, leaving him and Heaven alone.

"Perhaps you and I could go out to dinner sometime?" he asked.

"I would like that." Living in the halfway house with a bunch of women and working a job that paid minimum wage made Heaven feel like the ugly stepsister from the fairytale *Cinderella*. Heaven quickly jotted down the phone number to the pay phone on her floor and told him to call sometime.

Davis wasted no time. The following Sunday, he asked her out to dinner.

"I really don't have anything to wear. Why don't we make plans for next Sunday? I get paid next week and I'll be able to buy something pretty to wear on our first date."

"We could go to the mall and pick you up something. I'll pay for everything," he offered.

Heaven claimed she couldn't take advantage of

Davis's generosity, but he pressed her to accept his offer. After playing hard to get for over fifteen minutes, she finally agreed.

Davis bought her whatever she wanted at the mall. He bought her something from nearly every store in the mall. They went shopping for the next three Sundays. By the time Deacon Washington returned to church, Heaven had a brand new style. No more cheap, bargain basement markdowns for her. Now, only the best would do.

Chapter 9

"Ebony, I can't believe you tricked me into coming with you."

"I didn't trick you. I told you I saw a vendor selling Louis Vuitton bags at a cheap price. Your job at the supermarket isn't paying enough for you to buy one of those bags from out the store. You better get this hook up while you can."

"What good would it do me to have a new bag if I die from a heat stroke?"

The July heat had reached a record high of one hundred and ten. It was so hot outside, the state had declared a heat advisory for the entire area. Everyone was advised to stay indoors.

The vendor's stand sat right in front of the Walter Rand Transportation Center. Every bus, train, and cab made a stop at this depot and there were always plenty of people around. Commuters waited for their buses and tried to stay cool by standing in the shade, shielding themselves with umbrellas or simply fanning themselves with the daily newspaper.

When they reached the vendor, he remembered Ebony and pointed out the bags she had been looking at. As Ebony tried to talk the guy into giving her a deal, Heaven heard someone call out her name. She turned around and saw a woman walking toward her.

"Girl, I didn't know you were home. You look good." She hugged Heaven, but Heaven didn't recognize her face. The woman looked familiar, but Heaven couldn't recall how she knew her.

"I'm coming from the hospital." The woman took a puff from the cigarette she held in her hand. "My sister, Sherri, is recovering from surgery."

"Sherri. Oh!" Once Heaven heard Sherri's name it all came back to her. She remembered how she knew the girl. Her family lived next door to Nana. Heaven still couldn't remember the girl's name but she knew Sherri. The last time Heaven saw her, Sherri was tricking to support her habit. "How is she doing?"

"She's doing well. You should go up and see her. She looks good. She's cleaned herself up. No more drugs."

"That's good."

"Yes. She's been clean for almost three years. A few days ago she had a part of her liver removed to help save our uncle who needed a transplant.

"Wow! That's a big sacrifice. You must be proud of her."

"I think she's a fool. She should have let that bastard die."

Heaven was shocked by her choice of words. "Well, I have to be going. It was nice talking with you." Heaven hugged her one last time and they went their separate ways.

Chapter 10

The following day Heaven sat at the regular group session meeting waiting on Ebony. She had left Ebony upstairs on the phone screaming at someone on the other end.

Whomever Ebony was speaking with had made her so angry that Heaven heard a few curse words fall from her lips. This was not the Ebony she had grown to know and love. Ebony was usually full of smiles and pointed out the good in every circumstance. Her behavior today was out of the ordinary. Someone had made her terribly upset.

The chairs in the room were formed in a circle and Ms. Griffin stood in the center. Heaven admired Ms. Griffin. She was a perfect example of what every African American woman should stand for. She was stylish—always looking the part of a queen. A conservative dresser, her attire usually consisted of neatly pressed slacks complimented by shiny high heel black leather boots. Her short haircut was chic. She had eyes the color of coals and her lips were painted a perky purple.

She was educated. Every visitor who entered her office couldn't help but notice the number of awards, plaques, and diplomas that lined her office walls.

She was also uplifting. Ms. Griffin listened instead of judged when the residents spoke to her. She never talked down to anyone and treated every woman there with respect. Everyone loved her. They felt at ease around her and not like a burden.

Ms. Griffin pushed up her sleeves exposing five solid gold bangles on her arm. "Hello, ladies." Ms. Griffin was full of cheer. "Usually I ask for volunteers to share their feelings with the group, but today I have a story I would like to share. Is that all right with everyone here?"

"Ms. Griffin, no one here is going to stop you from doing your thing. Go ahead and share your story."

Everyone agreed with Fatima.

"Okay. A former resident of the halfway house contacted me last week. She had just received some good news and was eager to share it with me. While in prison, she had taken an interest in horticulture. She used the prison library to educate herself on different kinds of plants and how to best care for them. She became a master at flowers, plants, and landscaping. When she was released, she started her own business. Starting out small and investing in a cheap used lawnmower that cost her fifty dollars, she cut her elderly neighbors' lawns at discount. Word spread, and within a year she was making enough to hire two workers. She went back to school, took some college courses, and began building her business. A few days ago, she received a letter from the city of Camden. She won a bid with the city for a contract worth over one hundred and fifty thousand dollars." Everyone applauded. "She told me it wasn't always easy. She ran into a few obstacles, but managed to stay close to the Lord. She spent most of her time working, at the church, and on her knees." Ms. Griffin looked each of the residents in the eye. "This was her blessing. Something God had intended for her and she stayed focused and received her blessings. If God can do it for her, he can do it for you. Take the gifts God has blessed you with and maximize them to you benefit."

Toward the end of Ms. Griffin's story, Ebony stormed into the room and plopped down in the seat next to Heaven. Ebony showed up at the meeting in disarray. Her torn jeans and the wrinkled blouse that was buttoned wrong didn't go well with her the orthopedic shoes she usually only wore to work. She slouched in her seat and pulled out the tracks in her hair. It was clear she wasn't herself. Anger burned in Ebony's eyes and Heaven had never seen that much rage come from her before. It not only worried her, but it scared her too. Heaven wasn't sure if she should say anything, but she put herself in Ebony's shoes and did what Ebony would do naturally. "What's up?" she asked.

Her question led to Ebony gasping for air. She grabbed for her chest and it heaved up and down heavily. "I can't take this." Ebony yelled. She wrapped her arms around herself and rocked back and forth in her chair. Disrupting the meeting, everyone looked her way. "Why? Why me?" Surprised at her outburst, Ms. Griffin stopped talking and walked over to where they were sitting.

"God is punishing me. No matter what I do, it's not good enough," she cried out.

Ms. Griffin took a seat on the other side of Ebony. "Look at me." Ms. Griffin turned her face toward Ebony. "Do you want to go to my office to talk? Apparently something is wrong."

Ebony looked out of touch with reality. Worry lines filled her face. "I feel like getting high. I need some crystal meth." She turned and looked at the crowd. "Can anyone here get me some ice?" she screamed.

Ms. Griffin lightly tugged at her arm. "Let's go to my office."

Ebony pulled away. "No. Going to your office is not going to change anything. I want everyone here to see how drugs can ruin your life." She fell to the floor on her knees. "I've been rejected; rejected by my family. I don't know what to do. If I don't have my family then I have nothing to live for."

Ms. Griffin told Heaven to get Ebony a glass of water. She quickly got up and went to the nearest water cooler. She could hear Ms. Griffin tell the others the meeting was dismissed and everyone could leave. By the time Heaven returned, Ebony was crying hysterically on Ms. Griffin's shoulder.

They sat listening to Ebony pour her feelings out, but neither of them knew what was bothering her. Ms. Griffin had gotten her to calm down and drink some water, but Ebony was still disoriented. Ebony played with a dust bunny that lay beneath her feet.

"I've never been rejected. I try to be nice to everyone I meet. I treat people how I want to be treated, but today my husband . . . my ex-husband. He finally returned my phone call after weeks of me trying to get in touch with him.

"You have to understand, before I started using drugs, my family was the most important thing in the world to me. I loved my husband and I still do, but he's remarried and I can accept that, but I need to see my son. My son needs his mother."

"Did you ask your ex about setting up arrangements for a visit?"

Ebony nodded her head. "He said he thought it would be best if my son never knew I existed. My son thinks his father's new wife is his mother. Do you know how much that hurts? My little boy is the only reason I've wanted to get clean and push so hard to get my life back."

Ebony buried her head in her hands. She cried no tears. Probably because she had no more tears to cry. Heaven rubbed her back, hoping she would feel better.

"Ebony, I've seen how much your faith in God has grown since you've been here. Did you pray?" Ms. Griffin asked.

Heaven was glad Ms. Griffin was there. She always knew the right thing to say, because Heaven had no idea what to say to make Ebony feel better.

"God doesn't want to fix this. The Bible says we reap what we sow. I'm just getting what I deserve. Maybe I should have never stopped using drugs."

"If you start using again you are going to lose everything you've worked so hard for."

"Ms. Griffin, you're not hearing me. If I can't see my son then life isn't worth living. At least when I was getting high I could escape life's difficulties. Crystal meth took me away. One puff and all my worries would disappear.

She stood up in front of them. "I wish I had never started using drugs."

"If I had a dime for every time somebody said that to me . . . but Ebony, you can't change the past," Ms. Griffin said.

"This nightmare started with my husband. He is the one who got me to start using." Heaven had never heard Ebony sound so hostile. "I don't blame him for the things I did but all I wanted to do was spend time with my husband. We probably should have dated more than three weeks before getting married, but I was sure he was the one for me. I found out he was an addict shortly after the honeymoon.

"Once we moved into the house, he stopped coming home. Being a responsible person, he always made sure he took care of all household bills, but after that he would leave and sometimes not come home for two or three days.

"I thought he was having an affair, but after I confronted him, he told me the reason he stayed away was because he was ashamed for his family to see him using drugs. I couldn't stand him being out in the streets, so I told him he could bring the drugs home. This was the only way I could think of to protect my husband from being gunned down in the streets over a drug deal gone bad. He would take his drugs into the den and close the door behind him. I knew he was down there alone getting high and one day I joined him. I just wanted to try it. That's all it took and I too was hooked, although I didn't know it.

"My husband got tired of doing drugs and checked himself into rehab. When he was released, he was clean and he wanted me to get clean.

"The baby and I were still staying at the house, but my husband had decided to stay with his mother because he couldn't tolerate my drug use. I had tried to quit several times, but I could never stay clean. My ignorance of the drug's addictive power had me convinced I could get clean without anyone's help. To prove it, I promised myself that for one week, I would stop using crystal meth, but because I couldn't stop cold turkey, I used Xanax to keep me from feeling the effects of withdrawal.

"My husband had made plans to take our two-year-old son to the park that afternoon. While waiting on him to arrive I had taken a Xanax to take the edge off from not doing any crystal meth. I was laying on the couch, but I couldn't relax because the baby kept running around throwing things, turning on the radio, and playing with his toys. He was an active little boy, but that day he was overactive. Finally, I got fed up and went to the kitchen. I poured one Xanax out the bottle and smashed into a powder. Then I put it in the baby's drinking cup, filled it with juice, and made sure he drank every last drop. After he finished, he lay on the couch next to me and we both fell asleep. When I woke up the paramedics were at my house.

One was trying to revive me and the other my son. I was arrested at the hospital and they turned full custody of my son over to my husband."

Heaven was speechless. She didn't know what to say. If anyone else had told her that story about Ebony she would have never believed them. The woman she described in that story was not the same woman sitting next to her. Ebony had changed and deserved to see her son.

"If I was sober I would have never done that," Ebony cried. "All I want is a second chance."

Ms. Griffin patted her hand. "Ebony, everything is going to be all right."

Chapter 11

After Ebony's episode, Heaven helped her upstairs and into bed. Ebony softly cried herself to sleep. Heaven had a date with Davis. He had surprised her by getting them tickets to a concert in the park. Ms. Teena Marie was headlining and Heaven couldn't wait to see her live. She had heard that Teena Marie put on a great performance.

Heaven grabbed her jacket and was going to wait outside for Davis to pick her up, but when she walked out the door, he was pulling up to the curb. Davis had fixed them dinner and packed everything neatly in a picnic basket.

They arrived early and picked out a nice spot to lie out on a blanket and enjoy the concert. The concert started and the first performer on the stage was Stephanie Mills. Thousands of people had come and the park got crowded quickly. Heaven was snapping her fingers to Stephanie's song, "Home" when she happened to look a few feet away from her and saw her ex-boyfriend, Chrome. She was shocked to see him.

"Do you know him?" Davis asked, snapping Heaven from her daydream.

"No. He looked like somebody I thought I knew, but it's not him." Davis turned back to the concert. "Davis it's getting late. Can you take me back?"

"You want to leave before Teena comes on? I thought you wanted to see her."

"I do, but I'm so tired and I won't be able to enjoy her the way I want to. I'm sorry."

"If that's what you want, we can go." They packed up their things and Davis drove her back to the halfway house. When Heaven got back to her room, she was glad Ebony was still asleep. She needed some quiet time to herself without any interruptions.

During the first few months of Heaven's prison sentence she dreamt about Chrome's almond brown eyes and alluring cologne every night.

It looked like he had gained some weight. She wondered if he had found someone to cook him a few meals. She was happy if he had found someone else and was happy, but also a little jealous. *Why couldn't he have been happy when we were together?*

When she and Chrome were together she thought they had the greatest love affair on earth, but she was wrong. What they had was a drug affair, because Chrome had first been in love with her best friend, Keenyah.

Keenyah and Heaven had been inseparable friends since the first grade, but when Keenyah met Chrome, things changed. The things they used to do together Keenyah now did with him. Heaven felt like the start of Keenyah's new relationship marked the ending of theirs.

The day Keenyah died will forever be branded in Heaven's mind. That weekend, plans had been mapped out for them to stay at Heaven's house and do girly things like hair, nails, and talking about boys. Heaven was so excited.

This also happened to be the same weekend that Heaven's mom had been given a weekend pass to leave the psychiatric hospital and visit with her family. Heaven's mother had been institutionalized Heaven's entire life and her grandmother had always been her primary caretaker. Keenyah was the only person Heaven had ever told about her mother's mental illness.

Keenyah had gotten up three times to look out the window and by the fourth time Heaven had to find out what was up.

"Why do you keep looking out the window?"

"Chrome said he was going to come by."

"Tonight? Why? I thought you were going to hang with me? I went and rented our favorite movies and Nana bought us plenty of snacks."

"I am, but I promised Chrome I'd spend a few hours with him."

"So, you used me to get out of your parents' house because they won't allow you to see him?"

"No." Keenyah shook her head from side to side. "I miss him so much. I couldn't go the whole weekend without spending a few hours alone with him."

Heaven rolled her eyes and pouted. She was sick of hearing about Chrome.

"Heaven, don't be mad. I know I should have told you sooner, but I thought it would be better if I told you once I got here. I promise. Next weekend you can stay at my house and we'll hang out, just me and you." She wrapped her arms around Heaven's shoulder.

"That's what you said last weekend." Before Keenyah could make up another lie, Heaven went on. "Ever since you started dating Chrome, that's all you know. We don't talk on the phone anymore. I barely see you around school. You've changed."

"Heaven, I'm in love. We're in love. Chrome loves me. Aren't you happy for me?"

Heaven thought Keenyah had been brainwashed because at fifteen, what could Keenyah possibly know about love?

"Plus, nobody knows this but my parents but . . . I'm pregnant."

"Pregnant." Heaven jumped up from the floor. "You're not keeping this baby? Are you?"

She smiled and rubbed her belly. "Of course; I would never get rid of Chrome's first child."

Heaven couldn't believe Keenyah was planning on becoming a mother to that boy's baby. Chrome was a manipulator and Heaven was sure he had convinced her friend to keep the baby. That's why Heaven hated him. He pretended to be kind and caring, but she knew he was no good. It didn't help that he was a few years older than them.

Chrome was not what Heaven would consider

fine, but she later learned he was charming. That was probably how he charmed the pants right off of Keenyah and her too.

Heaven could feel her face turning red from anger and she wanted to take Keenyah by the arms and shake some sense into her. She was sick and tired of coming in second to Chrome. Once the baby arrived things would permanently change forever. The three of them would become a family and forget all about her.

"I hate you! I hate you! I hate you!" Heaven screamed at her. She had never screamed at Keenyah in her life and she was scared stiff when she did. "I wish I had never met you. Get out of my house! Get out!" Heaven flung words of insult at her and then walked over to her bedroom door and ordered Keenyah out.

"Heaven," Keenyah said as hurt filled her eyes. She reached her hand out to Heaven, but she slapped it away.

"I can't believe you're going to have his baby." Heaven glared down at her belly then back into Keenyah's eyes. "I hope your baby dies."

That was it. Keenyah knew Heaven was fed up. Heaven had said something that could not be taken back. Tears welled up in Keenyah's eyes, but she refused to allow them to fall. Heaven was glad Keenyah was upset. Now Keenyah could feel the same way Heaven had been feeling since Chrome came into the picture.

In haste, Keenyah grabbed her duffle bag and ran down the stairs and out the house. Heaven heard the screen door slam shut and she punched one of her bedroom pillows. Lately, she had been feeling angry all the time. Every morning she woke up and felt that if she didn't get some joy into her life soon, she was going to blow up and she had no idea when or where the explosion was going to happen.

She went in the bathroom, splashed cold water on her face, and looked at herself in the mirror. She wondered what she was going to do. Because of her lack of control, she had lost her best friend.

Regret soon set in and she cried over what she had just done. She wished she hadn't said what she did and she needed to take it back. She decided she was going to apologize when she saw Keenyah in school on Monday. Heaven blew her nose and walked back into her room.

She sat down on her bed and grabbed one of her stuffed animals. She held it tightly until she heard the sound of a screeching car tires and then a loud thump. Jumping up, she looked out her bedroom window. Down below she could see the bottom half of Keenyah's body being covered by the front end of a car. She panicked and rocketed down the stairs. She ran into the street she cradled Keenyah in her arms.

"Keenyah," Heaven screamed. The driver backed his car up, but Heaven refused to let her go. She just held her friend and cried. "Please, God. Please allow her to be all right."

Suddenly someone pushed her aside and caressed Keenyah's lifeless body. It was Chrome. He was the driver of the car. He had killed the woman he loved and their unborn baby. Blood ran down the side of her face. Chrome cried over her and Heaven stepped back. Chrome angrily cried at himself for being so careless. At that moment, she realized Chrome really did love Keenyah and she was full of guilt.

Heaven turned her head away in shame. The things she said to Keenyah had led to her death. She couldn't look in her friend's face knowing the things she had just said to her less than five minutes before, plus she knew she was probably the reason Keenyah ran into the street.

After Keenyah's funeral, Heaven became very depressed. She was to blame for Keenyah's death and she withdrew from everyone around her. She wouldn't talk to her grandmother or teachers. The school suggested her grandmother send her to a grief specialist, but Heaven refused to talk at any of the sessions. Heaven was allowed to stay home until Nana decided it was time for her to return to school.

Being in school without Keenyah was a hard adjustment. Each day she walked into class she expected to see Keenyah sitting in her usual seat waiting for her to arrive. A few times, she couldn't stand the ghosts that haunted her and she spent several class periods in the bathroom crying.

She finally got tired of going to school and started skipping classes. She would leave the house in the morning and end up spending the day at the park or mall. Until one day she ran into an old friend.

"What's up with you?" She shouldn't have been surprised to see Chrome coming out of the corner liquor store with a brown bag in his hand.

"What's up?" Heaven readjusted her book bag over her shoulder.

Smiling boldly, he acted like he was happy to see her. He hugged her hard and long. She was shocked by his reaction. She never considered them friends.

Judging by his appearance, it looked like his life had taken a turn for the worse. Heaven assumed he hadn't shaved in weeks from the looks of his full beard. Plus, he reeked from the stench of alcohol. From the look in his bloodshot eyes it looked like he hadn't slept in days. She had never seen Chrome looking this bad before.

The last time Heaven saw him was at Keenyah's burial. When they placed Keenyah's casket at her final resting place Chrome went crazy. He cried and screamed. Relatives, friends, and family tried to console him, but it was impossible. He tried to open the casket to get in with her. All he cried was no, no, no. He had disturbed the casket so badly it took five big men to hold him back. One guy lost his grip and Chrome took that as his opportunity to get in with Keenyah. The casket tipped over. The lid lifted up and Keenyah's exposed hand hung lifelessly over the side of the casket. He grabbed her hand and tried to pull her out. Her family had to tackle him in order to make him let go. They finally led him away from the burial. It was just too much for him to handle, but now he seemed no better.

"Ain't you supposed to be in school?" he asked.

Heaven gave him the evil eye. "Aren't you supposed to be at work?" she sarcastically responded.

He laughed at her. "I don't have a job anymore. They fired me . . . too many absences."

An awkward silence drifted between them. She

knew both of them were thinking about Keenyah, but neither wanted to say her name.

"Where you going?" he asked with his back turned. He walked in the direction of his car.

Heaven told him where she was headed and he offered her a ride. He unlocked the passenger side door to his car and he noticed her look. "I couldn't keep that other car. I traded cars with my brother." Now an old Ford Taurus replaced Chrome's shiny, always-clean Maxima. "I think this compromise makes both of us happy. He has a new car and I drive a vehicle that doesn't hold such bad memories."

The radio played the song "Humpty Dance" by Digital Underground in the background.

"Why don't you hang out with me for the day?" Chrome offered while he pulled a fifth of vodka out of his brown paper bag. He took a swig of it and then gestured for her to take a sip. She hesitated a moment before accepting his offer and swallowing a mouthful. Her first taste of liquor made her mouth feel like it was on fire. It burned as it painfully glided down her throat. She choked and grabbed her chest. Chrome laughed then snatched the bottle back.

"You have to take your time with this. Keenyah did the same thing when she took her first drink."

Chrome turned onto Federal Street and passed a few side streets until he pulled off onto a block full of abandoned houses. Chrome pulled over, turned off the car, and dug into his pocket, revealing a joint. She had smoked weed before, but not often. The last time she smoked was with Keenyah. Neither of them were regular smokers, but whenever Keenyah could steal a bag from the stash her brother was hustling, they would get high. That was the only way since neither of them had a job to buy the stuff.

It didn't take long for Chrome to spark it up and take a puff. When he exhaled, he had an amused look on his face. The weed must have been good to him. She noticed a difference in smell between what Chrome was smoking and what she had experienced in the past. What she didn't know was the joint was laced with cocaine.

He passed it to her and she readily took it, hoping to temporarily get away from the pain she felt over Keenyah.

"Don't you miss Keenyah?" he asked.

Heaven was disturbed by his question. She was trying to forget about Keenyah and he wanted to talk about her.

"I've been racking my brain trying to figure out what would make her run out in the street the way she did." Chrome said. "I told her I was coming to get her from your house and right before I pulled up, she ran into the street. Why Keenyah? Why?" Chrome banged his fist against the dashboard and cried.

Chrome blamed himself and Heaven felt he should have been pointing the finger at her. She needed to confess. Watching him torture himself over Keenyah wasn't fair. "Why was she outside waiting for me? Why wasn't she in the house with you?" Chrome looked to her for answers.

Heaven turned her attention out the window. The horrible things she said to Keenyah repeated themselves in her mind. That day kept chipping away at her until she couldn't hold it in any longer. Heaven turned to tell Chrome everything when her mind started playing tricks on her.

The way Chrome looked at her made her think he already knew about the argument. He stared at her as if he were reading her mind. She felt like he was trying to set her up to admit Keenyah's accident was her fault. The weed was making her paranoid and she grew nervous over what he was going to say next. Her heart raced and shot from one to sixty. In her mind she screamed that Chrome had to stop talking about Keenyah. She kept wringing her hands from nervousness, and the tension she felt pushed her over the edge.

Before she knew what was happening, she had climbed on Chrome's lap. Their lips brushed against one another and her mouth turned dry. She was scared and when he looked her in the eye she avoided him once again by kissing him on the mouth.

Chrome didn't respond to Heaven right away. He seemed unsure about whether what they were doing was right. It took him a minute, but he eventually came around and pulled her closer to him. It was really uncomfortable trying to make out behind the steering wheel, so they moved to the back seat. He laid her down on the back seat and she willingly gave away her virginity. He entered her with such force it hurt, but the feeling soon turned good. Her heart and emotions poured into him. She felt like she had fallen in love and she never wanted to leave him. Heaven wondered if this was the way Keenyah felt when he took her virginity. From that moment on, she was addicted to not only him, but also drugs.

The passion between them created their first-born son, Courtney. Then, a few years later, their daughter Odyssey was born.

Chrome was her new best friend and they were inseparable. Once she turned sixteen, she dropped out of school and moved in with him. The first few years were bliss. Although they weren't married, everyone knew they were a couple and Chrome spoiled her with whatever she wanted; especially drugs. Every payday Chrome bought a huge supply of drugs to last them through the week.

After Odyssey was born, Chrome's behavior changed. He was no longer the guy who wanted to make love to her all the time. Instead, he was distant and stayed as far away from her as possible. He would leave home, stay out all night long, and only come home to shower. She was worried he had found somebody else. Chrome wasn't the sexiest guy, but he was generous. A lot of women wanted to be with Chrome so he could treat them the way he treated her.

When Chrome did come home, they would fight. One day, things got so bad he packed his things and moved out. That was the last time she saw him. After Chrome left, she made sure she stayed high day and night. Heroin covered up all feelings of being abandoned and alone.

Chapter 12

After church, Heaven changed out of her dress clothes and slipped on something casual to wear to her visit with Nana.

"Where are you going?" Ebony asked.

"To go see my nana, she usually cooks a big dinner on Sundays. I know it's her first day back, but I figured I would surprise her."

Avery had pulled Heaven aside after church and warned her that Nana returned from her trip early. Nana called him the night before upset over a fight she had with her sister. She complained that she was worn out from the long train ride and wouldn't be in church this morning. He suggested she go see her as soon as possible.

"Mmmm!" She rubbed her belly. "I haven't had a home cooked meal in years. I hope you enjoy it. Anything is better than the stuff they feed us here." Ebony's words sounded more like a cry for help than well wishes.

Today was going to one of the most difficult

days she ever had to face. Seeing her nana for the first time after all these years was going to be really hard. Heaven felt like she needed to go by herself, but looking at Ebony's pleading eyes, she couldn't leave her behind. "Ebony, why don't you come along? I'm sure there'll be enough food for both of us."

Fifteen minutes later, they left the halfway house and caught the number three bus to the Fairview section of Camden. They passed by Morgan Village Middle School, the playground, and the basketball courts before stopping in front of Nana's house. The house looked so different than it did six years ago. Nana had replaced the old, faded blue siding with a perky bright yellow and installed a new steel gate to close in her yard. A bunch of wilted flowers filled the flower beds in the front yard. It was hard to believe she was standing in front of Nana's house.

"Are you ready?" Ebony asked. Heaven took a deep breath, pushed open the gate, and walked up the front steps. "Are you okay?"

"I'm fine, just a little nervous." She opened the screen door and knocked hard on the front door.

From outside, she could hear someone running toward the door. Nana peeked through her living room drapes. "What do you want?" she screamed. From where Nana was standing, she could only see Ebony standing on her front porch.

Ebony was dumbfounded and looked to Heaven for a response. Heaven shook her head. She didn't want Nana to know she was out there.

"Ms. Stansfield, I . . ." she hesitated a moment. "I'm a friend of your granddaughter, Heaven. She asked me to come here. I have some news I'd like to share with you."

Nana moved away from the window and cautiously opened the door. It wasn't until Heaven saw her grandmother's face that she realized how much she had missed Nana's warm brown eyes and wiry gray hair. The sight of her released a dam of tears.

When Nana saw Heaven, she covered her mouth with her hand and stared at her for a moment before saying anything. She opened her mouth to say something but nothing came out. Then she tried again. "God is so amazing." She cried before pulling her into her arms. Embracing Nana was therapeutic for Heaven's soul. Tears Heaven had locked away while in prison were set free by the one person in the world who loved her unconditionally.

"Nana, I'm sorry," she cried. "I'm so sorry for the way I treated you. I . . ."

Nana put her finger to Heaven's mouth to quiet her. "The important thing is that you're here now."

They stood in the doorway hugging for minutes before they realized Ebony was still standing behind Heaven. Ebony gave Heaven a tissue to wipe her face. Heaven then introduced her to Nana.

"Hello, it's nice to meet you." Ebony held out her hand.

Nana was the kind of grandmother who treated everyone she met like family. She pulled Ebony into her arms and gave her a loving hug. When they separated Ebony was crying.

"Girl, why you crying?" Nana asked.

"I don't know." She laughed. "Probably because

no one has ever showed me so much love, not even my mother."

"Well, Ebony, you can expect more hugs like that because you are now family." Nana motioned for them to follow her. "You girls come on in the kitchen so I can fix you something to eat," Nana insisted.

Once they were in the kitchen, Nana piled two plates full of food. She had prepared ham, collard greens, fish, and carrot cake.

"Nana, who is all this food for?"

"The girl next door. Her daughter passed away yesterday."

"Sherri?" Heaven asked.

"Yes, it's such a shame too. That family was just starting to heal some of its wounds."

"Nana, I saw Sherri's sister at the transportation center a few days ago and she said Sherri had just given a part of her liver to her uncle for a transplant."

"I can't remember the sister's name, but when that girl found out her sister had died she went crazy. She went up to that hospital and nearly choked the life out of that man. They had to call security to escort her out of there."

"When I saw her she seemed a bit bitter."

"Yes, the uncle who received Sherri's liver was her mother's brother. About three years ago, Sherri told her mother the uncle had molested Sherri and her sister for years when they were kids. He had even gotten Sherri pregnant and she had an abortion. It was a painful time for the entire family. I prayed the family would be able to make amends, but I don't think no one wanted to repair the damage that had been done more than Sherri. That is why she decided to give him a part of her liver, so she could free herself from all the hate she had for him. Unfortunately, she had complications and her liver failed."

"My condolences go out to the family," Ebony said.

"Where are you staying?" Nana asked.

"Right now I'm living in a halfway house downtown, but I'm more worried about you. I heard about the Grim Reaper. Have you been locking your doors at night?"

"Heaven, I lock my doors during the day. The city has gotten so bad, people are killing one another in broad daylight. They had a shoot out on the corner the other day. They just started pulling out guns and firing like it was the Wild, Wild West," she replied.

"Nana, you have to be careful."

"Yes, Ms. Stansfield, your son cautioned everyone and told them to make sure they took the necessary precautions to protect themselves."

"Please call me Nana," she said, before placing Ebony's plate in front of her. Then she looked at Heaven. "Girl, you've been to church?"

"Nana, don't make a big deal out of it," she warned.

"The Lord has answered my prayers." She finally put a plate in front of Heaven. "I prayed that you would return to church years ago. I had given up, but I guess all things are in God's timing and not our own." Nana took a seat next to Heaven. "Heaven, does Chrome know you're home?"

Heaven responded with a solemn no.

"Chrome brings Courtney by to check on me every once in a while. You need to go over there and see them. Chrome bought a house in East Camden near Stockton Station Apartments."

Heaven knew her grandmother meant well by suggesting she go see her son, but Heaven had decided it would be best if she stayed out of his life. Instead of telling her grandmother what was on her mind, she decided to keep her thoughts to herself. "Nana, listen. We really have to be going." Heaven took her plate and Ebony's and cleaned the scraps off in the trash. "We'll see you in church next Sunday." The two women kissed Nana on the cheek and hurried out.

Chapter 13

Thank you, Lord! Joy set off like fireworks in Heaven's soul when she entered church on Sunday morning and laid eyes on Deacon Washington. The sight of him temporarily numbed her legs and paralyzed her limbs from moving. She hadn't seen him in months, but it felt like a lifetime.

It had been a long summer and during that time Heaven and Ebony had acclimated well to living in a halfway house. Thanks to a strict regimen of church, meetings, and work they maintained their sobriety and had determined the best way for them to live with their addiction.

Ebony had developed a thirst for God. She prayed regularly, studied her Bible, and the thought of attending church and Bible study was exciting to her. Heaven liked God, but she didn't put her trust in him. She believed she had abstained from getting back on drugs because of her will to overcome. Heaven had no desire to get high. Life was good and now that she had no worries, she was free to concentrate on the one thing that had been missing from her life—a man.

Heaven and Ebony were seated just as Deacon Washington stood to address the congregation.

"On behalf of my children and me, we would like to thank the entire Mount Olive family for their overwhelming kindness and for all the words, cards, and thoughtful deeds during our time of need. A lot of people here knew and loved my wife and they know just how much she loved this church." Glancing up at the skylight, he continued. "I know she's smiling down on us this morning from heaven."

All the hallelujahs and amens made him cry. He wiped the tears from his eyes with a handkerchief and sat next to his mother, sister, and children in the pew.

Reverend Stansfield started off his sermon with a thought-provoking story. "Somebody said to me the other day, 'Why would I want to be a Christian?'" A lot of moaning sounded off in the church. "As I talked with this young man, he shared with me his thoughts. He said he had seen what being devoted Christians had gotten his family. His mother, father, and two sisters were all killed in a car crash; leaving him as the only surviving member of his family. He said his family went to church every Sunday. His mother was a Sunday School teacher. At least once a month he visits their graves and wonders why? Why would God take his entire family and leave him here to suffer?

"I understand why this young man is upset or perhaps even angry with God. His reasoning of why this had to happen to his family is a mystery to him. It's a puzzle he can't solve and he may never figure it out. He wanted to know why this kind of tragedy couldn't fall on someone who deserved it like a murderer or rapist. I told him it was because in God's plan, it was meant for you and only you. No one is exempt from pain or suffering. Not the saved or the unsaved. Everyone will carry their own share of burdens. Believe it or not, any problem or crisis you face was chosen specifically for you. Nothing happens by accident. God didn't choose you by drawing a lottery. There is a reason and a plan behind everything he does. There's a reason why Gail down the street got cancer and Sue didn't. The burden isn't the issue. It's how you handle that burden. . . ."

Ebony highlighted a few verses and scribbled a few notes on her program. She smiled at the things Reverend Stansfield preached about. There was nothing fake about Ebony's love for God.

Heaven wished she could be more like Ebony, but no matter how hard she tried, she wasn't interested in what Christ could do for her. Heaven had accepted the fact that maybe it wasn't meant for God to save her. She believed that job was meant for Deacon Washington.

He had been on her mind a lot since the funeral. She felt in her heart they were meant to be together. The conversation they shared the day of the funeral was so serene. He spoke to her like a lady. That's how she knew he was different and God had brought them together.

Reverend Stansfield finished preaching at precisely twelve fifty-one. The organist began to play a soft tune and Reverend Stansfield, Deacon Washington, and a few other deacons stood in front of the church. Deacon Washington looked debonair in a dark gray suit with a burgundy tie. The way he stood in front of the church and stared straight ahead showed that he was serious about the salvation of others, but when he lowered his head, Heaven could see how he was also a man who humbled himself before the Lord.

"Jesus is looking for you," Reverend Stansfield announced. His eyes scanned the crowd looking for anyone who wished to get closer to Jesus. He opened up his arms wide and invited anyone to join.

Heaven couldn't keep her eyes off Deacon Washington. There was something about him that was so alluring. Their eyes met and he smiled at her.

Reverend Stansfield continued coaxing folks to give their life to Jesus. "Open your heart to Jesus. Once you do, everything will be all right. You never have to be afraid again. Come to his open arms." Reverend Stansfield pointed to the floor in front of him. "Here is exactly where you need to be."

The time had come for Heaven to get closer to Deacon Washington. She lifted herself up from out of her seat and before she knew it, she was standing in front of the church. The congregation stood and applauded. Deacon Washington went to her and squeezed her hand lightly. Reverend Stansfield and Deacon Washington knelt down with her at the altar. Her uncle whispered in her ear, "Don't worry. You've come home. God is going to take care of you from this point forward."

Heaven nodded and bowed her head. The palms of her hands were wet with perspiration. Being so close to Deacon Washington made her nervous, but the nervousness subsided when she felt him place her hand in his.

Reverend Stansfield began to pray with her when she felt another pair of arms wrap themselves around her shoulders. Ebony came and squeezed in next to her at the altar. She too had decided to give her life to the Lord. Reverend Stansfield grabbed both of their hands and asked them to repeat after him. Ebony cried tears of joy during the prayer.

Once they finished praying, Deacon Washington escorted them out of the sanctuary and into a small room. Sister Stewart sat inside the room filling out paperwork.

"Sister Stewart, can you stay with these ladies for a few minutes while I help bring service to a close?"

"Sure!" she exclaimed. "Go ahead. We'll be fine." She got up from her seat and reached out to give them hugs. "I'm Sister Lizzie Stewart." She looked toward Heaven. "I know your Reverend's niece. I haven't had a chance to introduce myself to you yet. Your grandfather and I were very good friends." Heaven smiled in reply. Sister Stewart placed their hands in hers. "You two are going to enjoy being a part of Mount Olive. God is so amazing. He will never leave you alone. This is the beginning of a brand new day," she shouted.

"Yes, it is." Deacon Washington snuck up on

them from behind. "Sister, can I steal these two ladies away from you? I need to speak with them for a moment."

"No. I don't mind at all," she yelled loudly. "Oh! Deacon I got your message and whenever you're ready for me to pick up Celeste's things, give me a call." She placed her hand on top of his, "Remember, there is no rush . . . whenever you're ready." He nodded. "Girls, if you ever need any help, ask the pastor for my home number. I'm available day or night." She waved good-bye and strolled out the room.

Deacon Washington escorted them to the church office and offered them a seat.

"Ladies, from this day forward your lives are going to change. You don't have to ever fear anything again. God is now your father and he loves both of you." Ebony excitedly smiled. "The prayer you prayed with Reverend Stansfield is important. It means you are now covered by the blood of the lamb."

"Like the blood Moses instructed the Israelites to put on their doors the night the Lord passed through Egypt?" Ebony asked.

"Yes. That blood saved them and it has now saved you. That mark is a pass, a pass to get into heaven. So when you die, nothing is going to stop you from entering the kingdom of God. There is no reversal. Nothing you've done in the past, present, or future can stop you from going to heaven." Ebony beamed and tapped her feet excitedly.

Deacon Washington dug into his drawer and pulled out a few forms, and then handed them each a pen. "Please fill out these forms and I will set each of you up with a mentor. Your mentor will educate you on the structure of the church. They will study the Bible with you and make sure you are fully aware of who and what Christ represents. This will prepare you for baptism. Since you've already met Sister Stewart, I think it would be appropriate if she were your mentor. She is firmly rooted in the church and you can learn a lot from her." He pulled up a chair in front of them. "Since I met the both of you at the halfway house outreach service, I do want to stress that your addiction is just a bad habit. Everyone has habits that it seems like they can't get rid of, but with God anything is possible."

"That's what I want, Deacon. I want to leave the drugs in the past and start anew," Ebony said.

"That is what Jesus has allowed you to do. Start anew. From this day forward, your sins are washed away."

"Why can't you be our mentor?" Heaven asked. She had heard everything the deacon said, but Jesus saving her and making her a new person was not important. What was important was her spending time with Deacon Washington.

"Heaven, I don't think I can do that because I have so many things going on. You need someone who is able to devote their time and attention to you."

"I want you to be my teacher. I feel comfortable with you. Please don't misunderstand. I like Sister Stewart and I'm sure she's a wonderful teacher, but I would prefer to study with you." The deacon sighed deeply and took off his reading glasses. "Please, Deacon," she begged.

Deacon Washington was caving in. He didn't do well under pressure. He rubbed his temples and relented to her request. "I guess I can fit time into my schedule to have membership classes with the two of you."

"Thank you." She smiled. "I promise we'll be great students." She nudged Ebony to agree with her.

"Yes, Deacon Washington. We won't waste your time," she added.

"I know you won't." He walked over to his desk and flipped through his appointment book. "How about we meet on Thursdays? At 6:30. Is that time good for both of you?"

"That will be no problem," Heaven replied.

Chapter 14

"God, I know I don't call on you often, but I really need your help today." The leather-bound Bible the church had given Heaven was flipped open in front of her. She had been trying to make sense of God's word most of the day, but it seemed like an impossible mission. Fifty percent of the Bible was written in English that was too hard to understand and the other fifty percent was written in riddles. She needed the Children's Bible she had when she was a child.

The only reason Heaven was so determined to learn anything was because of Ebony. They had been meeting with Deacon Washington for a straight month and Ebony made her look bad at every class. Heaven was tired of looking like a dummy next to her every Thursday night. Each week she felt like Ebony had been chosen by God to bask in his knowledge while it was being intentionally hidden from her.

Ebony had become the star pupil of the class. She dedicated at least an hour in the morning and an hour at night to studying her lessons. She took notes, asked questions, and prayed regularly. Deacon Washington never missed an opportunity to commend Ebony on how much she had grown spiritually in such a short amount of time. He seemed to be more interested in her than in Heaven and she couldn't allow Ebony to get in the way because he was destined to be Heaven's man.

"Heaven, you have a phone call," Fatima yelled from the hallway. Heaven read one more line from the book of Psalms before getting up.

"Heaven." It was Deacon Washington. "I'm sorry but I have to cancel our class tonight. It's the baby. He's still not feeling any better and I don't want to leave him. You understand, don't you?"

"Deacon, I was really looking forward to seeing you this week. I have so many questions I was hoping to get answers to." She couldn't allow him to cancel. Her notebook was full of questions specifically for him and she had spent hours preparing for this class.

"Do you think we can hold off until next week?"

"We could, but I know Ebony was looking forward to attending class since she missed last week."

"Oh I forgot about Ebony." He sounded disturbed that Ebony would have to miss out on another class.

"She's been talking about nothing but meeting with you all week. Why can't we have classes at your house? Then you wouldn't have to take the children out."

He was silent to her suggestion because he thought it would be better if they resumed classes the following week. Before he could pass on her idea, she pushed a little more to convince him. "I promise Ebony and I won't disturb the children and as soon as class is over we'll leave." Heaven closed her eyes and crossed her fingers, hoping he would agree.

"I guess it'll be all right."

"Great! We'll see you at six-thirty." She promptly hung up before he could say good-bye. "Now for plan B." She had to get rid of Ebony, which would not be an easy task. She enjoyed class and would rather die first than miss another.

An hour passed before Heaven overheard Ebony in the hallway talking with Fatima.

"Have you heard anything about your son?" Fatima asked.

"No. Not yet. Two weeks ago Ms. Griffin gave me the number to this place that gives out free legal assistance to those who can't afford it, but when I called a woman took down my name and number and said someone would call me back. So far I've heard nothing."

"I wonder what's taking so long."

"I mentioned it to Ms. Griffin and she said she would make a call to see if there was anything she could do to help."

"I wish you the best. I know how much you want to see your boy." Fatima said.

"Yes, I'm praying every day."

When Ebony walked into their room humming to herself, Heaven pretended to be reading her Bible instead of eavesdropping on her conversation with Fatima. Soon Ebony's humming turned to whistling.

"Ebony, could you please quiet down? I'm trying to . . ." When Heaven looked up she was surprised of Ebony's new look. Her hair had been dyed a dark auburn with spiral curls that fell over her shoulders. No more of that bright orange color. Hair extensions made her hair not only longer, but also thicker. Eyeliner, mascara, and foundation had been expertly applied to her face. It was a new look for Ebony that made her look more sophisticated.

"I'm sorry. I didn't mean to interrupt," she apologized.

"That's okay." Heaven closed her Bible. "I love your hair."

"Thanks. I thought it was time for a change. I needed a makeover, not just on the outside but also the in. Talking with Ms. Griffin helped me look at the positive things in my life. She told me that faith, combined with a positive attitude, will take me where God wants me to be in life and I know she's right. Today I walked into work with a smile on my face and friendly thoughts in my head."

"Ebony, that is nothing new. You're always happy."

"I know, but today I went out of my way to help others. I got to work thirty minutes early and instead of waiting for my shift to start I immediately clocked in and helped the elderly customers shop for sale items. Mr. Walker, the manager, must have noticed the difference because he thought I did so well with the customers that he put me on the service desk." She pulled a few college brochures from out of her bag. "After work, I stopped by the college and picked up a schedule for their fall classes. I'm no longer going to allow my ex-husband's behavior to upset me. I realize how blessed I am to have you and Ms. Griffin as friends who will help see me through this. God is so amazing." She pulled her fingers through her new hair-do as if she were acting in a commercial. "I'm going to run out and grab a bite to eat. Do you want anything?"

"No, I'm trying to get in as much studying as I can before class tonight." Heaven pointed to the Bible.

"I told Mr. Walker if they needed extra help tonight they were going to have to call someone else. Nothing is going to stand in the way of my going to class." She slipped on her jacket and trekked out the room.

The week before, the supermarket called last minute and asked if their best employee, Ebony, could come in to work because they were short a few workers. Ebony was fast, efficient, and friendly at work. Mr. Walker loved her.

Ebony agreed to go in and work an extra shift, leaving Heaven and Deacon Washington to have class alone. The time they spent together was not what Heaven expected. The entire hour was wasted studying the Bible. She was hoping they would take a break to get to know one another better. Instead, they prayed, read scripture, and reviewed the church's doctrine.

Heaven tried to get him to pay more attention to her by asking some biblical questions. She figured if it worked for Ebony, why wouldn't it work for her? "I have a question about this." She pointed to a piece of scrap paper she pulled out of her purse.

"I Corinthians 10:13 'God is faithful; he will not let you be tempted beyond what you can bear. But when you are tempted, he will also provide a way out so that you can stand up under it,'" he read out loud.

"If I'm reading this correctly, God is saying I can overcome any thing I am tempted by because he will always provide a way out, but I don't see that happening in the world I live in. I see women, especially the ones in the halfway house, who admit they have no control over drugs. They claim they are powerless to drugs and love them more than their own life. If they could, they would die for it and they see no way out. For them there is no one to save them. They have no one to turn to."

"Heaven, that's not true. They do have an option, but they choose the easy way out. No one ever said giving up drugs was going to be painless, but if they put some effort into giving them up, it would be well worth it in the end."

His words stirred something inside of her. This was the first time he said something that actually made sense to her. She did use drugs to escape being responsible. It was so much easier than being rejected or hurt by those she loved. She meditated on his words for a few seconds before she felt him watching her.

"I apologize for staring," he said. "Your eyes are as green as the ocean. When I look in them, I see no ending. They are hypnotizing like my wife's. Her eyes weren't green like yours, they were baby doll brown."

Heaven was smiling on the outside, but on the inside she was screaming. Deacon Washington had mentioned his wife at every single meeting. It didn't matter what he was doing or discussing, everything reminded him of Celeste. Heaven was sick of hearing about Celeste. It felt like she had never died. Her name was constantly being mentioned in church. Several scholarships had been created in her name. The church was also planning on having a playground built in her honor. When were they going to put her memory to rest? Heaven fumed. When they buried her Heaven thought everything about her would also be buried.

His office phone rang and he excused himself to take the call. "Okay, Emalee. I'll be right there." He hung up the phone and turned to Heaven. "The baby has a slight fever and my sister is concerned. She thinks I should take him to the emergency room." He began gathering his things. "We can end here tonight. It's a good thing we didn't get too far. Next week I can quickly bring Ebony up to speed and pick up where we left off." He grabbed his briefcase and coat. "Heaven, I'll see you next week."

"Yes, Deacon. Same time, same place." He rushed out the church office, leaving her alone. Each official in the church had a photo taken with their spouse. These photos were hung along the back wall. Heaven glared at the picture Deacon Washington had taken with his wife. Love and happiness filled their eyes. There was no denying how much this man loved his wife. The only way Heaven would get the Deacon to come to her was if Celeste gave him a nudge in her direction and she knew exactly how to make that happen.

"Ebony, you had a phone call today," Heaven told Ebony when she returned from the store. "I forget the woman's name, but she said she was a lawyer and she would try to catch up with you at around seven o'clock tonight," she added.

"I bet the call has something to do with my son." Ebony sat on the side of her bed. "What am I going to do? We're supposed to meet with Deacon Washington at six-thirty, but I can't miss this call. I've been waiting for them to call me back for weeks."

"Ebony, you don't have to go to class."

"I know, but I missed last week. I don't want Deacon Washington to think I'm not taking this seriously."

"I'm sure Deacon Washington will understand. I'll let him know why you can't attend."

"Thanks, Heaven." She walked over and hugged her tight. "It's good to have a friend I can count on."

Lying to Ebony like that was not what Heaven had planned on doing, but it came so easily. She knew Ebony was going to be really upset when she didn't get that call at seven o'clock, but it had to be done.

Chapter 15

When Deacon Washington answered his front door Heaven was surprised to see him dressed so casually. No suit or tie. Today he wore gray jeans and a plaid button down shirt that made him look ruggedly sexy.

He invited her into the living room and offered her a seat. "I'm sorry about the mess." The floor was full of children's toys and blankets. "The children and I were watching a little television earlier." An episode of Bugs Bunny blared from his television set. "Where's Ebony?"

"She sends her apologies but she couldn't make it. She's waiting on a phone call concerning her son."

"Is she still trying to get visitation rights?" he asked. "The next time I see her I have to remember to ask her if there's anything I can do to help." He grabbed the remote and turned the television off. "The children and I were finishing up our dinner in the kitchen. Give me a second to check in on them and I'll be right with you."

He dashed out the room and into the kitchen. Minutes later, he reappeared with his briefcase, Bible, and books. "Now, let's see where we left off last week." He put his reading glasses on and opened his Bible.

Heaven searched in her purse for a pen. When she looked up, she saw Imani standing in the kitchen doorway with a fork in her right hand and a spoon in the left. A small morsel of her dinner was stuck to the side of her mouth. "Hello little lady, did you finish eating?" Heaven asked.

Deacon Washington turned around. "Imani, I thought I told you not to get up from the table until you were finished eating."

"I am. Sam keeps throwing food at me," she whined.

"I'm sorry. This will only take a moment." He got up to tend to the children.

"Deacon, do you mind if I use your bathroom?" Heaven asked.

"No, go right ahead. It's upstairs." Heaven remembered exactly where the bathroom was from the last time she was there. She climbed the stairs and walked right past the bathroom into his bedroom. She pulled a piece of paper from her pocket that would guarantee Celeste's memory would be erased from the house forever. She glanced at the letter one last time before gently placing it in with a dresser drawer full of Celeste's things. "Sorry, Celeste. It's time for you to say good-bye." Closing the drawer, she quietly snuck out the bedroom and back downstairs.

Before she got comfortable on the couch, Deacon Washington walked in with his children. "Deacon,

I hope you don't mind. I checked in on the baby. He's still sleeping."

"Great. It's rare for him to sleep for so long. It's also getting close to bedtime for these two little night owls." He patted his two oldest children on the top of their heads. "I'll be right back down," he said. "I need to make sure they change into their pajamas and brush their teeth then we can begin our lesson."

"No problem. I'll watch a little television until you return." Heaven remembered how well Ebony had connected with his children the day of the funeral. If they liked Ebony then she was sure she could get them to fall in love with her. She knelt down in front of them, "You two make sure you have a good night, okay?" She smiled at the children.

Imani showed her a mouth full of teeth and delightfully nodded her head. Samuel didn't look as happy as his sister. She could see malice in his eyes. "Get out!" He lashed out at Heaven. "Leave. I don't want you in my house," he screamed. Swinging his arm back, he struck her in the center of her lip with the video game he held in his hand.

Her bottom lip split open and she tasted blood. The pain that shot through her mouth hurt so badly, she wanted to cry. She covered her mouth with her hand and turned away.

"Samuel. You say you're sorry right now."

"No," Samuel defiantly screamed, then fled to the safety of his bedroom.

"I'm sorry. I don't know what's gotten into him," Deacon Washington apologized.

"That's all right," Heaven mumbled. "You better

go upstairs and see if he's okay. I'll be fine." The Deacon was reluctant to leave her alone, but she insisted. While he was upstairs she went into the kitchen to get a napkin and wipe away some of the blood.

Twenty minutes later he joined her in the kitchen. He found her sitting at the kitchen table holding a folded piece of paper towel against her lip.

"Heaven, I'm sorry. He's been having a rough time since his mother died. They were very close." He grabbed some ice cubes out of the freezer and placed them in a Ziploc bag. Using a dishtowel, he made an ice pack and pulled up a chair next to her. He moved her hand and placed the ice against her lip. "How does that feel?"

"Better." She tried to talk. "Samuel is just a child. He doesn't understand why I'm here in his mother's house. All he sees is this woman who is not his mother with his father."

"Still, that doesn't excuse his behavior."

Heaven was ready to give a list of excuses for Samuel's outburst, but the words got lost when she saw the way the Deacon was looking at her. He had finally taken the bait. She had caught his attention. He must have noticed his attraction to her because he pulled away.

"Why don't we continue with Bible study?" He ran back into the living room to get their materials. They spread their things out on the kitchen table and completed the lesson for the night in no time. Before she knew it he was walking her to the front door.

"Again, I'm sorry about what happened tonight."

"Deacon, stop apologizing. It was an accident."

"Are you going to be okay getting back to the halfway house on your own?" he asked.

"Yes, I'll be fine." He helped her with her coat.

"I'm going to suggest that you and Ebony be scheduled for baptism."

"Great! I can't wait to tell her."

With his pointer finger, he lightly touched her bottom lip. "It looks as though your lip may be swollen for a few days. Please don't tell anybody you got that here. People will start thinking that I hit on women."

"We wouldn't want that." She laughed. "They would start calling you the abusive deacon."

They laughed at her corny joke together and the chemistry between them glowed brightly. For a split second, she saw a look in his eyes that said he wanted to be more than her friend or teacher. This time she was not going to allow him to recoil his feelings. Hoping for the best, she kissed him softly on the lips. Her arms snaked themselves around his neck and she waited to feel his embrace. Relief flooded the core of her soul when she felt him pull her closer. She was lost in their kiss when he abruptly backed away from her. "We have to stop. I'm sorry. I don't know what came over me. I'm married."

"No. You *were* married," she reminded him.

He shuddered at the truth in her words. "I'm going to bed. Please let yourself out."

Chapter 16

A week later, Heaven stood in the mirror examining her lip. The mark Samuel left on her face had faded over time. Heaven knew the mark was payback for lying to Ebony about her phone call, but to Heaven it seemed well worth it. When she returned to the halfway house that night, Ebony wasn't upset that she didn't get her call. She simply said, "I've been waiting for them to call this long. I'm sure I can wait a while longer."

Heaven applied some make up to her face when Ebony swept into their room with the daily newspaper in her hand. "Heaven, listen to this. That Fentanyl Reverend Stansfield talked about in church killed twelve people over the weekend. On Saturday, ten people died in different parts of the city. They found a man's body in Fairview at ten o'clock in the morning and then there were seven OD's reported within thirty minutes of one another; all within a half a mile radius. 9-1-1 operators received a record breaking one hundred and thirty three drug-related calls all within a twenty four hour period.

"They interviewed one doctor at Cooper Medical Center and he stated that his staff was working double overtime and that the city's police department was under pressure to find out who's responsible for pushing Fentanyl throughout the city."

"It shouldn't be that hard. If they put some undercover cops on the street to make a buy then they've got 'em."

"It's not that easy. The police have arrested a few corner boys but they won't give up their supplier. The only clue they have is the small plastic bag that the heroin comes in. Each bag that is laced with the Fentanyl has the slogan, 'Get high on die tryin,' printed on it. Every time the police find one of these bags, it's lying next to a dead body and they have no one else they can question."

"What about the people who OD'd and went to the hospital?"

"So far any information we have received from victims has been unreliable," Ebony read from the paper.

Heaven pulled her hair in different styles before settling on a simple ponytail. "I don't even know why the cops waste their time trying to get that stuff off the streets. If those addicts end up killing themselves off that Fentanyl, then that's on them. That is one less crime the police have to worry about solving later on." She saw Ebony's mouth drop from her cruel words. "I have a one-on-one meeting with Ms. Griffin. I'll see you later."

Ms. Griffin updated Heaven on her progress in

the program. "Since you've been here you have been progressing well. You are attending church on a regular basis and Ebony told me the two of you are going to be baptized in a couple weeks. How do you feel about that?" she asked.

"It's cool, but I can't wait to get it over with. Everyone is making a big fuss when it's really no big deal."

"Sure it is. It symbolically means when you rise up from out of that water you are washing away your old life and you will emerge into a new one."

Deacon Washington had told her the same thing, but she was still confused about the significance of baptism. She was too embarrassed to tell anyone she didn't understand, so she kept silent.

"Have you given any thought to what I mentioned at our last meeting about having your grandmother sit in on a session?"

"I really don't think that's necessary, Ms. Griffin. My nana does not need to be burdened with my problems. I created them on my own and I'm sure I can solve them on my own."

"A lot of people who abuse drugs do it to escape or run from life, but you told me there was nothing in your past that made you do drugs. You did it because you wanted to, but if that was true, you wouldn't have a problem with asking your grandmother to visit with us." She paused briefly before continuing. "Tearing away that wall you've built up around yourself would be the perfect way to start your new life as a Christian, but it's your decision. I'll be here for you when you're ready."

Chapter 17

The Sunday of Heaven and Ebony's baptism had finally arrived. The ceremony was beautiful and one they would never forget. Several other people were also being baptized and the church was full of family and friends.

From the baptismal pool, Heaven could see Nana cry tears of joy. When it was Heaven's turn to be baptized, Reverend Stansfield said a few words and quickly submerged her head underwater. She was only under for a second, but in that time she expected to feel or see something. *Where was the bright shining light from God? Where was my angel from heaven?*

After church, the girls changed out of the white linens they wore for the baptism and back into their own clothes. Heaven saw Deacon Washington alone and quickly cornered him. His eyes darted around for someone to rescue him, but he was forced to face her. He had been distant toward her since the night of their kiss. During class, he avoided all eye contact with her and addressed most of his questions to Ebony. Plus, he made sure he was never left alone with Heaven.

Heaven didn't think the kiss was so bad that she deserved this kind of treatment, but to ease the tension between them she wanted to apologize for the remarks she made about his marriage.

"Hey Deacon, how are you this morning?"

"I'm good Heaven, how about you?" The official tone he used sounded so impersonal.

"How's the baby?"

"Much better, thanks for asking." He picked up his brief case and stepped around her. "Listen, I really have to go."

"Okay, I won't keep you. I'll see you around." On the other side of the church he greeted members of the congregation with a pleasant smile. She wished he would look at her that way.

Sister Stewart noticed Deacon Washington trying to get Ebony's attention and she gestured for Ebony to turn around. When she did, he had already rushed toward her and the two collided together. She practically fell into his arms. Heaven watched him ask her if she was all right while holding tight to her arm.

Heaven wanted to cry. Less than a minute ago, he barely had two words to say to her, but now he was making it a point to speak with Ebony. They laughed together and Heaven couldn't help but feel jealous over their relationship.

Nana startled Heaven from her thoughts. "Why do you look so down? Today is a joyous day. The skies have opened up and God's light is shining down on you and Ebony." She squeezed her hand.

"I'm so proud of you." Heaven's solemn mood didn't change. "What's wrong?"

"Nothing. I'm fine, probably just a little tired. It's been a long day. I might head back to the halfway house early."

"Are you sure? The church has cookies and punch downstairs."

She glanced at Ebony and the Deacon a second time and tried to make sense of what was going on between them.

"Hey, Heaven." Her somber mood grew worse at the sound of Davis's voice. She introduced him to Nana, who excused herself and left Davis and Heaven alone. "I bought you a present for your baptism. I was hoping you would come to my house this afternoon so I could give it to you."

A simple present was not the cure for her blues. Davis couldn't give her what she wanted and that was Deacon Washington. "Davis, I really appreciate the thought, but I'm not feeling well." Her eyes never left Ebony and Deacon Washington. "I think I need to lie down for a bit."

"You can lie down at my house if you like," he offered.

Deacon Washington held open one of the side doors leading out of the sanctuary for Ebony and him to walk through. She couldn't bear to watch them any longer; she was ready to leave.

"Sure, Davis, I'll come back to your house with you," she agreed.

They left the church and within minutes, he pulled up in front of his first floor condo in Cherry Hill. It was a brand new housing development with a unit specifically made to accommodate his disability.

His house was decorated in a traditional style. The living room had a fireplace, couch, and contemporary lamps sat on each cherry wood end table.

"Nice house," she complimented.

"Thanks. I would lie and say I decorated it myself just to impress you, but the decorator I hired did a better job than I could ever do."

He led her into the den and asked her to have a seat. With the assistance of his metal crutches, he walked over to a table and pulled her present out the drawer. On his way back to her, his foot got caught on the Oriental rug that was thrown across the floor and he tripped.

He fell on top of Heaven. With his face less than an inch away from hers she asked, "Are you all right?"

"Yes, I'm okay." They untwisted his legs from around hers and settled back on the love seat. "This is for you." He handed her a long, slender, burgundy gift box.

She loved presents; especially expensive presents. With everything that had happened that day, she thought she deserved to have something good happen to her. "That's what I like to see— that gorgeous smile," he said.

"Davis, you don't have to keep buying me presents." They had known each other for only a few months, but in that time Davis had managed to spoil her. He had flowers delivered to the halfway house at least once a week. They ate at the most expensive restaurants and he paid for her weekly visits to the spa.

"I know, but you are so beautiful. I really like you and hope one day you and I can be more than friends." His choice of words surprised her and she heard a lustful yearning in his voice she had never heard before. Her hands trembled from nervousness and she dropped the box to the floor. He picked it up, but instead of handing it back to her he opened it. Inside glimmered a platinum necklace with diamonds the size of peanuts.

"It's breathtaking!" She reached out to touch it.

"Before you ask." He took the necklace out of the box and told her to turn around. "It's the same necklace we saw at the mall. Except I had the original diamonds replaced with larger ones."

"Davis, this necklace must have cost you a fortune."

"It wasn't cheap, but neither are you."

He told her to look in the mirror. The diamonds looked huge around her neck. She couldn't believe he had bought this for her. Davis walked up close behind her and rubbed her arms. He stood so close she could feel how hard he was. She turned around and took a step back.

"Can I at least get a hug?" he asked. Heaven hugged him by standing as far back from him as possible.

"Are you ready to go?" She wanted to leave before he asked her for something she did not want to give up and she wasn't referring to the necklace.

He took hold of her hand and led her back to

the love seat. "Heaven, I was hoping you and I could spend some time together."

She recommended they watch a movie.

"Yeah, we could, but we could also do something else."

Heaven was afraid this was going to happen. She hoped Davis would be different because he was a church man, but he was just like the others. He did something for her and now he wanted sex in return. He stared at her like a dog in heat. She thought he was going to jump on top of her if she didn't say something soon. Heaven could feel the cool platinum against her skin. She loved the necklace he had gotten her and she wasn't about to give it back. She thought for a moment and decided to use this as a business opportunity. "Listen, if you promise to give me three thousand dollars, I'll give you some nookie, but you can't come shopping with me. I want to go by myself."

"Is that all?" He pulled his wallet from out his back pocket and counted out thirty one-hundred-dollar bills.

"You shouldn't carry that kind of money around with you."

"I usually don't, but I know when you're around, I have to make sure I have money because you're high maintenance."

"Do you have condoms?"

"They're in my bedroom." Without haste, he asked her to follow him. When she reached his bedroom he was already laid out on the bed.

"Can I use you bathroom to freshen up?" she asked.

"Sure, it's right through there."

She stared at her reflection in the bathroom mirror. She couldn't believe she was about to have sex with a crippled guy for three thousand dollars. This was one of those times she needed some dope to get her through. Instead, she splashed cold water on her face and joined Davis.

"Heaven, are you all right? You look flustered."

"Like I said earlier, I wasn't feeling too well." Davis had a king size bed. She climbed into bed and lay down next to him. "Are you a virgin?" Her question must have embarrassed him because he put his head down and his face turned red. "Don't worry. Everyone has to have their first time and I will make sure yours is unforgettable." She unbuttoned his pants and removed his boxers. Her eyes grew to twice their size when she saw how big he was.

"Can I get the condom?" she asked. The size on the condom said extra large. "I see someone was a bit confident."

He smiled boldly. She told him to lie down on his back. The skirt she wore allowed her to easily slip off her stockings and panties and climb on top of him. When he entered her his face looked like he had just experienced paradise. He reminded her of someone getting high for the very first time.

Like a teacher, Heaven educated Davis on how to make a woman feel good. Once he found his rhythm, she found herself enjoying her time with him. Perhaps having sex with Davis was what she needed. After he finished and she lifted herself up off him, she noticed the condom was missing.

"Where's the condom?" She panicked. "Please!

Please don't tell me that you released yourself inside of me." Davis sat up bewildered. "I don't believe this." She cried.

"Don't panic."

"I have a condom stuck up in me, and you're telling me not to panic." She ran to the bathroom and tried to use her fingers to pull it out, but felt nothing. He must have pushed it so far up she couldn't reach it. She walked out the bathroom in disbelief.

"You couldn't get it?" he asked.

"No I couldn't get it. Can you take me home now?"

They rode back to the halfway house in silence. Again, this was karma for doing anything for the love of money.

Chapter 18

Heaven had been under the weather the last few days. Depression had confined her to bed and taken away her appetite. The only thing she thought or cared about was how cold Deacon Washington had treated her on Sunday. He made her feel worthless and that resulted in her having meaningless, unprotected sex with Davis.

The sex was good and being in the arms of somebody who wanted her felt even better. That's probably why she had agreed. Davis may not have been who she wanted, but at least he bought her things. He would have never treated her the way the deacon had.

Ms. Griffin had warned her that rejection was a part of the recovery process and how she handled rejection would determine if she succeeded in the program or not. She suggested that if Heaven ever felt like all hope was gone, she share those feelings at one of the group meetings. That idea was not appealing to Heaven. She preferred to keep her feelings to herself.

Ebony assumed Heaven's depression was a cold. Every day she brought her bowls of chicken soup and herbal tea to help her feel better. Ebony made sure Heaven had undisturbed sleep and even volunteered to do her household chores. Ebony even called her out of work two days straight, but now her mini-vacation was over and she had to get back to work. If she didn't, Ms. Campbell was ready to send her to the doctor and then everyone would know there was nothing wrong with her.

The first person she saw when she walked into work was Zaria Evans. Already busy at work, Zaria managed to wave to Heaven in between checking out items, greeting customers, and bagging items. Heaven clocked in without speaking to anyone and went straight to her station. All she wanted to do was get through her eight hours and get back to bed. As soon as she flipped on the switch that opened her station, customers began lining up.

Zaria's laughter with her customers drifted into Heaven's ears. By the sound of the pleasantries she extended to everyone in her line, Heaven assumed Zaria was in a good mood. Heaven took a glimpse at Zaria from over her shoulder. She looked like she was on auto pilot. Like a robot, Zaria swiftly swiped items through her station, bagged them, and joked with every customer while taking their money. Zaria was a good worker, but Heaven had never seen her that productive. When Zaria stopped for a moment, she glanced at Heaven. Right away,

Heaven knew the reason behind Zaria's energy. She could see it in her eyes. Zaria was high.

It was hard for Heaven to look at Zaria and not be reminded of the things she had done when she was using. Those old feelings that she had suppressed for so long were making their way back to the surface. She tried to focus on her work and forget about Zaria, but she was fighting a losing battle.

Zaria had once admitted to Heaven that she often got high. She was a user of just about everything out there; crack, coke, weed, and prescription drugs. Her excuse was that she needed it to cope with life. When Zaria was high she was happy, friendly, and outgoing, but when she was sober she carried the weight of the world on her shoulders. She believed the only way she could get out of bed in the morning was by using cocaine. Before she went to bed at night she made sure she had a stash of either cocaine or heroin in her nightstand waiting for her in the morning.

As the day wore on, Zaria's enthusiasm died down. Her friendly greetings to each customer dwindled down to one every few people and it wasn't long before she was ringing customers out without speaking a word.

A young mother questioned the price of one of her items to Zaria. Annoyed, she responded with a nasty remark and the two started a screaming match. Mr. Walker came over and berated Zaria in front of the entire store. He apologized to the young mother for Zaria's unprofessional behavior and asked the woman to step to the customer service desk to resolve her problem. Zaria was coming down off her high and Heaven knew from experience that the best thing for everyone to do was steer clear of her.

After Mr. Walker walked away, Zaria turned the light off to her station and announced she needed a break. She walked away leaving three customers still standing in line. Heaven didn't want to see Zaria get in any more trouble so she politely asked the customers to get into her line.

Mr. Walker knew Zaria had taken her break and he kept walking past her station checking his watch. After twenty minutes, Zaria had not returned, so he asked Heaven to go to the employees' lounge and tell her to get back to work.

He was already upset with Zaria and Heaven didn't need him to be mad with her also, so she hurried to the break room, but when she looked around, Zaria wasn't there. There were only a couple places she could be. Heaven checked the back of the store, but there was no one there but a delivery man. The last place she searched was the women's bathroom.

"Zaria," she called out from the bathroom doorway. "Mr. Walker wants you back out on the floor. You better hurry up because he looks mad." She could see Zaria's shoes from underneath the stall.

"Heaven." Zaria pushed the stall door wide open.

Something told Heaven to turn around and go back to work, but she ignored her gut feeling and went to Zaria. When she reached her she was sitting on the edge of the toilet. In one hand she had a straw and in the other was a folded piece of paper full of dope.

"What's that?" Heaven nodded toward her hand.

"Your favorite," she replied. "Heroin."

Heaven stared at it lovingly and could feel herself succumb to the lure of it. It called out to her and she longed to hold it in her hands. Zaria held out the drugs to her and Heaven took them without hesitation.

She knew what she was about to do was wrong and that she should have run out of there when she first saw what Zaria was doing, but she couldn't turn her back on that high. Heroin had been silently calling out to her subconscious since she had returned back to town, but living under the careful eye of the halfway house had prevented her from indulging in her weakness.

Heaven took the straw from her and took a small sniff. The sensation it provided was so powerful that it could never be duplicated. Her first taste of dope was like making love to a lover she had been separated from for too long. She gripped the paper, taking sniff after sniff until there was nothing left.

"Do you have any more?" she asked.

"No, but if you have a couple dollars on you, I know where we can get some from."

Heaven pulled eight dollars out her pocket.

"That's enough to get us started, but first you need to get us out of work."

A few minutes later, Heaven walked into Mr. Walker's office. "Heaven, did you find Zaria?" he asked.

"Yes sir, she was in the bathroom." Heaven's eyesight was blurry from the dope and instead of talking to Mr. Walker she talked to a five foot potted plant that sat behind him.

"Are you all right?"

"I'm great. It's Zaria who's not feeling well. She's sick and feels like she can't make it home by herself."

He gave her a peculiar look. He grumbled under his breath about having to let two cashiers leave early, but he eventually said okay. Once Heaven and Zaria left the supermarket, they went straight to Zaria's friend's house in Centerville Projects.

Zaria walked straight into building 1B without even knocking. She hollered out to see if anyone was home and a female's voice responded. On the stairs leading to the second floor apartment, empty potato chip bags and crumbled soda cans lay scattered on the steps. When they reached the top landing, Heaven saw that the entire apartment was full of trash.

Trash bags overflowing with garbage sat in all four corners of the kitchen. Dirty dishes were piled high in the sink and dog waste waiting to be cleaned up was spread throughout the living room.

A small toddler wearing only a diaper ran around the apartment sucking from a bottle. The television blasted an infomercial and an older woman sat at the kitchen table puffing on a cigarette.

"It's freezing in here. What happened to the heat?" Zaria asked.

"Girl, my heat has been off since summer. When it was hot outside it was all right in here, but now that it's winter I'm trying my best to keep this place warm. Today is the first real cold day we've had. The weatherman kept saying winter was coming early and I didn't believe him. It's only October and the temperatures are supposed to fall into the low twenties."

"I think it's colder in here than it is outside." Heaven could see Zaria's breath as she spoke.

"That kerosene heater we have is running low. Bruce was supposed to go out and pick me up some. I'm still waiting on him to come back."

Zaria took a seat at the kitchen table and offered Heaven a seat. "Jill, this is one of the girls I work with down at the supermarket. We got off from work early and were hoping you had something for us to get into."

Jill eyed Heaven suspiciously. "How do I know she can be trusted?"

"She's cool. Trust me. She just got done doing six years in prison. She isn't going to cause any trouble."

Jill tapped the ashes from off her cigarette. "I don't have anything going on right now. Maybe when Bruce comes back he'll know somewhere we can get something on credit. You know Bruce has all these hook-ups. He should be back any minute."

Jill revealed a front row of rotted teeth when she spoke. Her hair had broken off in various places and it looked like it hadn't been combed in months. Jill used her fingernail to pick at a sore that hadn't healed properly on her face.

A dude the color of charcoal was sitting next to Heaven at the kitchen table. Usually Heaven would have admired his dark complexion, but because he was so ashy it was difficult for her to fairly judge him. His hands, lips, and face looked like chalk. Plus, his black pants and black hoodie were full of lint.

Zaria spoke to the ashy guy who hadn't said a word since they arrived. "What's up, Chris?"

"W-w-what's-s-s up? Zar-r ia?" he stuttered.

"How long has he been here?" Zaria asked Jill.

"For three days straight. He won't go home. I wish he would get up out of here because he needs to take a bath. You stank," she shouted toward him.

"How much dope did y'all do?" Zaria asked.

"We used his entire check. I'm sure he lost his job. Three days. No call, no show. Yeah. He's definitely fired," Jill concluded. She rocked back in her chair with the arm broken off.

Suddenly, someone swung the front door open and screamed, "I got it!" A big guy with a rough and rugged beard stormed up the stairs and into the kitchen. He held up a brown paper bag in one hand, and in the other was a red plastic gas container.

He walked over to the kerosene heater that sat in the middle of the living room floor and filled it back up. Then he walked back into the kitchen and dumped approximately forty bags of heroin that would sell for at least twenty dollars each on the street. From where Heaven was sitting she could see the words "Get High or Die Tryin'" printed on each bag.

"Bruce, where'd you get this stuff from?" Jill picked up one of the bags. "This is that good stuff everybody's been hunting down. I don't think I've ever seen so much dope at one time. You didn't steal this, did you?"

He looked insulted by her question, but the grin on his face proved his guilt. "Don't worry about that. What you need to know is that everyone here is going to have to pay to get high."

His eyes landed on Heaven when he said that. The small amount of cash Heaven carried in her pocket wasn't nearly enough to cover one twenty bag of dope. Any hopes she had of getting high had just gone up in smoke.

Chris discreetly reached his hand onto the table and tried to steal a bag without anyone noticing, but Bruce was like a hawk watching his young. He never took his eyes off any of those bags. Bruce slapped Chris's hand hard. "Oh no! Chris, you've been here getting high for the past three days. It ain't my fault you lost your job. You're going to have to pay for this like everybody else."

Jill eyed Chris pitifully then she laughed a hearty laugh. "Bruce, give the kid a break. You weren't complaining when he used his entire paycheck on us. Let him have just a few hits."

Bruce reluctantly agreed. Heaven thought it was unfair that even poor pathetic Chris was going to be allowed to get high and she was going to have to sit and watch them enjoy the drugs without her.

Zaria must have also been broke because she called Bruce into the living room while the unattended toddler ran around the room singing "Elmo! Elmo!"

Zaria whispered a few things in his ear. He looked in Heaven's direction and grunted a few times before nodding his head.

Zaria ran back, "All right, girl. Bruce has allowed us to have a little, but I had to promise to pay him back."

Heaven nodded her head in full agreement.

"It's a lot of us here. We're going to need something bigger than a spoon." Jill ran over to the kitchen cabinet and pulled out the lid to a mayonnaise jar.

Jill grabbed two packets of dope and dumped it into the lid. Grabbing the syringe on the table she filled it up with water and squirted it into the dope. She then took a lighter and held it underneath the lid until the mixture began to bubble. Jill cooked the dope to perfection, like she was a chemist in a laboratory. Bruce pulled cotton from out of a cigarette that lay on the table and dropped it on the cooked dope. Jill stuck the needle into the cotton and slowly pulled the plunger back until it was full of heroin. She stuck the needle into her arm and pushed the dope into her veins. Her head fell back and she was cast under its spell. That was the first time she had smiled all night.

Shooting up dope gave the best high and Heaven hadn't used a needle in years. There was only one needle in the house so they had to share. Heaven didn't think twice about the consequences of sharing an unclean needle with other drug users. Her thoughts were of how being high was going to help her forget about Deacon Washington. Jill passed Heaven the needle and she repeated Jill's routine. In an instant Heaven felt the same way Jill did. Her body relaxed and she passed the needle to Chris who greedily grabbed it from her hands. He quickly shot the dope into his neck.

Zaria snatched the needle from him, "Stop trying to be so greedy, Chris." Zaria took her turn and so did Bruce. They sat around that table for over two hours getting high. Before Heaven knew it, half the dope was gone and Bruce was beginning to put restrictions on who could continue getting high.

"All right, Chris, your time is up. You had enough of my dope and if you want to continue getting high you're going to have to hand over some doe."

Chris stared at Bruce like a zombie. Heaven thought Chris was so high he couldn't comprehend what Bruce was saying, but he woke up from his daze when Bruce walked over to him and pulled him out the chair. Chris realized Bruce was trying to put him out and he put up a fight. He scrambled on the floor and grabbed the kitchen table. He yelled out, "No-o-o."

Jill, Zaria, and Heaven tried to keep the drugs from falling off the table.

"Come on, Chris. You've got to go." One of the lighters had fallen to the floor and Chris picked it up. Bruce pulled Chris away from the kitchen table and tried to push him down the stairs. The two of them wrestled on the ground until Bruce lost his grip, allowing Chris to break free.

Chris ran toward the kerosene container sitting on the floor and lifted it high in the air, "Get-t-t b-b-back," he yelled.

Bruce froze where he was standing.

"Chris," Jill yelled. "Don't do anything crazy. You know we have a baby in here."

"Yeah, Chris," Bruce added.

"No, y-y-you were t-t-trying to g-g-get r-r-rid of me."

"No I wasn't." Bruce changed his tone. "I just thought it was time for you to go home. You haven't been home in days."

"Yeah r-right." Chris started throwing kerosene around the living room. The toddler had fallen asleep on the couch and was awakened by the commotion. Heaven stared at Chris. He was crazy and she thought this was the perfect time for them to escape. She didn't want to be around when he decided to light that tiny apartment ablaze.

Bruce tried to convince him one last time, "Listen Chris, let's start over and sit back down at the table. All of us."

Chris's face softened for a moment. That crazy look in his eyes conceded, but paranoia prevented him from trusting Bruce. Without a word he lit the lighter and threw it on the floor. Flames quickly engulfed the apartment.

Chapter 19

When Heaven opened her eyes the following morning her mind was still in a daze. She looked around and wondered how she had ended up back in her own bed.

"Good Morning," Ebony said. "How do you feel this morning?" Heaven lifted her head. The throbbing sensation pulsating against her temples forced her to lay back down on her pillow. Ebony stepped back into the bathroom. When she returned, her glare at Heaven was an indication that Heaven had done something wrong. "You were almost sent back to the prison last night."

"Why? What did I do?" Heaven's eyes widened with fear.

Ebony picked up one of her shoes that lay on the floor. "I went to the job last night to pick up my check and when I got there, Mr. Walker told me you had taken Zaria home because she didn't feel well."

Heaven started to recall what had happened the night before.

"You know that girl ain't anything but trouble. I don't know why you would go anywhere with her. I asked a few cashiers where Zaria lived and they told me she stayed on Norris Street. I walked up and down that block looking for your behind for over an hour in the cold. The wind was hitting me in the face and my feet were frozen.

"I looked for you until it was time for me to come back here. I knew for sure you were up to no good. Then I saw you staggering down the street about a block away and you didn't look good. Your eyes were half-closed and your mouth was hanging open. I tried to talk to you, but you were in such bad shape. You kept leaning against buildings and street signs to steady yourself. After you pushed me away a few times, you finally allowed me to help you. I prayed I could get you signed in and walk you straight to our room without running into Ms. Campbell. Unfortunately, she was the first person we ran into."

Heaven closed her eyes and moaned loudly. If she knew Ms. Campbell, she had probably already called the prison and told them to prepare her a cell.

"That's exactly how I felt when I saw her. You know how she claims to be part bloodhound. Sniffing out when someone is breaking one of the house rules and waiting for one of us to mess up so she can send us right back to the prison. She looked at you with her beady eyes through those bi-focal glasses. I just knew we were busted. 'Stansfield, you

all right?' " Ebony bellowed like Ms. Campbell. "I
tried to cover for you by telling her you were still
not feeling well. I don't know if she believed me or
not but she seemed concerned and suggested you
go see a doctor."

Heaven's heart rate accelerated to twice its normal pace. She stared at the door, scared the police
were waiting right outside her room ready to
storm in at any minute and take her back to the
prison.

"Heaven, what made you relapse?" Ebony's eyes
softened with sincerity.

Heaven couldn't tell her what happened between her and Deacon Washington. Ebony would
have thought she was crazy for going after him so
soon after his wife died. "Ebony, I got caught up in
something I shouldn't have been involved in. You
were right. I shouldn't have been with Zaria; she
ain't nothing but trouble. It's no big deal. I'll
never do it again," Heaven vowed.

"How can you be so blasé over something that
could have jeopardized your recovery and your
freedom? We were just baptized Sunday," she
shouted.

Heaven walked over and gave her a hug. "I'm
sorry." She didn't want Ebony to be upset with her.
She had come to really like Ebony despite her talking too much and being happy all the time.
"You're right! Me getting and staying clean is important and I promise, no more excursions with
Zaria."

Ebony pulled away and slipped on her coat.

"Where are you going?" Heaven asked.

"Did you forget? The church is having a meeting to discuss plans for construction of the new building."

Heaven didn't want to go. She wasn't ready to face Deacon Washington. After the night she'd had, she couldn't bear to see him talk with every member of the church then brush her off again. "I don't think I'm going. If anyone asks for me, tell them I'm sick."

After Ebony left, Heaven lay in her bed and tried to get some sleep. Each time she closed her eyes she saw a hypodermic needle flash before he eyes. She squeezed her eyes shut and tried to block out everything from the night before. Heaven refused to allow her relapse to destroy everything she had been working so hard for. She jumped up out of bed and threw on some clothes. Then she rushed downstairs and went to a group meeting. She felt a little better after the meeting was over. Ms. Griffin was right. It was therapeutic to hear other people's struggles with drugs. She went back upstairs and got in bed. Glancing at her arms, she could see the track marks left from the needle last night. Those marks scared her. She hated seeing evidence of what she had done to herself. She scrubbed hard and fast, trying to wipe away the track marks. She jumped up and used foundation from her make-up kit to cover them up. She then lay back down and prayed that God would save her.

When Ebony returned from the meeting, she placed a piece of birthday cake on Heaven's side of the nightstand. "What is that?" Heaven asked.

"It was Levi's birthday and the church had bought him a cake," Ebony replied.

Heaven unwrapped the dessert and dug into the chocolate cake. "How was the meeting?"

"The meeting was good. Davis asked about you. I told him you weren't feeling well and he practically ran over here to check on you."

Heaven groaned.

"You know he has a crush on you. It took me ten minutes to convince him not to come. I told him to stop by tomorrow and see how you are doing."

Heaven was glad Davis took Ebony's advice. She wasn't really up for visitors.

"Oh! Deacon Washington also asked about you. He seemed overly concerned when I told him you couldn't make it."

Heaven wished the deacon was concerned about her welfare, but after the way he ignored her on Sunday, she was sure he was probably faking concern because that was the polite thing to do.

Ebony gave Heaven a brief recap of what was discussed at the meeting. Then one of the girls on the floor yelled out. "Heaven, you have a phone call."

It was past nine o'clock. The only person who would call her this late was Davis. He hadn't stopped calling her since the day she spent at his house. If he asked her one more time when they were getting together again she was going to scream.

"Hello," she roared into the receiver.

"Heaven, this is Deacon Washington." Heaven was surprised to hear his voice. "I hate to have disturbed you at this time of night. Ebony told me you were ill. She said it wasn't serious, but I wanted to check for myself."

"I think it was just a slight head cold. A little rest and I'll feel a whole lot better."

"Good. I'm glad to hear that. I also wanted to apologize for the way I've been acting. I've had a lot of things on my mind and I took a lot of it out on you. That was wrong of me. I'm sorry."

"That's okay, I understand we all go through things every once in a while."

"Would you mind stopping by my house tomorrow evening? There is something I would like to talk with you about."

Heaven thought about how strange life was and how suddenly things could change. Yesterday she thought he hated her and today he was inviting her to his house. Heaven promised to stop by after her meeting with Ms. Griffin. When she walked back into the room, Ebony asked who was on the phone.

"It was Deacon Washington. He asked if I could stop by his house tomorrow."

"I think he likes you," Ebony sang out.

"He just lost his wife," Heaven reminded her.

"That don't mean the man can't be interested in you."

She had a feeling Ebony was right. Heaven dreamed Deacon Washington would fall to his knees and confess his true feelings for her. She couldn't wait to hear what he had to say.

Heaven was excited about her visit with Deacon Washington. She asked Ebony to help press her hair straight and then ran out to the store to pick up a bottle of Celeste's funky perfume. When she knocked on the door, he immediately answered, letting her know he had been waiting on her.

"Heaven, come in." When they walked into the living room, he had the fireplace burning and light music playing. "I hope you don't mind that I sent the children to Emalee's for the night. My children can be a handful and I don't want any more accidents like the one last time you were here."

They laughed together before sitting on the couch. "Heaven, I've been carrying this burden around and I've been too ashamed to share this secret with anyone." Heaven didn't think he would refer to his feelings for her as a burden. "I can't talk to Reverend Stansfield or anyone else from the church. I feel like my entire life has been a charade."

"Whatever it is that's bothering you, you can tell me."

"I found something." He gripped her hands tightly. "Something really disturbing. I prayed about it and the Lord told me to share it with someone and I thought about you. I hope it's okay if I lay my troubles on you for a moment. There is no one I can talk to about this because what I'm about to tell you affects my family greatly." He rubbed his hand over his face. "The day after you left here from our membership class I decided to begin packing Celeste's things away. A lot of her things I was going to give to Goodwill, but there were a few things I wanted to keep for the children. I invited

my sister over to help because she's good at organizing things like that. Anyway, I was in our bedroom packing away her sweaters when I lifted one
out the drawer and found a note hidden between
her clothes. It was a note from Celeste's lover."

"What?" Heaven had forgotten about that
phony note she'd hidden.

"That's exactly how I reacted." He pulled out
the letter from his pocket and gave it to her.

Celeste, I know you said we couldn't see one an-
other again, but I can't live without you. The
only thing keeping me alive is the endless memory
of passion we've shared together and the thought
of the life you and I created is growing inside of
you. Please see me. I love you.

"Is this for real?" she asked.

"I still can't believe it. When I showed it to my
sister, she refused to believe Celeste would have an
affair."

"What do you believe?"

"Heaven, this letter is dated at the time Celeste
was carrying Wesley. I can't ignore the possibility
that Wesley might not be my son. What should I
do? Ignore it? It's hard for me to believe Celeste
would deceive me in such a way."

"I think it's hard to believe anyone we love
would deceive us."

"I've been going over this letter in my head for
days. It just doesn't make sense. Celeste always ac-
counted for her whereabouts with me, not because
she had to but because she wanted to. If she was
having an affair, I had no idea."

"Sometimes those we trust the most are the ones who disappoint us," she replied. "What are you going to do?" she asked.

"I've thought about it and I'm not going to do anything. As far as I'm concerned, Celeste was still my wife and my memory of her will be the same as before. This changes nothing. As far as I'm concerned, Wesley is my son until somebody tells me otherwise."

Chapter 20

Heaven's plan had gone better than expected, but she wasn't finished yet. She needed a man to help her complete the job. She knew a lot of guys who would do anything for a bag, but she needed somebody who was confident. Someone who felt like the world revolved around him. Only one man came to mind and his name was Tyke.

Before going in to work, she stopped off in the Pollocktown section of the city to check out her old friend. Tyke didn't live in Pollock as it was called by city dwellers; but if she needed to find him, he was never far from the block. A bunch of young kids hustled drugs on the corner in front of a bar that had gone out of business called The Camelot.

The moment Heaven hit the corner, she was hounded with questions. Hustlers asking her what she needed and telling her they got her or can take care of her. Heaven remembered the days when she would appreciate the attention from dope dealers, but that was no longer her style. Today she had other matters she needed to attend to.

"I'm here to see Tyke," she told the crowd of boys. Curious eyes stared down at her, each one wondering who she was and what business she had with their boss. The crowd dispersed one by one, leaving one guy standing. This fella, unlike the others, had no forty ounce beer in his hand and his eyes were not yellow from smoking blunts all night long. He looked no older than seventeen and appeared to have a clear head.

"What you want with Tyke?" he asked.

"Tell him Heaven is here to see him. He'll know who I am."

He hesitated a moment before turning to his friends. "Watch her." A few feet away from where she stood he called someone on his walkie talkie phone. After a few words were spoken, Heaven heard a familiar voice say through the phone, "We'll be there."

Word on the street was that Tyke had moved up in the drug game. He had the best heroin in the city and every addict bought from him. Pushing heavy weight meant he was a threat to many. Heaven was sure Tyke had provided each one of his boys on the block with protection, just in case anyone tried to move in on one of his corners.

The kid who made the call sat back out of view and watched her from out the corner of his eye. The other boys on the corner went back to talking smack and cracking jokes on one another. Heaven watched the kids make their money. In less than five minutes, she witnessed at least twenty different sales take place. Being on the corner with so many drugs around her was tempting, but the halfway house had scheduled her to take a drug test in a few days. Plus, she was still waiting for the heroin to eliminate itself from her body. It was tempting being on the corner, but she could handle it.

The sound of screeching tires made Heaven turn around just in time to see a black Escalade pull up on the curb next to her. The back door swung open and the boy who made the call ordered her to get in.

She climbed inside and found Tyke sipping on a glass of brown cognac. Tyke had the sexiest smile and it always turned her on. He would always tell her his smile was reserved strictly for her. At times he was so convincing she believed every word he said.

He ordered his driver to drive around Camden. Then he leaned over and gave Heaven a hug. "What's up, girl?"

"What's up with you? I try to come check you out and I have to get clearance from the peanut gallery."

"That's my boy, Fitch. He's young, but he's proven to be one of the smartest cats I have on my team." He winked his eye at her.

Tyke had plenty of women and each one of them had probably fallen for him because of his alluring eyes. It wasn't the color of his eyes that was so appealing, it was that his eyes had a distinctive slant to them. A lot of people thought he was half Japanese, but he was always proud to tell everyone he was one hundred percent black.

Time had changed Tyke's style from Timberland

boots and sagging jeans to silk shirts, dress pants, and imported Italian shoes, but he still looked good.

"Would you like some Courvoisier?" he offered.

"I can't drink. I'm staying in a halfway house."

"That means your time is short. I can't wait to have you back home." He licked his lips and laughed as if he was remembering the old times between them. "So what's up? The only time you come looking for me is when you want something." He placed his hand on her leg. "Usually I'm the one hunting you down."

Heaven only loved two men in her lifetime and Tyke was one of them. They were never in a relationship with one another, but she loved drugs and he loved sex and those two things kept them cemented together.

Although Tyke had been in a steady relationship with the mother of his children since he was fifteen years old, it never stopped him from treating Heaven like anything less than a lady. He spoiled her with whatever she needed.

"I have a favor to ask of you."

His eyes turned to slits. That look was familiar to her and she knew him well enough to read his mind.

"Not that kind of favor." She turned to him. "I need you to go to this address tomorrow at around seven o'clock." She handed him a slip of paper.

"You going to meet me there?" he asked. "I heard you and Chrome broke up. I'm sure it's been a while. I'm willing to reminisce with you."

His driver turned down Broadway and slowed down to less than ten miles per hour. Tyke rolled down his passenger side window and pulled a gun out of his pocket.

No matter how much time passed or how much money Tyke made, he would always be a lover of guns. He was an avid collector. The older the gun, the more impressed he was with it. His most cherished collection was a set of guns he owned that were used in the Civil War.

"Tyke, can you tell your friend to drop me off on Mount Ephraim Avenue? I have to be to work soon."

"Can I borrow some money?" He held out his hand.

"Tyke, stop playing."

"I'm serious. I'm broke," he joked. "Upshaw, you can take her to work?"

On the way there, Tyke rolled down his window and pointed his gun at a few prostitutes walking the corners. He exercised his finger before placing it on the trigger.

"Tyke, what are you doing?" She grabbed at his arm. "Are you trying to send us both back to prison?"

"Girl, this gun ain't real. It's a BB gun." He pulled away from her and pointed it at a woman wearing a wig and a skirt too short for her long legs. With careful aim he pulled the trigger at his target. The woman jumped high in the air when that round silver ball hit her in the thigh. Once she realized what she had been hit with she yelled obscenities at Tyke as they rode away.

"Are you going to help me out?" She tried to refocus his attention on what she needed him to do.

"It depends," he replied.

"On what?"

"Whether you're going to help me out or not." He winked his eye and rubbed her leg.

"I'm serious." She pushed his hand off her leg. "Listen to what I have to say." Getting Tyke to go along with her plans was not going to be easy, but she was prepared to do anything he wanted.

After she finished giving him the details he looked unsure. "Heaven, that sounds a little risky."

"Tyke, I promise you nothing is going to happen. Once you do me this one favor, I'll never ask you for anything again."

"I've heard that before." Upshaw pulled into the supermarket parking lot and stopped in front of the store. "This is a big favor. You are going to owe me a lot."

She rolled her eyes at him. "What do you want?"

"You can start by hitting me off and we'll settle the rest later." He licked his lips and gave Heaven a sensual look.

She was willing to give Tyke some sex. They hadn't been together in a long time. Plus, she missed him. "We can't do it here," she said.

Tyke ordered his driver to go around the block a couple times. She straddled Tyke and allowed him to take off her blouse. "Is this what you wanted?" she asked.

He kissed her breasts and neck. "This is exactly what I wanted."

Chapter 21

Deacon Washington invited Heaven over to spend the evening with him and the children. Together the five of them sat in his living room watching Disney.

His daughter, Imani, was the friendliest little girl. When Heaven arrived at the house Imani led Heaven to her bedroom and introduced her to each one of her baby dolls. Now, as they watched the movie, Imani sat on her lap and talked as if they were old friends. She was adorable.

Unfortunately, the same couldn't be said about her older brother. Samuel stayed as far away from Heaven as possible. She tried talking with him but he tuned her out. It was obvious the kid didn't like her. That was something he and his aunt, Emalee, had in common.

During the movie, Heaven caught the deacon watching the baby play with his feet. The concerns he had about Wesley's paternity were manifested on his face. The baby laughed to himself and Hasani smiled lovingly.

A quick glance at the clock said the time had come for Tyke to make his grand entrance. At any moment, Heaven expected to hear chimes from the door bell. She jumped in her seat when she heard the door bell buzz instead of ring.

"Are you all right?" the deacon asked. "That loud doorbell will scare you if you're not used to hearing it." He laughed. "Let's put the movie on hold," he said to Samuel as he pushed the pause button before running to answer the front door. The children and Heaven sat quietly for a moment before she heard yelling. Heaven lifted Imani off her lap and told the children to sit still while she went to see what the commotion was about.

When she reached the front door, she could see Deacon Washington pointing his finger in somebody's face. "Wesley is not your son and you're going to have to kill me before I allow you take him from me," the deacon screamed.

"What's going on?" she asked.

"This man claims to be Wesley's father."

She looked to the other side of the door expecting to see Tyke. Instead, it was some guy she had never seen before. She stared at him with a blank look on her face. She was expecting to see Tyke and was really surprised.

"Look, I heard about Celeste and I'm sorry about what happened to her. I loved her probably more than you did, partner! But you are going to let me see my son." His threat seemed so real. She almost forgot he was acting.

"Over my dead body," Hasani shot back.

"That can be arranged." The guy exposed part of a pistol that was stuffed in the front of his pants.

Heaven stepped in the middle of their argument to ease the tension between the two men. She turned to the guy she assumed was sent by Tyke. "You don't have any proof that Wesley is your son and until you do, Hasani is his father."

"You want proof? I'll get you proof." The stranger stormed off and Hasani slammed the door shut behind him.

"Look at that punk!" Deacon Washington screamed. "Celeste would never hang around with a thug like him. I will never believe she slept with him. Someone is playing a sick joke and I don't think it's funny." He stomped around in anger. He had his back turned and didn't realized that Samuel and Imani had come running into the room.

From behind him Heaven whispered in his ear. "You're scaring the children."

When he turned around, he saw fear in their faces.

Deacon Washington asked Heaven to take the children back into the living room while he cooled himself down. Samuel refused to leave his father alone. Once Deacon Washington realized Samuel wasn't leaving without him, the four of them went back to finish watching the movie together. After the movie ended they put the children to bed. The Deacon and Heaven watched Wesley in his crib. One minute the baby was looking up at them and the next he was fast asleep.

Deacon Washington laughed. "He does the same thing every night. I think he tries to fight the sleep until it becomes too much for him. In the end, he conks out." They laughed together until he got seriously quiet. "I'm struggling to believe that Celeste wasn't unfaithful to me and then I'm hit with what happened earlier."

Heaven suggested they go down back downstairs and talk. In the living room, he gazed lovingly at a picture of Celeste in his hand.

"What's on your mind?" she asked.

"What if Wesley is his son? What am I going to do? What am I going to tell our family and friends?"

She pulled his face toward her, "You have to stop worrying about what Celeste may or may not have done. She is gone and you're here with three beautiful children who need you. No matter what happens, you're their father."

Her words softened him. "That's something Celeste would have said." Heaven gathered her things and was ready to leave. "Heaven, I'm glad you were here with me tonight. I'm not sure what I would have done if I were here alone."

"Everything is going to be alright. Wesley looks just like you."

"I wish I was as sure as you are."

She tried not to stare at his lips when he spoke, but she couldn't help it. She wanted him so badly. They stood at the front door in silence, like teenagers wondering what to say next. She was a little disappointed when he kissed her on the cheek and wished her a good night. She was expecting more, but could live with a simple kiss.

When she was a block away from the bus stop, that familiar black Escalade pulled up next to her.

Tyke was by himself and driving. "How'd it go?" he asked.

"I was expecting you to be there."

"I thought it would be better to send a professional. The guy I sent is taking acting classes down at the college. How'd he do?"

"He did a better job than you would have done; especially when he exposed the gun. He was really convincing to me, but not Hasani." Tyke waited for her to explain. "The type of guy you sent was some guy with braids in his hair, Timbs, and sagging pants. His wife would never deal with anyone like that. That's why I asked you. I expected you to show up in your silk shirt and expensive wool trench coat. He would have believed it if you would have shown up."

"Sorry, Heaven, but you know I can't put myself out there like that. I'm trying to stay underground." He stopped a few blocks away from the halfway house. "I assume you want this cat, but why are you going to all this trouble? If his wife is dead, you should have no problems. Plus, why would you have me lie and claim that child is mine when we both know he isn't?"

A smile crept across her face. "Because of doubt. I planted a seed of doubt in Hasani's mind. No matter what those test results say, in the back of his mind he will still wonder whether or not his wife was unfaithful and that will lead him straight to my open arms."

"I always knew you had some gangster in you."

Chapter 22

"Heaven." Fatima opened the door and stuck her head into Heaven's room. A sliver of light from the hallway landed on Heaven's face. She called out her name again until she answered. "Ms. Campbell wanted me to tell you that you have a visitor downstairs."

The clock on her night stand said it was after nine in the morning. Heaven sucked her teeth and leapt out of bed. Outraged that someone would come to see her this early in the morning, she searched around for her slippers. When she tripped over one of her high heeled shoes that lay in the middle of the floor, she cursed loudly. Now she was really upset. She grabbed her robe and stormed down to the front lobby.

She was shocked to see Davis at the front desk talking with Ms. Campbell. "Here comes Ms. Stansfield," Ms. Campbell announced.

"Davis, what are you doing here?" She pulled

her robe closer around her body. He was the last person she expected to see.

"I have a surprise for you," he gloated. "Why don't you run upstairs and get dressed? I'll be waiting for you right here."

"Davis, I don't think I'll be able to go with you. Today is my only day off from work and I made plans to spend the evening with my grandmother."

"I promise I'll have you back no later then six o'clock," he pleaded. "Don't I always take care of you? You are going to enjoy what I have planned."

Heaven was curious about what Davis had up his sleeve. He liked spending money and he never had a problem spending it on her, but Heaven wasn't being totally honest with him. The real reason she didn't want to go with him was not because of her grandmother, but because of Deacon Washington. The two of them had plans to have dinner together later that evening. She had been looking forward to their date and knew the more time they spent together the closer the two of them would become. She had invested too much time in the deacon to merely give him up for Davis.

"Ms. Stansfield, you can go with Mr. Davies but make sure you do your chores before you leave."

"See, the woman in charge has given her blessing." Davis pushed her toward the stairs. "Go do your chores, get dressed, and make sure you wear that outfit we picked up last week. The purple silk blouse, low rise jeans, and black high heeled boots would be perfect for the occasion."

Heaven sighed and went to get ready. After an hour of doing house chores and an hour of getting dressed Davis and Heaven finally left for her big surprise. Heaven kept asking Davis where they were going, but he refused to spoil the surprise. After she realized he wasn't going to spill the beans, she rested her eyes and took a short nap.

The car slowed down and the smell of salt water jolted Heaven from her sleep. She abruptly sat up just in time to see a sign that said WELCOME TO ATLANTIC CITY.

Heaven became alarmed. *What are we doing in Atlantic City?* This was the last place she wanted to visit.

"Are you surprised?" Davis beamed. "I thought it would be nice for you to get out of the city for a while. We can have a nice lunch and then do some shopping." Heaven gripped Davis' hand and her skin turned pale. "Heaven, what's wrong?"

She wouldn't answer him, but she kept squeezing his hand harder. Davis pulled over to try and calm her down.

"This is where I was locked up. The smell of the ocean reminds me of prison," she mumbled.

"Heaven, I didn't know. I'm so stupid. I never even thought about that. Do you want to go back?"

Heaven stared ahead at the casinos in front of them. For years she wished she was one of the millions of people who went to Atlantic City to enjoy a show, shopping, or gambling. Now she was free and able to enjoy it all, but she was scared. The sound of those prison bars being slammed shut rung loudly in her ears. The cold feel of her cell against her skin was fresh in her mind.

"Davis, I don't want to come back here. It's too much."

"Sweetie, I know being locked up must have been a horrible experience for you but you don't have to be afraid." He grabbed Heaven's hand. "I'm here and I'm not going to let anything hurt you. If you tell me you want to leave then I'll turn this car around and we can go back to Camden, but I had some special plans. I promise you will have so much fun today you won't even think about the prison."

Heaven trusted Davis and let go of her ridiculous fears. "Okay, we can stay."

Davis pulled in to the Trump Plaza Casino and Hotel. The valet opened their doors and Davis led her to one of the most exquisite restaurants in the place. They dined on a gourmet lunch, played a few slot machines, and shopped at the most expensive boutiques.

Heaven had searched every store for the perfect dress to wear with dinner later that evening with Deacon Washington. She tried on several different ones, but the last dress she found was flawless. It was a floor length, royal blue dress with spaghetti straps and it looked stunning on Heaven. It wasn't too tight and it wasn't too revealing.

"Heaven, you look like royalty in that dress," Davis told her.

Heaven beamed. That was just the reaction she was looking for. She told the saleslady she would wear it out the store.

"Davis, you know I have to be getting back soon."

"I know, but I have one more surprise." He pulled out a hotel key and flashed it in her face.

He pulled her to the hotel elevator doors and pushed the button for the Presidential Suite.

Heaven felt like their entire day had been a hoax. She should have known better than to trust Davis. The only reason he brought her down there was to get her into bed. The two of them got off on their floor and he opened the door with his key. She stepped inside and was immediately intimidated by the room's beauty. The view took her breath away as she looked out over the ocean.

"Do you like it?" he asked.

"I love it." She set her packages down by the door and inspected every room in the suite. After she was done, Davis wasted no time getting her out of that dress. In a rush to get out of there, Heaven went along with no objections. Before she got undressed she thought about making him put a condom on, but she remembered what happened the last time they were together. That condom had gotten lost in her and didn't show up until seven days after they had been together. She promised herself she would never allow that to happen again.

Davis wore her out. They stayed behind closed doors for over two hours before Heaven insisted that it was time for her to go. He didn't want to let her go, but he understood her need to spend the evening with her grandmother. After Heaven took a shower she put the dress he had bought her earlier back on.

Davis had decided to not allow the room to go to waste. He was going to spend the night and return home the following morning. He knew Heaven couldn't stay, so he had made arrangements to have a limousine drive her back to Camden. The one good thing about leaving Davis at the casino was that she wouldn't have to worry about him showing up to mess up her evening.

Chapter 23

When the limo reached Camden, Heaven instructed the driver to drop her off at the church. She was supposed to meet Hasani no later than six o'clock and she couldn't be late.

Heaven got out the limo and saw the deacon's car parked in the lot. She couldn't wait for him to see her in the new dress Davis had bought for her. If seeing her in this dress couldn't keep his mind off Celeste then nothing would. She told the driver to leave her bags inside the church while she went to find the deacon.

Heaven found him alone in the church office. He was sitting behind the secretary's desk with his head buried in the yellow pages. "What are you doing?"

He looked up startled. "I need to find the best family lawyer in the city." She could see Hasani was still upset over Tyke's friends visit. "I won't allow my son to be raised by that hoodlum." Heaven watched him hastily pick up the phone and dial a number from out the book.

She couldn't allow this charade to go on any longer. She walked over to him and took the receiver out of his hand, "Don't do that. What you should do is take Wesley and get a paternity test on your own. That way you will already have the paperwork proving he's your son and there will be nothing he can do about it."

"I thought about that, but I'm scared. What if the results come back negative?"

"Aren't you the one who told me and Ebony we never had to be afraid again because we had God in our hearts?" He looked amused that she had quoted something he said. Heaven then pulled him out his seat and grabbed their coats. "You didn't even notice my dress," she teased.

She stepped back and approval flashed in his eyes. "You look gorgeous."

"Thank you. Now are you ready to eat?" She took his hand in hers and the two of them left together.

Monday morning Hasani took Wesley to the paternity testing site and by Friday the results were in. When the letter arrived in the mail he was too nervous to read it himself so he asked Heaven to come over. The two of them sat at his kitchen table glaring at the envelope.

"Give me the letter," Heaven said. He stared at it a moment longer before handing it over to her. She opened the letter with confidence and pulled out the report. He looked at her face for any sign that it was good news, but she was straight faced. She held the paper out to him and he hesitated before taking it.

He scanned over it with his eyes. "God is so amazing. Thank you, Jesus!" he screamed.

"I told you Wesley was your son."

"Yes, you did say that and you didn't doubt it for a minute. I could tell by the way you opened that letter you had no doubt in your mind that Wesley was my son." He got up and strutted around. "I hope that guy comes back around because I can't wait to throw this in his face. I wish the kids were here."

"Where are they?" Heaven asked, surprised to not see them around.

"Over at my mother's with Emalee; I was scared I might break down and cry if the test results didn't turn out in my favor."

Heaven was happy the deception was over. She wanted to stay and celebrate but she had to get back to the halfway house. Ms. Campbell was in a bad mood when she left. She checked her watch and got up to gather her things.

"You have to go?" he asked. "They keep you girls on a tight schedule. It seems like I never get to spend enough time with you."

"Yes, they try to monitor our every move."

"Heaven, I appreciate you coming by tonight. As always, you're around when I need you."

This time he made the first move and pulled her into his arms. His lips kissed every part of her face until his kisses landed on her mouth. She parted her lips and their tongues danced together.

Her heart melted. She wrapped her arms around his neck and caressed the back of his neck. He held her tighter and their kisses led them to the couch. The two of them panted for one another. Hasani positioned himself between her legs and lust drove them to a place he had never been before. He stripped her naked and thrust himself upon her right in front of the fireplace. After it was over Heaven wanted to lay in his arms forever, but the clock was ticking and if she didn't move quickly she was going to be late getting back.

"Thanks for the great time but I have to go." She hurried out the door.

"See you in church on Sunday," he yelled out, right before she slammed the door shut.

Halloween was the time of year when drawings of witches and ghosts decorated the doors and windows of nearly every house in Camden. It was the first official holiday of the fall season. The weatherman had predicted warm weather for the days leading up to Halloween and everybody in the city was taking advantage of it—including Heaven.

There were three reasons why she decided to walk to work today. One was to enjoy the nice weather. Another was so she wouldn't have to call Davis for a ride. Every time she asked him to do something he wanted sex in return. She had created a monster who wanted to do nothing but climb on top of her. The last reason was so she could stop by the corner and pick up some drugs along the way.

Since that night Heaven spent with Zaria and her friends, she couldn't seem to shake that craving to get high again. The temptation lingered in her soul. During the day, she made sure to keep busy, but the moment she laid her head down she would have drug dreams. At night she was restless and unable to sleep. After the few hours of sleep she did get, she would wake in a cold sweat.

Every day was a struggle for her and it was getting too hard for her to resist. The temptation was slowly wearing her down. Earlier that day she had completed her scheduled meeting and drug test with Ms. Griffin. Of course she passed, but now that it was over she could indulge and not have to worry about being tested until the following month. Every once in a while, the halfway house would perform random drug testing, but she had never been selected. The staff thought that the testing was a surprise for the residents but that wasn't true. Somehow the news was always leaked before the test was announced.

Heaven often thought about the night she relapsed. She had promised Ebony that it would never happen again, but now she wasn't so sure. She assumed she would be able to forget about drugs and continue on with sobriety like that night never happened, but she couldn't. They haunted her every hour of every day. Abstaining from drugs was harder than she thought. Sometimes the urge was so strong, she felt like it would just be easier to give in.

Heaven cut through Centerville Projects looking for anybody who looked like they were hustling. She only wanted to buy a small bag; enough to satisfy her craving.

"Yo, you looking for something?" a young kid around thirteen years old called out. Heaven squinted at the kid's unfamiliar face. She was nervous about being back out on the block. She didn't trust anybody and if she bought drugs from the wrong person, it could land her back in jail. Not until the kid ran toward a car that had pulled over to the curb did she realize he wasn't talking to her.

She dug a crumpled twenty-dollar bill out of her back pocket. This was all the money she had. She let out a big sigh before stepping off the curb to go see what the kid was selling when a truck came charging at her from around the corner. It swerved to keep from hitting her. The driver put the truck in reverse and backed up until it stopped next to her. The driver's side window powered down and Tyke gave her a sideways grin.

"I've been looking for you. Get in!" he shouted. She peered at him while walking around to the passenger's side. She was tired of him giving her orders. When she climbed inside he drove off. "Let me guess. You're on your way to work?"

"How did you guess?" she sarcastically replied, looking down at her blue and red cashiering uniform.

"Well, today is your lucky day. I'm calling in that favor you owe me and you can make a few dollars in the process." Tyke usually didn't call in a favor until his back was against the wall. "Can you get away from the halfway house on Saturday?"

"Yes, but I planned on going to a special church service."

"With the deacon?" he asked. "I guess you've been servicing him since you haven't been hooking me up."

"Tyke, what do you want?" He was so irritating at times.

"I need you to go to Rahway Prison. You're going to visit with an inmate named Hercules Smith."

"Why are you sending me to Rahway Prison?"

"This is an old friend of mine and I owe him a favor."

"I hope you don't think I'm taking him a package because I'm not doing it. Tyke, I'm not even released yet and . . ."

"Girl, I didn't ask you to do anything except go visit the man." He relaxed behind the wheel.

"No message?"

"Nope."

"Then what?"

"Just visit him. Go there and talk with him. He's lonely and he needs somebody to talk to. I thought you would be the perfect person to go see him, but you have to go for three Saturdays straight. You have to go to the one o'clock visiting time and stay for at least two hours."

"This is crazy, but I guess I should be thankful that's all you want me to do. At least it's legal."

"My friend will be expecting you. He handed her a fake ID. You're going to be Tiffany Saunders."

"If this is legal why do I need a fake ID?"

"Did you forget you're still an inmate yourself? Being in the halfway house doesn't mean you're free." Tyke pulled his truck behind the supermarket and stopped in the back where all the deliveries were made.

"What are you doing?" she asked.

"Maybe you didn't hear me earlier, but I said I hadn't seen you in a while. I missed you." He leaned over and kissed her neck. Then he worked his way down to her breasts. Besides drugs, Tyke was her only other weakness. He was irresistible. She could never tell him no. Heaven was scared she would lose her job if anyone caught them so she asked him to hurry up, but Tyke never left her unsatisfied. He took his time and didn't care who saw them. After they were done he gave her one final piece of advice.

"Make sure you wear something sexy at every visit."

Chapter 24

For the next three Saturdays, Heaven sat in the Rahway State Prison visiting hall talking with Hercules Smith. Hercules was one of the ugliest and oldest men she had ever met in her life. He frequently reminisced about how fine he was back in the day, but it was obvious he had let himself go in his old age. His waistline had expanded into a pot belly that shook when he laughed. His face had morphed into that of a werewolf, because of a promise he made to himself over thirty years ago which prevented him from shaving his face until he was released.

The thing that annoyed Heaven the most was that this man was a pervert. He would subtly brush his hand up against her breast or behind every chance he got.

Most of their visits together were spent in silence with him staring at her chest. She tried to make conversation with him, but he didn't seem interested. All he did was gaze at her eyes, chest, and legs.

He bragged to all his jail house buddies that she was there to see him and he made sure everyone knew it. He introduced her to just about every prisoner and CO in the place. She even allowed him to take a few pictures of them together, including one scductive pose with her sitting between his legs.

During their last visit she did get him to talk about how he knew Tyke. That's when she discovered that this crazy man had been locked away for over thirty years and hadn't had a visit from a woman in over twenty. Apparently, Tyke told him he was sending her to him as a birthday present.

Visiting hours were almost over and Heaven was ready to go. "Well, Herc, it was nice meeting you, but my time is up and you know I won't be back next week."

"I know." His head dropped down in front of him and he stared at the pictures of them together. "If it's not too much trouble I was thinking maybe you could write me every once in a while. You know, not a lot, but maybe once a month. I've really enjoyed my time with you, young lady."

"Well, I'm really kind of busy." Heaven didn't want to lie to the old man. "But if I find some time, I'll get your address from Tyke."

He managed to show her a mouth full of gums. She felt good giving this man a little bit of hope; even if it was false hope. Hercules walked her to the exit. "Tiffany, can I have a kiss?"

Heaven's mouth dropped wide open. She was in

shock over his request. The thought of his lips touching hers made her cringe. Plus his lips were ashy and he had food stuck in his beard.

He noticed her hesitation. "I'll understand if you don't want to." He sounded pitiful.

"Yes." Again, she gave in under the pressure. "You can have a kiss, but just a quick peck."

He swiftly whisked her into his arms and smashed his mouth up against hers. He tried to stick his tongue in her mouth, but she refused. He finally let her go and stood back staring at her with love in his eyes. Heaven was so furious she walked straight out the room without saying good-bye.

She flung open the locker that held her purse and coat and pulled her things out. Her mind was focused on finding Tyke. She was fed up with him taking advantage of her generosity. He had done this to her in the past, but this time she was done with him. She slammed the locker door shut. There was fire in her eyes. She was so angry she almost ignored the call of someone trying to get her attention.

"Psst. Psst," she heard from behind the prison fence. When she turned around she saw a handsome gentleman in a CO's uniform. She had seen him before. Several times she had caught him checking her out in visiting hall. He called her over to the fence.

"What's a pretty lady like you doing wasting your time coming up here to see one of these knuckleheads?" he asked.

"Is it a crime to brighten somebody's day?"

"It's not a crime, just a shame. A shame you

would waste your time on someone who wouldn't waste their time on you." Inmates in the yard saw the two of them talking and started making a fuss in the background. "Don't worry about them. Why don't you take down my number and call me some time? I'd like to take you to dinner and treat you the way a queen is supposed to be treated."

Heaven dug in her purse in search of a pen. When she found one, she waited for him to rattle off his number. Before his mouth could form the first digit, gunshots rang out in the air and the cute CO fell to the ground. The inmates behind them also hit the dirt and she followed suit. Visitors who were leaving the prison hid behind their cars and screamed for help. The prison siren blared and the prison's Special Operation Response Team flooded the prison yard. Armed with facemasks, shields, and guns, they were ready for an attack from unknown sources. The guards rousted the inmates back into their cells and cries for help surrounded them.

Blood seeped from the CO's head and covered the ground. Heaven realized the guy was dead and she screamed out. She tried crawling away from the body. A guard came up behind her and helped her back to the prison.

Heaven sat in one of the prison offices being thoroughly questioned by police. She had a quick response for every question they asked. It was now clear to her why Tyke kept quizzing her before she left Camden. He was fully aware of everything that was going to take place.

The name Tiffany Saunders was cleared and the

police let her go. Heaven caught the bus back to Camden. She couldn't wait to get her hands on Tyke.

The bus let her off a few blocks away from her grandmother's house. When she entered the front gate, her grandmother was outside planting flowers in her garden.

"Good Lord! What happened to you?" Her grandmother got worried as soon as she saw the blood splattered on Heaven's shirt.

"Nothing, Nana. I just need to change my clothes and get back to the halfway house." Heaven rushed inside the house and up the stairs to her old bedroom. She searched around hoping to find something she could throw on temporarily. Her grandmother followed close behind her.

"Heaven, I hope you're not in any trouble."

She went into the bathroom to splash warm water on her face. She had to clear her head. "Nana, I don't know what happened. Some guy I was talking to was shot in the head."

Nana gasped. "I thought you were trying to turn your life around."

Heaven found an old pair of jeans and tee shirt in the bottom of her closet in her old room. She also found an old bomber jacket, it was two sizes too small, but she put it on anyway. "Nana, I am trying to straighten my life out. I had nothing to do with this guy dying."

Heaven changed her clothes and just before she ran out the door she kissed her grandmother on the cheek. Anger fueled Heaven's walk to Pollock. She was determined to find Tyke. It was a mile from her grandmother's house to where she expected to find Tyke, but it didn't matter. She was so angry the walk didn't bother her.

When she reached the corner, he was out there standing like a king amongst his people. She stomped toward Tyke with fire in her eyes. Her hands formed into fists. He saw her and opened his arms wide, but then Fitch stepped in between the two of them and blocked her path.

"Move!" she screamed. Fitch stared her in the eye like a guard dog ready to attack.

Tyke pushed between Fitch and Heaven. "Fitch, it's all right. She's cool." The tension around them was high. Tyke yelled out to Upshaw, "Take him to get something to eat. He's been on this block all night." He turned to Fitch and slid him a twenty. "Go to a restaurant and relax a bit."

He then pulled Heaven to the side. "Did you go to the prison to visit the ol' head?" His face did a strange twist when he saw her holey jeans and raggedy sneakers. "I hope you didn't go looking like that."

"Tyke!" she screamed. "You set me up and almost got me killed." She swung her fist at him, but missed.

"I forgot how violent you can be." He laughed. "Calm down. You didn't get hurt, did you?"

"No, but I should have never been there in the first place. You made me go up there as a birthday present to some senile old man. That's the last time I do something for you."

His employees laughed at her.

"Come on, girl." He pulled her toward his mother's house at the next corner. Before they left, she saw Fitch watching them from the truck.

Tyke told her to sit on his mom's front porch. "I'm sorry. You didn't get hurt did you?"

She wrapped her arms around herself, "No. I'm fine, just a little scared."

"I didn't mean to scare you." He lowered his voice to a whisper. "Heaven, I saw you today. I've been watching you for the past few weeks."

"What the hell have you been following me for?" she screamed.

"Can you keep your voice down? I don't want everyone to know what were talking about. A few weeks ago I got a call from a friend who is locked up in River Front State Prison. His time was short and he was about to come home when he got into a fight with another inmate and ended up killing the boy. There were a bunch of inmates around and one Correctional Officer saw the murder. Of course, none of the inmates are going to testify against him, but the CO has to testify or lose his job. My friend told me he would pay me fifty grand if I got rid of him. So I started following him and I found out he had been transferred to Rahway, for his protection, until after the trial was over."

"Was that the CO I was talking to?"

"Yeah, that was him. I had been watching him for weeks. He has a car, his own place, a girl, and a baby. He also had a lot of women on the side and a lot of the woman he picked up were coming from the prison, visiting people on the inside. That's how I knew he was an easy mark. I had seen him holla at different women who were nowhere as near pretty as you. I knew he would try to talk to you when he saw you. That's why I needed you to do this for me. Plus, I wanted to see if you were still loyal."

"Loyal?"

"Yeah. I trusted you to go up there and see my boy for three Saturdays straight and you did as I asked. That shows I can trust you. Anyway, today was my last chance to get at him. I was glad when he approached you."

"If you trust me, why didn't you tell me what you were up to?" Heaven stood up and looked him straight in the eye.

"It was best if you didn't know anything. The police might have picked up on it and I couldn't take that chance."

"Why did you involve me in this when you know I'm trying to get myself together?"

"Heaven, I said I was sorry." He stood up. "Don't you want your cut of the money?"

Heaven held out her hand.

"Stay right here. I'll go get it." He ran into his mother's house and came right back out with a brown paper bag. He shoved the bag into her hand.

"How much is here?" she asked when she looked inside the bag.

"Five thousand. Plus an extra two thousand for all your trouble."

"Don't bother getting in touch with me ever again." Heaven left Tyke, took the money back to Nana's, and hid it in the bottom of her closet.

Chapter 25

The month of October began with temperatures below normal, but the days grew milder as the month progressed on. The first Sunday in November had proved to be a beautiful day for the church to hold their annual fall festival.

Each year, the members of Mount Olive Baptist Church looked forward to their pilgrimage out to the country. The congregation and their families were offered the opportunity to temporarily escape urban life and partake in life on a farm.

A friend of Reverend Stansfield's owned a huge farm and he made the event worth looking forward to. He provided horseback riding lessons, allowed the children to feed the animals, and had enough food to feed two churches.

Deacon Washington invited Heaven to tag along with him and the children in the car. The two of them had been spending a lot of time together both in and out of bed. Their relationship had turned from formal to informal when Deacon

Washington told Heaven to call him by his first name. The children were adjusting well to her being around and she was making herself available to the Deacon as much as possible.

Today would be their first church outing together and every member of the congregation was sure to take notice. Heaven was nervous about how people were going to react. She had told Nana and Ebony about Hasani and they were glad she found happiness. The church bus, followed by Hasani's car, pulled onto a dirt road that led to the farm. Once the bus came to a stop, people poured out and into the parking area.

"Dad, can I go?" Samuel watched a group of children line up to get pony rides.

"Yes, son, but be careful."

"Daddy, can I go too?" Imani whined.

"Yes, baby." When their father helped them from the car, they ran to join a crowd of children. Hasani had chosen to leave Wesley with the babysitter. He didn't want to chance him catching another cold with the unpredictable weather.

Heaven and Hasani followed a bunch of people into the barn. Inside was a buffet of food, decorations, and plenty of seating to accommodate all the guests. Heaven could feel members stare and gossip as she walked by. But the hardest stare came from Emalee. She was livid because her brother had brought Heaven with him.

"Hasani, can I speak with you a minute?" Emalee blocked their path and looked Heaven in the eye.

He excused himself and Emalee led him out the barn and toward the area where the pony rides were being given. Heaven sat on a bench alone. Ebony saw her sitting by herself and called her over to the table she shared with Nana. Heaven got up, but before she could move, Davis stopped her and he looked upset.

"Is that what you needed my money for?" Davis asked. "So you could buy a new outfit to come to the festival with Deacon Washington?"

Heaven didn't want to cause a scene. She knew the church had enough things about her to talk about. "Davis, I know you're not upset because I came here with Hasani."

"Oh! It's Hasani. He's no longer Deacon Washington. Your relationship with him must have changed. Did that happen before or after you started sleeping in his bed?"

"Davis, please let's not do this here," she begged him.

"When I asked you were you coming to the festival you said no."

"I wasn't, but when he asked me to help him with the children I couldn't tell the man no. His wife just died. The poor man needed help."

"Well, the two of you looked mighty close when you pulled up today."

"Davis, we're just friends. . . ."

"I'll race ya," Hasani yelled from the meadow. Seconds later, he and the children stood next to them out of breath.

"Are you guys hungry?" Heaven asked the troops.

"Can I have some juice?" Imani asked.

Heaven went to the nearby punch bowl and poured her a small cup.

"Hey, Davis, I'm surprised to see you here," Hasani said. "I thought you would be over with the rest of the congregation watching them milk cows."

"I was, but it got boring. The men are more afraid of the animals than the women."

"Yeah, I know what you mean." Hasani turned toward Heaven and over his shoulder.

Davis' eyes told her to beware.

"Do you want to sneak away for a minute?" Hasani held out his hand and she reluctantly took his hand.

"What about the children?" she asked.

"Emalee and my mother can keep an eye on them. We won't be long." Before leaving the barn he asked Emalee to watch the children. Then he led Heaven to the horse stables. When they stepped inside, Heaven was intimidated by the big bulging eyes and loud noises the horses made. She timidly followed Hasani to a bench and took a seat next to him.

"You don't have to be scared. They don't bite. Well, Ms. Stansfield, Did you notice how everyone was staring at us today?"

"How could I not notice? Over a hundred pair of eyes staring at me. I felt like I was being observed under a microscope."

"You should be used to it by now. We always have three tiny pair of eyes watching us."

"You're right. I think the kids have made some kind of vow that Daddy must always be accompanied by one of his children."

They laughed together.

"I'm glad you invited me. I know how hard it

must have been for you to do this. I'm sure you miss doing things with your wife and it's no secret your sister doesn't approve of me."

"My sister will be fine. She misses my wife. I think she feels threatened because I found somebody else so fast after Celeste. Heaven, I really like you and I know it hasn't even been a year since Celetse passed, but I feel drawn to you. Our relationship has moved rather quickly, but I need you to know I want to get to know the real Heaven better. Let's slow things down. Allow me the chance to really court you."

Heaven smiled. She had never had a man court her before. She wondered what that consisted of. She looked forward to things progressing with Hasani. "Tell me about your childhood?"

"Well, I was raised by my nana in Fairview."

"It was just you and her? No parents?"

Just a moment ago, there was no where else she would have rather been than with him, but now she wanted to hide from him and his questions about her past. She wasn't comfortable talking about her mother; it hurt too much. Instead of dancing around the question she gave her generic response. "My mother died when I was young and I have no memories of her. I've never known my father."

"I'm sorry. It must have been hard growing up without a mom or dad."

"You can't miss what you never had and Nana did the best she could. The only thing I've ever wanted to do was make her proud, but I got mixed with drugs and then I went to jail. I feel like I disappointed her."

"Don't be so hard on yourself. You may have made mistakes in the past, but now you're trying to do the right thing." He turned toward her. "Heaven, since you mentioned your history with drugs, I think this would be the perfect time for me to let you know what's been on my mind.

"I feel really lucky to have you in my life. It's not too often someone loses a wife and finds a woman just as special so quickly, but I don't think I could move forward with our relationship if I didn't ask you about your past drug use. I know you've been in rehab and you're changing your life around, but I have seen first hand how people have relapsed. I can't have drugs or people who use drugs around my children. I need you to tell me your life with drugs is over."

"I understand, and I would never disrespect you or your children by exposing them to anything like that, but you don't have to worry because I'm never going to do drugs again. I'm hoping what we have is special and I don't want to ruin it. If my uncle can overcome drugs, so can I."

"Good." He stood up. "Are you ready to rejoin the party? I'm getting hungry."

Heaven got up and stepped in a pile of cow manure. "Hasani, look at my shoe."

He laughed at her. "Wipe it off on the ground."

She walked over to the side and scrapped her foot against the wooden stall. Hasani leaned against the barn doors when he accidentally hit a lever. The handle came down and a chute opened above Heaven's head. Several bales of hay landed on her head, knocking her unconscious.

Chapter 26

"Heaven, can you hear me?" Ms. Campbell's loud, harsh voice echoed in Heaven's ears. *Why is she screaming?* Next, a beam of bright light shined brightly in her eyes, bringing her to. Heaven could see Ms. Campbell standing next to a white man in a lab coat through the slits in her eyes. Her first thought was she had been sent back to the prison. Heaven felt around her wrists for handcuffs, but was glad when she didn't find any. She looked toward the windows for bars but saw none. "Where am I?"

"You're in the hospital?" Ms. Campbell hissed.

"Heaven, you had an accident. Do you remember what happened?" the man in the lab coat asked.

Heaven placed her hand on her throbbing head to stop the pain. She closed her eyes again to ease the pain.

"She may still be a little disoriented," the man said.

"When can she be released?" Ms. Campbell inquired.

"I'm going to keep her for a few more hours. I didn't want to do an MRI because of her condition, but since she did wake up we'll see how she does and then I'll have her released."

Heaven opened her eyes when she heard the man leave the room. Ms. Campbell's loathing eyes peered down at her through her bi-focal glasses. "What did the doctor mean by my condition?" Heaven asked.

"Heaven, you can stop the act. I already know," she replied belligerently.

"Know what?"

"About your pregnancy."

"What pregnancy?"

"I guess it's safe to assume Deacon Washington is the father. Is that why you've been spending so much time with him? Having dinner at his house; participating in various church functions; going to the fall festival together." She paced back and forth in front of Heaven's hospital bed taunting her. Ms. Campbell would stop every few steps and look at her with disgust. Heaven placed her hand on her belly. She was pregnant. This was great. She had gotten pregnant and she wasn't even trying.

"Why would the doctor tell you I was pregnant? Isn't that a violation of the rules? Doctor patient confidentiality or something like that."

"Heaven, you're still a ward of the state; your medical condition is my business. I have every right to know you're pregnant. At least you have no one to answer to. The parole board is going to want to know how I allowed this to happen."

"Does Hasani know?" Ms. Campbell was the least of Heaven's worries.

"Does Hasani know what?" Hasani pulled away the curtain that isolated them. "The doctor said it was all right if I came in."

Ms. Campbell rolled her eyes at him behind his back.

"You had me scared. You were out for a while."

"I'll leave you two alone." Ms. Campbell excused herself.

"What's wrong?" He sat on the side of Heaven's bed.

Heaven was anxious to tell him her news. She was unsure of how he was going to react, but she couldn't keep this to herself. "I'm pregnant," she blurted out.

He clasped the bed sheets tightly and his face looked like he had just eaten a handful of sour grapes. He got up and ran his fingers through his hair. "I don't know what to say. I guess I shouldn't be surprised." He turned to her. "I assumed you were on some kind of birth control."

"We never talked about it, but if you're not happy, I understand. This is just as much a surprise to me as it is to you."

"No. I'm just a little surprised, but I'm going to be a man and do the right thing."

Heaven wasn't surprised by his willingness to take responsibility for his actions. He was a good man. "We're getting married?" she asked with excitement in her voice.

"Married?" Hasani questioned.

"I thought that was what you meant by doing the right thing." Confusion flashed across his face.

"Never mind. I just assumed." The smile on Heaven's face slowly disappeared.

He walked to her side and caressed her hand lovingly. "You're right. I don't want to treat you like you're something I should be ashamed of. What kind of example would that be for the children? We will get married."

Heaven smiled broadly.

"But can we keep this quiet until I tell my sister and mother? Then we can make a formal announcement to the church."

"I love you, Hasani." She wrapped her arms around his shoulder and squeezed tightly.

Chapter 27

"Can we go get our pumpkins now?" Imani asked her grandmother. Church service had ended, and the children were going with Emalee and their grandmother to pick pumpkins.

Ms. Washington placed Imani on her lap and kissed her on the cheek. "We sure can."

"Hello, Ms. Washington." Heaven walked up behind them with Wesley in her arms.

"How are you, Heaven?" Ms. Washington embraced Heaven and kissed her on the cheek. It was always a pleasure when Heaven spoke with Hasani's mother. They had such a good relationship, and Heaven hoped once Ms. Washington heard the news of her son's pending nuptials her feelings for her wouldn't change.

"I'm good; thanks for asking," Heaven replied.

Emalee played with Wesley in Heaven's arms without speaking a word to Heaven. Then she turned to help the children put their coats on. It had become customary for Emalee to ignore

Heaven. It happened so often that Heaven was used to it.

Emalee was taking the children back out to the country to pick pumpkins. They ran out of time at the festival and Emalee promised to take them back later on. "Let's go," Emalee announced.

On their way out the door Imani asked, "Is Wesley going with us?"

"No. Not this time, honey," Emalee replied. "But I promise we'll bring him a pumpkin back from the farm and we'll put his name on it. Okay?"

Imani shook her head in agreement. When they opened the door the brisk fall air swept into the church. As they stepped over the threshold Hasani called Emalee back in. "Can I talk with you for a moment?" he asked.

Emalee saw the serious look on her brother's face and felt something was wrong. She wasn't sure if it had something to do with him or the children, but something wasn't right.

"Mom, why don't you wait here?" she told her mother.

Heaven watched them disappear down the hall together. She wondered how he was going to break the news to her. She knew Emalee was not going to be happy. Emalee hated her so much she would probably wear black to the wedding. Heaven took a seat on one of the pews and waited for the two of them to return. Ms. Washington sat down next to Heaven and the two of them talked briefly about upcoming church events and the children.

Sister Stewart stopped to speak with them and then she asked to hold Wesley. "He's getting so big," she commented. She sat on the other side of Heaven and played with the baby. Imani and Samuel sat quietly looking through their Picture Bibles. The three women chatted until Emalee came storming into the sanctuary searching for Heaven. When she found her she ran up in Heaven's face.

"You whore!" she screamed. Everyone in the church stared. "You couldn't wait to pounce on my brother. You knew damn well my brother was vulnerable after the death of his wife. How did you do it? How did you get him to ask you to marry him?"

"Emalee, stop causing a scene." Hasani tried pulling his sister out of Heaven's face by grabbing hold of her arms.

"Why should I stop now? Let me tell the soon to be Ms. Hasani Washington exactly what I think about her. You may be marrying into my family but you will never be a Washington. You will never be the kind of mother Celeste was to her children."

Hasani grabbed Emalee and pulled her into the vestibule. Everyone could still hear her yelling. "Hasani, I'm telling you, Celeste loved you and those kids more than life itself. She would never cheat on you."

Heaven's face had turned red from embarrassment. Members stole quick glances at her and turned away in whispers. She wanted to get up and walk out, but it was pointless because Emalee had already broadcasted all her business. There was nothing left for the church to hear.

"Pregnant!" Emalee screamed from the vestibule. Heaven had forgotten about that news. Emalee ran back into the sanctuary. "You did this on purpose. You seduced my brother," Emalee accused her. "Is the baby even his? Hasani, you don't have . . ."

"Emalee, stop it! Stop acting like a fool!" Hasani yelled. He had finally gotten her to calm down. "This is not Heaven's fault. I knew what I was doing." Hasani blew air out his mouth and turned to his sister. "Emalee, you know how much I loved Celeste, but she's gone and I have to move on."

"And this is how you honor her memory . . . by getting the first whore you meet pregnant?"

Hasani stared at Emalee. "I have never heard you speak like this before. I don't even know who you are. I'm tired of talking to you." He walked out the church.

Heaven chased after him and on her way out the door Davis stared at her. She could see the hurt in his eyes.

"I'm sorry," Hasani said to her once she caught up to him outside. "She loved my wife very much, but I never expected her to react like that, but don't worry. She'll accept you over time."

Heaven hoped so. If not, their wedding was going to be a disaster.

Chapter 28

Heaven's life had turned upside down. She had no idea there were so many details to planning a wedding. Since Emalee's outburst, Hasani didn't think it was necessary to announce their engagement to the church, but she felt it was important for them to get married before she started showing. They had planned to get married a week before Christmas. She had bought her gown, ordered flowers, and reserved the photographer.

Her dream of having a winter wedding was coming true. They had invited everyone from the church and of course Ebony would be her maid of honor. All three children were in the wedding and now all she had to do was wait for the day to arrive.

"Did you get your invitation?" Heaven asked Ms. Griffin.

"Yes and thank you. How are the wedding plans going?"

"Crazy. I never knew all the work that goes into

planning a wedding. I've barely had time for myself. In between working, making sure I attend all my meetings, and of course, next week I'm released."

"Yes, I got a copy of your parole papers today. The board approved your release. Your last day here is the day before the wedding."

"Yes, I'm so excited. Ebony and I are being released on the same day and afterward I convinced her to stay with my nana. I feel better knowing there will be someone there with her."

"Have you thought about the added responsibility of being a wife?"

"I'm pretty sure I can handle it. I know you always say not to take on too much and to take one day at a time, but I'm ready to do this."

"Heaven, you have done beautifully in this program. You have demonstrated how serious you are about your recovery and the story of how God brought you and the Deacon together is a remarkable love story, but one thing I am concerned about is the pressures of being married. Marriage can be tough, but it's going to be even harder on you because you are stepping into a marriage and becoming a stepmother to three. Plus, the church will look to you to provide leadership from time to time. That is a lot for somebody who has been clean for less than a year."

Heaven put her head down as if she were being scolded by her parent.

"Heaven, I'm not trying to put you down. I want you to remember that you can't do it all. A lot of people are going to rely on you and you shouldn't feel pressured to do it all. If you begin to feel over-whelmed ask for some help. No one is going to look at you any differently."

"Ms. Griffin, I remember what happened when I was out there using. I never want to use again," Heaven lied with ease. Less than an hour before her meeting she had finished off a twenty bag of dope.

"Satan uses your confidence as a weakness. Drugs are literally Satan's candy. I attended a church conference a few years back and the pastor talked bout the rise of drugs in the inner city. He said Satan put drugs out there to deceive, confuse, and cloud the judgment of millions of people."

"Ms. Griffin, I've been there. I know. I've been caught up in it, but I feel so much better being clean than being high."

"Heaven, if you ever feel as though life is being a burden, I'm here for you and if for some reason you can't get to me, take it to the Lord."

"Thanks, Ms. Griffin. I'll keep that in mind."

Chapter 29

"Heaven, you look beautiful." Nana's smile was genuine. It was Heaven's wedding day. A day she would treasure until the day she died. Ebony adjusted the veil on Heaven's head and pulled down a few strands of hair against her back

"I agree. Heaven, you look stunning. Hasani's heart is going to melt when he gets a look at you in this dress." Ebony added.

The three ladies were in the ladies lounge of the church getting dressed. Heaven stared at her reflection in the three-way mirror. Her dress was a replica of the Walt Disney classic Cinderella with glass slippers to match. The strapless gown was a one of a kind. The seamstress who made the dress was as a member of the church and had spent every waking hour carefully sewing every bead on the dress by hand. A masterpiece of symmetrical artwork decorated its long sweeping train.

The sounds of stifled sniffles drifted from Nana. Heaven knew it was a bad idea for her to be present while she was getting dressed, but Ebony insisted. She said Nana had every right to see her only grandchild get ready for her wedding.

Heaven applied a final coat of lipstick to her plump lips. Then Nana had another outburst. "Your momma would be so proud," Nana cried.

Heaven sucked her teeth. "Can we not talk about her? Today is supposed to be my day."

The mood in the room quickly changed from cheerful to tense. Ebony sensed the women needed some time alone and she excused herself.

"Heaven, you know your mother is sick. Why do you hate her? It's not her fault she wasn't able to raise you."

"Just once, I would like for the focus to be on me and not her," Heaven yelled so loudly at her grandmother that she immediately felt awful. "I'm sorry. I shouldn't have yelled. I'm just excited about today and I want everything to go perfectly."

Nana struggled to get up from her seat and when Heaven went to help her up she broke away from her grasp. "It's almost time. I'm going to take my place upstairs," she said with her back turned.

As a child, Heaven would leaf through photo albums full of pictures of her mother, Amelia. She could hear her grandmother at night earnestly asking the Lord to grant her a miracle and heal her daughter, but he never did.

Nana was a very strict parent who made sure her children were raised to love and serve the Lord. Especially Amelia, who served on the junior usher board, sang in the children's choir, and had read the entire Bible by the age of ten.

When Amelia turned eleven she changed. One day Amelia withdrew from her family and the world around her. She seemed to have slipped into a depression and it happened so suddenly her mother didn't even know what was happening.

Nana was worried about Amelia's mental state and wanted to take her to the doctor, but her husband said it was just a phase and insisted she would grow out of it.

That same night, Nana was awakened by noises coming from Amelia's room. Nana got up to check on her, but stood at her bedroom door listening for a moment before knocking. She could hear Amelia telling someone to shut up. She sounded so angry. Nana thought it was strange that someone would be in her room at that hour. She was also worried because her daughter had not said more than three words to her all week. It hurt her because the two of them had been so close.

She opened Amelia's bedroom door to find Amelia dressed in all black sweat clothes, a scarf wrapped around her neck, and her hair flying wildly over her head. It was the middle of summer, but her bedroom window was closed and the air conditioner had been turned off. The heat was suffocating and Nana thought her daughter would have a heat stroke at any moment.

Amelia paced the floor and screamed at no one, but when Nana stepped into her room she gave her the hardest and coldest stare she had ever seen. The joyful spirit she usually saw in her child's eyes were gone. She thought a demonic spirit stood before her. Nana was so scared she immediately closed the door. She could hear Amelia go back to pacing the floor and screaming out for someone to shut up.

Nana never mentioned the incident to her husband. The following morning when Amelia came to the table for breakfast she was quiet. Nana could see dark circles under her eyes and realized the child hadn't slept all night.

One day, while her husband was out of town for a church conference, Nana came home early from work. When she walked into the house she heard banging coming from upstairs. She walked up the stairs and into Amelia's room. Amelia was banging her head against her bedroom window and looked like she was trying to stick her head through it. Amelia's head was bleeding and the window pane was cracked. Nana tried to stop her. She grabbed her from behind and pulled her away from the window. Amelia was a lost soul. She fought her mother and the look in her eyes was one Nana had never seen before. It seemed like she was possessed with a demon that was ready for a fight. Amelia pushed and hit Nana and finally Amelia bit her hand. Nana ran out of her bedroom and closed the door. She could hear Amelia tearing the room apart. Nana was frightened and had no idea what was wrong with her daughter. It had all happened so fast.

She called the police and they called an ambulance to restrain Amelia. They put a straight jacket on her and she was taken away to a psychiatric hospital for evaluation. Later they told Nana her daughter was schizophrenic.

Nana couldn't believe what the doctors were

telling her and was determined to pray that demon out of her. The doctors convinced her to allow Amelia to stay at the hospital until they could be sure she wouldn't be a danger to herself. Eventually it was decided that the severity of the disease was so bad the medication they were giving her did no good. She wasn't responding to it so they had her permanently institutionalized.

Nana visited her daughter every chance she got and at each visit her daughter seemed to slip further and further away from her. She knew she had lost her daughter the day she went up to visit and Amelia didn't recognize her.

Chapter 30

Heaven looked at her reflection in the mirror. Her whole life was going to change after today. She would have a husband and a family.

A tapping sound against the window stirred her from her thoughts. Heaven thought it was some kids playing. She went to the blinds and peeked through. It was Tyke and he motioned for her to come outside.

He was the last person she expected to see. She picked the bottom of her dress up so it wouldn't get dirty and snuck out the back door.

"What are you doing here?" She was frantic. "Hasani is right inside."

"Wow. You look hot. I'm jealous. That deacon sure is lucky. I don't know if he deserves you. Do you think he can handle your sexual appetite?" Tyke moved toward her with greedy hands.

"Back off." She gave him a stern look. "Nobody is touching me but the man standing across from me at the altar."

Tyke undressed her with his eyes and seductively licked his lips. "I heard you were getting married. This wedding is a big thing. Everybody is talking about it."

Tyke's sex appeal made Heaven's panties moist with desire. "What do you want, Tyke? I thought I told you I never wanted to see you again."

"Heaven, you and I both know you didn't mean that. You were just mad at the time. How many times have you been upset with me and said you didn't want to see me again?"

He was right. She had cursed him out, punched him in the lip, and once she even tried to hit him with her car, but none of that mattered because he had a way of luring her back into his world. Tyke reminded her of a giant spider that spun a web so beautiful that its prey was drawn to it, but once it touched the web, it couldn't get out. That was their relationship, it looked beautiful from the outside but it was always a sticky situation.

"I don't need you in my life."

"Oh now you don't need me, just because your marrying a deacon." Tyke bounced his shoulders up and down. "Well, guess what? I need you and I need you today. I have another job to do and it's really important for you to come with me."

"You have got to go." Heaven pointed in the direction away from the church. "I'm getting married today."

"Come on, girl. You know I wouldn't be here if it weren't important. I need you to come with me for less than thirty minutes."

"Tyke, you have got to get out of here." She

peeked inside the church to make sure no one was coming. "My wedding starts in less than an hour."

Tyke folded his arms and planted his feet firmly on the ground. "I'm not going anywhere unless you come with me." Being just as stubborn as him, she folded her arms and tapped her foot on the ground. She was not going to be manipulated by his antics. "Suit yourself. I'll just go grab a seat in the church and when your fiancé asks who I am, I'll pull him to the side and tell him what good friends we are." Tyke stroked the side of her face and opened the door to walk inside. Heaven heard Ebony call out her name so she quickly pushed Tyke behind a bush out of sight.

"Heaven," Ebony stuck her head outside. "What are you doing out here? You're going to get your dress dirty." Ebony picked up the bottom of Heaven's dress and tried to usher her back inside the church.

She inhaled deeply. "I needed to get some air. Isn't it beautiful out here?"

"Yes, but not as beautiful as you're going to look walking down the aisle. Now let's go back inside." She opened the door wide.

From behind her back, Tyke stepped out from hiding. "Ebony, it's so hot in that church. Can I get a few more minutes out here by myself?"

Ebony looked suspicious, "Heaven, are you sure everything is all right?"

"Yeah, I'm fine. I'll see you inside." Heaven pushed her inside and closed the door. Heaven listened for a moment before she heard Ebony's heels walk back toward the chapel.

Tyke came out and grabbed her wrist. "Come on. Let's go before someone else comes looking for you."

Without giving her a chance to put up a fight, he shoved her inside his truck and closed the door.

Chapter 31

"Tyke, you couldn't wait for me to change out of my gown?" She looked down at her spotless gown. She couldn't allow a speck of dirt to get on it.

"I promise you ain't nothing going to happen to you or that dress."

He filled her in on what he wanted her to do while he drove.

"Tyke, I don't know why you don't get your girl to do this with you. You two could be Camden's version of Bonnie and Clyde."

He laughed at her. "I would ask her but she's not as strong as you are. I know I can trust you. "

"You can't trust your girl?"

Tyke concentrated on the streets of Camden as if it was his first time seeing them. "Sometimes I question her loyalty." His tone turned serious. "I know she's down with me, but that's because I can give her anything she wants. What would she do if danger came my way? Would she hold me down or run for cover? She's not like you. You're not scared of anything. Heaven, you're a bona fide gangsta chick. Someone I'm proud to have on my team."

Heaven used to think being on Tyke's team was a good thing. She was admired by plenty of people because Tyke took care of her on the side. He always lived life to the fullest. Money, cars, drugs, and diamonds were all at his disposal and he always treated those around him well, but lately she could see a change in him. Something different was driving him. His life had taken a turn for the worse. "Tyke, why are you doing this? Going from a drug dealer to a hit man . . . Why the sudden change?"

He wasn't sure if he was ready to share the truth with her, inevitably deciding in the end to trust her. "Do you realize how many cats are killed everyday over a measly corner or dime bag of crack?"

"That's nothing new. It has been going on for years."

"I know, but as I mature I can see the young heads coming up and setting up shop, taking over corners, and getting their own workers. These young cats are harder and bolder than ever. They're hungry for money and they hold no fear of trying to take out the biggest dealer in town to get to the top."

Surprised by his admission, she asked, "You scared?"

"I'm not scared, but I don't want to die young. When I took out the Correctional Officer, even though it happened so fast, there was a moment I could see the look of fear in his eyes. There was nothing he could do to escape death. It's something about that look in the victim's eyes that makes me feel powerful."

Heaven's cell buzzed in her lap. It was Ebony. She was expecting her to call. She answered. "Heaven, where are you?'

"I had to run out for a minute. I'll be back in time for the wedding."

"You have to get back here, now."

"Ebony, I'll be there and if I'm a little bit late stall them." She ended the call just as Tyke pulled onto an abandoned block. It was a narrow deserted street. The entire street was lined with houses that were boarded up, and trash was lying around in the front yards. There were a few local residents passing through, using this street as a shortcut to their final destination.

He turned off the ignition and turned toward her. "This is going to be easy. There isn't going to be any blood shed. I've been following this boy for over a week. This hit comes as a request from his father."

"His father? What could this man have done to make his dad wants him dead?"

"The son is an addict. He's stolen, lied, and has been in the hospital over a dozen times within the past year from near fatal overdoses. I think the father is desperate and doesn't know what else he can do. He's tried tough love, but the mother always allows the son back in the house. The father feels like Doctor Kevorkian and just wants to stop his son's pain."

"By having him murdered?"

"It's not going to be murder. It's going to be an overdose. I can't blame the father for feeling this way. Wait until you get a look at this guy. He's already dead. All that's missing is his grave. He's a living corpse; walking around breathing, but not alive. I feel sorry for the brother. It's best if he's put out of his misery."

"How do you know the father isn't setting you up?"

"The father is a friend of my dad. I know my dad wouldn't set me up with anybody I couldn't trust." Tyke pointed across the street. "This is where he usually gets high." They sat and watched the house for less than five minutes before a guy wearing a baseball cap pulled down low on his head walked up the block and entered the house. "That's him right there and he's right on time. He's comes here every day between ten and eleven o'clock." Tyke handed her a dime bag of heroin. Looking at the bag in my hand, she noticed the slogan, 'Get high or die tryin'. "Go in there and give him this."

"Where did you get this from?"

"That's not important. What is important is getting him to use this stuff.

"You want me to walk up to this guy and hand him a bag full of dope. Don't you think it seems a little odd that I'm wearing a wedding dress?"

Tyke reached in the back and gave her his jacket to cover up with. "Tell him it's a present from his friend the mailman."

"The mailman?"

"Yeah, maybe three or four times a week this guy searches the neighborhood for the mailman. I've seen him chase down the mail truck on foot. Once he catches up with him he gets inside and they drive to an alley somewhere and climb into the back. Now I can't say for sure what exactly is going on in that truck, but the truck gets to rocking…" Tyke rocked back and forth in an attempt to imitate the truck. "But I'm sure they weren't sorting mail. I'm thinking they get busy in more ways than one. When ol' boy leaves out of there he was swaying to one side. I could tell by the way he kept nodding as he walked down the street they had gotten high."

Heaven jumped out the truck in a hurry. She wanted to get this over with so that she could get back to the church.

"Don't be long," he screamed. "Heaven, what you're about to see will be very disturbing." He pushed out his chest and took in a deep breath. "Suck it up, be a man."

She rolled her eyes at him and ran across the street. Once she made it up the steps leading to the front door, she pushed open the door. It was a typical squatter's house. It was drafty and there were small rays of sunshine seeping through the boarded-up windows. She carefully walked across the dusty floors and scanned the rooms for the guy with the baseball hat. She searched the living room and then saw him in the next room sitting at a raggedy kitchen table looking blankly at the wall. Heaven walked up to him but it took a moment for him to notice her. The cap on his head prevented her from clearly seeing his face. She pulled out the clear plastic bag of heroin Tyke had given her and held it out for him. He snatched it from her hand. Heaven thought it was odd that he never said anything to her. She turned to leave but the smell of crack being smoked stopped her.

She turned back toward him and watched him grab his backpack from off the ground and pull out a lighter and spoon. The lighter he was using was nearly out of fluid. He repeatedly tried to get a flame by flicking the lighter over and over again. Finally he got a spark and held the lighter underneath the spoon. He cooked the dope and loaded it into the syringe. The needle he used looked unclean and was bent from repeated use.

The way he focused so intently on the drugs and blocked out everything around him scared her. She had seen how an addict could be calm one minute and hysterical the next. She hoped he didn't get violent.

She watched him take off the heavy sweatshirt and set his baseball cap down on the table. Her eyes opened wide in horror. His skin was scorched. He had been badly burned in a fire. His face was distorted and part of his face was covered with bandages and the other part exposed pieces of his flesh. Looking away, she felt nauseous. She held her stomach and prayed she wouldn't get sick all over her wedding gown. She held onto the wall to steady herself. When she looked up again, he steadily inserted the needle into his arm where the skin had been burnt away. He dug the needle past the open flesh and into his exposed veins.

He leaned back and enjoyed the few seconds of high the heroin gave him before sticking the needle back into the cooked dope and repeating the process. Heaven watched him carefully as he stuck the needle again into his arm, but before he could pump more dope into his arm he stopped and looked up at her.

That's when Heaven noticed something familiar in his eyes. She had noticed it earlier, but she thought she was being paranoid. She recognized those eyes. It was him. It was Chris. The guy from Jill's house the night she got high with Zaria. He was the one who lost it and threatened to burn the place down.

Chapter 32

"Oh my," she whispered. Chris did sct the place on fire. His burns were a result of that night. She remembered how Chris used to look. He was now a completely different person.

He saw her staring at him and held out the needle to her. He motioned for her to take it. That urge she had been trying to suppress reared its ugly head. Once again, she couldn't control her craving for that poison.

The lure of the needle drew her closer to him. She swallowed hard and balls of sweat formed on her head. She sat across from him, forgetting she was getting married. She took the needle out of his hand and tied the rubber hose around her arm. She inserted the needle in a fresh vein. The relief she felt sent chills through her body and immediately took her to another place. She was no longer shooting dope in her arm. Instead, she saw herself wandering through a field of cushiony soft clouds.

The sound of hard footsteps echoed in her head and stopped in front of her. She couldn't see who it was. Her vision was blurred.

"No, Heaven!" Tyke cried. "What are you doing? You told me your were clean!"

She and Chris sat at the table nodding off to sleep. He peeled her fingers from around the syringe. Tyke pushed her out of the chair and she fell to the floor. He made her get up and screamed in her face, "Come on, we have a job to finish."

He walked around to Chris and held him from behind so he couldn't move. Incoherent, Chris didn't make any effort to break away from Tyke's hold. He quietly sat in the chair.

Tyke shoved the dope in her direction. "Fill it all the way up." Her body was so relaxed that it took a few seconds for her to understand what Tyke was saying. "Heaven, get your behind up. I need you to fill that syringe with heroin and shoot him with as much as you can."

She lazily grabbed the syringe and did as he said.

Chris awoke from his drug-induced stupor, realizing something wasn't right. He fought to get away from Tyke's grasp. Tyke held him tighter and Chris's eyes grew with fear. He was scared of what they were going to do to him.

"Heaven, you have to stick him in the vein," Tyke yelled.

His arms were a blur in front of her eyes. She couldn't clearly see his veins from the burns on his arms. She wiped one of her sweaty palms along her dress and started to shake from nervousness.

"Can you do this?" Tyke asked.

She ignored him and searched Chris's arm for one good vein. After looking over both his arms twice, she finally found a spot on the side of his neck. Steadily inserting the needle, she placed her thumb on the syringe lever, but she couldn't press it.

Her conscience began weighing down on her. She had second thoughts until Tyke started yelling at her again. "Heaven, do it now." Tyke's screaming scared her and she quickly pushed the lever all the way down. Chris's body slumped in the chair, but he was still breathing. His head dropped down in front of him.

"All right do it again," Tyke told her. "This dope is lethal. One more hit and he's done."

Listening to Tyke's cold words, she shot him up one more time. This time the drug was too much for his body to handle. Chris started foaming at the mouth and he went into a seizure. His body shook involuntarily.

Tyke let him go and allowed his body to slide to the floor. His head jerked a few more times, but his eyes eventually closed for the final time. "All right that's it. Let's get out of here."

Tyke wiped their fingerprints off the syringe and pressed Chris's hands all over it. He then led Heaven out the house. Before they left, Heaven turned and looked at Chris's body one last time. Her heart was heavy with guilt.

Back in the truck she laid her head back. She couldn't believe she helped murder someone she knew. She tried to close her eyes, but Tyke's yelling distracted her. "Heaven, you almost messed up my deal. I thought you were done using dope."

She remained silent.

"Yo, I'm talking to you. You could have blown the whole deal. There's a lot of money riding on this being done right. I told his father there would be no loose ends."

She opened her eyes and glared at him. The combination of drugs and leaving Chris dead on the floor had numbed her body. She didn't know what Tyke was saying, but she knew it wasn't good from the look on his face and the way he waved his hands at her. He finally pulled up to the church.

Every time Heaven used dope there were periods of time she couldn't account for and this was one of those times. She remembered Tyke pushing her out his truck and then she was back in the ladies lounge at the church and Ebony was lightly placing a cold rag against her face.

"Heaven, where have you been?" When Ebony took Heaven's hand in hers she got a good look at the fresh tracks left on her arm. "I knew it. I knew you were up to something when I found you outside." She lifted her to her feet. "Come on, girl. You have got to get it together. You are already a half hour late for your own wedding."

A soft knock on the door stopped Ebony's attempt to sober Heaven up. "Is everything all right in there?" It was one of the women from the women's auxiliary.

"Yes, Sister Daniels. Everything is fine. Please ask Reverend Stansfield to give us ten more minutes and you can start the wedding."

Heaven's eyelids were heavy and she just wanted to sleep, but Ebony wouldn't let her. She wet the washcloth again and laid it on Heaven's forehead.

Then she pulled foundation from out of her make-up bag and applied it to Heaven's arm to hide the tracks. "Heaven, I don't know what made you go out and get high today, but I know today is something you've been waiting for. I'm going to make sure I see you through."

Forty minutes later, after Heaven's high wore off, she stood at the altar across from the man of her dreams. She was still in a daze from the heroin, but before she knew it, she and Hasani were cutting the cake and sharing their first dance together as husband and wife.

Chapter 33

After a weeklong honeymoon in the Poconos, the newlyweds returned home to a living room full of boxes. Hasani pushed things to the side, trying to dig a path for them to walk through.

"I didn't know you had so much stuff."

"Neither did I." She stared at the various objects lying around. Everything she had ever owned must've been brought over from her nana's house. She saw a bean bag she hadn't sat in since high school. There were stuffed animals and several boxes of mementos; things she hadn't seen in years.

"Heaven, I'm sorry about this," her husband apologized. "I told the deacons to bring your things over, but I had no idea they were going to leave the house in such a mess."

Heaven pulled one box open and started taking things out. "Well let's start going through each box. We need to have this place cleaned up by the time Emalee brings the children home."

The doorbell rang and Hasani returned with Deacon Daniels. "How are you, Mrs. and Mrs. Washington?"

He was the first person from the church to address her as Mrs. Washington. She liked the feel of that title. She felt honored.

"I'm good, Deacon Daniels, thanks for asking." Heaven got the feeling that Deacon Daniels wanted to speak with her husband in private so she excused herself from the room. "Hasani, I'm going to take a few of my things upstairs and start to unpack." She attempted to lift one of her suitcases when Hasani took it from out of her hands.

"Heaven, I think this is too big for you to carry. I'll bring it up later."

She was going to object but she knew he was right.

"Okay, I'll go into the kitchen and see if there is anything in the fridge."

Heaven wondered what the deacon wanted to talk with her husband about. Whatever it was must have been important for him to come over on their first day back.

Heaven went into the kitchen to give Ebony a call. After the wedding, Ebony made her promise to call her as soon as they came home from their honeymoon. She called Ebony on her cell phone and she answered on the first ring. "Girl, I've been waiting for you to call me for hours."

"My husband and I just came home less than twenty minutes ago." Heaven giggled. "I love the way it sounds when I say 'My husband.'" The words rolled off her lips.

"Heaven, I was so upset when I found you outside the church leaning against the church sign stoned. You are so lucky I'm the one who found you and not somebody from the church." Heaven rolled her eyes at the phone. Ebony worried too much.

". . . and did you forget you are pregnant? Aren't you concerned about the baby's health?"

Heaven had the cordless phone propped against one ear as she searched through the refrigerator for something to eat. By the time she saw Hasani walk in, she had grown tired of hearing Ebony chastise her like a child so she disconnected the call without saying good-bye. "Honey, we need to go to the store and buy some groceries. There's nothing here to eat. The kids need snacks and I have a craving for black licorice and yogurt."

When he didn't answer, she closed the refrigerator door. The look on Hasani's face said Deacon Daniels had been the bearer of bad news. "What's wrong?" she asked.

"Deacon Daniels just told me Sister Lizzie Stewart's son was found dead while we were away. He OD'd on drugs the day we got married."

Heaven's heart sunk to the bottom of her stomach and her lips trembled. Panic stirred her soul and she silently prayed that Chris was not Sister Stewart's son.

"They said he overdosed on heroin." Heaven grabbed hold of one of the chairs. "Heaven, you look pale. Are you all right?' He rushed to her side.

"I'm okay. I think it's the baby. I'm going to go

lie down for a moment." She walked out the kitchen and struggled to climb the stairs. She never thought her situation could get any worse. This wasn't how she expected her life with Hasani to begin.

Chapter 34

"Heaven, it's time to wake from your slumber. You need to get dressed." Heaven looked up at her husband from underneath the covers. Hasani was fully dressed and drinking from a coffee mug. It looked like he had been up for hours. Heaven turned back over and tried going back to sleep. "Heaven, the funeral starts in a few hours," Hasani called out again.

Heaven had a horrible night's sleep. When she left Hasani in the kitchen, she had gone to bed and had not gotten back up until now. "Hasani, do we really need to be there? We haven't even been home for twenty four hours."

He sat at her bedside. "You know my duties at the church require me to do certain things and now that you're my wife I also need you to be there. There are going to be times like this when we have to be places that we're not too excited about being at." He leaned down and kissed her on her forehead. "Now get dressed and I'll meet you downstairs for breakfast."

Being at Chris's funeral was worse than Heaven could have imagined. It was a closed casket service and in the front of the church an easel held a blown up picture of Chris.

The photo showed Chris laughing. He didn't resemble the Chris she knew. He looked healthy with a plump face, bright eyes, and clear skin. He had all his teeth and he looked quite handsome.

Once they were seated, Heaven was filled with anxiety. Her nerves were bad and she felt guilty. Although no one but Tyke knew what really happened the day Chris died, she felt like all eyes were on her.

Davis was asked to read the eulogy and Ebony helped as an usher. Sister Stewart sat in the second pew screaming out, "Christian! Christian!" The women of the church gathered around her trying to soothe her sorrow.

Heaven got up to leave. She couldn't watch Sister Stewart suffer any longer. "Where are you going?" Hasani asked.

"I can't take this any more. This is too sad."

Hasani pulled her back down in her seat. "Don't leave. It's almost over."

Heaven was consumed with guilt. Every time she looked at Chris's picture she saw the sins she had committed against him. The results of her deception were being played out in front of her very own eyes. The flowers, pictures, Sister Stewart's cries; it was all too much for Heaven. She regretted what she did and she shed a river full of tears over

Chris and the secret she would have to carry with her for the rest of her life.

After the burial, she thought Hasani was taking her home, but he wanted to stop at Sister Stewart's house to pay his last respects. "It's the least I can do after the way she took care of the children after Celeste died," he said.

Sister Stewart was the first person they saw when they walked into her house. She looked a lot stronger than she did at the funeral. Her eyes lit up when she saw Heaven and Hasani.

"Thank you both for coming. I'm sure this wasn't what you were expecting to come home to on your first day back from your honeymoon."

"No, it was an unpleasant surprise," Hasani replied. "If there is anything you need from us, just give us a call."

"Christian was a good son; very polite and re-spectful. He never caused me any trouble until he started using drugs. I've been blaming myself since his death. My husband keeps telling me it's not my fault, but I can't help but wonder." Heaven didn't realize Sister Stewart was married. She didn't see her husband at the funeral. "Being an ex-offender myself . . ." Heaven was startled by her words. She turned to Heaven with a warm look. "Yes, Heaven, I used to abuse drugs and I used quite often, especially when Christian was a child. A lot of times I took him with me when I did drugs. It wasn't until he was in high school that I cleaned myself up, but maybe if he hadn't seen me snort so much coke up my nose, he wouldn't have felt it was all right to do it himself. I wish you could have met him," she said to Heaven.

She had no idea Heaven was probably the last person Chris had laid eyes on before he left this earth.

Chapter 35

It was a glorious Sunday morning and Heaven felt like the sun was shining down directly on her. She was excited because it was a new year, she had a new family, and today was her first Sunday service as Mrs. Hasani Washington.

Before the wedding, Nana and the women of the church sat her down and told her what it meant to be a deacon's wife.

They explained that her life was no longer her own. Being a part of the church meant there was always something that needed to be done. For the women, this included cooking dinners, organizing church functions, devoting time to charities, and doing all these things with a pleasant attitude.

Heaven gladly accepted everything the ladies told her. She even embraced it. A lot of the duties the ladies listed were things Celeste used to do. That's why it was so important for her to do everything Celeste did, but better.

One obligation she was looking forward to was being named director of the church's new day care center. Celeste had been named director of the day care center because she was married to Hasani. With the long hours needed to get licenses, permits, and business plans, the church thought it would be more convenient for a husband and wife to oversee the project. Now that she was the new wife, she expected to be appointed the position. Nana hinted that Avery would probably make the announcement that day in church.

Emalee wasn't the only person bothered that Heaven had married and was pregnant by Hasani. A lot of people in the church disapproved and treated Heaven cold. Even Davis had stopped speaking to her. She felt shunned by the people she sought approval from the most. Heaven planned on using her position as director of the daycare center as a way for them to look at her differently.

"Good morning, Mount Olive." Deacon Daniels addressed the congregation. He read a few death notices and made a few announcements concerning various church revivals. "Last but not least," he announced. "I'm sure everyone is eager to find out about the day care center arrangements."

Amens were shouted throughout the church. Currently, the church had a small day care center that provided low-cost services to the residents of the city, but a lot of members were concerned about what would happen to the center once the church closed down to undergo construction for the new church that was being built.

"I'm glad to say the church has temporarily

secured a building on Cooper Street. The daycare center will be housed there until the church construction is complete."

The church's current center opened two years ago and had grown considerably since the first day. A lot of single mothers left their children at the church with the peace of mind that their children were being taken care of properly. It also gave the church the opportunity to bring more children into church. A lot of the day care children had never been to church, but by reaching out to the parents, their children were now attending. As a result, Sunday School and church services had grown considerably.

"Also, I'm pleased to announce that Sister Ebony Collins has been asked to be the new director of the day care center. She will work closely with Deacon Washington to get the day care center ready to reopen at its new location. Sister Collins has her master's degree in child development and worked for the Camden City School District for eight years. She was also certified as a day care teacher and worked as a kindergarten teacher for five years."

The joy Heaven felt had been burst like a bubble. She couldn't believe Ebony had been named the new director of the children's day care. That position was supposed to be hers. Sister Stewart along with other ladies of the church hugged Ebony and congratulated her. Heaven glanced up at Avery, but he wouldn't look her in the eye.

"Congratulations, Ebony." Deacon Daniels clapped and the entire congregation gave her a round of applause. Ebony stood up and waved like she was Queen Elizabeth.

Once the church quieted down, Deacon Daniels said, "Also, the church is also looking to increase the staff at the daycare center. If anyone in the congregation knows of anyone who has a degree or is in school working toward a degree in child development, psychology, sociology, or elementary education, invite them to come down to the daycare center next Wednesday, Thursday, or Friday for interviews."

After Deacon Daniels sat down, Heaven whispered to Ebony, "Congratulations! I didn't know you were so smart and that was a beautiful thing you did volunteering to head this project."

"I love children and it's important to nurture their young minds," Ebony whispered back. "But I didn't volunteer. Reverend Stansfield knew about my background and he asked me to approach the Deacon Board about the position."

Appalled, Heaven forced a smile on her face. She sat back and tried focusing on the rest of service, but she was so angry. Jealously controlled her thoughts. She was sure that position was hers. Heaven started to sweat and her body temperature rose. Beads of sweat formed on her hands and face. She had to get out of there.

Imani was sitting beside Heaven and she held Wesley in her arms. Samuel sat in the pew behind them with Emalee. Heaven turned around and whispered to Emalee, "Could you take the baby and keep an eye on Imani for me? I need to use the ladies room."

Emalee eyed Heaven suspiciously while taking the baby from her. Heaven told Imani she would be right back. She got up to leave and Imani yelled, "I want to go with you." Imani jumped up from her seat and wrapped herself around Heaven's legs.

Imani was loud and people started to stare at them. Emalee saw the commotion Imani was causing and told her to sit with her while Heaven went to the bathroom. Heaven darted toward the bathroom before anyone else tried to stop her.

When she entered the bathroom, only one other woman was in there and she left right after checking her makeup. Heaven entered one of the stalls and hastily dug around in her purse until she pulled out a small bag of dope she had left over from a few days ago.

Heaven had returned to using drugs on a regular basis. She justified her use by telling herself that she wasn't doing anything wrong. Her use added up to once a day and when she did it was such a small amount it was barely noticeable, but that small amount helped. She had no idea how hard it was going to be taking on three children and a husband. Plus, she was pregnant and tired a lot of the time. Her life had gone from super slow to over drive overnight.

Heaven had bought some dope after Chris's funeral and promised herself what she didn't use she would flush down the toilet, but she couldn't do it. It was a good thing she had stuck that little bit in her purse because she wouldn't be able to make it through the rest of service without it.

She pulled out a spoon and dumped the contents of the bag inside. Within minutes she was high and all of her anxieties were released. A rush went through her body. She couldn't believe how good she felt sitting on the edge of the toilet. Her head hit against the stall wall.

She had no idea how long she had been in the bathroom, but she must have fallen asleep because Emalee woke her up by calling out her name and banging on the stall door.

"Heaven!" she screamed. "Heaven, what are you doing?"

She was still a little groggy but she knew where she was. "Emalee, I'll be out in a second."

"Imani wants you. She's been asking for you since you left and that was almost forty minutes ago. What are you doing?"

Heaven was feeling too good to argue with Emalee. She had been gone for a while and knew she had to get back to the service. "Emalee, go back to your seat. I'll be right there."

"We'll wait," she arrogantly replied. Heaven knew Emalee's only reason for sticking around was so she could be nosy and report back to her brother.

Heaven got up and flushed the toilet. When she turned around to grab her bag the spoon she used to cook the dope fell to the hard floor. It made a rattling sound and Heaven knew Emalee saw it fall.

Heaven placed it back in her purse. When she came out of the stall Emalee looked at her with a smirk on her face. Imani stared at the two women. Heaven went to the sink to wash her hands and then took Imani's hand from Emalee's.

"What were you doing in there, Heaven?" Emalee asked from behind Heaven's back.

"Emalee, if you have something to say—say it!"

Emalee walked back to the stall she was in and looked into the toilet. "You look nervous . . . maybe even guilty. Were you doing something in there you know Hasani wouldn't approve of? Did you flush evidence down the toilet?"

Heaven laughed. "Evidence! Evidence of what?"

"Your drug use. I know you're using again. Hasani may trust you and be blinded to the truth, but you can believe I'm onto you and when I catch you I'm going to expose you for what you truly are—an addict."

Heaven had the impulse to slap Emalee for saying that in front of Imani, but she stopped herself. Emalee was trying to push her into an altercation. Heaven wasn't going to do it. Instead, she turned and left with Imani, leaving Emalee in the cold, small bathroom.

Chapter 36

By the time Heaven returned to her seat the service was nearly over. She sat down just in time to hear Avery give his final remarks. Heaven hastily swung the baby's diaper bag over her shoulder. When she looked up, she saw Emalee standing in the back of the church watching her with a smirk on her face. Then Davis walked up and whispered something in her ear. The two of them shared a laugh together.

Hasani came over and took the baby out of Heaven's arms. "Heaven, Deacon Daniels's wife has invited us over for coffee. Do you want to go?" he asked.

"No, I would rather go home. It's been a long day." Heaven's voice was flat and Hasani knew what had her bothered.

"Okay, let me go tell them we won't be able to make it and I'll meet you at the car." Before Hasani could walk away, Avery approached them.

"Hello, Reverend. Great sermon today," Hasani complimented him.

"Thank you, Deacon Washington. It's a joy to preach the word of God." He turned toward Heaven. "I know you and your family are looking forward to getting out of here, but I was hoping I could speak with you for a moment in my office."

"Uncle Avery, I'm sure whatever you want to speak with me about can wait. I'm tired and we need to get the children home."

"It will only take a minute of your time. I won't keep you long." he replied.

"Honey, I'll meet you right here." Hasani held his hand out for Imani and told Samuel to follow him.

Avery escorted her down to his office and asked her to have a seat. When Heaven sat down she hoped her uncle wasn't going to ask her to head up another ministry because she really had her heart set on the day care center.

"Well, I'm sure your wondering why I would call you into my office."

"Yes, I am kind of curious." She chuckled. "What was so important that you couldn't speak to me in the sanctuary?"

Avery folded his hands in front of him and his face turned serious. "Well, I'm going to get straight to the point. Davis Davies has come to me with upsetting information involving you." When she heard Davis's name she knew it was not going to be good.

"When you first started attending church, I did notice the two of you were close. I was aware he had taken you out to dinner and had bought you a few things, but I had no idea the two of you were having sex."

"Avery . . ." she tried to interrupt him.

"Let me finish." He insisted. "You are my niece, but this man is still a part of my church and I can't allow such scandal to run rampant inside these walls. I know you're not fully to blame. You may have gotten caught up in a situation between two honorable men and didn't know how to get yourself out, but I can't have these kinds of love triangles going on in my church. The Lord doesn't like confusion and that's what this is. That is why I proposed to the board that they consider Ebony for the director position instead of you. I truly feel you aren't mature enough to handle a position with so much power. The person I want to fill this position must be focused on Christ and not themselves."

"Uncle Avery, how could you make a decision like that without first asking for my side of the story? I don't know what Davis has told you, but I think there has been a mix-up. Davis may have been interested in me at one time but I made my intentions clear. I did not lead him on in any way and I certainly did not have sex with him. Maybe he is upset over the fact I married Hasani."

"Heaven, I've known Davis for a long time. I believe every word he's told me. He wouldn't lie about something this serious. That man would rather die than tell Deacon Washington he had been with his wife, but Davis believes the child you are carrying could be his."

"This is absurd. This baby is my husband's. I don't believe you would believe Davis over your own niece," Heaven screamed.

"I don't think you would lie, but I do believe you would try to cover up the truth and you can't do that."

She swallowed hard and wanted to curse Avery out for being in her personal affairs but she thought that might make her look even more guilty. She stood up to leave. "Is that all?" she asked through clenched teeth.

"No. Sit back down," he demanded. "The reason I called you down here was because I don't like to keep secrets and I don't plan on keeping this from someone I respect and work with every day. I'm giving you advance notice so you can tell your husband about your relationship with Davis. You have one week. Please don't force me to tell him." He offered her the door. "You may go now."

She slammed the door behind her.

The car ride home was quiet. Even Samuel and Imani avoided their usual buzz of playing and talking to one another. The mood was uncomfortable until baby Wesley squealed loudly. Heaven saw him flash a mouth full of gums. It was amazing how such a beautiful baby could brighten her day and soften her heart with just a simple smile. She glanced over at Samuel and he put his head down to avoid looking at her. He still wasn't used to having her around.

They pulled into their driveway and everyone piled out of their SUV. Heaven went straight to the bathroom to take a shower. She stayed in there for more than thirty minutes. The heroin she did earlier was beginning to wear off and she was getting irritable. After drying off, she walked back into the bedroom and Hasani was waiting for her.

"What did the Reverend want to speak with you about?"

"Oh nothing," she sarcastically replied. "He told me he was the reason I wasn't selected as director."

"I heard."

"How did you know?" she asked.

"Once you left I asked Deacon Daniels what happened. He told me Reverend Stansfield suggested Ebony. He had gone to her and asked her to consider the position. She showed up at the last meeting to give a whole presentation. She had blueprints and diagrams outlining a child's development from infancy to grade school. She provided reports on how to make sure kids in the urban communities succeeded. Deacon Daniels said he was impressed. I asked if the reverend gave an explanation for why he asked Ebony to consider a position that was meant for you, but he wasn't sure."

"I know why. He told me the reason was because he thought I was too self-centered instead of Christ centered."

"What would make him say something like that? I have never heard Reverend Stansfield be so callous."

"I don't know. Maybe he sees me as the deceitful whore who seduced the godly deacon and tricked him into marrying her."

"You know that's not true."

"Why isn't it? You should have seen the way he

talked to me." Heaven was trying to hold her lies together. She had no idea how she was going to keep her affair with Davis a secret.

"If you want me to go back to the board and tell them you would like to be considered for the position, I will."

"Don't you dare! Then everyone at church will think I was upset over not getting that position; especially Emalee." She went to the closet and looked around for something comfortable to wear. "I don't want any of the members thinking they intimidate me in any way. Ebony can have the position."

"Honey, I know this was an unexpected blow. You don't have to act strong in front of me." He walked close to her and wrapped his hands around waist.

"What do you want me to say?" She turned and pointed in his chest. "Hasani, you know how much I was looking forward to heading that project. I had so many plans. I even showed them to you. We discussed each and every activity for every age group," she exclaimed. "I feel like Ebony did this intentionally. She knew how much I wanted that position."

"She is one of your closest friends. I don't think she did this on purpose. I'm sure Reverend Stansfield and a few other members at the church probably encouraged her." He hugged her tighter. "Ebony will be an excellent director and she loves children. Let's wish her well and enjoy the extra time we'll have together now that you won't have to work."

"But I was looking forward to working with you every day, since you are a part of this project."

"Don't worry about it. Now you'll have a chance to miss me during the day."

They kissed and she laid her head against his chest. A soft knock at their bedroom door let them know one of the children needed them.

"Come in," Hasani said.

Samuel pushed open the bedroom door. "I think Wesley needs to be changed. He keeps crying."

Hasani moved toward the door. "I'll get him."

Heaven laid down and thought about Avery. She couldn't believe how he had taken away something so important to her with so much ease. She wanted to forget about it, but she couldn't. Thoughts of revenge filled her mind. She needed to find Tyke.

Chapter 37

After she dropped Samuel off at school and called a babysitter for Imani and Wesley, Heaven went to find Tyke.

She pulled out of her driveway and headed straight to Pollock. She was so angry with her uncle. Heaven wanted to ask Nana to intercede on her behalf, but then she would have to explain why Davis thought the baby she was carrying was his. It looked like she would have to take care of things on her own.

Less than five minutes later, she was slowly scanning the block for Tyke. The kid who called Tyke that first day she went looking for him was sitting in his usual spot. He saw her and slowly shook his head no. He was telling her Tyke wasn't around.

Heaven pressed down hard on the gas pedal and sped down the narrow street like a bullet. She slammed on the brakes at the next stop sign and tried to think of where to look next.

She rode down Mount Ephraim Avenue hoping

she would find him shopping on the busy street. She stopped at a traffic light directly in front of Dazz's Record Shop. The elementary school across the street was having a fire drill. Dozens of kids crossed the street in front of her and as she waited for the crossing guard to move she saw Tyke's truck parked a few feet away. She quickly parked and combed the nearby shops in search of him. He couldn't be far. Tyke was too lazy to walk more than a couple feet. She stuck her head in a few small shops and still saw no sign of him. She stood on the sidewalk and looked around. That's when she saw him. He was in the barbershop sitting in the barber's chair.

"That should have been the first place I looked," she said out loud.

When she walked in all eyes fell on her. The place was full of customers. Men, women, and children were all waiting their turn to get into the barber's chair. Tyke was in the middle of telling a story about his cousin who was killed a few years prior when he saw her.

One of the barbers asked could they help her.

"Man, she's looking for me." He saw the slight bump in her belly. "Am I gonna be a father?" he joked before getting up out the chair. He laughed.

"Could you stop joking around? I need to speak with you," she whispered.

They turned and walked toward the door. "Yo man, I'll be back. Don't let no one take my spot." He yelled out to his barber. Once they were outside he said to her, "Why didn't you tell me you were pregnant?'

"Why would my pregnancy concern you?"

"Oh! Now I understand why you and the deacon got married so quickly. You're going to pass the baby off as his."

"No, the baby is his."

"I hope it's a boy this time. You know I already have four girls." He pulled a piece of spearmint gum out of his pocket and popped it in his mouth. "Didn't I tell you the only time you come looking for me is when you want something? What's up?"

"I need you to take somebody out for me."

"Yo, somebody must have really made you mad because I've never heard you talk like that." He laughed. "Who is it?" he asked.

"Reverend Stansfield."

"Yo, isn't that the short guy whose face is on every billboard in the city?"

She nodded.

"Heaven, you can't take out a guy like that. He has strong political ties to the community. Taking him out would be like murdering the mayor. If we killed him every cop in the city would be on a man hunt."

"Can't you make it look like an accident?" she asked.

"Isn't he related to you?"

Heaven nodded her head.

"What did this guy do to you to make you so angry?"

"I have my reasons."

"Well, whatever they are, they ain't good enough to kill a reverend." Tyke tried to step around her, but she stopped him.

"Please, Tyke. You said there was no one that

you trusted more than me and I feel the same way. I trust no one but you to do this for me," she begged.

"Girl, you're asking for the impossible. Think about what I just said. If we get caught we're both going back to jail for a long time."

"You won't get caught—because you're good." She winked at him.

"You're even better because I can't believe I'm going to do this for you. I'm going to end up dead messing around with you."

Her face lit up. "Nothing is going to happen to you. Now listen to me. I need you to make sure you give him one to the head like you did that CO."

"I can't believe you're telling me how to do this. I thought you said I was good."

"You are, but I can't afford for him to get back up after this is done."

"Would you quiet down?" he hushed her. "Do you want the world to know what were talking about? Listen, I will do this my way but I need you to promise to stay away from me for a while. A high profile murder like this and the police are going to question everybody and it would be best if they found no connection between me and you."

"Fine." She turned back toward her car and he grabbed her arm.

"Heaven, be prepared to pay me for this. I want fifty thousand. I can't do this for you for free."

"Where am I supposed to get that kind of money from?"

He shrugged his shoulders.

"I'll give you back the money you gave me and

we can make arrangements for the remaining amount. Deal?"

"Deal," he replied and went back into the barber shop.

Sister Stewart had talked Heaven into coming to her house for lunch. Heaven had been dreading this date for weeks. Every time Heaven saw Sister Stewart, she was reminded of Chris. There were days she was so ashamed of what she and Tyke had done, she couldn't look Sister Stewart in the face.

Heaven wasn't sure if the connection they shared was because they had both endured the loss of a child or if it was because they had both suffered from drugs.

Sister Stewart stood in front of her house sweeping trash away from the front curb. When she saw Heaven, she greeted her with open arms. "Hello," she said, then she gave Heaven air kisses on the cheek. "Come on inside." Sister Stewart placed her hand on Heaven's belly. "I love feeling the tummies of expecting mothers. It's a miracle to be able to bring another life into the world."

Heaven thought she was thinking of Chris. They entered the house together, and Sister Stewart took her coat and placed it on a nearby chair.

The aroma of pasta called Sister Stewart back to the kitchen. "Heaven, I wanted to fix something good and filling for our lunch today," she yelled. "I know how it is to be pregnant. Plus, you have a new husband and three children to take care of. Life will get hectic for you, but you have to make sure to take care of yourself."

While Heaven waited for Sister Stewart to return, she looked at the pictures of Chris scattered around the living room. Each photo seemed to show a different Chris. There were various photos of him as a baby. He was a plump little boy with big eyes and no teeth. Heaven smiled. He looked nothing like the Chris she remembered.

"When a woman has a baby she never considers the possibility her baby may one day grow up to be a drug user. I know I never did."

Heaven was startled. She didn't see Sister Stewart watching her. Heaven's hand lay against her stomach. She prayed her baby wouldn't inherit her disease. Although, the possibility was great because Heaven was still using while pregnant.

"When I look at you, I see so much of myself. The struggle that lies within you is dangerous. Every day you get up unsure if you can make it through the day without using and that uncertainty will result in you relapsing." Heaven felt like Sister Stewart was reading her innermost thoughts. "There is no need to be afraid. I'm here to help."

The front door opened and in stepped a big, brawly man. The man looked like he had been working in a oil refinery. His overalls were covered in smut and oil and his hands were filthy. He stood at the door taking off his boots before he walked any further into the house.

"Lizzie," he roared.

When he turned around and saw them watching him from the couch he blushed. "I'm sorry. I didn't know you had company."

"Heaven, I don't believe you've met my husband,

Bruce." Their eyes met and they immediately recognized one another from the night Chris set Jill's house on fire.

Bruce waved hello to Heaven and turned back to his wife. "What you cooking?"

"Sorry, honey. You didn't tell me you were coming home for lunch. I only cooked enough for Heaven and me. Do you want me to call down to the sandwich shop and order you something?"

"No, that's all right. I'm only home for a second." He ran upstairs and left them alone.

Tyke had told Heaven Chris' father wanted him dead because the drug use was killing his son, but now she knew Chris' father was also on drugs. Heaven wondered what the real reason was behind him wanting his son dead.

Lunch was ready and the women ate in the kitchen. Sister Stewart fed Heaven well with a plate of steaming pasta and shrimp dripping in a creamy white sauce. It was delicious.

Heaven admired Sister Stewart's kitchen while they ate. It looked like it had just been renovated. Everything in there looked new. "I'm serving you today on my new china; all courtesy of Christian. We finally got the money from Christian's life insurance company and Bruce took me out to get all new appliances since Christian had stolen most of them from us."

Sister Stewart confided in Heaven like they were old friends. "I feel so guilty about my son's death. I didn't force him to do drugs but I enabled him to do it. Now that he's gone, I think about all the times I should have said no. I shouldn't have given him money whenever he asked for it. I shouldn't have looked the other way when he stole my engagement ring, sold our water heater, or siphoned the gas out my car to get drugs."

Heaven could hear the regret in her voice. "Heaven, it was so crazy around here. I never thought my own son would steal from me, but I know how it is when that dope has a hold of you. You'll do anything. One day I came home and the television was gone. I would buy food and he would come in right behind me and steal it out the refrigerator. When Bruce found out what was going on he put him out. He told Christian he had to go.

"Then one day I found Chris at the front door crying for me to let him back in. When I looked in that boy's eyes and he told me that he didn't steal from me I believed him. There was something in his eyes that said he was telling the truth. Bruce told me I was just seeing what I wanted to believe. After things kept disappearing I believed Bruce was right, but to hear my baby cry like that broke my heart. It's a hard thing to turn your back on your only child; even when you know it's for the best."

Sister Stewart cried and Heaven hugged her. Heaven felt sorry for her and wondered how much of Sister Stewart's pain her husband was responsible for.

Chapter 38

The following Sunday the church was holding a bake fair and Heaven had promised to bring a Chocolate Swiss Cake. It was her favorite as a little girl and the only cake she knew how to make from scratch. Unfortunately, time slipped away from her. Imani caught a cold, Wesley was teething, and Hasani used her car all week because his was in the shop. She had too many things to do and baking a cake was not a priority. She wanted to call Nana and ask her to bake one for her, but she knew Nana had also promised the church a few cakes. If she knew her grandmother, she was sure she was making them all from scratch.

"Hasani, can we stop at the grocery store?" The entire family was in the car and on their way to church.

Hasani pulled into the local supermarket and stopped out front. Heaven opened the door and Imani yelled out, "Can I go with you?"

"No," Hasani told his daughter. "She's coming right back."

Heaven got out and when Wesley noticed she was leaving, he also screamed. He held out his hands for her and she gave in. "I forgot. I ran out of pampers this morning. I can't carry cake and pampers by myself."

Hasani didn't question his wife's sudden need for pampers. Instead, he allowed her to get back in the car and everyone accompanied her inside the store. It didn't take her long to find what she needed. She found what she needed. Then she and her family waited patiently in the express lane.

Ten minutes later, the line had barely moved. Impatient, Heaven looked at her watch. "We're going to be late for church. What is taking so long?" She looked ahead to see what was holding up the line. At the front of the line the cashier was having a lengthy conversation with another customer. "What in the world is he doing?" she asked.

"It's all right, Heaven. There's no rush," Hasani reasoned. He never let anything bother him.

"Sure there is. We're members of a big church and we both have duties and responsibilities. We need to be there when church begins." She watched the cashier as he slowly counted out his customer's change. Then he straightened out the money in his drawer before helping the next customer in line. He greeted them with a big smile and asked about their day.

"We don't have time for this," Heaven complained. "He can chit-chat another time." Heaven impatiently tapped her foot on the ground as another ten minutes passed. By the time they got to the front of the line Heaven was furious. "Young man," she chastised. "you shouldn't be fraternizing with customers when you have a whole line of people waiting."

The boy looked at Heaven timidly. "Ma'am, I'm sorry for the delay," he mumbled.

Heaven looked at the boy's name tag, "Rocco, you need to take more pride in your job. This is the express lane," she stressed. "As a matter of fact, I want to speak to the manager. Please call the manager." She raised her voice. Heaven knew she was overreacting; maybe it was because she had run out of dope that morning. She continued to degrade the boy. Customers from other lines were looking to see what all the fuss was. Patrons who were trying to pay for their items and leave were now being held up by her insistence to make a point. The boy was reluctant to call his manager, but he knew if he didn't his customer was bound to make a bigger scene.

Shortly after the checkout boy paged the manager to his station, a tall, thin white man appeared. "Rocco, is there a problem?"

"This woman wants to speak with you."

"Hi, I'm the manager. Is there something I can help you with?"

Hasani nudged her and whispered in her ear, "Heaven, don't do this, you're going to make us later than what we already are."

"No, I want this man to know how poor of a job his employee is doing and if he expects to continue to have our patronage, he'll do something about it." She placed her hand on her hip, "Sir, this is supposed to be the express lane and your check out boy is anything but express. He is doing a terrible job, talking with the customers and asking how their day is going. His conduct is holding other people up. My husband," she pointed at Hasani, "is deacon at a well-known church and we are trying to make it to morning service, now we are going to be late. Do you come to work on time every day?" she asked.

"Yes ma'am," the store manger replied.

"Well, our family also needs to be to church on time." She shoved her finger in his face to get her point across. Hasani dropped his head in embarrassment and even baby Wesley looked at her oddly. "I'm very upset and I will be sure to tell our congregation not to shop here because the service is so bad."

"Ma'am, I apologize for the inconvenience, but we do encourage our cashiers to talk with our customers as if they're old friends."

"Can you teach your cashiers the meaning of being efficient because that is something they are not?"

"If you'd like, we can have another clerk check you out and I'll be sure to take ten percent off your total for all your trouble."

"Ten percent? That's all? We have a congregation of hundreds. If word got out that you didn't know how to treat your customers, I can guarantee you would lose thousands."

"Okay ma'am." He grabbed her things and placed them in a bag for her and handed them to Hasani. "You can take your items and go. It's on us."

After the Washington family left the store they got stuck in a traffic jam. "Damn," Heaven said out loud. Hasani looked at her strangely. He had never heard her curse before.

"Ohhh, she said a bad word," Imani pointed out.

"Heaven, just because you have an attitude today didn't mean you had to take it out on that cashier. He was just a kid."

"You know what?" she screamed. "Shut up! Just shut up!" She slammed her trembling fist against the dash board. The children watched her in horror. "I don't want to hear it any longer."

Her behavior scared her husband and the children. He pulled over to the side of the road and yanked her out the car. "Heaven." He grabbed her face. "You have got to stop acting this way. I don't know what's wrong with you, but ever since you missed out on being named director you've been mean and nasty to everybody in the house and I want it to stop right now. You are going to get back in the car and act like a lady. Do you understand me?" Hasani shouted at her in a stern voice

"Yes," she solemnly replied. They got back in the car and she thought about her actions in the store. She couldn't explain why, but she was losing control.

They finally pulled onto the church's block, but were stopped by a barricade of fire engines, paramedics, police cars, and news vans.

"What is going on?" Hasani said. He pulled over to the curb and told Heaven to stay in the car with the children until he returned.

Heaven and the children tried to see what was

going on. Church members were being helped out by rescue workers. Two paramedics walked through the front doors carrying a stretcher with a white sheet pulled over a body. Heaven became scared and told the children to cover their eyes.

She wondered what was going on when she saw Sister Stewart sitting on the curb crying hysterically. "Stay here," she told the children. Heaven ran over to Sister Stewart. "What happened?" she asked.

"Oh Heaven, it happened all so suddenly. I just couldn't believe it was happening. What are we going to do?"

Heaven rubbed her back and tried to get her to calm down. "Can you tell me what happened?"

She took a deep breath. "Sunday School had just started and a boy from one of the classes pulled out a gun and started shooting. All I heard was gunshots from the classrooms in the back. Deacon Daniels went to see what was happening and ended up getting shot in the shoulder."

"Is he all right?" Heaven asked.

"I suppose. He was taken away in the ambulance not too long ago, but," Sister Stewart whispered to Heaven, "the boy did kill little Raven Harper."

"No," Heaven cried. "Deacon Harper's granddaughter?"

"Yes, I saw them carrying her body out."

"What am I going to tell Samuel? He has a play date with her every week." Police rushed by them. "Who was the boy who did this?"

"I don't know; I've never seen the boy before."

Heaven thought about her grandmother. Nana usually came to church early. She liked to help out with Sunday school and then stay through the eleven o'clock service. "Sister Stewart, did you see my nana in church today?"

"I saw her earlier, but not since the incident."

Hasani ran toward them. "Heaven, I want you to take the kids home. It's chaotic in there and I . . ."

"Hasani, did you see my nana?"

"No I haven't seen her, but that doesn't mean she's not here."

Over his shoulder Heaven saw her being helped out the church by a paramedic. "There she is." They ran to her. "Nana, are you all right?"

"Yes dear, I'm all right."

"Did you get hurt?" Hasani asked.

"No, I'm fine; just a little shaken up," she replied.

"Hasani, I'm going to take Nana home with us if that's all right."

"That's fine. I'll be there as soon as I can."

Hasani helped them to the car and went back into the church. Heaven put the car in reverse and glanced over to a crowd of spectators who had gathered to watch the commotion. Tyke stood within the crowd. He winked his eye at her and turned to walk away. She wanted to go after him and ask him what he had to do with this, but she had to get her family home. She would make sure she talked with him later.

Chapter 39

Heaven was overcome with relief when Hasani finally walked through their front door. "I'm glad you made it home. I was worried."

He joined her in the kitchen and took off his suit jacket, draping it on the back of the chair next to him. "How's Nana?" Hasani asked.

"She's a little shaken. I fixed her some tea and she's feeling much better. I didn't want her to leave so I called Ebony and told her Nana was going to spend the night with us."

"That was a good idea. She enjoys being around the children."

Heaven went to the kitchen cabinets and pulled out a dinner plate. "So what happened to the kid who did the shooting?"

"The boy was arrested and taken down to the station."

"Why did he do it?"

"I don't know. He won't give a reason why."

"Are you hungry? I cooked beef stew. I can heat you up some."

"I'm really not hungry." Hasani was distant. Heaven thought it was because of the shooting, but she had to make sure.

"What's wrong?" Heaven asked.

"Heaven, did you ever think any more about what happened this morning at the grocery store?"

"You're still upset over that? I'm sorry for the way I acted."

"That's not what I'm talking about." Hasani sat her down in front of him and spoke lightening fast. The adrenaline rush he got from helping people at the church had not worn off yet. "After the chaos settled down I took a moment to ask God why. I had to know why a child had to lose her life at Sunday school. Why had this tragedy happened at our church? Then all I could think about was how you were yelling at that kid today in the store." He rubbed his head. "For some reason, that scene stayed in the front of my mind. Then it occurred to me that it was meant for us to be held up this morning." Heaven listened to his words. "Imagine if we would have gotten to church on time this morning. That could be one of our children laid out in the morgue."

"Don't say that," she mumbled.

"It's the truth," he yelled. "Heaven, you owe that boy an apology. God used him to keep us and our family safe and you went on a rampage." Hasani got up and walked to the other side of the room. This was the first time she had ever heard him raise his voice at her. "I'm going to bed." He stormed out of the kitchen, leaving her alone with her thoughts.

The following day, Hasani was still upset over what happened at the grocery store. The tension was high in the Washington household. Hasani wouldn't speak to Heaven unless he had to and Heaven feared her marriage wouldn't be able to withstand the strain much longer.

Hasani left the house early that morning to take Samuel to school. She knew Hasani would spend most of the rest of the day at city hall applying for permits for the day care center.

Heaven was depressed. Her husband wasn't speaking to her and she had not heard from Tyke. She was sure he had something to do with the shooting, but she needed to know why he would do something like that.

Heaven had a list of errands she had to take care of. She feared if she took the children with her they would slow her down. So she called a babysitter.

The first place she hit was Corinne's. Corrine's was a Soul Food Restaurant that sold the best baked goods in the city. Heaven had volunteered to bring the desserts for a meeting the women of Mount Olive had scheduled for Sunday. This meeting was being held to discuss the upcoming Women's Day event. Instead of trying to do it all herself, she decided to place an order at Corrine's.

She walked into the restaurant and up to the take out counter. Corrine was sitting at the counter looking over receipts when Heaven walked in. She welcomed Heaven to her establishment and asked what she needed.

"I need an assortment of desserts. Our church is having a meeting Sunday and I wanted to bring something good for them to snack on."

"That shouldn't be a problem. We're not that busy today. What church do you belong to?"

"Mount Olive Baptist Church?"

"Oh! We have a bunch of ladies from there in here today." Heaven turned in the direction Corrine pointed. Seated at several tables in the next room was just about every female member of Mount Olive. Everyone she was supposed to meet with tomorrow was there, except for Sister Stewart.

No one saw her walk into the room, but she overheard Sister Daniels say to Emalee, "I sure do miss Celeste. She was such a beautiful person. I don't understand how your brother could marry a white girl and expect us to accept her into the church."

"She's not white," Emalee replied. "You know she's Reverend Stansfield's niece."

"Well, she looks it," Sister Daniels replied and the women laughed together.

Heaven stood and listened to the women's conversation before clearing her throat. Emalee saw her first and then Ebony.

"Heaven." Ebony stood up to greet her by giving her a hug. The other women in the room refused to look in Heaven's direction, except for Emalee who smiled at Heaven while eating her desert.

"What's going on?" Heaven asked.

"The ladies from the church came to discuss plans for the Women's Day." Heaven could see the meeting had just about concluded by the number of dirty dishes set on the table.

"That meeting wasn't supposed to be until Sunday."

"It was," Emalee spoke up. "but we decided to change it. A huge snowstorm is supposed to hit the area Sunday. We called around and since everyone was free, we changed the meeting to today."

"Emalee, you didn't think about calling to let me know?" Heaven screamed.

"I forgot," she replied, then turned back to the ladies with her notebook. "Ladies, we only have a few more items left on the agenda and then we're done."

Heaven's cell phone rang in her purse. When she pulled it out the number flashed unknown on the Caller ID. Heaven gave one last look at the women and walked out. Ebony called after her but Heaven kept on going. Once she was outside she answered her call.

"Hey, lady!"

"Tyke!" she shrieked.

"I thought you would have come looking for me by now. Like I said, you only come looking for me when you need something."

"What do you know about that shooting that went on at my church?"

"Shooting? What shooting? I don't know what you're talking about."

"Tyke!" she screamed. Heaven looked around and quickly jumped in her car.

"Relax. I had that young boy come into the church and light it up. You told me you wanted to get rid of your uncle. That little boy has been pestering me for years to give him something to do to earn some cash. I thought this was the perfect opportunity. I promised him his own corner that he can run anyway he likes."

"An innocent little girl was killed."

"I know, I heard. I told him to be careful. Maybe that gun had a bit too much power for him."

"Did you ever consider the consequences? That boy could have shot one of my children. My family attends that church."

"Heaven, what do you want me to say? I thought he understood."

"How do you know this kid is not going to crack under the pressure and tell the police everything?"

"This kid is tough. He has no family and has practically raised himself. No father. His mother is a regular customer. He's been in and out of foster homes his whole life. He's not going to break."

Heaven saw the ladies of the church leaving Corinne's. "What's up? Since it failed the first time, I owe you."

"Tyke, forget it. I got into this problem myself, I can get out myself." She ended the call.

Chapter 40

Tuesday was laundry day and Heaven had washed every dirty piece of clothing in the house. Samuel was at school, Imani was downstairs watching television, and Wesley was napping.

She walked into Imani's room to put her clothes away when she saw a picture of Celeste sitting on her night table. It bugged her every time she walked into one of the children's room and saw Hasani's dead wife smiling back at her. Looking at Celeste's picture made her feel inadequate; like she had to constantly compete with her ghost. Before Heaven moved in, Emalee had given the children portraits of their mother as a reminder of who their real mother was.

Heaven remembered how the women from the church ignored her at Corinne's. It really hurt her to hear them talk and laugh at her. Heaven was trying her hardest to fit in, but she could not be Celeste.

She walked over and picked up the picture of

Celeste and Hasani holding each other with love in their eyes. The way he looked at her was the way she wished he would look at her. The more she stared at their picture the angrier she got. She hated Celeste and wished she was more than dead. She wished she had never existed. She slammed the picture back down on the nightstand and turned to walk away, but she could still feel Celeste's eyes mocking her.

She snatched the glass frame, raised it high above her head, and smashed it against the nightstand. She did that repeatedly until there was glass all over the room. Then she took the photo and started to tear it into tiny pieces. She crumbled the photo in her hands. "I hate you!" she screamed. "I hate you! I hate you!" Hatred raged inside of her. Heaven was determined to make Celeste go away forever.

Imani heard Heaven screaming and ran to her room. When she got there, she saw Heaven down on her knees smashing Celeste's picture to pieces. She watched in horror and tears rolled down her face. When Heaven finally noticed what she was doing, she looked at all the blood on her hands from the cuts.

"Oh honey, I'm sorry."

Imani watched her carefully.

"I don't know what came over me." Heaven reached out to Imani and she ran away from her. Heaven heard the doorbell ring and then the front door open. "Imani, don't answer that door," she screamed.

"Hey pumpkin, where's everybody at?" Ebony's voice drifted up the stairs. The sound of footsteps climbing the stairs warned Heaven that Ebony was on her way up. She sat on the edge of Imani's bed holding her hand.

"What happened?" Ebony asked in horror when she saw all the blood.

"I had a slight accident."

She grabbed Heaven's hand and looked down at the shards of glass still lying on the floor. "You have to go to the hospital. These cuts look deep."

Ebony helped her up, gathered the children, and drove them to the emergency room. There was a long line when they arrived so they had to wait for Heaven's name to be called.

"What happened?" Ebony asked again.

"I told you, I had an accident," Heaven emphasized.

"No, what really happened?" Ebony asked. Heaven didn't know what to tell her because she wasn't sure herself.

"My new mommy was angry at my other mommy and she hit her picture and that's how she hurt her hand," Imani tattled as she ate potato chips from a bag.

"Is that what happened?" Ebony asked.

"Imani, why don't you go and see what toys they have in the play area while I talk with Ms. Ebony." Heaven pointed to an area specifically sectioned off for children.

Once she walked away, Heaven turned to Ebony. "I don't know what happened. I lost it. I'm so sick of seeing Celeste presented as the proverbial Virgin Mary. It's bad enough I have to continually prove myself at the church, but it was getting to me that I have to prove myself in my own house.

I shouldn't have to be haunted with pictures of Celeste all over."

"Well, she is the children's mother," Ebony replied.

"Yes, a mother who is dead," Heaven replied.

"Does this have anything to do with you seeing us at Corinne's yesterday?"

"That's part of it, but I'm tired of being treated like I'm the bad guy when I have done nothing wrong, but fall in love."

"Why don't you talk with Hasani about it?"

"I've been wanting to but I've been scared of what he's going to say."

"Well, you're going to have to tell him what happened to your hand. Now seems like the perfect time."

When Hasani got home at five o'clock, Imani ran to tell her father what happened while he was away. Heaven was in the kitchen and could hear Imani repeat the entire scenario. She detailed everything from Heaven screaming at the picture to them going to the emergency room. Next, she heard him tell her to sit down and then he walked into the kitchen.

"Is everything she said true?" Hasani asked when he came into the kitchen. He looked at the bandage on her arm. Heaven nodded her head. "I think you scared her."

"I scared myself. I didn't realize that looking at Celeste's picture every day was affecting me in such a way. My anger boiled over and I went crazy."

"Why didn't you tell me you were uncomfortable with the pictures of Celeste in the children's room?"

"I was scared of what you might say. I didn't want to upset you."

"Heaven, this is our house. You shouldn't feel uncomfortable in your own home. Emalee is the one who put pictures of Celeste in each one of the children's rooms. If that bothers you, we can take them down."

"Really?" She was surprised. "It's not that I don't want the children to remember Celeste. I just don't think it's healthy. I told you about my mother and it was very difficult being constantly reminded of her by Nana, but not have her around."

"I'm sure the children will understand," Hasani replied. Heaven kissed him on the cheek for being so understanding.

The following morning, after Hasani took Samuel to school, Heaven got up and put every picture and every knick-knack that was a reminder of Celeste in the basement.

Heaven wouldn't have to worry about Celeste again until Emalee realized what she had done.

"Excuse me." Emalee barged into the kitchen where Heaven was flipping through a new baby catalog. Wednesday was Emalee's regular day to spend time with the children. She usually took them out, but since the weather was unfavorable she stayed inside with them. "I just came from the children's room and the pictures I put of my sister-in-law are gone. Do you know what happened to them?"

"Emalee, I don't know if you've realized it or not, but I am now the woman of this house, not Celeste. I felt uncomfortable having pictures of my husband's dead wife all over the house, so I put them in the basement." Heaven challenged Emalee with her eyes.

Emalee laughed. "You felt uncomfortable having my sister-in-law's picture in her children's room, but you didn't feel uncomfortable moving into her house, you didn't feel uncomfortable marrying her husband less than seven months after her death, and you didn't feel uncomfortable sleeping in her bed," Emalee spat at her.

"Look Emalee, I know you're upset. But getting angry at me is not going to make the situation any better. You may as well get used to the idea. I'm here and I'm here to stay."

Emalee stormed out of the house without saying good-bye to the children. Heaven knew it was best for Emalee to leave before she got violent and did something she may regret later.

Chapter 41

Sunday had arrived again and Heaven walked into church late because she brought a special guest with her. Heaven, the kids, and her guest crept to her normal pew and took their seats. When Deacon Daniels stood to make the announcements he asked if there were any guests visiting the church for the first time.

The boy sitting next to Heaven stood up. "Hello, my name is Rocco and I was invited here by Mrs. Washington. I had no idea I was coming to church this morning," He chuckled at his supermarket smock and jeans. "But when she came into the store this morning and asked me to come to church with her, I felt like God was answering my prayers. I've only been to church maybe once or twice in my entire life, but the things going on in my life have made me seek God. My mom is sick. The doctor told her that she needs certain medications to get better, but my mom's insurance company won't approve the prescription." Tears welled up in Rocco's eyes. "They keep sending us letters saying they are not covered. I've called everyone I know, but no one will listen. Finally, I called on God."

Heaven cried and hugged Rocco.

The two of them sat down and a bunch of member's came over to introduce themselves and to give him hugs and kisses. A few members even reached out to Heaven and told her she did the right thing by asking Rocco to church.

Hasani came to them and reached out to shake the young man's hand, and then he kissed his wife. "I love you," he said.

Heaven didn't ask Rocco to come with her so Hasani would stop being mad with her. She asked him to come because her actions were wrong and she knew saying she was sorry wasn't enough.

Heaven rubbed her growing belly. It was getting bigger and bigger every day. She couldn't feel any movement yet, but it was evident there was life growing inside of her. At times she couldn't believe she was going to have another baby. Her growing baby and growing drug use were two worlds she wanted to keep separate from one another. That is why, in her fourth month of pregnancy, she hadn't been to any prenatal doctors visits. She was scared that once the doctors tested her blood she could no longer pretend she didn't know her baby was going to be born addicted to heroin.

She never made it to her first appointment because she was too high to even get out of the car. She sat in the parking garage sniffing dope up her nose and then she nodded out to sleep. By the time she awoke, all the cars were gone and she was the only one left. Heaven planned to reschedule her appointment, but the longer she waited, the harder it got.

Earlier that week, Hasani gave her money for a doctor's appointment she never had. She took the money and planned on getting high with it. She made a deal with a hooker to split the dope in exchange for her making the buy, but Heaven gave her the money and she never came back. That was all the money Heaven had, so she went without all week long. It was the longest she had gone without any drugs and she wasn't feeling that bad. The first few days she was a little irritable, but after that, she felt good.

The men's choir had begun to sing another hymn when Heaven's eyes focused on Levi standing in the front row of the choir box. His head kept bobbing up and down and he could barely keep his heavy eyes open. Heaven studied him for a moment. She knew the look. Those eyes were the eyes of an addict. She couldn't believe Levi was high in church. Ebony whispered in Heaven's ear, "Doesn't Levi seem different to you today?" She had the same thoughts Heaven had.

After church was dismissed, dozens more people came over to talk with Rocco. While they talked, Heaven excused herself so she and Ebony could corner Levi. "Hey, Levi." He was trying to hurry out the church. "What's up with you?"

"Hey, Mrs. Washington," he replied.

Ebony saddled up close to Levi. "Sister Washington and I were watching you his morning and we noticed that you had a hard time keeping your eyes open. It looks like you had a long night."

"As a matter of fact I did. I was out late with some friends. I should have made sure I went to bed early, but I'm going home right now to get some rest." He turned to leave, but Ebony stepped in his path.

"Levi," Ebony said. "You looked the same way I used to look when I was using drugs."

"Drugs?" He laughed. "Sister Collins, I don't use drugs."

"It didn't look that way to me."

Sister Stewart walked up behind them. Heaven was glad to see Sister Stewart. Levi couldn't fool her. Sister Stewart could spot drug use a mile away. The three of them had Levi surrounded and Heaven expected him to confess.

From over Ebony's shoulder, Heaven could see Emalee and Hasani engaged in a heated discussion. Emalee snapped her neck, waved her hands, and pointed her fingers in his face. It wasn't unusual for Emalee to be upset, but she usually directed her frustrations at Heaven and never her brother. Hasani looked like he was trying to calm her down, but there was no satisfying her. Heaven wondered what was going on.

Hasani then walked over to their small group. "Hello, Sister Stewart, Ebony, Levi, can I speak with my wife for a moment?"

"Sure, you two go ahead. Ebony and I can handle it from here." Sister Stewart and Ebony walked Levi to a secluded part of the church while Hasani pulled Heaven into an empty pew. They sat down.

"Honey, did you hear Rocco's testimony this morning? I feel so bad for the way I treated him. That poor kid has got so much going on right now. It must be hard for him to be so cheerful at work and then go home to see his mother suffering. Isn't there something we can do for him?" Heaven asked.

"Yes, the church is going to see if we can offer him any assistance, but there is something else I need to speak with you about." Heaven waited for him to apologize for the way he had been acting all week. "Heaven, did you notice how upset Emalee was this morning?"

"I saw she had an attitude, but that's nothing out of the ordinary; especially when it comes to me."

"Yeah, that's true, but sweetheart why didn't you tell me you were going to wear this . . ." He pointed to her dress. ". . . to church this morning?"

She looked down at her attire and was confused. "You're upset because I wore maternity clothes? You knew I was going to start showing soon. I thought we discussed this."

"No, I'm upset because you wore Celeste's maternity clothes to church this morning."

"Is that what Emalee is so upset about?"

"Well, can't you understand why she would be a little upset over this?"

Heaven thought she could get away with wearing one of Celeste's dresses without anyone noticing. She should have known Emalee would be the one to recognize her outfit.

Ever since she married Hasani, Emalee had

been a thorn in her side. She scrutinized everything Heaven said and did. Heaven wished she could find a way to get her out of her life.

"Hasani, I'm sorry. I only wore it because I didn't have anything else to wear. My waistline is expanding so quickly and I found a box of her things down in the basement so I figured I'd just throw this on for today and go buy myself some new things tomorrow. I didn't mean to upset Emalee."

"Well, to tell you the truth Heaven, you not only caught her off guard, but also me. It startled me when you walked into church this morning."

"Are you mad?"

"No, I'm not mad I just wish you would have said something to me before you did something like this. Emalee might not have been the only one who noticed you wearing Celeste's clothes."

"I would have told you, but you left early."

He sighed heavily. "Don't worry about it. It's a common mistake. I guess anybody would have done the same thing you did. From now on, can you just give me a heads up before you do anything like this?"

She leaned over and gave him a kiss. "Sure, honey."

"Before I forget to tell you, I'm going to ask Levi to take you and the children home in the church van, that way you can leave the car with me."

"You're not coming home with us?"

"No, Ebony and I are going to work together on preparations for the new daycare center and I don't expect to get home until later."

"How much later?" she asked.

"I'll be home in time for dinner."

Heaven felt uneasy about the two of them working together. As a matter of fact, she felt uneasy every time he mentioned her name. Although Ebony was her best friend, she couldn't help but remember how impressed he was with her when they were in membership classes together. He may have been attracted to her.

"I can see the concern on your face. If you're worried you won't be able to manage the children by yourself, I could ask Emalee to go home with you. I promise. She won't cause you any problems."

"I don't need her help. I'll see you when you get home." Heaven walked over to Hasani's mother. The children were gathered around her. "Children, could you go gather your things so that we can go home?" Heaven asked.

"No!" Samuel screamed through clenched teeth. He was getting more difficult to handle every day. Samuel never listened to anything Heaven said and screamed every time she wouldn't allow him to have his way. She felt like he was growing up to hate her.

"Heaven, if it's all right with you, Emalee is coming over my house for a while and I would love to spend some time with the children," Ms. Washington intervened.

"I don't know. You know we're supposed to get that really bad snow storm tonight," she replied.

"Isn't Hasani staying late to work at the church tonight? He can pick them up on his way home. This will give you the chance to get some rest," she reasoned.

"Please!" Imani pleaded. Heaven could never

tell her no, so she allowed them to go. Then she made sure to tell Hasani where he could pick the children up.

Heaven grabbed Rocco and the two of them joined Levi in the church vestibule. When he saw her coming he looked behind her. "Deacon Washington said you and the children needed a ride," he said

"They're going to spend the afternoon at their grandmother's, but we need to drop Rocco off at work."

"Cool. Since it's just you two, I can take my car. That way I won't have to come back here."

After they dropped Rocco off, Heaven talked with Levi. "What did the ladies say to you?"

"Well, you know how loud Sister Stewart is. She came down hard on me. She told me she never wanted to see me like that again. I told her I wasn't doing anything, but she didn't believe me. She thinks I would lie in church."

"Would you?" Heaven asked.

"I didn't really lie."

"Well, what is it that had you nodding all morning?"

"I told the ladies it was cough medicine, but the truth is, I had taken a few Valiums last night, that's all, nothing big."

Prescription pills. She forgot they made people high. She wondered if he could get his hands on some OxyContin for her.

He pulled into her driveway. Heaven was scared to approach Levi because she wasn't sure if she could trust him but it wasn't going to hurt anything if she asked him a question. "Do you have any pills on you right now?"

"Mrs. Washington, I don't carry that kind of stuff around with me."

She knew he was lying. When Heaven frowned down at him he dug into his pocket and pulled out a baggie full of different colored pills.

"Are there any OxyContin in here?" She took the bag from him and carefully looked through the bag.

"Why? Is that what you're looking for?" Heaven got out the car and hurried to the house, but before she went in Levi called out to her, "Ms. Washington, we're having a farm party at this address in a few weeks. You can come if you want. A lot of kids usually show up and we have a lot of fun." He had written the address down on a piece of paper.

"Thanks, Levi. This sounds like fun."

Chapter 42

When Heaven walked in the house she went straight to bed. She was so tired. The further along she got into her pregnancy, the more tired she got. She took a nap and didn't wake up until later that evening when Hasani walked into their bedroom. "Hey baby, I didn't mean to wake you."

"That's okay. What time is it?"

"Almost ten o'clock."

"Wow. I must have been really tired. I didn't realize I had slept for so long. Did you pick the children up?"

"Yes, and when I did, Emalee brought up the subject of my mother living with us again."

"Hasani, I thought we agreed that I'm in no condition to care for three kids and keep an eye on your mother, especially when I have another baby on the way."

"I know, I tried to explain that to her, but she just doesn't understand."

"Why doesn't she move in with her?"

"I don't know. I think it would be a good thing for her to live with Mom. That way she could keep an eye on her. It's not going to be too long before she is going to need someone to watch over her full time and I would prefer it be Emalee instead of a stranger who doesn't know us or Mom. Have you noticed how much weight my mom has lost? The dementia seems to be getting worse."

"She is looking thin."

"That's because my mom hasn't been eating. Emalee said when they go out for a meal mom won't eat because she thinks she's already eaten. She keeps forgetting to feed herself. That worries me because there could be other important things she is forgetting."

Heaven wanted to change the subject. "Is it snowing outside?"

"Yes, the weather man said that Jersey may get up to three feet of snow. I'm not going in to work tomorrow and I'm sure the schools will be closed."

"It'll be nice to have everyone home on a snow day."

Hasani snuggled up close to her and wrapped his arms around her swollen tummy. "I was really proud of the way you reached out to that kid." He nibbled on her ear.

She pulled back to look him in the face.

"What's wrong?" he asked. "Is the baby all right?"

"No, I'm fine. You're the one that is acting strange. I've never seen you act like this before."

"When I looked at you from the pulpit today it was if I was seeing you for the very first time. You looked radiant."

"Maybe it was because I had on Celeste's clothes."

"No. This has nothing to do with Celeste. I never thought I could love anyone as much as I loved Celeste, but now I know I was wrong in thinking that way. I know it's been hard for you to live in Celeste's shadow, but I want you to know that I'm in love with you. I didn't marry you because you were pregnant with my child, but because of who you are on the inside."

That was the sweetest thing he had ever said to her. They kissed and she slowly unbuttoned his shirt. "Where are the children? I don't want them to walk in on us."

"Sound asleep," he replied.

He took his time, gently kissing every part of her body; even kissing her stretch marks. He massaged her thighs, legs, and breasts with baby oil. While kissing on her belly, he talked to the baby, "Hey, little fella. I hope you're all right in there," Hasani joked.

Heaven laughed, "How do you know it's a boy?"

"I don't; it could be a girl." He placed his lips on her belly and sucked hard forcing her to laugh. ". . . and if it's a girl, she is going to be just as beautiful as her mommy."

Hasani took his wife in his arms and made love to her for the first time ever. They had engaged in sex before but this was the first time Heaven felt like he was actually making love to her. Their sexual escapade on this cold snowy night was something she had never experienced before. It was a pleasure she would never forget.

Hasani had fallen asleep and the sweet aroma of their love still lingered in the air. While lying in her husband's arms Heaven could feel the bad vibes she often felt by living in Celeste's house lift from off her shoulders. She could see Celeste's presence fading from the lives in the house. The way Hasani made love to her was proof that he was finally letting Celeste go. For the first time she felt like she belonged with this man and his children.

Hasani stirred in his sleep. He was surprised to see Heaven awake. "What are you doing up?"

"Just thinking, about how much I love you."

"I love you too."

He fell back to sleep and Heaven laid in his arms for another hour before she got up. She quietly crept down to the kitchen with her purse. Heaven sat at the kitchen table and pulled out the small baggie full of the pills Levi had given her. There were several different kinds and colors of pills. She wondered what they were. She poured herself a glass of water and took all twelve pills at once. Her eyesight blurred in front of her. She felt dizzy and she had to put her head down. She didn't expect the pills to take effect so soon.

The phone rang loudly in her ear. She quickly answered before it woke up the entire house.

"Hello?" Her voice was groggy and she sounded like she was sleep.

"Hello, Heaven. I'm sorry for calling so early in the morning, but I was hoping to speak with Hasani."

"He's asleep right now." Heaven was short with her mother-in-law.

"Well, I think the oil in my heating tank has run out and I don't have any heat in my house. It's getting colder and colder in here by the minute. I know it's hard for anyone to get out with the amount of snow that has fallen, but I was hoping he would know somebody to call. It's an emergency."

Heaven didn't hear anything that Ms. Washington said. "Ms. Washington, I'll tell him you called." She hung up the phone and passed out at the kitchen table.

Heaven was asleep for hours and when she woke up she was back in her bed. She turned over to wrap her arms around Hasani but he was gone. Heaven lay in the bed for a while before the smell of bacon and eggs called her downstairs. The children were watching cartoons in the living room and a fire blazed in the fireplace.

In the kitchen she found her husband behind the stove. "What are you doing this morning?"

"I'm cooking lunch for my beautiful wife. Have you seen her?" He laughed. "I thought we would have a stress free, work free day."

The clock said it was after one o'clock in the afternoon. It had been a while since Heaven had slept so late. It must have been those pills.

"You know I found you down here knocked out at the table." He pointed toward the table with a spatula in his hand.

"I was wondering how I made it back upstairs."

"I knew you were tired. We can blame you being worn out on either the pregnancy or the love making we had last night." Hasani grinned. He grabbed her by the arm and turned her in the direction of the living room. "Now you go back into the living room while I finish up here, but first I'm going to give my mom a call." Heaven's face turned pale. He saw the look on her face. "What's wrong?"

"The baby kicked me really hard," Heaven lied.

"I told you we have a football player in there." He dialed his mother's number. "Let me make sure my mom is all right. The weatherman said it snowed over three feet. "

Heaven remembered talking with Ms. Washington but she couldn't recall the exact details of their conversation. She did remember her saying the words emergency. Heaven prayed her mother-in-law was all right.

"She didn't answer. Let me call Emalee, maybe she's heard from her." He called his sister. "Emalee, have you talked to Mom?" His eyes fell and Heaven got nervous. Heaven was scared that Ms. Washington told Emalee she had spoken with her last night. Hasani was going to want to know why she didn't wake him. "All right, Emalee. Don't worry. Neither of us can get over there now because the state has declared a state of emergency, because of all the snow. I'll call down to the police station and see if there is anything they can do."

Hasani called the police station and spoke with a long time friend of his who was a sergeant in the department. Wesley was crying and probably hungry, so Heaven carried him into the kitchen and put him in his high chair. Hasani called his sister back. "Sergeant Jenson said he would send somebody around there to check in on her but they are busy so it may take a while. I'll give you a call as soon as I hear something."

A few hours later the sergeant called back and told Hasani he sent a few uniformed men over to his mom's house. When she didn't answer the door, the police had to break it down to get in.

They found her lying on the couch barely breathing. Apparently she had been inside that cold house all night. The officers said it felt like the cold wind was blowing right through the house. She was taken to Cooper Hospital.

As soon as the roads cleared, Hasani picked up Emalee and they went to the hospital.

Hasani called Heaven from the hospital to give her an update on his mother's condition. "Heaven, my mother keeps saying that she talked with you last night."

"She said that?" Heaven's heart dropped to her knees.

"Yes, but the doctor said it could be the dementia. She forgets things and imagines others. She must have forgotten to pay her oil bill. I feel so guilty. I should have been following up on her bills. It was foolish of me to take her word that she had paid things." Hasani blamed himself. "Somebody should have stayed with her last night. The doctor said she's in bad shape. When she fell asleep the cold made its way into her bones and that wasn't good for her legs. She has a really bad case of hyperthermia."

"Is she going to be all right?" Heaven asked.

"Well, the doctor estimates she was in the house for at least eight to ten hours before anyone found her. It looks like she has frostbite on the lower extremities of her body, particularly her legs. They tried everything to revive her legs but it was impossible. They had to amputate her legs."

Heaven gasped.

"They had no choice. It was either her legs or her life." Hasani sighed. "She is aware of the surgery and I'm surprised her spirits are high. I told the doctor I wanted to be the one who told her and when I did she told me, 'Don't you look so down. It's okay, it was only my legs.' "

"At least she took the news well."

"Yes, I'm glad for that. Emalee and I are going to spend the night up here with her and then I'll give you a call in the morning."

Chapter 43

After Hasani's mom was released from the hospital, Emalee was forced to move in with her. Heaven felt this was God's way of taking care of her problem with Emalee. Emalee would be too busy caring for her mom to worry about what Heaven was doing. She was thankful that Hasani's sister would now be out of her hair.

It was late in the afternoon and Heaven was on her way to pick up the children. Hasani had asked Emalee to keep them while Heaven went to her doctor's appointment.

Heaven skipped out on another appointment and bought some dope. She enjoyed her day. She went home and got high in the privacy of her bathroom.

Emalee left Heaven a message for her to pick up the children from the church's new daycare center on Cooper Street. Emalee had been hired as a teacher. She and Ebony had spent the day cleaning and getting the place ready for opening day.

Heaven got out of her car and walked in the front doors. She was still a little jealous over Ebony getting that position, but she was trying not to dwell on it.

From the entrance, she could hear Emalee talking. Heaven stood at the door and listening. "I know that's your friend, but does she realize she's twenty-nine not nineteen? The first time I saw her was at my sister-in-law's funeral. She wore this black wrap around dress that was too small for her big behind. The material was so flimsy I could see the cellulite in her thighs."

Ebony laughed in the background.

"Why did you allow her to go out looking that way? Does she think she's cute?" Emalee asked.

"You know what? I don't judge people on what they want to wear because I'm so big I probably couldn't fit my arm in that dress. You should get to know Heaven. She is really a nice person. We became really close when we were in the halfway house together. "

"Everyone knows I don't like Heaven. For some reason, she is not who I saw my brother taking as his next bride. You want to hear something funny?"

"Sure," Ebony replied.

"When I met you at the funeral, I was sure God had sent you to be with Hasani."

Ebony laughed and Heaven's eyes grew.

"I don't trust that Heaven. She's ugly; with all the bumps and scars on her face from the acne. The only reason any man would be attracted to her is because of her light complexion and those green eyes."

"I never told anyone this, but I was attracted to your brother. I thought he was an honorable man with three of the most beautiful children."

"I knew it," Emalee screamed.

"But the time of our meeting wasn't right and when it was, he was already interested in Heaven. He now belongs to her."

Heaven had heard enough. She knocked loudly on the door and all talking came to a halt. Imani ran from the corner of the room, "She's here!" she cheered.

Heaven bent down and gave her a big hug. "Hey, Baby, are you ready to go?"

The four-year-old quickly shook her head.

Emalee was standing on a ladder stapling construction cutouts to the wall. When she saw Heaven, she stepped down. "How was your appointment?"

Heaven was upset by what she'd overheard, but she shouldn't have been surprised. Emalee never hid how she felt about her. Heaven's jaw tightened around her words, "I'm good and the baby is fine. Can you get the children ready? I have to go." She was stern with her request.

"Let me get their coats." Emalee picked up Wesley from out of the playpen and asked Imani to follow her into the next room.

Heaven walked around the room examining all the new renovations. It looked as if they could open any day. Ebony had done a lot to change the place around. Brightly colored cartoon characters covered the walls and multi-colored miniature desks and chairs were scattered around the room. They had even set up a space for the teacher's lounge.

"It looks good in here, Ebony."

"Thanks, but a lot of this was done by your husband. He insisted on staying with me. It required a lot of late nights, but it was worth it." She sipped on her coffee. "Do you know what you're having?" She pointed to Heaven's stomach.

"No, we want it to be a surprise. Hasani told me you have a hearing today regarding visitation with your son."

"Yes, I have to take a drug test this morning. I've been jumping through hoops for these people, but so far, my case manager said everything is going well and this position I got through the church has really helped. All I have to do is pass the drug test and the courts will make arrangements for my first visit with my son for this weekend."

"That's wonderful."

"Yes, and I owe a lot to you and Hasani. You both have been great; especially your husband. Did he tell you he was going to take some time off from work to be there with me during the hearing?"

"No, he didn't tell me that." Heaven was surprised. "Hasani didn't mention it." Heaven wasn't sure if he purposely didn't tell her or if it slipped his mind, but whatever the reason, she thought he and Ebony were getting too close and spent too much time together. They'd been working fourteen hours a day trying to get the daycare center together.

"It's almost time for my appointment." Ebony looked at the clock and took another sip of her coffee.

"Ebony, can you help me find the children's coats? I don't know where they're at," Emalee yelled from the next room.

Ebony ran to help Emalee, leaving Heaven all alone. Heaven couldn't help but think about Ebony's words. Her interest and gratitude toward Hasani worried her. Heaven hoped she failed her test. If she failed, then the church would have to get rid of her and find someone else to fill the director's spot. Heaven eyed Ebony's coffee cup, opened up her purse, and pulled out the last twenty bag of heroin she had bought. She didn't want to waste her dope on Ebony, but she felt like life was treating Ebony too good. She spent a great amount of time with someone else's husband, everyone liked her, she had a great job, and she was about to get visitation with her son. Heaven wanted her to know what disappointment felt like. She poured the half the dope into the Styrofoam cup Ebony was drinking from, stirred it with a stirrer that was lying nearby, and replaced the lid. By the time Ebony, Emalee, and the children returned she was patiently waiting.

"Are you guys ready to go?" Heaven asked the children. She took Wesley from Emalee's arms and watched as Ebony finished off the rest of her coffee.

"I'll walk out with you if you'd like," Ebony said to Heaven.

"I would like that."

Chapter 44

Heaven stopped by the school to pick Samuel up before heading home. When they walked in the house Samuel started his homework and Imani went to her bedroom to play. Heaven was playing with the baby in the living room when her husband came in and walked straight back to his study.

When Hasani had bad news, he had a habit of going straight to his Bible and reading the book of Job. Reading about Job's unshakable faith during the adversities that fell upon him was an example of how he could also endure his own trials in life.

When Heaven got up to ask Hasani what he wanted for dinner, she saw his Bible flipped open to the book of Job.

"What happened?" She knew something was bothering him.

"Ebony failed her drug test today." Hasani stopped reading and she could see how disappointed he was.

"Oh no!" Heaven put her hand to her heart as though she was surprised.

"They found traces of heroin in her system. It wasn't a lot, but enough."

"What's going to happen to her?"

"Because she's still on parole, she has to see her parole officer and she may end up going back to jail."

"Did you ask her about it?"

"Of course, and she swears she hasn't used any drugs. I thought there may have been a mix up at the lab but her case manager said that the lab has less than a one percent error rate. She left the courtroom in tears, but you should have seen her husband. He caused a scene outside the courtroom by stepping in Ebony's face and yelling that she would never see her son because she was nothing but an addict."

"Can he keep Ebony away from her son?"

"Yes he can. I don't know what happened but this will set her back. I can't help but think this is the church's fault. She has been taking on a lot of extra responsibilities with the new daycare center and maybe it just got to be too much for her. She needs a friend. I think you ought to go see her."

"I don't know, honey. She might want to be alone."

"Sweetheart, if you don't go talk with her, I think she may do something drastic."

"Like what?" Heaven asked.

"I don't know and I don't want to find out."

* * *

The first place Heaven checked was Nana's house. Nana said Ebony had been there earlier but left upset. Heaven went by the church, a few local restaurants, and she even called Emalee. When everyone said they hadn't seen or heard from her, Heaven wondered where she could be.

Heaven went by a few well known drug corners thinking maybe Ebony had gone there, but she saw no sign of her. When Heaven passed one drug corner she had to drive down a dark secluded one way street in order to get back to the main road. There were a lot of abandoned houses on the street and when she reached the middle of the block she saw two people coming out of one of the vacant houses.

She looked a little closer and noticed one of them was Ebony. Ebony stumbled out of the crack house laughing and giggling. She looked a mess. Her hair was wild and she was hugging on some guy with braids in his hair. Heaven couldn't believe Ebony would revert back to her old ways. She watched her trip over her own feet and fall to the ground.

Heaven stopped the car and shouted, "Ebony."

"Who dat?" Ebony shouted in Heaven's direction while clinging to her friend for safety.

Heaven got out of her car and ran onto the sidewalk underneath the street light. "Ebony."

Ebony squeezed her eyes tightly shut and quickly shot them open. "Hey, Mrs. Washington," she said in a derisive manner.

"What are you doing out here?" Heaven asked.

"I hooked up with an old friend of mine and . . ."

she looked over her shoulder at her friend and they both laughed together. "We've been catching up on old times."

"Come on, baby." The six foot tall guy tugged on Ebony's clothes. "I thought you were coming home with me."

"Heaven, I have to go," Ebony shouted. Heaven got back in her car and watched them stagger up the street together. She was angry. It wasn't supposed to work out this way. Ebony was supposed to be hurt from not being able to see her son. Heaven should have found her in tears; instead, she was treating herself by getting high. Ebony cheated Heaven out of seeing her in pain. Even if she could have seen Ebony struggle with the desire to use then that would have been gratifying, but for Ebony to willfully cave in wasn't enough.

Heaven got in her car and planned to go home. There was nothing more she could do. As a matter of fact, she didn't care what Ebony did. That was on her. But the more Heaven thought about it, the more upset she got. She turned her car around. Ebony had to suffer some kind of consequences for her actions. Heaven started looking for her again. She searched the streets and immediately found Ebony and her friend strutting together down Morgan Boulevard. Heaven pulled over and rolled down the window. "Get in this car right now," she ordered.

Ebony squinted at Heaven before she recognized her. "Hey." She sounded drunk. Ebony stopped walking and got in the car without saying a word to her friend. She laid her head back on the seat and closed her eyes. "It feels so good in here."

Heaven drove to Elgin's diner.

Once they were seated, Heaven ordered a glass of orange juice for herself and a mug of black coffee for Ebony.

The smell of freshly brewed coffee woke Ebony up. "That smells good," she said.

They watched the waitress fill her cup and place Heaven's orange juice in front of her. Once the waitress was gone, Ebony lifted her mug underneath her nose and looked Heaven in the eye.

"Did you drug me?" Ebony asked.

Heaven was surprised by Ebony's question. She diverted her eyes to avoid looking Ebony straight in the face. She was scared her eyes would tell on her. "Excuse me?"

"Did you drug me? I've been thinking about this all day. I'm no dummy. You could have slipped something in my coffee this morning. That is the only way those test results would have found something in my system. Why would you do that? I thought you were my friend."

Heaven reasoned that Ebony was high and not really aware of what she was saying. Although she was telling the truth, Heaven couldn't admit to anything. Ebony was a smart girl. She should have known she would have figured it out.

"Ebony, do you think I would drug you?"

Ebony tried looking her in the eye, but Heaven kept her attention focused elsewhere.

"Don't try to place this blame on me. Maybe it's like you said, God is punishing you."

When Heaven said that, she could see the effect of her words. Ebony suddenly looked ashamed.

"Ebony, God is very upset with you and he is not going to forgive you for the things you've done."

Ebony covered her face with her hands. "God is going to forgive me," she mumbled. "Just like I'm sure He has forgiven you."

Heaven gave her a quizzical look.

"I knew you were using when we were in the halfway house and I'm sure that if I knew so did everyone else in the house."

"That's not true."

"Sure it is. Plenty of nights when you thought I was 'sleep I could hear you go into the bathroom to get high. If God can forgive you, I'm sure He'll excuse me this one time."

"Ebony, I hate to tell you this, but I haven't used since that time with Zaria. I don't know what you think you saw or heard, but I've worked hard to stay clean. I'm not like you, I didn't stumble at the first sign of trouble. I'm baptized and married to a righteous man, so even if I did get high once He'll forgive me before He forgives you."

Addicts have an uncanny ability to tell when they are being told a lie. Heaven knew she wasn't fooling anybody but herself. She refused to talk about her moments of weakness and concentrated on keeping the attention focused on Ebony.

"What happened, you were doing so well?"

"Heaven, I don't know what happened today." Ebony went from sounding accusatory to regretful. "I lost my son, and then I lost control. The next thing I know, I was buying a bag of crystal meth."

"What happened to you being strong and enduring through the hurt and pain?"

Ebony cried in her seat and then Heaven's cell phone rang.

"Heaven, where are you?" Hasani asked from the other end.

"I'm at the diner with Ebony."

"It's kind of late for you to be out by yourself." He sounded like he was concerned.

"Yes, but there are some things I need to talk with Ebony about."

Hasani could hear her cries in the background. "Is everything all right? Do you need me to come there?"

"No. I'm helping Ebony work through some problems. I'll be home soon." She hung up before he could ask any more questions.

Ebony was stronger than what she appeared to be but Heaven planned on making sure Ebony lost all self-confidence by the end of the night. "Ebony, you know just as well as I do that losing control is an excuse to revert to your old ways. Using drugs and throwing yourself a pity party is being self centered."

"I'm sorry," she cried.

"No, you can not apologize for this. This is a mistake that may cost you God's love. Was getting high worth you losing God's love?" Ebony looked at her through watery eyes. "I think God made a mistake by choosing you to be one of His children."

"What?" Ebony shrieked.

"You heard me. I don't think God wants you to be one of His children any longer. I wouldn't be surprised if He didn't love you any more."

Tears rolled down her face. She was sobbing

and grabbed a few napkins to wipe her face. Heaven was relentless and would not let up. She wanted Ebony to hurt the same way she hurt when she saw her at Corinne's with all the women from the church.

"If you want God to forgive you then you have to stop this." Heaven said to her.

"I'll do whatever I have to do. I don't want to lose God's love."

Ebony's voice was filled with sorrow. She sounded sincerely sorry for what she had done.

"Ebony, I'm going to drop you off at Nana's and I want you to meet me at the church tomorrow afternoon. I'm going to help you fix this. Okay?" Heaven stood up and gathered her things.

Ebony didn't move from her seat. Instead, she stared out the window at the passing cars. Heaven wondered what had caught her eye and when she looked out the window she saw one car veer into oncoming traffic and strike another car head on.

"Oh my goodness!" Heaven screamed. "Someone dial 9-1-1." Patrons in the diner ran to the window to see what the commotion was about. Ebony didn't flinch. They watched as the ambulance and police came. Bodies were pulled out of the wreckage and covered with white sheets.

"Do you think the people who died in that car crash were saved?" she asked rhetorically. "Do you think they're going to heaven? Do you think because of all the wrong I've done that when I die I won't go to heaven?"

Heaven stared at her, "Ebony, I can't answer those questions. We'll just have to wait and see."

* * *

The following day Heaven pulled up to the church right on time for her meeting with Ebony. It had been a hectic day for her. Imani didn't want to get up this morning and Wesley refused to stay with the sitter. After getting the children settled she was able to run a few errands. She was hoping things would go a lot smoother with Ebony.

Heaven had thought about what she had done to Ebony overnight and she felt horrible. Her intention was to make Ebony feel bad about herself, not make her feel like God didn't love her. She regretted telling her those lies about God. All she wanted was for Ebony to go away. Her goal today was to convince Ebony to move away. She would tell her it was best for her move to another town and start over.

Heaven parked her car in front of the church. On her way inside, she saw George, the church's handyman, fiddling inside his work truck.

"Hello, George,"

"Hey, Mrs. Washington, how are you doing today?"

"I'm doing all right, but every day it gets a little harder for me to get around." She rubbed her belly. George had always been one of the few members Heaven was friendly with.

"I understand. My wife and I had seven children and I think she said with each pregnancy it got easier and easier."

"Well, I don't know about that, George. After this one Hasani and I are going to take a break. Four kids in one house is a lot."

"I agree with you there."

She waddled away.

"Mrs. Washington, if you're going into the church be careful. I have a lot of tools lying around in the sanctuary. Reverend Stansfield asked me to take down the ceiling fans. I think he wants to put them up in the new church."

"Oh, yes I did hear him say something about that. I was supposed to meet Ebony Collins here; perhaps we can meet somewhere else."

"Oh Ebony, she's already inside. I think she's in the sanctuary waiting on you."

"Okay, I'm just going to go get her so we can get going." Heaven slowly climbed the stairs and entered the church. Heaven took off her sunglasses and gasped loudly at the horrific sight in front of her. She grabbed one of the pews and leaned against it for support so that her legs would not fall out from underneath her. Ebony's body hung from a rope tied around her neck. She swung in the air suspended from the rafters.

Chapter 45

A paramedic handed Heaven an oxygen mask to help with her breathing. Since discovering Ebony's body she had been short winded. She pushed the mask away and bent down as far as her waist line would allow her to go. "I'll take it," Hasani told the medic. He pushed her shoulders back and made her use the mask. "Honey, this will help." He placed it over her face and she inhaled deeply and finally regained control of her breathing.

"Mr. Washington, it's official. The coroner has declared the victim's death a suicide by hanging," an officer reported. Heaven cried some more and Hasani pulled her closer to his chest. The officer then held out a slip of paper to her. "Mrs. Washington, she left a note addressed to you."

Slowly taking the note from the officer Heaven opened it up. Inside Ebony had written, "Proverbs 26:24-26 People with hate in their hearts may sound pleasant enough, but don't believe them.

Though they pretend to be kind, their hearts are full of all kinds of evil. While their hatred may be concealed by trickery, it will finally come to light for all to see."

"Heaven, why would she leave you a note like this?" Hasani inquired. "Do you think she's talking about herself?"

"I'm not sure." Heaven folded the note and slipped it in her purse. Heaven knew she had pushed Ebony, but she never thought Ebony would do this to herself.

"She fooled us all; especially me. We spent so much time together and I never thought she would take her own life. Perhaps I was blinded by her positive attitude and great outlook on life. That was just a disguise to cover up the truth of her using drugs again. I feel like a fool. How did she appear when you were with her last night?"

"Fine," Heaven wiped a few more tears away from her face. "A little down because of her son, but she didn't say anything along the lines of suicide."

Hasani hugged her tighter. "I'm sorry, honey. This must be hard for you. I know how close the two of you were."

She closed her eyes. "Yes, it's really hard," she mumbled.

Since finding Ebony's body, Heaven hadn't used once. Times like these, when she felt guilty, sad, and hurt, she needed to block out the world and the only way to do that was to get high. She wanted to get high, but she couldn't because no one would leave her alone. Someone was with her at all times. If it wasn't one of the children, it was Hasani, Sister Stewart, or Nana. Heaven felt like everyone was scared she was going to start using again because of Ebony's death, but what they didn't know was that she was already using.

It was so sad having to put a good friend like Ebony in the ground. Ebony's funeral wasn't elaborate, but very warm. Just like her. The church was full of every kind of yellow flower. Reverend Stansfield said the yellow represented her everyday smile.

The most upsetting thing for Heaven was seeing Ebony's ex-husband show up with their son. The only time he would allow their son to see his mother was in a casket.

Heaven lay in her bed and turned on the television.

"Honey, do you want me to run you a bath?" Hasani asked. "You look stressed."

Heaven was stressed, but that was because she hadn't used in almost six days. "No!" she screamed.

He felt the tension in the room and left her alone. "I'll go make the kids dinner."

Hasani left and Heaven lay on the bed watching television. Imani came into the room and asked if she could she watch TV with her. Heaven allowed her to come in. Imani climbed onto bed next to Heaven and they watched the news. Heaven wasn't really watching the program. She was trying to think of a way to get out of the house without anyone wanting to go with her. Then a plan came to mind.

"Hasani." As soon as she yelled for him, he came and stood in their bedroom doorway. "I changed my mind. I would like a bath."

"I'm glad you changed your mind. I think it will relax you." He left and a few seconds later she could hear him running bath water. Imani had fallen asleep, so while Hasani was in the bathroom, she slipped downstairs grabbed her keys off the key rack and went out the door without anyone noticing.

She got in her car and when she hit the end of her block she realized she didn't have her purse with her. She searched the car and realized she didn't have any money. No debit card, driver's license, or anything.

She punched her fist against her hand. She had to get some drugs. This could be her only chance to get high. She started driving and ended up back on Tyke's block. Heaven pulled over and got out. She looked for Fitch since he seemed to be in charge. She walked up to him. "Remember me?" she asked him.

He looked at her face for a brief second then went back to watching the fellows on the corner.

"Listen, I need for you to do me a favor. I'm broke, I don't have no money on me. I need you to extend me some credit until I get my hands on some cash."

He still didn't say anything. He just sat there. "Listen, you can call Tyke and ask him if it's all right. I'm sure he'll be okay with it."

Fitch ignored her. She was desperate and had to get her hands on some dope. She got in his face.

"Get Tyke for me now," she screamed, but he didn't budge.

Heaven slapped her leg. She was out of options. This kid wasn't going to give her anything. She thought about asking one of the other kids hustling for some credit, but that became an afterthought when a couple pushed by her in a hurry. The pair quickly purchased some drugs and walked away with that small plastic baggy in their hands. Jealousy, anger, and fear consumed Heaven. That's when she lost it and went crazy on that corner. She balled her hand into a fist and stepped in front of the woman. She looked at Heaven wondering what she wanted. Then Heaven pulled her hand back and punched the woman in the center of her chest. She had already sized up the woman, who probably weighed less than one hundred and ten pounds. She was sure she wouldn't fight her back, but Heaven didn't think about the man who was with her.

As soon as Heaven snatched the dope from the woman's fingers, that big, brawly man slapped her with his open hand. Blood spattered from Heaven's mouth and over her clothes. She felt her mouth balloon. The guys out on the corner were laughing at her. She turned to run, but before she could get away he slapped her again. This time her body slammed into the ground. He reached down and took back the drugs they had purchased. He helped his woman step over her body.

Heaven lay on the sidewalk, still in a daze from the butt kicking she had just received. She should have left after the kid refused to give her anything. Cold chills seeped into her bones from the concrete.

She glanced up and the kid turned his back to her. Heaven crawled over to a stop sign that sat on the corner and used it to help pull herself up off the ground. Her mouth was full of blood. She'd had enough of the corner so she staggered back to her car.

Tears blurred her vision as she slowly drove home. When she entered the house Hasani rushed to her side. "Heaven, where did you go? You took off and . . ." He saw the bruises on her face. "What happened?" He wiped blood off her face. "The baby! We have to take you to the hospital."

"No," she cried. "I'm fine. I just need to go to bed." Heaven was going to lie to him and tell him some thugs tried to carjack her, but she was tired of lying. She placed her head on his shoulder and cried.

Chapter 46

It was Heaven's first Sunday back in church in over a month. She refused to go out in public with the bruises from her beating still visible on her face. She hid in the house until her face healed.

A lot of people asked about her, but Hasani made excuses for her absence. The night following her beating, Heaven confessed to Hasani that she'd had a moment of weakness and was going to go buy some drugs. She described in detail how some users on the corner attacked her for no reason at all. He was very understanding and suggested she start seeing a therapist. She agreed.

This Sunday the church had arranged to do a small tribute to Ebony for the numerous things she did for the church. Heaven was still curious about who Avery was going to ask to replace Ebony. Since they hadn't asked her, she figured Avery was still blocking her from being nominated

Avery got up and said a lot of kind things about Ebony and afterward, he asked Heaven to say a prayer for her. Heaven asked everyone to bow their heads. She thanked the Lord for Ebony's friendship and for the way she brightened the lives of everyone she came into contact with. While she was praying she looked up to see a lot of people shed tears for Ebony. It was a shame Ebony would never know how many people treasured her. Heaven was about to bring her prayer to a close when she looked to the back of the church and saw Tyke looking inside the church doors from the vestibule.

She knew he was there to see her. Heaven quickly said amen and rushed out the church to catch him before he could slip away. Spring was right around the corner and Heaven could smell the flowers on the verge of blooming in the air. A strong wind blew through her hair. She looked up and down the street for his truck, but saw no sign of him. Heaven walked to the corner but she still didn't see him hanging around. She didn't know where he went, but she knew she could catch him on the block later. It would be hard for her to sneak away, but she would think of an excuse.

When she turned to walk back toward the church she heard his voice behind her, "Hey Heaven." She stopped in her tracks and prayed her ears were deceiving her. When she turned around it was Chrome. It had been such a long time since they stood face to face. The last time they were together they were two completely different people. When she saw him at the park the day she was with Davis she hoped to never see his face again.

He looked the same; except he had a bald head

and little extra weight had softened his mid section, but he still looked good.

"Chrome," she softly whispered. His eyes searched hers to see if she was happy to see him or not. "You look good," she said. Chrome had been her man for years before he abandoned her and never came home. "What are you doing here?" she asked.

"I came to speak with you," he replied. "I see you're doing well for yourself." He looked down at her bulging belly.

"I've been doing okay."

"Heaven, I need to speak with you."

"About what?"

"I think you already know the answer to that."

"Heaven." The sound of Emalee's voice made Heaven cringe. She spun around to see her standing behind her. "My brother asked me to come outside and make sure you were all right. Is everything okay?"

Heaven didn't think things could get any worse than they were at that moment. "Emalee, everything is fine. I'll only be a few more minutes."

Emalee watched her and Chrome cautiously. She was always trying to catch Heaven doing something. Emalee slowly inched her way back to the church. Once she was far enough away, Heaven whispered to Chrome, "I can't talk right now."

"Then I'll wait. I'm not going anywhere until I speak with you."

Chrome was stubborn and she knew when he said something he meant it. She took a deep breath, "Meet me after church down by the battleship at Wiggins Park. I'll be there as soon as I can."

* * *

Once church let out Heaven lied and told Hasani she was going to attend a support group for recovering addicts. She left the children with him and told him she would meet him back at the house. As she approached the church's exit doors she heard Avery call out her name.

She hadn't spoken to him since he threatened to tell Hasani about her and Davis. She was going to keep walking, but he placed his hand on her shoulder and asked her to come to his office. There was something important he needed to talk with her about.

"Avery, whatever it is can wait. There is someplace important I need to be."

"Heaven, this will only take a minute. I need to apologize to you." She was shocked and thought she had heard him wrong. Once they reached his office he closed the door behind her.

"I'm not going to keep you long. I know the last time we met it wasn't under the best of circumstances. I came down on you kind of hard." Heaven rolled her eyes and looked away from him. "What happened with Sister Collins has got me to thinking. She had so much going on in her life that I never thought she may have needed someone to listen. It's tragic. Her whole life was unraveling right before her eyes and it finally pushed her over the edge.

"I don't want to push you to do the same thing she did. I trust that you will do what's right for you, your husband, Davis, and the baby. I'm going to stay out of your marriage and not say anything to Hasani." She breathed a sigh of relief.

"Don't misread what I'm telling you. If you bring this mess you created inside my church, I will tell everything and you won't like the way I break the news." Avery's face was very serious. "Also, if you still want the director position I can have the announcement read next Sunday."

Heaven couldn't believe her ears. Her uncle had really had a change of heart. Her lips smiled and she thought about the plans she had waiting for her back at home. "Avery, I would love to accept that position."

"Great!" he sang.

". . . but I'm not going to. I refuse to allow this church to treat me as some second-rate stand in. You won't stick me with that position because your first choice is gone. Sorry, Rev, pick somebody else." Heaven threw her coat on and strutted out his office.

Chapter 47

Heaven's high heeled shoes sounded loud against the pavement. She could see the New Jersey Battleship docked on the Delaware River. The spring weather was trying to push its way up the Atlantic Coast, but the cold air wasn't going anywhere just yet. The sun glistened over the water and the winds were high. Pulling her hat down farther on her head so it wouldn't fly away, Heaven saw Chrome sitting on a nearby bench. When she reached him she sat and waited for him to speak first. Not saying a word, he continued to look out over the water. He looked like his mind was elsewhere; somewhere peaceful and serene.

Heaven spoke up, "How did you find me?"

"I read about the girl who hung herself." Chrome's eyes followed a speed boat skimming the water. "They put your picture in the paper. Was she a friend of yours?" She slowly nodded her head. "I'm sorry for your loss."

"Listen, Chrome, if you have something to say

then just say it. My husband is going to get worried if I'm gone for too long."

"Your son misses you." Once those words left his mouth, she immediately regretted meeting him.

"How is he?"

"Physically he's fine. Emotionally, he's hurting." He got up and walked over to the rail. "Why didn't you come looking for us when you were released?"

"I couldn't. I was tired; so tired of using drugs. I needed to change my life around. My drug use was destroying my life. I had lost my child, you, and even myself. That's why I had to make a new life for myself. Being married to a deacon has allowed me to make a clean start."

"So you were just going to forget about the son you left behind?"

"When the public defender told me Courtney had been put in foster care, that bothered me; him living with strangers. I vowed to get clean, come home, and get my son, but with each passing year the thought of getting clean seemed less important.

"My prison counselor stressed to me how important it was for my rehabilitation to change not just my life but also my lifestyle. That included my friends, my environment, and everything I did. I wasn't sure if I was ready to give up all the things I enjoyed. In my mind, I convinced myself that my son was better off in foster care than with me. I spoke with Patsy Riley a few times and you know how she likes to gossip. She told me you had gotten yourself together and Courtney was with you. I was glad to hear that because I knew you would take good care of him." She rubbed her hands together to keep warm. "How did you find out where Courtney was?"

"After you were arrested Patsy saw me at the bar and told me that Courtney was taken into custody by the state. This was six months after Odyssey died. When Patsy told me Odyssey was gone, I felt like the world had stopped spinning on its axis. My legs buckled underneath me and I fell off the bar stool and onto the floor. I cried so hard.

"At the time I wasn't working. I barely had a place to lay my head, but I couldn't leave my son in foster care. I signed up for outpatient rehab and the people there were really helpful. They helped me get a job, a place, and custody of Courtney. It took a little over a year, but things are much better now." He rubbed his mouth. "I'm clean now. I haven't used in over five years."

"That's beautiful. I wish you and Courtney nothing but the best and . . ."

"Wait a minute." He held up his finger. "What do you mean you wish us nothing but the best; I want you to come home with me. I want you to see Courtney. He's grown so much. He's going to be so happy to see you."

"I can't go with you. I'm sure he blames me for what happened." A sparrow flying above caught her attention. "Does he talk about that day?"

"He used to talk about Odyssey a lot, but as time moved on he's talked less and less about her." She saw a sparkle in his eyes when he talked about Odyssey. Chrome always did love his children. "Heaven, can you talk about that day?"

"Why should I? You know what happened"

"No, I was told you were arrested for child neglect and involuntary manslaughter. I've heard rumors, but I want to hear your side of the story."

Heaven looked into his eyes and she saw their daughter's eyes. The pain and memories were coming back to her. She swallowed back the tears. "I can't. It's too painful."

"Heaven, can you please try?" He held her hand. "I love you."

"Love me!" She jumped up from her seat. Now she was laughing. "Chrome, the most valuable thing I realized while in prison was that what we had wasn't love. You never loved me and I never loved you."

"I am in love with you. You may be married to someone else, but I will always be in love with you," he insisted. "I may not have always showed it or done right by you and the kids but you can't tell me I didn't love my family."

"Chrome, if you loved your family so much you wouldn't have left us," she screamed in his face. "Nearly a year had passed since me or the kids had seen you. The only thing we shared a love for was dope. That was our bond and both of us allowed that needle to come before our children. Odyssey had to sacrifice her life so you could finally get clean and I could find someone who truly loves me."

Chrome put his head down. Heaven had nothing more to say. She took two steps away from him when he said, "I did love you."

"No. You were in love with Keenyah." His head shot up. He couldn't believe she had said her name. "You have always loved her. Even in the ground. I knew you carried a picture of her in your wallet when we were living together. You probably still have it." He turned his head away, confirming her suspicions. "I also knew you took our son to her grave on her birthday."

"It's amazing how you can stand here and condemn me for the feelings I have for someone who is dead, but what about the person still living that you won't let go?"

"What are you talking about?"

"I saw Tyke leaving from out the church. He showed up just before I did. I saw him enter and leave and then you came out a few minutes after. You've always been in love with him. You just refused to admit it because you knew he was with Chantel." Heaven gave him a ridiculous look. As far as she was concerned, the conversation with him was a wrap. She turned to flee the scene.

"Heaven, I should have never said that."

"Don't worry about it because I'm not. Do me a favor and leave me alone forever."

"What about Courtney?" he asked.

"Tell him I'm dead." The sunlight followed her from the park.

Chapter 48

Heaven parked directly in front of seventeen Whitman Street, the address Levi had given her. She parallel parked her SUV close to the curb and helped the children out the car.

Levi's invitation to a kids' party seemed a bit out of the ordinary. She knew he didn't have any children, so why was he so excited about a farm party? Every week he reminded her not to forget the date. She was expecting this to be a fantastic party with real farm animals, food, and games for the kids.

Imani held Heaven's hand tight in hers and swung back and forth. The little girl was happy and had been looking forward to this day. Heaven had allowed her to pick out what she wanted to wear and she chose her purple corduroy dress with white tights.

Seeing Imani smile again made her happy. After Imani witnessed her breakdown, she was scared to be alone with Heaven. The little girl who used to run into her arms at the sight of her was timid and unsure. Heaven regretted her behavior that day, but was sure the time they spent together today would make them close again.

"Do you think we're going to see a chicken?" Imani asked.

"I hope so," Heaven replied.

"I can't wait for Samuel to get out of school so I can tell him about the party."

They crossed the street and climbed the steps until they stood in front of a huge red door. Heaven knocked once. She could hear a clamor of activity going on over the rap music inside. She waited thirty seconds before knocking again. This time a teenage kid answered the door. He stumbled back and held the door wide open for them to enter. Heaven nudged Imani to enter first. The kid kicked the door closed behind them and staggered away.

Heaven's mouth dropped wide open from surprise. She was expecting children around Imani's age to be there. Instead, all the kids looked old enough to be in high school. She pulled Imani through the crowd and held onto Wesley tight in her arms. They walked into the living room which was crowded with more teenage kids. They were everywhere, lying on the sofa, sitting on the floor, and a few sat on the stairs smoking blunts. The house looked like it was full to capacity.

Heaven looked around for Levi. When she didn't see him she wondered if they were at the wrong house.

Imani tugged on her coat. "I'm scared." The ruckus the kids were making in this obviously unsupervised house concerned Heaven. She was scared of what could happen with no adults around. She was making a trail back to the front door when she ran into Levi.

"Hey, Mrs. Washington, I'm glad you made it." He popped a few kernels of popcorn in his mouth from the bowl he carried in his arms.

"Levi, I thought you said this was a kid's party?" Heaven was upset that Levi had misled her.

"I didn't say a kid's party. I said a pharm party." He clarified. Then he noticed the baffled look on her face. It took him a minute to realize why she was confused. "Oh farm. You thought I meant farm like oink, oink." He imitated a pig. "Naw, I meant pharm." He pulled her into the living room and picked up a snack bowl from the middle of the coffee table. He tilted the bowl so that she could see the contents.

Inside were pills of all different colors: white, peach, lavender, blue, green, pink and black. "This is a pharm party. Pharm, as in pharmaceutical. My boy has one of these parties at least once every other month. A bunch of kids from the neighborhood raid their parent's medicine cabinets and steal different prescription drugs. We bring them all together and pour them into bowls. You just take a handful…" Levi bent down and grabbed a handful of pills and swallowed them all without any water "and enjoy."

A girl dancing by with a bottle of Grey Goose in one hand stuck her hand in the bowl Levi was holding and popped a couple in her mouth as if it were candy.

Levi knelt down in front of Imani. "I guess that's

why you brought the kids. Want some popcorn?"
he asked her. Imani was a popcorn lover. She stuck
in her tiny hand and pulled out a load of popcorn.

"There's nothing in there, is it?" Heaven asked.

"Naw, it's clean." Levi stood straight up. "I'm
sorry, Mrs. Washington. I just assumed you knew
what I was talking about."

She watched the teenage kids dance around the
room, drinking beer and getting high. "Whose
house is this?"

"My boy lives here. His mom and dad are both
doctors. They stay out of town a lot on business.
Plus he can usually get his hands on the most pills.

"Levi, I'm going." Heaven held her hand out for
Imani. "This is not what I was expecting."

"Mrs. Washington, before you go, you can look
through a few bowls." He noticed Imani watching
his every word. ". . . and pick out a few treats if you
like."

Heaven had been trying to stay away from
heroin. Perhaps she would take some pills with her
just in case she needed something to calm her
down. "Thanks! I'll look around and then we'll be
going."

"All right. Take your time. We have bowls throughout the house." Levi went into the kitchen. Wesley
was becoming restless and he squirmed in her arms.
She moved him from her left arm to the right and
told Imani to hang on tight to her coat and not let
go. They moved from room to room looking
through bowls. Nothing was labeled. Heaven didn't
know what the pills were or how they would make
her feel, but if they could make her high she didn't

care. She picked out a few black, peach, and lavender pills.

They excused themselves down a narrow hallway that was full of smoke from burning blunts. Heaven used her arm to shield herself from the smoke getting in her face. She glanced behind her to make sure Imani was still close to her. This was no place for a child to be. Once they checked that last room they were leaving.

They entered the den. It was practically empty. One couple lay on the couch making out. They were practically having sex. The guy was already undressed all the way down to his boxers. Another couple watched from the floor and passed a blunt back and forth between them. Heaven saw the bowl she was looking for sitting on a nearby table. She walked toward it and passed a boy laid out in a recliner chair.

She studied his face for a second. It was familiar to her; his caramel colored skin, jet black straight hair, and eyebrows that arched up. Her heart dropped down to her stomach. She couldn't believe it. It was Courtney; her only living child. She wheezed for air and grabbed at her chest because she couldn't catch her breath. Heaven fell to her knees and lifted his hand but it went limp. She was scared he was dead. His face was still warm so she assumed he was still breathing.

A bunch of kids stumbled over them. "Get away!" she yelled, then she turned back to help her son. "Courtney, can you hear me? Courtney!"

Heaven couldn't even hear her own voice over the loud music and chaos in the room. She tried waking him up, but he wouldn't respond. Wesley began to cry and so did Imani. There was no one around who looked sober enough to get help so she stood up and patted Wesley. "Don't cry."

She grabbed for Imani's hand and pulled her back down the hallway. She searched a bunch of faces until she found Levi sitting on the counter in the kitchen. He had replaced his popcorn bowl with a bottle of gin in one hand and a handful of pills in the other. Heaven stood in the doorway waving her arms to get his attention. After he took a swig from his bottle he looked up and saw her. He noticed the serious look on her and rushed to her side.

"What's wrong?" He worried that something was wrong.

"I need you to keep an eye on Imani and the baby for me." She passed Wesley to Levi and the baby screamed ever louder, kids trying to get by stared at them.

"Why?" He rocked Wesley trying to stop his tears.

"My son is here and he's unconscious. I'm trying to get him to wake up but he won't respond." Levi gave her a confused look. He followed her back to the den. When he caught up with her she stood towering over Courtney's unresponsive body.

"I didn't know Courtney was your son," Levi said.

"Levi, he needs medical attention." She reached into her handbag and pulled out her cell phone.

"What are you doing?"

"I'm calling an ambulance. I've got to get him to the hospital."

"You can't do that. The police will be all over this place."

"Levi, he may die if I don't get him to the hospital. Take the children out to my car and I'll be there as soon as I can." Levi turned to leave with the children when an operator answered Heaven's call. She told the operator her son was unconscious and the address of where they were.

Levi must have warned a lot of people that she was calling the ambulance because by the time the paramedics arrived the place was just about empty. The EMT asked Heaven a lot of questions and she answered them to the best of her ability. As the medics lifted Courtney's body on the stretcher they saw a bowl of prescription pills sitting on a nearby table. They picked it up and took it with them. Courtney was wheeled out and Heaven followed.

When she arrived at the hospital, she told the nurse she was there to see Courtney. She considered telling the nurse she was Courtney's mother, but she didn't feel as though she had the right. She hadn't been his mother in years. What right did she have to use that title now?

The nurse asked her to wait in the waiting room until a doctor came out to see her. Heaven was desperate to know what was going on, but the hospital would only discuss Courtney's condition with his father. She paced the waiting room floor for forty-five minutes before a nurse told her they had to pump Courtney's stomach and he was resting. She also told her that the hospital had been in touch with his father. He was on his way. "Ma'am, would you happen to know how old the patient is?

It would help if we had that information." The nurse asked her.

"He's twelve years old," she solemnly replied.

Two police officers approached Heaven with questions. She provided them with the vague details she remembered. She made up a lie about the church witnessing in the neighborhood to explain how she discovered the house full of kids using prescription drugs. When the officers found out she was a member of Mount Olive and married to Hasani they conveniently wrapped up their questions and apologized for disturbing her. As soon as they left, Chrome walked through the emergency room doors. "Where's Courtney?"

Chrome's clothes were covered in smut and oil. He must have come straight from work.

"The nurse said he's resting. Chrome, they had to pump his stomach."

He rubbed his head in anguish. Heaven felt so guilty. She was sure he was going to lose his temper and take his frustration out on her. "Chrome, I'm so sorry. I should have listened to you." She was still holding Wesley now asleep in her arms. "If I would have known . . ."

Chrome hugged her. "Heaven, it's not your fault. I'm his father. I should have been there. I know you're upset and so am I, but the most important thing is for us to let Courtney know that we're there for him. Are you willing to do that?"

Heaven sighed heavily. She was now being backed into a corner and had no choice but to face her son. The new life she had become accustomed to was slipping away. The time had come for her to acknowledge Courtney. She couldn't allow him to suffer any longer for her actions. If she didn't it could cost him his life. "Yes, Chrome. I'll be there."

"Are you Courtney's parents?" a doctor asked. Heaven and Chrome both stepped up at the same time and said yes together. "We pumped Courtney's stomach and retrieved over twenty four different prescription pills from his stomach. There were Xanax, Vicodin, Percocet, and a few E-pills. You were lucky to get him in to us when you did. That young man was in danger of slipping into a coma and possibly never waking up. A lot of kids don't realize that prescription drugs can be just as dangerous as street narcotics. I have arranged for Courtney to meet with the hospital psychologists while he's here, and if possible, I would like for you two to also meet with her." He handed Chrome a slip of paper. "This is the number to her office. Give her a call in the morning to make an appointment for the three of you. The nurse is still getting him settled in his room, but once she's finished, I'll be sure to have her come get the two of you." Chrome shook the doctor's hand and thanked him.

Chrome looked at Heaven. "Are you willing to see this doctor?"

Heaven was terrified, but not as scared as when she found Courtney unconscious. She wondered what Courtney was going to say when he saw her for the first time after all these years.

"Do you want me to stay with you?" she asked.

Chrome looked over at Imani asleep in the chair and Wesley knocked out in her arms. "No, you go on home; it's late."

Chrome helped her carry the children out to the car. "Chrome, call me." She gave him her cell phone number. "I really want to be there when you talk to the doctor."

"Don't worry. I will." He waved good-bye and she headed home.

Chapter 49

When Heaven pulled up into her driveway she saw that every light in the house was on. When she saw Emalee's car was parked out front, she remembered Samuel. She had forgotten to pick him up from school. When she didn't show up, the school probably called Emalee. The minute she turned the engine off, her front door swung open. Hasani stood in the doorway then rushed out to her and the children. When Heaven looked up again Emalee stood in the doorway watching.

"Heaven, where have you been?" Her husband sounded more concerned than upset. Emalee slowly walked up behind him. Imani was awake when her father opened the back passenger door. "Daddy, we were at the hospital," she screamed. Alarmed, he glanced at his wife and then scooped his daughter into his arms.

"Is everything all right, Heaven? We were concerned when you never picked up Samuel and then we couldn't reach you by your cell phone."

"They don't allow cell phones in the hospital," Heaven shot back. Emalee had taken Wesley in her arms and then everyone went back in the house.

"Sweetheart, what happened?"

Heaven sat down on the couch and swallowed her pride. There was going to be no easy way for her to tell him the truth. She turned toward him and saw Emalee standing right behind him ready to listen to every word she was about to say.

Heaven looked past Hasani to Emalee. Emalee realized Heaven wasn't going to talk while she was in the room, so she excused herself and put the children to bed.

"Before I tell you this story, I want you to know I've changed. Since you and the children have come into my life, I've changed. I'm not the same person I used to be."

"Honey, you don't have to tell me that. I knew that before we married."

The reassurance of his smile gave her enough courage to say what was on her mind. "I never told you this, but I had children before I met you." She could see the questions in his eyes. "You're probably wondering why I never told you before." She stared down at the floor and then lifted her eyes to meet his. "I was scared you wouldn't love me if you knew who I really was."

He lovingly rubbed the back of her hand. "I will always love you. There is nothing you can say to change that."

She took his hand in hers and lingered a moment before she asked him something she had wondered about for months. "Did you ever wonder what it was I did to land in jail?"

"Nope, because it didn't matter to me what you did in the past. My heart was leading me forward with you, not back behind you. I knew your crime had something to do with your addiction, but that was all."

For the next hour, Heaven recapped the horrible day her daughter died. During it all, Hasani lovingly caressed her and wiped away her tears.

"It wasn't his fault. He was only trying to help his sister feel better. I'm a horrible mother."

"Heaven, that is all in your past." He hugged her tight. "Now that you have released all your pain, things are going to get better."

"That's not all there is to the story. Courtney's father called Nana and told her that Courtney had been rushed to the hospital. He overdosed on prescription pills."

"Heaven, I'm sorry."

"That's why I was at the hospital. It looks like he's going to pull through it, but I know I'm to blame," she cried.

"Don't worry. We're going to help your son the best way we can." Her husband stroked her hair and kissed her forehead, making her feel at ease.

Chapter 50

Heaven was surprised when Fatima called and asked if she could she go to church with her on Sunday. Her call aroused suspicion in Heaven. They hadn't seen each other since Ebony's funeral. It seemed strange that Fatima would want to start coming to church; particularly her church.

When they were in the halfway house together, Ebony asked Fatima to come to church with her several times, but she always claimed church wasn't her thing. Heaven figured Fatima either had troubles or she was causing trouble. Whatever the reason, Heaven was sure she would find out sooner or later.

Fatima met her outside the front of the church and the two of them walked in together. Once they were seated, the men's choir opened with their first selection. The men's choir was always good. Their voices harmonized perfectly with the tenors and bass. Mount Olive could always look forward to a holy ghost-filled service when the men's choir was singing. Once the men sat down and everyone settled back in their seats, Avery got up to say a few words before the scripture lesson was read.

Fatima leaned over to Heaven, "Do you know that kid in the front row?" Heaven's eyes looked in the direction Fatima pointed in. "Oh yes. That's Levi. He's a good kid." Heaven studied him for a minute to make sure he was clean. His eyes were alert and he seemed aware of his surroundings. "Why?"

"That's my son," Fatima replied.

Heaven looked in her eyes for an explanation, but a rumbling sound that roared from the back of the church stole her attention away. Heaven thought a herd of buffalo were storming their way through the church; instead, it was a swarm of police officers. Cops were everywhere. They seemed to come in from the front, back, and side entrances.

Avery walked down the center aisle and a host of men from the church crowded around behind him in rank order.

"Reverend, I'm sorry to interrupt your service but I had no choice. We have reason to believe a member of your congregation is connected to a string of murders."

"Who are you referring to officer?" Avery asked.

"Get you hands off me," Levi screamed out. Two officers handcuffed Levi and pulled him out of the choir box.

"Officer, there must be some mistake. Levi couldn't have killed anybody."

"Reverend, I can't get into the details but we have strong evidence that makes Levi a suspect in a crime that was committed last night against an elderly couple. I'm sure you already know about the series of murders that has been waged against senior citizens."

"You can't possibly think Levi is the serial killer." The pastor stared at him with disbelief in his eyes.

"I wish I was wrong about this one, but the proof we have is pretty strong."

Humiliated, Levi hung his head down as the cops escorted him out in handcuffs. Fatima got up and stood in their way. "Officer, this is my son. Where are you taking him?"

"Mom?" Levi asked.

"Don't worry, son. I'm coming straight to the station. I'm not going to leave you to deal with this by yourself."

The police walked around her and put Levi in the back of a cop car. Fatima ran down the steps and Heaven followed behind her. She ran toward her car but Heaven convinced her it would be better if they rode together in her car.

Reverend Stansfield dismissed church early and met them down at the police station. While they waited for some news about Levi, Fatima and Heaven talked.

"Fatima, are you all right? I know you've been looking for your son and as soon as you find him he's arrested."

"When I saw him in that choir box my heart practically stopped. I've been looking for Levi all over this city and every lead I had turned into a dead end. When we were in the halfway house, Ms. Griffin told me some people choose God as a last alternative. Once they had exhausted all other possibilities and felt as though there were no other choices, they came looking for God. I felt that way today. I refused to listen to God whispering in my ear. Once I got tired of doing things my way, and I decided to seek God, he led me straight to Levi." She laughed. "Imagine if I would have come to church sooner. If I would have come to church last week or last month I would have found him earlier. This might have been prevented."

"Fatima, you showing up today was a blessing. You came at a time when Levi needed you most. I can't say what would have happened if you had come to church any earlier, but perhaps God's using this incident as a bridge to help fill the gap between the two of you."

One of the arresting officers came up to them and told Fatima she could see Levi. She squeezed Heaven's hand for support then followed the officer down the corridor. Heaven said a silent prayer for her as she walked away.

Heaven laid her head back against the wall and closed her eyes. It had been a long day and she was tired. "I overheard what you said to Fatima." Hasani sat down next to her.

"When did you get here?" she asked.

"I just walked in the door. I had to make sure Emalee was all right with the children." Heaven could see approval when he looked at her. It seemed like their marriage was getting stronger every day. "I'm proud of what you said." They watched a few officers drag in criminals in handcuffs. "What do you think of all this?" he asked.

It wasn't often that Hasani asked for her opinion. This was turning out to be a day full of surprises. "I can't see Levi being a serial killer."

"I thought the same thing." He smiled and placed his hand on top of hers. When she looked up, she saw Fatima rushing back visibly upset. Heaven handed her a handkerchief from out her purse to wipe away the tears.

"What happened?" Heaven asked.

"Heaven," she cried in her arms. "He hates me."

"That can't be true." She rubbed Fatima's back to try and soothe away her pain.

"It's true. I knew he'd be upset, but he told me to get out and never come back. He said he could fix this problem on his own and then he asked for you."

"Me?"

"Yes, he wants to see you," she cried.

Both Hasani and Avery seemed interested in why Levi would want to talk with her. Heaven gestured to the officer that she was ready. He escorted her to a small room. Inside Levi was alone with his head face down on the table. When she walked in, he lifted his head and the puffiness around his eyes showed he had been crying.

She pulled out a chair and sat down next to him. "Levi, what's going on?"

"My mom? You know my mom?" he asked.

"Yes, we were in the halfway house together."

"I didn't even know she was alive." He blew air out his mouth. "She's the reason I'm in here."

"Levi, you can't blame your mother for what's going on."

"Yes, I can. Mrs. Washington, you don't know

everything I've gone through with her." He
slammed his fist down on the table and hollered.
"She can kiss my behind the same way she turned
her back on me when I was repeatedly raped to
support her habit. I don't want to have anything to
do with her, ever."

Heaven was already aware of the things that had
occurred between him and his mother, but she decided to keep that to herself. "Levi, why did you
ask to speak with me?"

"Mrs. Washington, you have to do me a favor. I
know that you're friends with Tyke."

Heaven was surprised when he said Tyke's
name. She had no idea he knew Tyke and she was
even more surprised he knew of her friendship
with Tyke. She was going to deny any association,
but she was caught off guard and didn't know what
to say. "He's told me things about the two of you."

"Levi, I don't know what your friend has told
you, but he's a liar," Heaven tried to defend herself.

"Don't get upset. I would never repeat any of
the things he told me, but I need a favor. You have
to find Tyke for me. Tell him where I'm at and my
charges. He needs to get me a lawyer."

She wondered how much Levi knew. Tyke had
been talking about her behind her back to members of her church and never told her. She couldn't
wait to talk with him.

Heaven left Levi. She told Hasani and Avery
that Levi was ready to see them both. With hope in
her eyes, Fatima looked at her for any sign that
Levi may have forgiven her, but Heaven slowly
shook her head and Fatima cried even more.

Chapter 51

Heaven took Fatima back to the church to pick up her car. Once she promised to call Fatima with any news concerning Levi, she sped off toward the block. When she hit the corner of Louis and Lansdowne, she drove her car up on the curb and jumped out. "Yo, I need to see Tyke. Right now!" she screamed to everyone out there. Heaven was acting like her old self again and she was ready to call out everybody on that corner. A few fellas ran for cover while others gave her hard stares. Fitch watched from the stoop.

When she saw him she demanded to know where Tyke was. "Yo, you gonna get hurt if you run up on us again like that," he said. She wasn't worried about threats from a teenager. "I ain't seen Tyke, but I'll let him know you came through." She thought he was lying, but she figured she did the right thing by coming up there the way she did. He was sure to tell Tyke she was looking for him.

When Heaven got home, Emalee was there watching the children. Since Emalee had the children, Heaven wanted to go back out and look for Tyke, but she didn't want Hasani to come home and she not be around. He told her she had to start getting more rest. She was seven months pregnant and it wouldn't be long before the baby came.

Heaven walked into a quiet house. "Where are the children?" Emalee sat in the living room watching the news by herself.

"Wesley is napping. Samuel is next door and Imani is up in her room."

Her curt responses were typical Emalee and Heaven had learned to ignore her. Heaven rubbed her belly. The baby had been kicking all day and she was tired. She moved toward the stairs to lie down in her bed when Emalee stopped her.

"Did you see Levi?"

Heaven nodded her head.

"How is he?" She seemed genuinely concerned about Levi so Heaven gave her a brief recap.

"I only spoke with him for a minute, but he seemed all right. I'm sure Hasani will have more information when he gets home."

A newscaster on the six o'clock news reporting on Levi's arrest caught their attention. Emalee turned up the volume. The female reporter stood in front of Camden Police Headquarters giving a summary of Levi's charges, which amounted to fifteen counts of homicide.

"It won't be long before all the stations pick up the story and it goes nationwide." Emalee turned to Heaven. "I had no idea that Levi's mother was still alive."

Heaven tried to end their conversation by flipping the television off. "What difference does it make if you knew that his mother was alive or not?"

"No need to get upset, Heaven. I just assumed that since the two of you were in the halfway house together, she also did time for a drug-related crime." Heaven was tired of talking with her. She turned toward the stairs. "I think it's a shame when a mother chooses drugs over her own child."

Heaven's jaw tightened and her eyes bulged out. She wanted to jump on Emalee but because she was pregnant she ignored her. "Levi will be fine." She was sure there would be another day when Emalee would overstep her bounds with Heaven and that would be the day Emalee would get exactly what she deserved.

"No thanks to his mother. The only mother figure the boy had in his life was his grandmother and when she passed, the poor boy probably felt like he was all alone in this world."

"Grandmother?" Heaven didn't know Levi was raised by his grandmother. Fatima never mentioned any relatives. She wondered if Fatima knew about Levi and his grandmother. Emalee continued talking but Heaven blocked her out. Her mind was full of thoughts concerning Tyke and Levi. She attempted to escape Emalee's vicious attitude when something she said caught her ear.

". . . then she just stopped taking her medication. It was so unlike her. Her condition deteriorated and then she died."

"What did you say?" Heaven asked.

"Levi's grandmother," Emalee repeated.

"No. How did she die?"

Emalee sucked her teeth to show how upset she was that Heaven wasn't paying attention the first time. "His grandmother wasn't taking her medication like she should have. I remember visiting with her one day and she was in so much pain. The woman could barely talk. I told her she had to remember to take her medication and she looked back at me with tears in her eyes. She looked like she wanted to tell me something but couldn't. It's best she moved on. At least she doesn't have to suffer any longer. It would probably kill her to see Levi in jail."

Levi. Prescription drugs? Was he taking his grandmother's meds?

Heaven's mind was running on overload. She had so much to do in so little time. If she could find Tyke then he could clear up her suspicions concerning Levi.

It was late when Hasani came home. The clock said it was after one in the morning. He tried slipping into bed without waking her, but she was already up.

"What happened?" she asked.

"He won't talk to anybody. Reverend Stansfield called in one of the best lawyers in the city. The man came down ready to work with Levi and get him released, but he wouldn't talk. I don't know if he's scared or if he's trying to protect somebody."

Heaven stroked the side of his face with her fingers. "It's going to get better."

"What did he say to you?"

Hasani never turned on the lights so he couldn't see the look on her face when he asked her that question. She had been so focused on finding out the connection between Levi and Tyke that she forget to think about what she was going to say to Hasani when he asked what Levi had talked to her about.

"Well, we prayed together and he asked me about his mom and that was about all."

"Does it seem odd to you that a boy you barely know doesn't ask to see a lawyer, his mother, or pastor but wants to speak with you?"

Hasani was suspicious, but she wasn't about to tell him the truth. "Hasani, it's not like the boy is a stranger to me."

"I know but you've only known him a few months and the people who can help him the most, he rejects."

She turned away from him. "Like you said, maybe he's scared." She pretended to go to sleep, but Hasani kept talking.

"I meant to ask you about the missing money in our bank account."

Tension filled her body. She had been dreading this conversation. She knew it would only be a matter of time before he found out about all the money she had taken out of the bank. She grew hotter with each passing second.

"I was balancing our check book earlier in the week and we were short twenty eight hundred dollars. I thought it was a banking error but when they sent me a copy of all transactions it looked like it was money you had withdrawn with your bank card. Do you know anything about it?"

"I went and put some things on layaway for the baby."

"Heaven, you know I don't mind you spending money, but twenty eight hundred dollars in a month is a little bit much." She never answered him. "Are you using drugs again?"

"I can't believe you would ask me that," she screamed. "Do you really think I'm using again?"

"Heaven, I had to ask. It wasn't too long ago you admitted that you tried to buy drugs and ended up getting your mouth split open. We have all this money missing and unaccounted for and some days you act like you're losing your mind. I need to know. I deserve to know what's going on with you. Then, with Emalee whispering in my ear . . ."

"This is about Emalee telling lies about me," she shouted.

"No." He gave an aggravated moan. "I'm sorry. Maybe I'm being paranoid, but the amount of money you're spending will make us homeless."

"I suppose I got a little carried away. I'm sorry, it will never happen again. From now on any large purchases I make will be discussed with you first."

"Well, I guess I need to tell you this before you try to withdraw any more money. I've cut off all your credit cards and you can't withdraw any money out of our account without both our signatures."

She turned to face him. "Why would you do that? You don't trust me?"

"It's not that I don't trust you, but you spend more money than I make. Our entire family lives off my sole income. I pay all the bills and I have to make sure there is always enough money in the bank for me to do that. This is a safety precaution so that there is never any miscommunication about how much money is being spent. It's not like you won't ever have any money. I will give you a weekly allowance."

"Allowance!" she shouted. "I don't believe this. My husband is restricting me from the funds in our account. Fine, Hasani, if that's what you want but as soon as I have the baby, I'm getting a job so you better be prepared to make arrangements to have somebody pick up Samuel because I'll be too busy making my own money." She turned over and went to sleep.

Chapter 52

Heaven went to the nurse's station on the third floor of the hospital and asked which room Courtney was in. The nurse on duty directed her down the hall. When Heaven approached Courtney's room, the door was slightly ajar. She didn't want to walk in without Chrome's permission, so she quietly stood just outside the door and listened. Inside she could hear Chrome, Courtney, and the hospital psychologist talking.

When Heaven and Chrome talked, he suggested she come up to the hospital a little later than the scheduled time they were supposed to meet with the doctor. He thought it would be best if he and the doctor spoke with Courtney alone first.

When Heaven left the house that morning Hasani was still asleep. She was still furious with him for putting a restriction on money that he had promised would always be accessible to her. He was supposed to come to the hospital with her, but she changed her mind and decided to face her son alone

"Courtney, can you tell me about your mother?" she heard the doctor ask. There was silence and he never answered the question. "Do you know where she's at?"

"Jail." Hearing her son's voice for the first time in such a long time sent chills down her spine. He no longer sounded like a little boy, but more like a man.

"Do you know why?" the doctor asked. Again he was silent. "Can you tell me about Odyssey?"

"Dad, do we have to do this? I know y'all think there is something wrong with me because of what happened, but I'm fine. I'll never do anything so stupid again."

"Courtney, there's more to it than you think," Chrome replied. "This doctor is here to make sure you're healed mentally as well as physically. Cooperate with us and I promise it'll be over sooner than you think."

"Courtney," the doctor interrupted, "Can we talk about what happened when you were a little boy? Your father has told me you had a rocky start before you started living with him. Can we talk about that?"

"No," he sulked. "I'm tired of talking."

"If he doesn't want to talk we can't force him. Maybe we should let him rest and then come back later," the doctor suggested.

Chrome and the doctor walked out the room and saw Heaven standing at the door listening. The three of them walked further down the hall together. "Did you hear everything he said?" Chrome asked.

"I heard enough." The psychologist looked between the two of them before Chrome introduced them. They shook hands.

"It's nice to meet you," the psychologist said. "As you heard, Courtney isn't displaying too much emotion. He's keeping it locked inside and that isn't a good sign. Since he doesn't want to talk, I can't pinpoint his problem. It could be that he doesn't remember or doesn't want to remember."

The doctor took her glasses off and cleaned them with her shirt. "I'm hoping when Courtney sees you he will react, whether it's positive or negative, at least we will know what direction we should proceed in." She looked at her watch. "Listen, I still have an hour before I have to move on to my next patient. I'm going down to the cafeteria to get a coffee. Once I come back we can go in and talk with Courtney again."

When the doctor left, Heaven turned to Chrome. "How do you think Courtney is going to react when he sees me?"

"I'm not sure. At first I thought once he saw you it would help, but now I'm not so sure. I thought what he was missing was his mother, but he seems so cold. Nothing like the little boy you would remember."

They sat outside Courtney's room talking until the doctor returned. When she did she asked Heaven to sit outside the room until she sent Chrome out to get her. When they went back in the room she was interested in what the doctor was going to say to Courtney. She couldn't help but hope he would be happy to see her. Finally, Chrome came out. She took a deep breath and walked in with him.

"Courtney, your father and I have a surprise for you," the psychologist announced.

Walking into his room, the first thing Heaven noticed were his green eyes, which he had inherited from her. He was so handsome.

"Mom." He stared at her in shock.

"Hey, slugger." She used the name she used to call him as a kid. Chrome called her closer to Courtney's side. "It's me and I'm here to see you."

He looked scared and she saw a few tears fall from his eyes. She held out her hands to give him a hug. She had waited so long to hold her son in her arms again. When she moved closer to Courtney, he grabbed the steaming cup of coffee the doctor had placed on the nightstand next to him and threw it in Heaven's face.

Her face was on fire. She used her hands to try and soothe the burning pain. She screamed loudly and backed away from him. The drink scorched her face. Nurses rushed into the room and helped Heaven out into the hallway. They immediately put her in a wheelchair.

"My face. My face," she screamed.

A nurse came and placed a cold compress to the burns and another brought some cream. Heaven was moved to an examining room. Chrome tried to help, but a nurse told him they would be back out to get him once a doctor looked at her face.

An hour later Chrome came in to see how she

was doing. The doctor had wrapped her face in gauze. "How do you feel?" Chrome asked.

She moaned in response.

He pulled a chair up to her side. "Heaven, I had no idea he would react that way. The doctor said you shouldn't have any permanent scarring. It was only first degree burns. Your face will be red and puffy for a while, until the skin begins to heal itself."

"What did Courtney say?" she asked

"I don't know, he refuses to speak to anyone."

"Maybe my coming back into his life wasn't such a good idea."

Chapter 53

By Friday, the redness in Heaven's face was starting to fade. She still had a few red blotches, but she used makeup to hide them. Tonight was Imani's dance recital and her little princess was so excited. Hasani planned on being at the police station most of the day, but promised to meet his wife later at the dance studio.

Heaven had not given up on her hunt for Tyke. She still had questions for him, but she figured he was hiding out from her because he hadn't called her.

It was three o'clock—time for her to get Imani ready for her recital. Heaven poked her head inside Imani's bedroom door and told her to grab her gym bag and meet her down stairs. Heaven hurried to the den to pick up a bag full of costumes she had made for all fifteen little girls in Imani's dance class. Not forgetting about her sewing kit, she carried everything she could out to her car.

On her way back in the house she felt a small pain strike her in the abdomen. It wasn't severe so Heaven ignored it. She figured it was the baby telling her she was doing too much and not getting enough rest. Once the recital was over and she had a chance to speak with Tyke she made a promise to herself that she would relax for the remainder of her pregnancy.

Emalee had come over to stay home with Samuel and Wesley until Hasani came to pick them up. Heaven and Imani left the house and rode down Federal Street.

When Heaven stopped at a traffic light she heard someone call her name. It was Zaria and she was standing on the side of the road with a forty ounce in her hand. She strolled up to the driver side window and asked could she catch a ride. Heaven was in a hurry to get Imani to her recital, but she told her to get in.

"You're pregnant!" Zaria roared when she saw Heaven's belly.

"Seven months," Heaven replied.

"I guess that means you don't want any of this." Zaria pulled out a bag of dope and dangled it in the air.

"My daughter is in the car." Heaven stressed and her eyes shifted toward the backseat. Zaria turned and waved to Imani. Imani waved back, hanging on to her baby doll tightly.

"You dropping her off?" Zaria asked.

"No, she has a dance recital."

"Well, what about afterward? Can we go out somewhere?"

Heaven had wanted to get high all week long,

but because of the way her face looked she couldn't get out of the house. Courtney, Levi, Tyke, and Hasani were all stressing her out. "Can you sew?" Heaven asked her.

"Sew?"

"Yeah, I have to finish sewing the kid's costumes, but if you can wait for me until after the recital is over, we can go out somewhere."

"If I can't sew I'll learn," she replied.

The dance studio parking lot was full of overactive little girls. Once Heaven parked, Imani ran over to her classmates and her teachers escorted her into the auditorium where they usually rehearsed. Heaven waved to the teachers. Then she went into the dressing room to finish sewing the girls' costumes.

"Everything is done except for the wings." She showed Zaria what had to be done by carefully stringing the thread through the needle. She attached the wings to each leotard.

Zaria held one of the costumes up. "What are they?" she asked.

"They're bumblebees." Heaven laughed.

"Who taught you how to sew?" she asked.

"I took a class when I was in the prison. Actually I was forced into it. My prison assessment counselor said I wasn't doing anything productive and I needed to do something beside sleep all day, so she signed me up to take sewing. I never thought it would come in handy one day."

Zaria and Heaven sat for over two hours sewing bumblebee wings. When they finally finished, they had less than an hour before the recital was scheduled to begin. Heaven sat back in her chair and sipped on a bottle of water one of the dance instructors had brought to her. A few feet away, from her Zaria pulled out a dime bag of dope and took a sniff.

"Are you crazy?" Heaven hollered at her. "Anyone can walk in here at any time."

"Look, I've been with you for hours and I just needed a little pick-me-up. Stop tripping. Nobody saw me." She stuffed the bag back in her pants pocket. "Do you want a quick hit?" she asked.

Heaven was ashamed of her lack of self control. She should have been able to at least wait until Imani's recital was over, but she couldn't. She gestured for Zaria to throw her the bag. Heaven snorted a small amount up her nose.

The minute Heaven exhaled her water broke. Water seeped down her leg and onto the floor. Zaria laughed and pointed at her. "What you going to do now?" she giggled.

Heaven had no idea what she was going to do. She wasn't due for another ten weeks and she hadn't been feeling any contractions. She grabbed her purse and threw her keys to Zaria. "Follow me," she ordered.

"You're not going to leave the costumes lying out like that are you?" she referred to how they had left the costumes spread out all over the chairs and desks in the dressing room.

"Yes," Heaven shouted. She didn't want Imani to see her in the condition she was in. Heaven was feeling a light buzz from her high and she had a wet spot on the back of her pants from her water breaking.

They made it back to Heaven's car and pulled

off. "Do you have any more dope on you?" Heaven asked.

"Nope. That was all I had and I'm short on cash," Zaria replied.

Heaven directed Zaria to the bank. While holding her belly Heaven went to the ATM machine. When she slipped her card in and punched in her pin number the word "Denied" flashed across the screen. Heaven banged her hand against the machine. She had forgotten that Hasani had restricted her access to their money. All she had in her pocket was twelve dollars. Her belly was starting to feel more uncomfortable. She told Zaria to take them to the nearest drug corner.

If Heaven wasn't in so much pain she would have noticed that Zaria had taken her to Tyke's corner. Zaria told the kid on the corner she only had twelve dollars and that she wanted a twenty bag, but he wouldn't sell it to her without all the money.

Zaria was a true hustler because she not only convinced the boy to give them a twenty bag of dope for twelve dollars, but she also got them a little something extra. When she pulled away from the corner with the dope in her hand she asked, "Where to now?"

"The hospital," Heaven replied. She couldn't take it any longer. They pulled into the hospital emergency room parking lot and she unbuckled her seat belt. Zaria opened the car door, but Heaven stopped her from getting out. "Let's do this first," she said, referring to the dope.

"Now?"

"I don't want to take this stuff in there with us," Heaven replied.

Zaria agreed. By the time Heaven took her last hit, she couldn't take the intense pains any longer. They had to go in.

Zaria helped carry her into the emergency room. As she walked across the parking lot the pains in her stomach had become extreme. Heaven walked slow and stiff while putting most of her body weight on Zaria.

A nurse saw them and immediately put Heaven in a wheelchair. Then she was wheeled to a private cubicle so a doctor could examine her. Zaria stayed and kept her company while a nurse asked her a lot of questions.

"How many weeks are you?" the nurse asked while writing on her clipboard.

"I don't know." Heaven's response caught her off guard. She put down her clipboard and gave Heaven a strange look. "I should be around seven months."

"When was the last time you were at the prenatal doctor?"

She hesitated a moment. "I haven't been."

The nurse picked up her clipboard and scribbled notes down on paper. Then she called an orderly over. "Please take Mrs. Washington up to room 521. I'm scheduling her for an ultrasound."

Heaven was quickly admitted with no problems. She was placed in the maternity ward. A nurse came and connected Heaven to a few wires. She inserted one IV in her arm and told her it would help to subdue the pain. Nurses rushed in and out of the room, setting up machines and preparing for the ultrasound.

Finally, thirty minutes later, the doctor walked into her room. "Okay, Mrs. Washington. Let's see what's going on with your baby." The doctor, a happy fellow, reminded Heaven a lot of Ebony. His bright red hair, red freckles, and corny jokes made her feel at ease. He pulled a stool over to her bedside and stared at the baby on the monitor. His enthusiasm quickly faded and he squinted to get a good look at the screen. He face was full of concern.

"Doctor, what's wrong?" Heaven asked.

"Mrs. Washington, I see some complications with the baby's development that bother me. I'm going to order the next available operating room. I don't want to wait any longer. I'm going to deliver the baby tonight." He stood up. "Heaven, this is an emergency delivery so things are going to be a little out of the ordinary. I will order you an epidural, you'll be prepped for surgery, and I'll be back to see you before we go into the OR."

The doctor left and Zaria spoke up. "Heaven, he talked like there was something seriously wrong with the baby."

"I know." His choice of words scared her. She prayed nothing happened to her baby. She realized she hadn't been the best mother by doing drugs and skipping out on her prenatal appointments. She couldn't stand to have another child die because of her mistakes.

"All this seriousness is making me have to pee," Zaria said, and she headed for the bathroom door. "I'll be right back."

The nurse came in and gave Heaven some forms to sign and she said that they had contacted Hasani and he was on his way. "Mrs. Washington, I'll be right back with the anesthesiologist. He will be the one administering your epidural today." The nurse informed her.

As soon as she walked out the room Heaven could smell a faint odor. She looked toward the bathroom door. She knew Zaria wasn't doing what she thought she was doing.

Heaven slipped out of bed and took the IV she was connected to with her. As quietly as possible she tiptoed over to the bathroom door and swung it wide open, catching her in the act.

Zaria sat on the floor, leaning against the tub barely conscious. Beside her was a whole roll of toilet paper sitting in a pile. That quick, she had unraveled the toilet paper tube and used it as a pipe to smoke some heroin. She glared up through half open eyes. "Hey, Heaven." She laughed.

Chapter 54

Heaven stepped in the bathroom and closed the door behind her. She snatched Zaria's homemade pipe up from off the floor, "Zaria, you had drugs on you the whole time." She couldn't believe Zaria would get high without her. "You are so selfish. I would have never hidden any drugs from you. I always share."

"I know," she chuckled. "That's why I came in the bathroom. So you wouldn't find out." She could see Heaven was upset by the look on her face. "I'm sorry," she slurred. "I just needed one hit. I could be here all night."

Heaven lowered herself down on the floor next to Zaria. The small bag that held the drugs was nearly empty except for a small corner. "Where's the foil?"

Zaria looked around in a daze. "Oh, here it is," she laughed. "I was sitting on it." She pulled it out from under her behind.

Zaria held the foil while Heaven dumped what

was left of the dope on it. Then she held the flame from her lighter underneath it. Seconds later, Heaven was inhaling a small morsel of smoke that left her craving more.

The nurse returned looking for Heaven. She knocked lightly on the bathroom door. "Mrs. Washington? Mrs. Washington, are you in there?"

"Yeah . . . I had to use the bathroom."

"Mrs. Washington, we would prefer you not use the rest room. If you have to go, I can bring you a bed pan."

Zaria laughed and Heaven had to cover her mouth to shut her up. "Okay. I'm almost done. I'll be out in a few minutes."

"Do you need any help?"

"No," Heaven insisted. "I'm fine. I'll be right out."

"I'll be back in a few mintues with the anesthesiologist." The nurse's footsteps could be heard walking away.

Heaven gently rocked Zaria to get up. "Zaria, I need you to go get me some more dope." Zaria clumsily stood up and nodded her head. "Go now. Okay?" Zaria nodded at her in agreement again.

"Heaven, I don't have any money." She groaned.

"Zaria, you never have money. Turn some tricks if you have to, but don't come back without some dope." Heaven splashed cold water on Zaria's face to wake her up and then the two of them walked out the bathroom together. They were both startled to see Hasani sitting on the window sill looking out over the busy street below. Zaria hung onto Heaven, barely able to stand. Hasani turned to his wife and he looked angry.

Zaria saw his look and she got nervous. "Heaven, I-I-I'm going to get out of here," she stuttered. "I'll come check on you later." She sprinted out the room.

"Hi." Heaven crawled back into her bed.

"Were you getting high?" he accused her.

"I had to use the bathroom," she lied.

"You usually take your friend with you to use the bathroom?" he sarcastically replied. "Heaven, I could smell the smoke." She could tell he was about to release his fury on her but they were interrupted by the nurse and anesthesiologist.

The nurse asked Hasani to leave so Heaven could get the epidural. Thirty minutes later, the doctor returned with Hasani right behind him. "Heaven, are you ready?"

"Doctor, can I come in the operating room with her? I'm her husband."

"I saw you hanging around outside I was wondering who you were. It's nice to meet you. Did Heaven explain to you that by delivering the baby today I'm trying to avoid any further complications?"

"The nurse explained everything to me." Hasani cut his eyes at Heaven.

"I'm sure your wife will be more relaxed with you being in the delivery room. I will have a nurse get you something to put on and she'll escort you down to the operating room."

Being in the O.R. made Heaven nervous. When she gave birth to Courtney and Odyssey it was so much easier. She never had to leave her hospital room. The doctor opened her legs, told her to push and there they were. This time she didn't know what to expect and it didn't help that she was beginning to go through withdrawal. The doctors thought all her sweat was from the bright lights beaming down on her.

As the doctors explained everything that was going to take place, she saw Hasani silently say a quick prayer. He was a man who always put his trust in God. When he finished praying he walked over and held his wife's hand.

When the surgery started, her doctor used a scalpel to cut open her abdomen. She was so numb she couldn't feel anything but a lot of pressure. Hasani kept peeking to see if he could see anything. It didn't take long before the doctor called out to one of the nurses.

"Nurse, I'm going to pull the baby out and I need you to immediately take it from me." The nurse did as instructed. Once the baby was delivered, the doctor called for a pediatric surgeon to start operating on the baby. Hasani's eyes filled with fear. Heaven and Hasani had no idea what was going on. They could see the nurses hook the baby up to different monitors. Heaven watched an older Asian surgeon hover over her baby.

"Mr. Washington," Heaven's doctor spoke to Hasani, "your wife will be stitched up and moved back to her room. I will be there shortly to explain about the baby and answer any questions you may have."

After Heaven was taken back to her room, her doctor entered looking much more serious than she wanted him to be. "I'm sorry to have to tell you this, but your daughter has some serious life threatening complications. I checked on her right before I came to see you. The baby's intestines developed outside her body. This is not a common thing. It is most commonly seen in mothers who abuse drugs." His eyes shifted to Heaven. "The baby tested positive for heroin. The law requires the hospital to call in the authorities. Someone from the Department of Youth and Family Services will pay you a visit before you're discharged from the hospital."

"Doctor," Hasani spoke up. "What about the baby?"

"Another doctor has stabilized her. We will keep a close eye on her overnight and if she makes it through the night, we plan to perform more surgery in the morning."

Chapter 55

Hasani and Heaven sat in her hospital room in silence for more than three hours. She knew he was mad and wondered what he was thinking. The way he sat in the chair next to her bed with his hands covering his face scared her. She expected him to lash out at her at any moment, but he just sat unmoved.

When he finally broke the silence, Heaven was leery of how calm he seemed to be. "Why did you lie to me? Every time I asked you how the doctor's appointment went, you said fine." His voice was steady with no signs of anger.

"Hasani, I really thought you weren't interested in me or the baby. You were always too busy with the new church, new daycare center, or Ebony, everything except what was going on at home."

He thought her excuses were ridiculous. His eyes blazed with fire. "Don't you dare accuse me of neglecting my family. The truth is your drug use was more important than your child." He pointed in her face. "Now my daughter is in there fighting for her life because you're weak."

She could see the veins in his face swell. "I'm sorry," she whimpered.

"Don't be sorry now. The damage has been done." He cut his eyes at her. "You better pray my daughter makes it." He stormed out the room.

She felt like she was living a horrible nightmare she couldn't wake up from. Her daughter was fighting for her life and Heaven felt like drugs had once again won. Thoughts of how she had once again allowed one of her children to suffer the consequences of her drug use filled her mind. Children are innocent and shouldn't be punished because of their parent's sins.

All emotion had left her body and she felt numb. Hasani made her feel awful, but she deserved every word he said. After everything Heaven had been through, she wished she would die. Then she wouldn't have to worry about disappointing so many people around her.

The following morning Heaven woke to the same dull gray walls that helped her drift off to sleep. The IV's had been removed from her arm and Davis was sitting at her bedside. She was glad to see him. She knew he wouldn't be mad at her. He was one friend she could depend on.

"Davis, how did you know I was here?" She smiled at him, but he looked upset.

"I happened to be with your husband when he got the call you were in the hospital." He grimaced.

She hoped he hadn't said anything about their affair. "Did you see Hasani?" she asked.

"When I came in he was sitting in the waiting room waiting on news about the baby."

"Davis, I don't know what to do. I feel like my whole world is being snatched away from me."

"Can you stop thinking about yourself for once?" he shouted. The tone of voice Davis used was unexpected. "Your daughter could be dying and all you can talk about is yourself." Again she felt ashamed, "Heaven, you and I both know that baby could be mine . . ."

"Davis," she interrupted him before he could go any further. "I already told you that baby is my husband's."

"I know what you told me, but you don't know for sure. We were together around the time she was conceived."

Heaven couldn't bear to take any more abuse. She wasn't going to allow everyone to beat up on her; especially someone she wasn't even married to. "So what?" she yelled back. "Are you going to tell Hasani you slept with his wife and that the child he is so worried about might not be his?" The smug look on his face disappeared. "I didn't think you would."

Davis studied her face. "Heaven, you are so sure I won't say anything, but I haven't even seen that little girl yet and she has already stolen my heart. I love her more than I ever thought I could love you, and for that reason, I'm going to do what's best for her. You aren't fit to raise a fool. So I'm going to petition the courts for a DNA test and if she is my daughter, I'm seeking full custody."

"You can't do that," she cried.

"Watch me. Even if she turns out not to be mine, I'm sure Hasani will end up leaving you and taking his daughter with him."

"No. You can't. That would destroy my family. Please don't. I'm begging you." She clasped her hands in front of her and pleaded with him.

"Forget begging. It won't work this time."

"To hell with you then." She turned indignant. "No matter what you do, no judge is going to give you a baby. You can't even walk without those crutches. You will never raise my baby."

Davis left her room in a huff. Heaven was so mad about the way Davis talked to her that she wanted to throw something. That demon who always whispered in her ear when life became too much for her showed up. It told her some dope would make her feel better.

Heaven looked toward the door, expecting Zaria to walk in any second. She wondered where she could be. The girl hadn't come back like she said she would. Zaria had probably found somebody else to get high with and ditched her.

Unable to sit in the hospital any longer, Heaven dragged herself to the bathroom and threw her clothes on. She looked at the bandages that covered her abdomen and it hurt when she bent down. It was killing her to move but nothing could keep her in that hospital any longer.

Heaven staggered to the door and she overheard a few nurses say that Family Services was on their way to question her. She knew she had to hurry up and get out of there before they arrived and possibly locked her back up if her daughter didn't make it.

She slid down to the floor and crawled past the nurse's station on her hands and knees. Fortunately, no one saw her and she was able to slip out the door without anyone seeing her.

Chapter 56

Wandering the streets of Camden with nowhere to go, Heaven felt faint. She was tired and the pain from her surgery the night before was so severe, she could barely move. She needed to get to Nana's and rest but it was too far for her to walk.

She staggered into a brand new laundromat that had had been open less than a week. Everything inside was new and clean. No trash littered the floors and the most modern washer and dryers lined the walls. Heaven took a seat in the back of the laundromat and rested. She suffered from pain.

While she sat watching dozens of people wash their clothes her cell phone vibrated in her purse. She watched it ring before sending the call to voice mail. It was Hasani. He was trying to reach her, but she didn't want to be found.

The humongous dryers gave off enough heat to warm the entire place. The heat made Heaven tired and she drifted off to sleep. A few hours later, she heard a bunch of rowdy boys enter the store.

She kept her eyes closed because she didn't want anything to disrupt her sleep, but they were causing such a ruckus she had to open her eyes.

She saw Fitch with seven other boys standing around him. He stared at her with an odd look in his eye. Heaven knew Tyke was fond of this kid, but she thought he was weird because he was so quiet. He never talked. He left his friends and came toward her.

"Fitch, I'm so glad to see you." She didn't expect him to respond so she kept on talking. "Listen, can you loan me twenty dollars until I get some cash on me? You know I'm good for it and you know you're going to see me."

Before he dug in his pocket and pulled out a wad of bills he looked toward his friends. He peeled her off a twenty.

"Thanks, I appreciate it and I need one more favor. Can you call Tyke for me? I need to get in touch with him, it's important."

Fitch looked around as if he was scared somebody would hear him talking. "Tyke is busy. You'll have to hook up with him later. If you come by Time and Place tonight, that's where he'll be." Time and Place was another popular bar in Pollocktown.

"Thanks, Fitch. I really appreciate this."

"Yo Fitch, you coming?" his friends called for him. Fitch turned and looked at her one last time before walking out the door."

Heaven stayed in the laundromat until the owner started closing up the place at ten o'clock. She pulled out her cell phone and called a cab to take her to Time and Place.

When they pulled up in front of the bar she paid the cab fare and got out. Her legs were still a little wobbly but the rest she managed to get during the day helped her feel a lot better.

She stumbled up to the bar entrance and Tyke caught her right before she hit the ground. He was leaving the bar with his entourage.

"What's up, girl?" He helped her stand up straight. "I see you had the baby. Is it a boy or girl?" he asked.

"Girl."

"Then she's definitely mine. I can't seem to get a boy to save my life," he joked.

"Tyke, can you let me hold some drugs on credit until I can get some cash?"

"I don't have anything right now. Come back later. You shouldn't be using that stuff anyway. You just had a baby."

"That's why I need some." She reached out for him and wrapped her arms around his waist. "Tyke, I'm begging you. I'm in so much pain. Please, I need something," she pleaded. "I did all that stuff for you and was never paid for what I did."

He thought about it and knew she was right. "Listen, I really don't have anything on me right now," he checked his watch. "But if you really want to get high, I can get my driver to take you to the Shooting Gallery."

"What's the Shooting Gallery?" She hung on to his arm tight.

"Heaven, are you sure you shouldn't go to the hospital? You look pale."

"I'll be fine." She pulled away from him and

leaned against a nearby tree. She saw Fitch whisper something in Tyke's ear. She was sure he was telling her that she had borrowed twenty dollars from him earlier that day. "Fitch, I didn't forget about you. I told you I would pay you back and I will," she yelled.

They spoke in a hushed tone for a few minutes before Tyke turned back to Heaven. "Heaven, the Shooting Gallery will satisfy your need to get high." Upshaw pulled the Escalade around and Tyke opened the back passenger door for her to get in. "After you get done come spend the night with me? You don't look like you're in any shape to go home."

"You're not going with me?" she asked.

"No. Fitch volunteered to go with you. You don't look too good and I'm sending him to look after you." Fitch jumped in the front passenger seat next to Upshaw. Tyke turned and went back into the bar.

Upshaw drove down Kaighn Avenue and made a right onto Haddon Avenue. During the drive, Heaven realized she had forgotten to ask Tyke about Levi. She would make sure to ask him when she saw him later.

They passed Our Lady of Lourdes Hospital and made a final left hand turn into Harleigh Cemetery. It looked like they were entering the black hole. There were no lights except for the headlights from the truck. Upshaw came to an abrupt stop in front of a cement building. They got out, leaving Heaven in the back. "You coming?" they shouted to her.

Heaven didn't know where they were going, but

she wasn't going to be left in the center of a cemetery alone.

They entered the building and the first thing she saw was a huge steel plated chamber that occupied the entire right side of the room. There were plain wooden caskets piled up on top of one another against the wall. To her left was a hoard of people, all using drugs. Everyone in the room was shooting up. Junkies were placing needles in their arms, feet, behinds, anywhere they could find a fresh vein. Dim lighting revealed several card tables set up around the place. Upshaw handed Heaven a dime bag of dope and told her to go in. She walked over to a nearby table that had boxes full of brand new syringes.

"Is this for real?" Her question was directed toward Upshaw.

"The boss likes to keep his customers happy," Upshaw replied. Heaven taste-tested her dope by dipping her finger in the bag. It was the real stuff. She looked behind her. Fitch looked just as surprised as she was. He had taken a seat in a nearby corner and watched, as if he were on the block.

Before going to find a seat, she took one of those hypodermic needles for herself. Several people had already migrated to the corners of the room with kits that consisted of a needle, spoon, and lighter.

It was like the cold, damp room had transformed into a utopia for the users. The room was so quiet and a strange aura filled the air around her.

Heaven needed seclusion. She spotted a table in the far corner that was empty and migrated toward it. She passed several tables that were already full, but at one table she saw Zaria with her head nearly an inch away from hitting the table. Heaven gave her a slight push. "Zaria, what happened to you? You were supposed to come back."

Zaria looked at the distorted figure in front of her. She wrinkled her brow as if she didn't know who Heaven was. "Heaven?" she guessed. "Hey girl! I'm sorry I couldn't come back for you. I got caught up in something."

"I can see that." Heaven referred to the dope residue left on her nose. Zaria tossed her head back, closed her eyes, and her mouth dropped open. Heaven grabbed a seat next to her and took a lighter from off the table. When Heaven flicked the lighter to cook her stuff, the woman at the table next to her went into a seizure. The woman fell back, her chair tumbled over onto the floor, and her body trembled. A thick white liquid oozed out of her mouth. She tightly gripped her right arm with her left hand and tried to gain control of her body, but it was no use. When she did stop moving, she was dead.

Everyone in the room saw what happened but no one stopped getting high. No one tried to help her; instead, the people who sat at the woman's table stole her bag of dope. Others went back to shooting and sniffing the stuff, trying to get as much as they could. Heaven stared at the woman's body. It was strange seeing someone die from an overdose. It reminded her of her daughter.

Upshaw ordered two other guys who worked for Tyke to help him get rid of the woman's body. They walked over, picked her lifeless body up by her feet and hands, and carried her over to a waiting casket.

"She'll be ashes by morning."

Heaven turned to the guy on her left.

"That's how they get rid of the bodies. Why do you think we're in a crematory? No body. No evidence."

"That's what this is?" she shouted. "Who owns this?"

"Sweetheart, I don't know. You know their boss has connections. The more money you have, the more power you have."

Upshaw circled the room with his gun and ordered everyone to put the drugs they had into the wastebasket he was carrying. A few people obeyed while other's tried to hide what they had left, but they couldn't fool Upshaw. He took his gun and pistol-whipped a few men and women until they gave up what they had.

Upshaw then took what was left outside and when he came back he carried a fresh load of drugs. He handed out tiny dime bags to everyone. Without haste everybody dug into their bags like it was Christmas. They couldn't wait to shot, snort, or smoke it. This was especially true for Zaria, who had gotten over her previous high and was ready for more.

Heaven stared at her bag. She didn't understand why they would take one bag from her and then give her another. "You better hurry up and get as much of that as you can. Before you know it they'll be back around wanting it back."

She leaned close to her new friend. "I don't understand. Why do they give us the drugs and then take it away from us?"

"They aren't really giving us drugs, they are testing their product. They can't put something out on the street that is so strong it'll kill everybody, so they use us as test dummies. The batch they just gave us killed ole' girl, so they go back out and get another batch that isn't as strong. If nobody in here dies off that batch then they'll push that out in the street."

Her friend tapped his arm, looking for a fresh vein. Unable to find one, he injected the needle in between his toes. The image of that woman flashed in her mind. She couldn't think of anything else.

"Heaven!" Upshaw yelled so loudly she jumped. "Is something wrong? Why aren't you trying out any of this stuff? It's the best your boy has got."

Her eyes drifted to the needle sitting beside her. She picked it up and got ready to stick it in her arm when she heard a loud thump. A guy across the room had fell out on the floor. Upshaw checked his pulse. He shook his head and the man's body was also dumped into an empty box.

Heaven was scared. Too many people were dying. This was the first time she ever felt afraid of what could happen to her. Upshaw pointed his gun at a few people. She felt like they were being held hostage. Upshaw stood blocking the door with his gun.

Upshaw's helpers came around to collect the remaining dope and she ran toward Upshaw. "I got to get out of here," she told him.

He laughed. "Sorry. No one leaves until the night is over." Heaven scanned the room. She was the only one who looked like she wanted to leave. Too scared to argue with Upshaw, she slowly retreated to her seat. As she crossed the floor, a woman who appeared to be around sixty-five years old fixed her eyes on Heaven. The woman's mouth dropped wide open and Heaven thought she would be the next one to overdose, but she didn't. She just kept staring.

It was hopeless. Heaven felt like she was going to die in that place. She sat back down next to Zaria. Heaven lifted her eyes. "God," she silently prayed. "Please help me. I repent and am so sorry for the wrong I've done. Help me now."

Suddenly, the door they entered through was torn off the hinges. "Everyone on the ground," an officer yelled and several others pointed their guns. Everyone looked around in fear, but nobody left any dope on the table. Instead, they stuffed as much as they could in their pockets.

Heaven sat at the table unsure what to do. She saw the cops push a bunch of people against the wall and then one cop came over and pushed her to the floor. She cried out in pain.

"Yo, she needs an ambulance," Fitch told the cops with his head face down on the ground. "She just had a baby."

The cop went over and told her to turn over. When she did, she could see her wounds had started to bleed through the bandages. The blood seeped through her clothes.

"This one needs an ambulance," the officer said out loud. Heaven's face was in agony. The officer helped her into a nearby chair and then he hand-cuffed her hands.

Within fifteen minutes, the police had lined everyone up and marched them out to the paddy wagon. Heaven was laid on a stretcher. As she was being carried out by the paramedics, she could see the moonlight shine on Celeste's grave. Heaven could clearly read her tombstone:

Celeste Washington
Devoted wife, Loving mother
. . . an Angel Heaven Sent

Chapter 57

Heaven was taken back to the hospital, but this time they didn't put her on the maternity floor. She was placed in a regular room with a guard posted outside her door. The doctors reexamined her. Her staples had busted and once they were reinserted, the doctor and nurses allowed her to rest.

Heaven closed her eyes and thought about everything she had been through that night. Nothing like that had ever happened to her before. She thought about all the people she had watched die. It was horrible to watch somebody OD, but to know that their body was going to burn into ashes was even worse. Heaven cried tears for those souls that were lost that night. She could not help but feel sorry for them and their families.

Heaven knew she had to leave the drugs alone. She could have died then been cremated and no one would have ever known what happened to her. In the past, she never worried about whether or not the drugs were going to kill her, but after watching people's bodies being disposed of like dead dogs, it made her flinch.

"Mrs. Washington, the doctor said it was all right for us to speak with you." A young black man came in and handed Heaven his card. "I'm Detective Hughes and this is my partner Detective Jones." He pointed to a man standing behind him.

Detective Hughes pulled up a chair beside her bed. "You do understand you are under arrest and as soon as you're able to leave the hospital we have to take you down to the station?" She nodded. "The charges we have against you aren't serious. We know you're on parole and if you cooperate with us, we can make this easy on you."

The detective behind him pulled out a note pad and pen. "Mrs. Washington, we have reason to believe you have information on Troy "Tyke" Townes that could help us put him away for a very long time." She shifted her eyes away from them.

"Listen, I know this guy is a friend of yours, but we have reason to believe Tyke is responsible for the Fentanyl that has been killing people throughout the city. We were hoping you could help us point the finger at him. We know the two of you were close."

Heaven glared at the officer from the corner of her eye.

"I'm sure you weren't aware of this, but we were following you tonight."

At first Heaven thought he was teasing, but he never cracked a smile.

"The police were alerted when it was discovered you left the hospital."

Heaven put her head down in shame and puddles filled her eyes.

"Your room was searched and when they found that empty bag of Fentanyl in the bathroom, we felt it was urgent that we speak with you."

Jones held up a clear plastic evidence bag. Inside was the dime bag printed with the words "Get High or Die Tryin' " she and Zaria had used.

"An APB was put out on you. It was easy to find out you were at the laundromat. The police waited for you to leave and then followed you straight to Tyke."

Heaven wasn't sure what to say and what not to say. She wasn't sure whether or not the cops were trying to set her up. "After your friend Troy "Tyke" Townes had his driver take you to the . . ." He flipped back through the pages of his notebook. "Oh this is it. The Shooting Gallery, we followed you and that is how we knew where you were. After we raided the crematory, Tyke was also taken into custody."

"On what charges are you holding him?" she asked.

"We found a gun on him. On that one charge he can be out in the next hour, but if you help us out we can hold him." Heaven didn't say anything. She listened to what they were offering. "We've known for weeks that Tyke was behind the Fentanyl, but we had no way of proving it. All the evidence we have is circumstantial."

The other detective finally came out of the corner and spoke, "If you have any information that could connect Townes to the Fentanyl, I guarantee your charges will go away. Otherwise, we have a list a mile long of reasons for you to be back in your cell at Jefferson Reformatory for Women within the hour. Plus, I don't think your daughter is doing too well. If she doesn't make it, then that would make two of your children who have died at your hands."

Tears rolled down her eyes. She wondered why God had saved her to make her go through hell all over again. Heaven didn't want to go back to prison, but she wasn't sure she could betray Tyke. "What kind of info are you talking about?"

"Anything. Have you ever seen him holding one of those little bags?" He pointed to the bag on the table. "Have you ever heard him talk about Fentanyl? We can use anything. With enough circumstantial evidence, a jury might send him away for a long time."

"If I turn, then I want immunity and I want papers stating that. Then I'll tell you everything I know."

After Heaven was discharged from the hospital, the police escorted her to police headquarters for booking. Once she left there she realized she had no where to go. She was sure she wouldn't be welcomed back at Hasani's house, so she had no choice but to return to Nana's. When she walked into the house using her house key, she found her grandmother sitting quietly at the kitchen table sipping on coffee. There was no radio or television playing. The table was clear except for her Bible, which was turned open to the book of Revelations. Heaven slumped down in the chair across from her and waited to hear Nana tell her how much she had messed up.

Nana read her Bible and drank her coffee. When she finished the chapter she was reading she said, "What are you going to do now?" Her words expressed no hurt and no anger.

Heaven finally cried. She had been holding back her tears all night long. Heaven fell to her knees and sobbed in Nana's lap. "I've done so much wrong that I don't how to fix it."

Nana held Heaven's hands in hers and closed her eyes. "My Father," she prayed, "one of your children has found themselves in the eye of a catastrophic storm. The enemy has sent a cyclone that has threatened to destroy the life she's worked so hard to rebuild. The winds of this storm are so strong and fierce she can't find a way out.

"We realize the remedies and quick fixes we apply to our lives are only temporary cures to our wounds. But if we seek your spirit, the solutions you provide are permanent.

"We ask that you allow Heaven to feel your warmth. Her life has fallen into the depths of darkness with no light for her to see. For weeks, she has been trying to climb out of this pit only to fall back down again deeper than she was before. Help her, Lord." Heaven wailed loudly. "God, give her hope. Give her the strength and courage to boldly face her problems. Amen."

Chapter 58

"Nana, I knew you were forgetting something." Heaven swung her front door open and stuck out the umbrella she held in her hand.

"Hello, Heaven." Heaven's eyes nearly fell out their sockets. If someone would have told her Tyke's baby momma would be standing on her front stoop with two of their four children, she would have never believed it.

"Chantel, I thought you were my grandmother." Chantel held one toddler in her arms and another one stood besides her dragging her baby doll by its hair.

"Aren't you going to invite us in?" Chantel pushed her way into the house and told her daughter to sit on the couch. Heaven hadn't seen Chantel in years. In shock, Heaven forgot to ask who told her where she lived.

Chantel sat her youngest daughter down on the couch and sashayed up in Heaven's face. "Can we go somewhere to talk in private?"

"Sure." Chantel followed Heaven into the kitchen and slid into a seat across from her at the kitchen table. Chantel hadn't changed a bit. She was still ghetto as ever. She had cut all the weave out her hair and she wore it short, but she still wore a lot of makeup. Plus, the thing that always annoyed her about Chantel was the way she cracked her gum when she talked.

"I'm sure you're wondering why I'm here."

It was no secret Chantel despised Heaven. The two had never gotten along and it was all because of Tyke. Chantel viewed Heaven's relationship with Tyke as a threat. Tyke had plenty of women on the side and Chantel knew about all of them. But most of those affairs never lasted more than a month except for his relationship with Heaven. They had been messing around for years. Heaven and Tyke were a part of one another and she was someone he would never leave alone.

"Heaven, I know you and I never got along . . ." Chantel talked with a smile on her face and for the first time she showed no signs of animosity toward Heaven. Heaven was apprehensive around Chantel. She knew how quickly she could turn from a pussy cat to a tiger. The nice way she was treating Heaven was out of the ordinary. "But I had to come here and face my greatest fear." She batted her eyes and her demeanor turned meek. "I came to tell you face to face that Tyke admitted to me that he is in love with you."

Heaven laughed in her face. "Chantel, I don't know what kind of game you're trying to play, but I'm not listening to anything you have to say."

"I know you don't believe it, but it's true."

"Let me get this straight. He told you this?"

She nodded her head and Heaven laughed even harder.

"I can't believe you came over here to tell me your man is in love with me."

"I know it may seem hard to understand but he called me earlier this week and we had a long talk. When he told me you were going to testify on behalf of the state, I expected him to put a contract out on your head, but he fooled me. He talked about you like you were the one who had given him four beautiful daughters. He believes you're not going to testify against him. When I asked him why he was telling me this he said it was because you two had a bond that was stronger than anything him and I would ever have."

Chantel took a tissue out her pocket and wiped at her eyes. It was hard for Heaven to believe that Tyke had said that to Chantel. It didn't make sense for him to say this to her when he needed her the most.

"When I hung up with him, I had to face reality. The only man I have ever loved was in love with somebody else. Do you know how much that hurts? He has always been in love with you." Chantel slipped into a trance when she spoke. "I remember how good he treated you and he never hid your relationship like he would with the others. Friends and family would come back and tell me they saw the two of you shopping at the mall, he's brought you to my house, and you've played with my children." Tears flooded her eyes. "But I don't care. I don't mind being number two, because I know he would never leave me and the children. I can't live without him in my life."

"Why are you telling me this?"

"Heaven, I'm begging you." She gripped Heaven's hand. "Please don't testify against him. He will go to jail. The police are under pressure to pin this Fentanyl on anyone and Tyke is the most likely candidate. He is going to be blamed for the death of every addict in the city who has OD'd off that stuff. You are the only connection the police have connecting Tyke to that Fentanyl." The more she talked the more hysterical she became. "Our children need their father." Tiny footsteps patted into the kitchen. Her one-year-old daughter ran into her mother's arms. "What kind of life will the girls have to look forward to visiting their father in prison every week?"

"Chantel, I don't think you're aware of everything Tyke and I have done."

"No, he's told me everything."

"The police have a weak case against him. Even with my testimony there's no guarantee they will get a conviction."

"Then why don't they drop it?" she asked.

"Because like you said the police department is under a lot of pressure to finger somebody and arresting Tyke is the closest they've ever come to solving the case."

"If you exercise your Fifth Amendment rights you don't have to say anything. Then that will weaken their case even more."

Chantel looked so desperate. Heaven had never seen her look so vulnerable. She had seen plenty of people run a con, but there was something sincere in the way Chantel pleaded. At that moment, Heaven could see Chantel wasn't there for herself but for the sake of her children. Tyke was her life. The only life she had ever known. "I can't promise you anything, but I'll think about it."

"That's all I can ask." She got up with her daughter in her arms. She talked to her baby. "Give Miss Heaven a hug. If we're lucky she'll help us bring your daddy home." The baby held out her tiny arms for Heaven. While holding the little girl in her arms she wondered if she would ever get to hold her own daughter. The baby smiled at Heaven with that distinctive smile her father said he saved only for her. Her daughter looked exactly like her father. Heaven didn't know what to do.

A whole two months had passed and Heaven hadn't heard from Hasani, Davis, or anybody from the church. Sister Stewart did stop by to see her and Fatima came by periodically. Aside from the two of them, Heaven felt like she had no friends or anybody who cared.

Nana would come home from church on Sundays and tell Heaven everybody there had asked for her, but she didn't believe it. She knew no one at that church liked her and they were probably glad she was gone.

Heaven was concerned about her daughter. Hasani wouldn't speak to her and she had no idea how she was doing. Avery did call her the day the baby was released from the hospital to say the baby was doing much better.

Depressed, Heaven moped around the house with nothing to do until Nana suggested she give Chrome a call. After seeing Courtney's reaction to seeing her at the hospital she was sure she had made the right decision to stay out of his life, but that didn't stop her from missing him. She blamed herself for her son's emotional pain and wished there was something she could do to stop him from hurting.

Out of curiosity, she called Chrome to find out how Courtney was doing. They talked for over thirty minutes before Chrome suggested she come visit at his house in East Camden.

A few days later, she caught the bus and it dropped her off right at the end of his street. When she got off she bumped into an older lady who she immediately recognized. It was the old woman from the Shooting Gallery who was staring at her strangely. They smiled at one another and the woman allowed the bus to leave without her.

"Since that night I've often thought about you." The woman started walking with Heaven. "Honey, I don't know who you are or where you come from but when I saw you walk across the room that night you weren't alone." Heaven thought the woman was delusional and probably still getting high.

"At first I thought my eyes were playing tricks on me but now I see the truth. You were sent from God." Heaven chuckled out loud at her comment. "That night I saw a light shine down on you so bright it made you glow. That light was a beacon for the police to see. If the police hadn't showed up that night I'm sure half of us would be dead."

When Heaven stopped in front of Chrome's

house the woman stopped talking. "You take care and remember God has you here for a reason." Heaven watched her walk off until Chrome called her into the house. He stood on the porch wearing an apron. She walked up and gave him a light hug then they went into the house together.

"Were you cooking dinner?" she asked.

"I was trying to make Courtney something before his track meet tonight. You can have a seat in the living room. I'll be right with you."

Heaven looked around at the nicely decorated house. It reminded her of her Nana's with all the photos. This house looked nothing like the apartment they had shared together. There were plenty of pictures of Courtney from the age of seven until now.

Heaven noticed he didn't smile at all in his youngest picture. There was no glow in his eyes. In each picture taken after that one she could slowly see the life coming back in his face. The most current picture of him showed him very happy and full of joy.

It was obvious to Heaven she was the reason why it took so many years for her son to smile.

"How's it going?" Chrome wiped his hand on a dish towel. The apron was removed and she could smell the aroma of barbeque chicken drift past her nose.

"I'm doing well," she replied. "Do you smell something burning?"

"My macaroni and cheese!" he screamed and ran back into the kitchen.

Heaven laughed and followed him back into the kitchen. She picked up a box that was lying on the table. "You burnt macaroni and cheese from out the box? You're hopeless. Where is that apron at? Let me help you out."

Chrome handed her the apron he wore earlier and she put on another pot of boiling water while they talked.

"Have you been attending meetings?" he asked.

"Yes. I think that's the only way for me to stay out of trouble. I've been attending meetings and staying away from people who I know are users. I have to stay clean. I can't afford to get in any more trouble before I go back to court."

"I'm glad to hear that. Maybe we can attend a meeting together sometime?" She agreed. "The reason I invited you over was because I feel like I'm fighting a losing a battle with Courtney."

"Why? You're doing a marvelous job with Courtney."

"If that was true, I would have known that he had skipped school to go to a pharm party and almost killed himself using prescription drugs."

"You can't blame yourself for that."

"Heaven, I need help."

"What do you want me to do?" She poured macaroni into the boiling water and looked in the refrigerator for milk. "It's obvious Courtney doesn't want me in his life. I've seen his wrath."

"The psychologist at the hospital referred me to the therapist Courtney and I have been meeting with for the past month. Last week, he suggested you come sit in on a meeting with us. What do you think?"

"I don't know. I have so much going on in my own life. How much help can I be to anyone else?

I'm not even sure I could deal with any more of his hatred toward me. That may send me over the edge and back to using. What did Courtney say?"

"I haven't said anything to him yet. I wanted to talk with you about it first." Heaven heard the front door open. Chrome got up and walked into the living room. "Courtney, are you ready to eat?"

"Dad, is it all right if I eat over at Daniel's house? Afterward his dad is going to take us to our track meet."

"Where's his dad at?" Chrome asked.

"Out front." Chrome looked out his front door and waved to Daniel's dad.

"Sure, it's okay, but let me talk to you before you leave. I know your mother is not someone you wanted to talk about in the past, but I need to know how you would feel about her coming to one of the therapy sessions with us."

Heaven heard silence. "Courtney, it will do us both some good to resolve some issues and we can make her feel good in the process."

"Dad, I don't want her there. I told you. I have no mother. I wish she were dead. Why can't she leave us alone?" Daniel's father blew the car horn. "Can I go?"

"Sure. Go ahead." After Heaven heard him leave, she came out into the living room. "Well, at least now I know how my son feels about me. The same way I feel about my mother."

Chapter 59

The prosecutor looked hard at work mulling over mounds of paperwork. "Excuse me," Heaven whispered.

"Heaven, I'm glad you're here." The young white lawyer jumped up from his seat to shake Heaven's hand. Nana and Heaven had just arrived in the courtroom and had found a couple of seats in the front row right behind the prosecution table. "You look nice."

Heaven tried on several different suits that morning and had decided on the one that made her look most like an upstanding citizen. The navy blue suit she found at the consignment shop made her look conservative. She had pulled her hair back in a bun and wore very little makeup. Today it was important for her to win over the jury and have them believe her.

The prosecutor told Heaven her only charge was accomplice to murder. Her assistance in Chris's murder was going to be dropped to a lesser charge in exchange for her cooperation. The prosecution had waged a war in convicting Tyke and she was their greatest ally.

Levi, also a witness for the prosecution, had information that was supposed to corroborate her story. She had no idea what that information was, but she figured it had something to do with the ties that linked Levi and Tyke.

Since Chantel's visit all she could think about was her testimony. The prosecution was counting on her to say she received dope laced with Fentanyl that killed Chris from Tyke, but it was going to be hard for her to turn against someone she had always stood by.

The evidence the state had was all circumstantial and she was probably the only person who could put Tyke away. Every part of her testimony had been picked apart and analyzed by a legal team. They had rehearsed her delivery, words, posture, and look. This was one case they were hoping to win. It was up to her to convince a jury he was guilty.

Levi was escorted into the courtroom in shackles. He had lost so much weight Heaven didn't recognize him. Levi's bail had been denied. He had been sitting in jail for the last three months and she hadn't spoken to him since the day of his arrest.

Suddenly, there was a lot of movement in the courtroom. Several police officers entered the courtroom at once. Two stood at the entrance. Two stood near the side windows and another stood next to the defendant's table. Once everyone nodded their heads acknowledging the place was secure, Tyke walked in with his hands bound behind his back. His lawyer greeted him and the officers took off the cuffs. Heaven watched him sit with his lawyer discussing their strategy for getting him acquitted.

Heaven stared at her former lover and noticed he had lost something. Every time she and Tyke were together he was so egotistical. His swagger said he was so sure of himself and his smile reflected his confidence that he could have any woman he wanted. Most people wore bling. Tyke *was* bling.

But inside this courtroom, he looked so casual. He had on cotton Dockers and old dusty loafers instead of silk pants and Armani shoes. He too was playing a role to coax the jury into believing his story.

"Heaven." She followed Nana's gaze to the courtroom doors. Hasani, Sister Stewart, and Fatima entered together.

She was glad to see Sister Stewart and Fatima, but she was overcome with emotion when she saw Hasani. God had answered her prayers. She prayed Hasani would forgive her for lying to him and for using drugs while pregnant. More than anything, she wanted her marriage to work. She held no hope it would ever happen until that day.

Hasani took a seat beside Heaven and kissed her on the cheek. "I've been praying about what to do about us. We are a family and when a family has a crisis they deal with it. I love you." He gripped her hand warmly. She felt relieved to know her husband was behind her.

Sister Stewart and Fatima sat next to Nana and

before court started, Sister Stewart reached over and gave Heaven a huge hug. "I told you I would be here to support you." Heaven's heart felt warm. Sister Stewart was one of the few people who loved her and could understand everything she was going through, but she wasn't sure if Sister Stewart would be so supportive once she heard her testify on the stand.

The bailiff announced that court was now in session and the judge took his rightful place on the bench. Tyke turned in Heaven's direction and winked his eye at her. Then Chantel walked in with all four of their children. They played the part of being the supportive family sitting behind the defense table. Heaven felt sorry for Chantel. It must be a terrible thing to know the man you love is in love with someone else.

Levi was the first witness called to the stand. The prosecutor stood before Levi and the first question he asked was how he knew Tyke.

"I met him a few years ago. I was a runaway living on the streets and he took me in," Levi stated.

"How long did you live with him?"

"I stayed with him and his family a little over a year before I went to live with my grandmother."

"Over the course of that year did you ever see or hear Mr. Townes talk about Fentanyl?"

"Yes. Before he picked up his first shipment from his supplier he bragged about how he had gotten his hands on some stuff that was going to make the city go crazy. After he pushed it out on the street people started dropping dead."

"What about these bags with the slogan 'Get

High or Die Tryin,' have you ever seen him with one of these bags?"

"I've never seen him with one of those printed bags, but I remember him telling me that he needed a slogan. Something to let his customers know they were buying the good stuff from him. That's when he came up with the phrase, 'Get high or die tryin.' "

"Levi, I want you to explain to the jury how manipulating Mr. Townes can be." The prosecutor paced in front of the jury. "You were charged with fifteen different counts of murder. Can you tell me why you would do something so horrendous?"

"Because he asked me to." Levi pointed at Tyke. "Tyke referred to each murder as a promissory note. If a customer owed him a lot of money he would arrange to have their grandmother or grandfather killed and once the insurance money was collected, Tyke would get his money back. Plus interest."

"Why did these people owe Mr. Townes money?"

"Unpaid drug debts."

"What did Mr. Townes do when he heard you were arrested?"

"Nothing. He refused all my calls and never came to see me. He acted as if I didn't exist."

"I thought the two of you were friends," the prosecutor said.

"No. We were never friends," Levi paused for a moment. "Only lovers."

Heaven was shocked by Levi's testimony. Tyke turned to his lawyer and whispered something in his ear then they laughed together. Heaven watched

Chantel's reaction to this news. She shifted uncomfortably in her seat, but it didn't look like Levi's confession was a surprise to her. The Chantel she knew would have stood up and called Levi every name she could think of, instead, she sat quietly and tried to ignore Levi's accusations.

The prosecution sat down and Tyke's lawyer cross-examined. "Young man, isn't it true you have a drug problem?"

Levi hesitated before answering. "I dabble every once in a while."

"As a matter of fact, I have documentation that says when you were arrested you had high levels of prescription drugs in your system. Isn't it true you killed all those elderly people to support your own drug habit?"

"No, Tyke is the one who told me to do it."

"No, Mr. Garrett, the truth is, you tortured senior citizens and killed them for their medications. Just like you watched your grandmother suffer in agony while you stole her prescription pills."

"That's a lie!" Levi screamed.

The prosecutor stood up. "Your honor, I object."

The judge told the jury to strike the last statement from the record, but the damage had already been done. Levi stepped down and it was now Heaven's turn to take the stand.

"Heaven, the drugs used to kill Christian Stewart, who gave them to you?"

The courtroom was quiet and the tension high. Everyone waited in suspense for her to answer. Chantel wanted her to say nothing. The prosecutor expected her to do the opposite.

"I don't know." When Heaven responded the prosecutor was looking down at the floor, but he abruptly raised his eyes to meet hers. "I used a dime bag of dope I had bought earlier."

He pulled out a sheet of paper from his file folder and waved it in Heaven's face. "I have a signed affidavit from you that accounts the details surrounding Christian Stewart's death." He grimaced at Heaven's unexpected performance. "In it you describe how Troy 'Tyke' Townes gave you a bag of heroin with the Fentanyl in it and forced you to shoot a lethal amount of dope into his arm. Is that true?"

Heaven looked over at Tyke, who studied her every move. She started crying, "We were together and I did stick the needle in his arms but I don't know where I got the drugs from. I had bought them early that day," she cried.

Tyke lightly clasped his hands together like he was praying. He knew Heaven wouldn't let him down. Heaven watched Sister Stewart shudder when the lawyer described how Chris had really died. When Heaven looked her in the eye, Sister Stewart looked away.

The prosecutor quickly moved on to his next question, "Heaven, you were arrested at the crematory on May twenty-first. Can you tell the jury how you got there?"

Chantel sat on the edge of her seat waiting for Heaven's reply.

"Tyke had his friend give me a ride."

"Who told you about this Shooting Gallery?"

"A friend told me," Heaven mumbled.

Tyke looked at her with admiration in his eyes. The prosecutor slapped his leg with the papers he held in his hand. He took off his glasses. It was obvious he wasn't happy with her answers. He told the judge he was done questioning her. The defense chose not to cross-examine her since Heaven's testimony helped the defense more than the prosecution.

Heaven stepped down from the stand. When she went back to her seat the prosecutor turned to her. "Thanks a lot, Heaven. Any chances we had are now blown."

"Don't worry about him," Hasani whispered. "You told the truth. That's all that matters." Hasani hadn't made her feel any better. She felt worse. Chantel glanced her way and threw her a sly grin.

The state had very little additional evidence. At around five o'clock Tyke was called to the stand. He humbly took the stand and swore to tell the truth. Although, Tyke was trying to be humble in front of the jury his charm was intoxicating. Chrome's words filled her head. The day they were down at the waterfront, he accused her of always being in love with Tyke. *Perhaps, he was right.* For the first time since she had gotten out of jail, she longed to be with Tyke.

"Troy, you are being accused of a lot of crimes. We have already heard Heaven Washington's testimony stating that you were at the scene when Christian Stewart was given a lethal injection of Fentanyl."

"Yes, I was there," Tyke replied.

"And what were you doing there?"

"Heaven asked me to come there and hold him down while she pumped the dope into his arm."

"Do you know why she wanted him dead?"

"I have no idea."

"Why did you go along with it?"

"We're friends, she asked me to do her a favor and I did."

"That's an awfully big favor for a friend, don't you think? Being an accomplice to murder."

"Well it wasn't just a favor. In exchange for me doing something for her she would do something for me." He laughed.

"So the two of you were close?" his lawyer asked.

"Yes."

"Intimate?"

"Yes."

"You had a sexual relationship with the married Mrs. Washington?"

"Yes."

"Is this the only favor she's ever asked you for?"

"No. She asked me to hire somebody to come to her husband's house before they were married and pretend to be his dead wife's lover and the father of their newborn."

The jury gasped. Hasani had held her hand tight throughout the entire trial, but now, he pulled away from her.

"I have two more questions for you Troy. Did you have anything to do with the serial murders and were you ever in a relationship with Levi Garrett?"

Tyke answered no to both questions. His lawyer

turned toward the judge and announced that he was finished.

During the prosecutions cross examination Tyke answered all questions with confidence. He made sure he looked both the lawyer and the jury in the eye when he was speaking. Tyke was such a good manipulator. Watching him speak, anyone would have thought he was speaking the truth straight from the Bible.

Before the prosecution had rested their case, they reserved the right to call in a witness later in the trial. The judge allowed it. Once Tyke stepped down from the stand, the prosecution got up and announced they had another witness to call to the stand.

"The state would like to call Shane Wilson to the stand," the prosecutor said.

"Your honor, this witness is not on the list of witnesses I received." Tyke's lawyer protested.

"We could not allow this witness's identity to be revealed until now. This man is an undercover police officer who has vital information pertaining to this case. He is being called in as a last resort."

The judge heard both sides and allowed the testimony. When the bailiff went out the courtroom to get the witness Heaven was surprised to see Fitch dressed in a suit and tie.

"He's just a kid." Heaven said out loud. He was sworn in under oath and took the stand.

The prosecution questioned Fitch thoroughly. He said he was twenty years old and had been working undercover for the past year. Within that year he had managed to learn a lot about Tyke's drug operation, but one thing he was never told was where the Fentanyl came from or how it was obtained.

Fitch described to the jury how he found Heaven in the laundromat the day after she gave birth to her daughter and how he had called in to the police station and told the police where to find her.

"I knew those cops were lying," Heaven said to herself out loud. Then she continued listening to Fitch's testimony.

Fitch then explained how he knew about the Shooting Gallery, but only people who were hand picked by Tyke knew of its location. He refuted Heaven's testimony by telling the jury he was there when Tyke sent Heaven to the Shooting Gallery. He also said he was wired that night and that was how the police found them. The last thing he said before stepping down off the stand was probably what helped Heaven's case the most.

"Although, Mrs. Washington may not have been aware of it, if it weren't for her, I may have never found the Shooting Gallery."

Shane was dismissed and the defense waived their right to cross examine. Heaven thought the state had lost because of her lack of testimony, but with Fitch's testimony she thought they had a good chance of winning.

After both sides gave their closing remarks, the judge spoke to the jury. He instructed them to re-view all the evidence and come back with a verdict. He then adjourned court for the day.

Chantel gathered her children to go, but before she did Heaven stepped in her face. "You set me up." Chantel tried walking around her but Heaven wouldn't move out the way. She aggressively grabbed her arm. "You are going to hear what I have to say." Heaven was furious.

"What do you want?"

"How could you come to my house and tell me a bunch of lies? You and Tyke used me."

"Stop playing the victim. You sleep with my man for years and you expect me to let that go. He has always turned to you. I'm the one sleeping in his bed, but he confides in you. Finally, he comes to me for help. Do you think I was going to turn him down? Instead of worrying about me and my family, why don't you concern yourself with what's left of yours?" Heaven shifted her eyes to Hasani. He was talking with Nana and he didn't look happy. Heaven rushed from Chantel over to Hasani.

"Can I speak with you for a moment?" She tried to lace her fingers through his but he snatched his hand away.

"We have nothing to talk about." He was irate.

One of the guards was leading Tyke out of the courtroom when he hollered, "Yo, partner."

Hasani turned around.

"Make sure you kiss my daughter good night." He laughed.

Hasani's face dropped and his head spun to Heaven. The guard pushed Tyke along and they disappeared out the side entrance. Hasani barged out the courtroom doors. Heaven couldn't let him leave without trying to explain. She rushed after him, but Sister Stewart stopped her.

Heaven was ashamed to look her in the eye. She dropped her eyes to the floor. Sister Stewart forced Heaven's face up. "Sister Stewart, I'm so sorry. I had no idea Chris was your son until the funeral and then . . ."

"Ssshhh, darling." She pressed her fingertips to Heaven's lips. "There is no need to explain. I understand what happened. The truth revealed in this courtroom has opened my eyes. I know who is responsible for my son's death and I'm going home to confront that person." She gave Heaven one last hug and walked out the doors.

Heaven sat down and quietly cried to herself. She saw the prosecutor talking with Fitch on their way out the door. "Man, thanks for coming through for me on this case. I knew I couldn't trust that addict to do what she was supposed to do. I've worked enough cases to know people on drugs will always protect their dealer."

Heaven was humiliated. She sat in the courtroom with her nana and cried to herself.

Chapter 60

Three months later Heaven stared at the rain pouring down outside her window. It was a cold, damp day and she was waiting on Ms. Griffin to arrive with her nana. Heaven had finally agreed to have a group meeting with her family.

Tyke was cleared of all charges accusing him of distributing Fentanyl. He was found guilty on gun possession charges and accessory to commit murder. He received seventeen different counts for each person they found at the Shooting Gallery that night. Tyke was sentenced to fifteen years in prison. He would be eligible for parole in seven. Levi had his trial and he was sentenced to two consecutive life sentences in prison. He was currently filing an appeal.

Although Heaven hadn't kept up her end of the bargain, the prosecution still asked the judge for leniency in her case. Fortunately, the judge was a black woman and she had mercy on Heaven. Instead of jail time, she thought Heaven would be better off in a two year inpatient rehab facility in Piscataway. Being forced into rehab wasn't as bad as Heaven thought it was going to be. This time she was serious about getting better and when she realized she needed her family around for that she called Ms. Griffin and asked if they could now have a group meeting with her family.

She pulled a picture of her daughter out her pocket. Hasani had named her Mahogany Heaven because the baby had her eyes and a beautiful walnut brown complexion. She was beautiful. Heaven sat around in the waiting room waiting for her guests to arrive. When she heard the doors open she stood. The first person to walk in was Nana. Heaven gave her grandmother a long hug.

They separated and the next person to enter was Hasani. Ms. Griffin said she was going to ask him to come, but Heaven doubted he would show. He kept his distance from Heaven and she could tell by his actions that he was still angry with her.

Ms. Griffin walked in last. She asked everyone to take their seats so that they could get the meeting started. "Now that we're all here, it's important to realize that Heaven's recovery begins today. Right here in this room. I've spoken with Heaven and we have discussed her life at length. She's told me about her childhood, her mother, and a few other things. These factors have all contributed in some way to her drug addiction."

"Excuse me." Everyone turned around. Heaven was surprised to see Chrome and Courtney. "Ms. Griffin, you did say it was all right to bring my son. Didn't you?"

"Of course." She jumped up to meet them. She added two more chairs around the table. "Heaven, I forgot to tell you that your grandmother suggested we invite Courtney and his father."

Heaven nodded her head in agreement.

"As, I was saying, if we can get everything out in the open this will allow all of us to better understand her pain. A lot of the hurtful things that happened were not Heaven's fault. It was her addiction." She turned to Heaven. "Heaven, why don't you begin?"

It was hard for her to say out loud a lot of the thing she had been ashamed of her whole life. Things Nana never knew. "Well, I began abusing drugs after my best friend, Keenyah, died." Heaven paused for a second and she looked at Courtney. Like her husband, he too refused to look at her.

"Heaven, it's okay," Ms. Griffin encouraged her. "No one here is going to judge you."

Heaven recalled the events of that horrible day and recanted the story exactly as she remembered it. "I think Chrome and I were both in mourning and the drugs helped both of us live with what we had done. I couldn't get over the horrible things I said to her. I killed my best friend. If I hadn't said those terrible things to her she would have been in the house and would not have run out in the street."

Chrome rubbed his face as he heard Heaven's confession. He couldn't believe what she was saying.

"Oh Lord," Nana said aloud. "I had no idea."

"I'm sorry, Nana. I never meant to hurt you."

Heaven knew the tears in Nana's eyes were from disappointment.

"I . . . I . . ." Nana tried to say something.

Ms. Griffin grabbed her hand. "Ms. Stansfield, is there something you want to say?"

"Yes, I think it's about time. A lot of people have suffered because of my silence."

"Ms. Stansfield, this is not your fault," Ms. Griffin said. "It's not Heaven's fault either. That's why we're all here; to help her face her demons and take responsibility for her actions." Ms. Griffin looked toward Heaven. "Heaven, there is no way you could have prevented your friend from running into the street and getting hit by the car. The only person you can control is you."

"I was jealous. I was jealous of her relationship with Chrome. She died thinking I hated her and her baby."

"Heaven stop saying such things," Nana said.

"Nana, it's true," Heaven cried.

"Heaven." She crossed the room to hug her. "You are not responsible for Keenyah's death. I'm sure you think you are but there are things you don't know about that night." Heaven could see her nana had a confession in her eyes. "The day Keenyah died I was on my way home from the market and I saw your mother standing on the sidewalk arguing with her."

This was news Heaven never knew. She cringed at the mention of her mother.

"I saw your mother grab Keenyah and Keenyah tried to break away from her, but she stumbled out

in the street. That's how she got hit. You didn't
have anything to do with her death.

"Why was mom fighting with Keenyah?"

"You know how your mother is. She has always
been overprotective of you. She told me she heard
the two of you fighting upstairs in your room and
she confronted her. She kept on saying Keenyah
was shouting at you.

"After Keenyah was hit the focus was on her. So
I pulled your mother into a nearby alley. I told her
to stay there until I came and got her. I couldn't
bear to see her go to jail. It was an accident that I
felt horrible about. It wasn't too often that your
mother was allowed to come home from the hospital and the one time she does somebody ends up
dead."

"I remember you packed Mom's things that
night. You told me you were cutting her visit short
and taking her back to the hospital. I thought you
were sending her back because you were worried
about me."

"That was part of the reason. With your mother
around I couldn't give you my undivided attention
and you needed that. I tried to protect both of
you."

Heaven's tears flowed freely down her face.
Everyone in the room had a somber look on their
face.

"Heaven, if I knew you felt responsible for that
girl's death I would have told you sooner. I'm sorry
I kept it from you all these years."

Heaven cried uncontrollably and Hasaan com-
forted her by wrapping his arms around her,

"Heaven, you told me your mother died when you were too young to remember," Hasani said.

"That was a lie. I was too embarrassed to tell you the truth about my mother." Heaven turned her chair in his direction. "The truth is that my mother, her name is Amelia, has been locked up in a psychiatric hospital since she was eleven years old."

"I'm sorry. I had no idea," he said.

"Heaven, I'm also sorry," Chrome said. "I had no idea you had so much grief buried inside and the things I did by leaving you with two children didn't help any."

"Chrome, we can't change the past, only the future. I pretended my mother was dead when she really isn't." Heaven looked over at Courtney and they stared at one another for a moment. "Maybe if I was honest with myself I would have been a better mother to my children."

"If your mother has been institutionalized since she was eleven years old then where is your father?" Hasani asked.

"I told you the truth about that. I have no idea who my father is."

"Heaven's paternity is a mystery to us all," Nana added. "Amelia was only fifteen when she gave birth to Heaven. The doctor said Heaven was just as much a surprise to them as she was to me. They had no idea my daughter was pregnant until the night she went into labor. Amelia tried to keep to herself and she would never allow anyone to touch her, so she was able to hide her pregnancy.

"Amelia had apparently gotten pregnant by either another patient or somebody on the hospital staff. They did an investigation, but they were unable to pinpoint who the father was and Amelia would never say. The only thing we knew for sure was that the father was white."

"Ms. Stansfield, isn't the hospital responsible for things like this? They were supposed to keep an eye on their patients."

"They gave me a whole lot of apologizes about how they couldn't keep an eye on all the residents. They said it was hard taking care of mentally ill patients because they were more sexually inquisitive than most." Nana smiled. "When that nurse placed that beautiful bundle of joy in my arms I knew she was something special. Amelia had already named her Heaven and I thought it was a perfect name, so I kept it."

"I hate to have to ask you this, but did you have anything to do with Ebony's death?" Hasani asked. "I know the police ruled her death a suicide but the note she left was so weird."

Heaven cried at Hasani's feet. "Hasani, you have to believe me. I didn't know she was going to kill herself. Ebony was never doing drugs. I slipped something in her coffee so she would fail the test. I was jealous of her getting the position and she spent more time with you than I did. I said some really mean things to her but I didn't think she was going to kill herself I just wanted her to go away." Hasani stared at her in disbelief.

Ms. Griffin walked over and helped Heaven back to her chair then she gave her a hug.

"Heaven, I think a lot of your problems stem from you feeling like you weren't loved. You've had a lot of separation in your life. Your mother wasn't a big part of your life. Then when you found out Keenyah was pregnant you thought you weren't going to have her in your life any longer. She dies then you get with Chrome and he ends up leaving you. Heaven, you focused on all the people who left you but what about those who stuck around? Your nana. Your husband. God."

Then they heard a light tap on the door. The hospital was telling Ms. Griffin that their time was almost up.

"Heaven, we have to go. Do you want to say good-bye to everyone? I don't know how long it'll be before you see them again." Ms. Griffin stepped back and Nana hugged Heaven tightly. Heaven couldn't stop crying in her arms. She loved her grandmother so much and didn't want to let her go.

Next Hasani walked up to her. Heaven was surprised by how emotional he was. "Heaven, I never told you this, but the day Celeste died she urged me to go to the halfway house that night with the church. I wasn't going to go because she hadn't been feeling well but she told me to go and that's when I met you. Then exactly one year later our daughter was born that same day. I've always felt it was Celeste who brought the two of us together, but after hearing the truth about your past I'm more confused then ever about our future together." He hugged her tight. "I was going to file for divorce but I need to give it some thought. Don't worry about the baby. She's growing and gaining weight. I'll be sure to send you some pictures." He kissed her hand one last time. "Oh! I forgot to tell you. I asked Davis to be the baby's godfather."

"Godfather?"

"Yes, the night the baby was born he stayed and prayed with me. He never left my side. I know the two of you were friends and I was touched by his concern. I know he doesn't have any kids and I thought he would be a good choice."

Heaven was glad Davis had decided not to say anything. That was one secret she would hold on to until the time was right.

Ms. Griffin stepped up. "Heaven, I'm not sure if you remember how anybody hardly attended our Group Session Meetings that were open to the public."

"How could I forget? Half the time we were the only ones there."

"Well, I think word got around about how the heroin users were being held at gunpoint and their bodies cremated and that scared a lot of people into wanting to get clean. Every meeting this week has been standing room only."

"I guess something positive did come out of this," Heaven replied. She turned around and saw Chrome and Courtney standing in the corner of the room.

Chrome walked up and wrapped his arms around Heaven's neck. "I love you," he said.

"I love you, too." She wiped tears from her eyes.

"Okay, we'll be going but Courtney has something he wants to give you."

Courtney shuffled up to his mother. He held

out a tiny slip of paper toward her. She picked it up and read it. "You are loved."

"Odyssey had gotten it from her fortune cookie the day she died. I know she couldn't read it but she said she was going to give it to you. Now it's yours."

She reached out and wrapped her arms around her son with tears in her eyes, Then she hollered, "God is so amazing! G.I.S.A. God is so amazing."